Cassie Linden Finds Her Sweet Spot

Linda Avellar

Black Rose Writing | Texas

This is a work of fiction. Names, characters, businesses, places, events, and incidents are either the products of the author's imagination or used in a fictitious manner. Any resemblance to actual persons, living or dead, or actual events is purely coincidental.

ISBN: 978-1-68513-692-5
LIBRARY OF CONGRESS CONTROL NUMBER: 2025941908
PUBLISHED BY BLACK ROSE WRITING
www.blackrosewriting.com

Printed in the United States of America
Suggested Retail Price (SRP) $21.95

Cassie Linden Finds Her Sweet Spot is printed in Garamond

*As a planet-friendly publisher, Black Rose Writing does its best to eliminate unnecessary waste to reduce paper usage and energy costs, while never compromising the reading experience. As a result, the final word count vs. page count may not meet common expectations.

Praise for
Cassie Linden Finds Her Sweet Spot

"Smartly observed... Avellar excels at making her two leads both charming and relatable."
–Kirkus Reviews

"*Cassie Linden Finds Her Sweet Spot* is thoroughly absorbing...engrossing, realistic, and hard to set aside."
–Midwest Book Review

"*Cassie Linden Finds Her Sweet Spot* is a wise and poignant exploration of the fears that hold us back from connecting with the people we love and with ourselves. An absorbing debut from an author to watch!"
–Jamie Beck, *USA Today* bestselling author

"Linda Avellar's new novel is a layered, meaningful exploration of that phenomenon known as the 'sandwich generation.' You'll feel for Cassie as she spies that sweet spot in the distance and root for her as she seeks to navigate her way there."
–Barbara Josselsohn, bestselling author of eight novels, including *The Lilac House*

"This book is perfect for anyone who loves a happy ending and books that make you feel the depth of love - of family, friends, and romantic relationships. A heartwarming tale of finding love in the most unexpected ways."
–Kim McCollum, author of *What Happens in Montana*

"I loved this book. Cassie Linden is an everywoman, facing the challenges of caring for her aging dad, helping her son figure out college and worrying about her own future...and present. Warm, intelligent and steeped with emotion...a gorgeous debut."
–Kristan Higgins, *New York Times* bestselling author

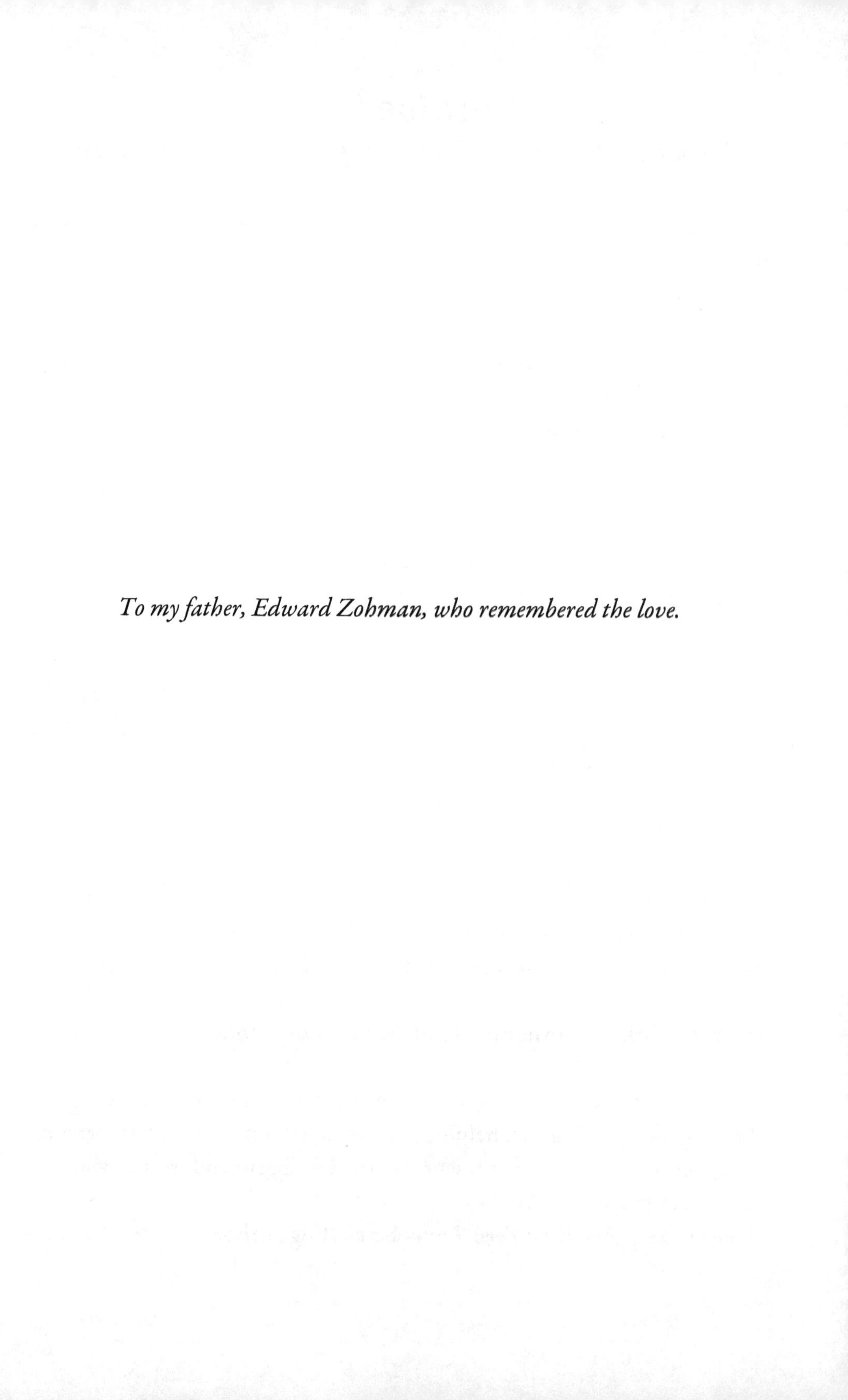

To my father, Edward Zohman, who remembered the love.

Cassie Linden Finds Her Sweet Spot

Chapter One

Halfway up the driveway Andrew's ringtone brought her to a stop. Cassie had just spoken with him the day before, and he didn't usually call again so soon. She threw the rental into park and rummaged in her bag, trying to grab her phone before he disconnected. Once he was gone, she'd never get him back.

"Mom?" His voice was wobbly, and she knew in an instant something was wrong. Her mind raced through a dozen scenarios: he was hurt, sick, in trouble. All kinds of misfortune could befall a kid away at college.

"Sweetie," she said, her heart suspended, "what's going on?"

"The frat had a party last night..."

"Okaay." She waited. Nothing good could be coming.

"It kinda got out of hand. People were drinking and stuff, and...um...a kid fell and hit his head."

"Oh Andrew." Her stomach lurched in a sickening way. Those damn fraternities with the drinking culture. Worse in New Orleans, where it was always a big party. "Is he all right?"

"I don't know. He's in the hospital."

"Did you see it happen?" She felt ill at the thought of this poor boy, hurt so badly he'd landed in the hospital. Then a shameful rush of relief that it wasn't her son.

"A few of us were goofing around. I didn't see him fall, but he hit his head on the tile floor." He sounded like he was about to come apart, and she wanted to wrap him in her arms like when he was little. Only he was nineteen and thirteen hundred miles away. "Were you drinking too?" she asked without much hope. Of course he'd been drinking. Things like that didn't happen when kids were sober.

"A little. I mean, yeah, a lot, actually. Campus police came, then they called New Orleans P.D."

A gust of fear blew through her. He had no idea. "Did you talk to the police? No one pushed him, right?"

"No, no one pushed him. He just fell. But they took statements from all of us."

"Andrew." She tried to keep her voice calm so she wouldn't upset him further. "Why didn't you call Dad or me right away? You shouldn't have said anything to the police without an attorney. One of us could have flown down."

"I realize that now, but it happened so fast, and they said they just needed to find out what happened. I didn't do anything. It was an accident." A hint of defensiveness, like maybe there was more to it. But she couldn't think of that right now. The immediate issue was her son could be in legal jeopardy.

"If they're questioning you, you need a lawyer." A boy was seriously hurt, maybe brain damaged. The police or the university could be looking to set an example. "I'll come right down. I'm sure I can get a flight tonight or tomorrow. Where are you now, at the frat house?" She'd call Shelly and let her know what was happening. Dad would be all right for a few more days until she settled things with Andrew.

"No, don't come." He'd pulled himself together a little. "There's nothing you can do. If the police want to talk to us again, I'll say I want a lawyer. I won't do anything without talking to you or Dad first."

"I think I should come down there."

"Mom, no. Don't come."

"Are you sure? I hate the thought of you dealing with this all alone." Every maternal instinct told her to get on a plane, but she didn't want to be a helicopter parent either, swooping in at the first sign of trouble. He needed to learn to deal with the consequences of his actions.

But still. He was her son.

"Yeah, I'm sure. It's better if you don't come."

"You could stay with me in a hotel for a few days, get out of that frat house." She'd had reservations about Tulane, but Phil had gone there and Andrew had grown up hearing about the French Quarter and Mardi Gras and Phil's frat buddies, who were still his best friends. She'd tried to interest him in other schools, but there was never a question of Andrew going anywhere but Tulane.

"Mom!"

"All right. Okay." She gave way reluctantly. "But let me know what's happening and how that poor boy is doing. And for God's sake Andrew, if the police contact you or there's any disciplinary action from the university, I want to know right away. Understand? This was beyond stupid of all of you."

"I know. I understand." He sounded contrite. He was basically a good kid, had never been in any real trouble before. She knew drinking and carousing went on in the fraternity, but this was serious.

"I love you," she said, a hitch in her voice. "It'll be okay, we'll get through this."

"I love you too," he mumbled.

She stowed her phone but couldn't banish the feeling he hadn't told her something. Even with all the drinking, how would a boy fall and hit his head like that? She left the car and walked into the field, zipping her jacket against the brisk spring breeze. Her parents had more than a grassy lawn. The Lindens had five full acres with stone walls that dated to colonial times. And just across the street was another twenty acres of undisturbed woods that had never been developed. Her parents, refugees from the city, where it was hard to come by a tree, had fallen in love with all that open space. But to Cassie, it had always felt oppressive. Too much green. She much preferred Manhattan, where trees were tidily contained along the sidewalk, and even if you hated your neighbors, at least they were in the building.

She picked her way carefully across the field, which was pocked with rocks and holes where small animals lived. And of course, her father's beehives, which she gave a wide berth.

Andrew was withholding, she was sure of it.

But she hadn't been honest with him either. Not for his whole life. She knew she needed to tell him, especially now with her own concerns. She glanced up at the house but saw no sign of her dad. A spring day like this, she'd expected to find him outside with his hives.

She hadn't been home in too long. Shelly, who lived all the way across the country, knew more about what was happening here than Cassie, who lived in New York City, an hour away. "He's slipping," her sister had insisted. "You need to check on him." So Cassie had packed a bag—a small one—and left Phil a message that she was going to Connecticut for a few days. Were you supposed to notify your ex of your whereabouts? She doubted Phil would care one way or the other, but part of her—the part that couldn't believe her marriage was over—was still going through the motions like a clock whose battery had run out of juice but kept on lurching forward anyway.

She started back to the car and continued up the long driveway. One thing at a time.

•   •   •

The smell hit her the minute she stepped into the house.

Something was burning!

"Dad!" She rushed to the kitchen where smoke curled from a blackened pan. She grabbed a dish towel and yanked the pan off the burner. Then turned off the flame and cranked open a window.

"Dad!" she hollered again. "Where are you, are you okay?"

"Shelly, is that you?" He came down the stairs slowly.

"It's me, Cassie. You left the stove on. What were you cooking?"

"I was going to make a grilled cheese." He had on a rumpled flannel shirt, and his hair stuck up like he'd just awakened from a nap. "When did you fly in?" He opened his arms for a hug, and she went into them, a lump rising in her throat that he thought she was Shelly.

"I'm Cassie," she said. "Cassandra."

"I know who you are." He pulled back to look at her. "You think I don't know my own daughter? Is your sister here too?"

"No, she's in California."

"California?" Her father looked uncertain. "Shelly said she was coming."

Cassie swallowed. "That was me. I called to tell you I was driving up, remember?" But clearly he didn't. He seemed smaller than she remembered. Her father had never been a large man, but he'd had presence. Whether you liked it or not, her dad, with his opinions, commanded a room. Always Mr. Linden to her friends, while her mom insisted they call her Maggie.

"How about I make you another grilled cheese?" Cassie said. "I'll have one too." She'd normally opt for a salad, but her dad looked pleased she'd offered and followed her into the kitchen. The smoke had cleared, and she made a mental note to change the batteries in all the smoke detectors. God knew when he'd last done it and what else was about to fall apart around here.

Her father watched closely as she took out four slices of bread and set a pat of butter in a pan, standing behind her in a way that always used to annoy her. Her dad had a right way to do everything—coffee was scooped precisely, the toaster set exactly to medium, never light or dark. Her dad was a stickler for protocol.

"Fruit? Why do you want fruit?" he said suspiciously as she scoured the fridge for an apple or pear or something the slightest bit healthy. "You still on that crazy vegetarian diet?"

She took a breath, but no point rehashing that old argument. "Not vegetarian; I eat chicken and fish. Just no red meat." Actually, she was surprised he'd remembered. But that was how dementia worked. She'd learned that with her mom. Early on, especially, there didn't seem to be any rhyme or reason to what she held on to. Things that packed an emotional punch, maybe. Although as the disease progressed, her emotions had become all out of whack. She'd weep at a TV commercial but stare at her girls blankly.

Cassie found a couple of apples, cut them up and set them out with the sandwiches. Her dad ate slowly, but he always had. Her father was a deliberate man. A tax attorney who drew up spreadsheets for family vacations and insisted on packing the trunk himself because no one else could possibly do it right. Cassie used to argue with him about what should go where while her mother and Shelly sat patiently in the car, waiting for them to sort it out. Always knocking heads, the two of them.

It became worse when her mom got sick, Cassie unable to see how much she was slipping. The day her father refused to let her mom drive to the mall, Cassie called him a bully.

"I'm happy to drive you," he'd said, but her mother drooped with shame as he took the keys. He took everything from her mom—her independence, her dignity—that was the way Cassie saw it back then. And over the years, it became harder to unsee even though she knew it wasn't fair.

She picked at her sandwich. She wasn't hungry. She'd eaten mainly to get him to eat. "So I thought I'd stay a couple of days and see how you're doing."

He swallowed a bite of sandwich. "Doing fine."

"Is Elena still coming once a week?" The house didn't look too bad, newspapers piled on the counter, dishes in the sink. Phil had been a whole lot messier. Now that he was gone, the apartment was spotless. And empty.

"Her sister comes now."

"What happened to Elena?"

Her father shrugged. "I don't know. She's busy." Elena had been with her father twenty years, and in one day a week managed not only to clean the house but cook him several meals. Elena was a godsend.

"Shelly didn't mention her leaving," Cassie said dubiously.

"She's going back to college." Her father said this firmly, the way he said everything, like there could be no argument.

"College?" Elena was close to sixty, with grandkids. It seemed unlikely, but you never knew.

"What's her sister's name?" Cassie would confirm this with Shelly. Cassie felt a tug of guilt that it had been so long since she'd seen him. But even before her own problems consumed her, it had been painful to come home. She'd been sixteen when her mom was diagnosed. Her vivacious mother with her sparkly outfits and wit to match dissolving into someone utterly unrecognizable.

Her mom had tried to hold on to herself, picking out her own clothes even as the Alzheimer's advanced, putting on makeup. Cassie had been horrified when she came home from college one Thanksgiving to find her mother weeping in the bathroom, lipstick in hand, unsure what to do with it. She'd swiped it along her eyelid, then realizing her mistake, tried to rub it off. Her lid was streaked bright pink, her face blotchy from crying. "Can you help me?" she moaned.

Cassie had put a drop of cold cream on a washcloth and gently cleaned her mom's eyelid. Then as her mother stood trembling, Cassie carefully applied the lipstick to her mother's lips. "Rub them together," she said. "Like this." She rolled her own lips together to demonstrate, dying inside that her beautiful mother didn't remember something as simple as lipstick.

Every time Cassie came home it was worse, until she finally stopped coming. Her father wouldn't hear of a facility and kept her mom at home until the end. By then, Cassie was in law school and Shelly was already out west, starting her photography career.

Their mother was fifty-four when she died.

Cassie's father finished his sandwich and dabbed up a few crumbs with his fingers. He looked tired. "Who were you talking about?"

"Never mind. It's okay." He had a right to be tired. He was eighty-five. Old people got tired. Sometimes they forgot; it didn't mean he had dementia. Maybe Shelly was overreacting.

Cassie picked up the plates as he shuffled off to the family room to watch TV. Coming home always made her twitchy. Here in the house where she grew up, the nagging fear of dementia trailed her from room to room. Ridiculous, but there it was—that somehow the house itself might be the point of contagion. That something inside—radon or dust motes or lead in all those layers of paint—scrambled the neurons.

Her mother was about Cassie's age when it started. Small things at first—mixing up words, losing her keys. Who didn't do that? But now as she approached fifty, every name Cassie forgot felt like a warning. She tested herself constantly—the names of colleagues' kids, her aunt's birthday. The day she forgot *eggplant* felt like the beginning of the end. "That purple vegetable," she was reduced to telling Andrew as she struggled in the market. "Grab a couple of those." The word came to her in a rush of relief ten seconds later. "Eggplant," she'd blurted. But ten seconds was too long to struggle with the word eggplant.

Shaking off the memory, she washed their lunch dishes and scrubbed out the sink. Vacuumed and mopped the floor. Wiped down the stove. Her dad hadn't changed a thing since her mother died. The house had been built eighty years ago and the bones were still good. A solid house built to last. Her parents had done some updating over the years, but after her mom got sick, everything stopped. Her dad hadn't cared enough to pick out new paint or change the cabinets, and the kitchen was frozen in time with forty-year-old appliances that somehow kept chugging along. The only thing he'd bought was a big screen TV.

And of course, his bees.

By the time Cassie finished up in the kitchen, her dad was dozing on the couch with the news on. She'd originally planned to stay a day or two, but who was she fooling, her father was barely managing. She couldn't leave without sorting this out.

She needed a plan. That was the way she'd always proceeded. Actionable steps. That was how she'd gotten through law school, how she'd always attacked life. Until lately, it had worked pretty well.

She carried her bag upstairs, lingering in front of a row of framed pictures in the hallway. Her mother; forever hip in seventies bell bottoms and a tie-dyed top. She couldn't have been more than late thirties. Ten good years left. Was her mom's mind already retreating there, a decade before she started showing symptoms? Did she notice changes even then? And the thing that tormented Cassie—could there be something brewing even now in her own brain, a slurry of toxic proteins slowly amassing strength, a treasonous army that would eventually overrun her? Shelly, who had dodged the genetic mutation that guaranteed early onset, was forever haranguing her to get tested. "At least you'll know what's going on," she said.

"I'll think about it," Cassie said, and she did. She thought about Alzheimer's every day. Every missed word, every lapse in concentration unnerved her.

She had never told Andrew any of this. He only knew his grandmother had died young. If Cassie had the mutation, Andrew had a fifty percent chance of inheriting it too. She knew she needed to be honest with him about their family history, but she could barely think of it herself.

Because if it was coming, did she really want to know?

Chapter Two

The next morning, Cassie got up early and went for a run. Her father was already sitting with the paper and coffee, but she had to move first. She ran nearly every day unless it was icy or snowing. She had a gym membership for extreme weather but preferred to be outside, heading west on 79th Street, bouncing impatiently at the lights or ignoring them if there wasn't much traffic. Hitting her stride after she crossed the West Side Highway and gained Riverside Park, with the Hudson on her flank. The city, on steroids, muscling to the water. She ran with her earbuds in, listening to podcasts or music. Or sometimes just the sounds of the city revving up for the day.

Running was almost a religion to her. Five miles. More on the weekends. Phil used to urge her to skip it once in a while and spend a lazy Sunday morning with coffee and bagels. Looking back, maybe she should have. Staying in shape was part of it. No question. But more than that, all the research showed a connection between exercise and cognitive function. They didn't know exactly why, only that people who moved had sharper brains. Less likely to get dementia. So she ran like her life depended on it.

There weren't many cars out early on a Saturday, especially on the back roads of Laurelton. It felt like country up here, with the narrow winding roads and old stone walls. The trees hadn't leafed out yet, about a week later than in the city. Everything was slower up here—neighbors even said hello, which would never happen in New York.

She crossed the road and jogged up the hill onto the undeveloped land next to her father's property, coming upon a grassy area where, surprisingly, someone had installed dozens of bee hives. She kept well away, imagining how many insects must be churning inside.

The woods had the expectant feel of spring—leaf buds about to unfurl, ivy emerging from leaf litter on the forest floor. She and Shelly had once buried a time capsule here with a detailed letter about what was happening on Earth in 1978: the first woman astronaut, Reese's Pieces, a test tube baby.

She paused at a speckled boulder. That might be the spot, but maybe not. Who could remember after all these years? She'd bet even Shelly, who had a faultless memory, couldn't find it. But the doubt persisted as she ran on. Her mind, which had always been her biggest asset, played games with her, taunting her with what she thought she knew or should have known or might have forgotten. Should she have remembered the rock? Would Shelly have remembered, would anyone? She had no way of knowing. All she had was the dread that paced her, no matter how hard she tried to outdistance it.

She almost missed the sign. *Luxury homes by Weber Properties.* The rendering showed a high-end gated community. Pretentious construction. No charm, just big and new. The acreage next to her dad's house apparently was going to be developed.

For a moment, she felt a piercing sense of loss. Her parents had always loved that their land backed up to all this open space, that they couldn't see another house from where they sat. She had nothing against change. In fact, economic development for the city of New York was what she did for a living, crafting the legal framework for historic preservation and affordable housing projects. The city was a living, breathing entity, always evolving. Even here in Connecticut, life moved on. But her dad would be upset the property was being developed. She wondered if he knew, or if he'd known and forgotten.

She was still stewing about the development when she reached town with its tidy shopping district, the library on one corner and police station on the other. Laurelton had a studied quaintness, the kind of place that had managed to avoid chain stores, where kids could walk to town for ice cream without anyone worrying. If only Andrew were younger and she could tuck him away in a place like this. She'd hoped growing up in New York would immunize him from the allure of New Orleans. He was already a city kid, had been to museums, knew how to navigate the subways. But apparently the mind-bending freedom of college had seduced him.

The coffee shop was packed. The woman in line ahead of Cassie, who had hold of a toddler, groaned in exasperation. "I don't know why they can't get more help on the weekends. It's always busy. You'd think someone would figure that out." The little boy wriggled free, making for the granola bars and bags of veggie chips that were supposed to be better for you than regular chips but really weren't. The mother dashed after him, thanking Cassie for saving her place in line.

"Don't worry about it," Cassie said when the woman returned but missed what else she was saying because she'd caught a glimpse of the newspaper rack.

"Oh God, that nightmare," the woman said when Cassie ducked back in line with *The Laurelton Tribune*. "I'm in real estate so I'm all for building, but that guy Weber wants to put up a bunch of McMansions. It'll ruin the town's character."

"Who's this Weber Properties?" Cassie said. "Have they done anything else around here?"

Until now, Laurelton had escaped the frenetic development of Stamford a few miles away, probably because it was too far from the train. Laurelton had stayed small with strict zoning. Half acre lots in town, at least two acres farther out. Her parents had one of the few five-acre parcels. But now it appeared the zoning laws had been relaxed because Weber Properties was poised to build forty homes on that twenty acres.

"Some outfit from New Haven. They've done a couple of other projects around here." She gave Cassie a curious look. "You haven't heard about this? It's all anyone's talking about."

"I live in the city. I'm just here visiting my dad."

The woman set down the toddler, who'd begun to twist. "Beth Tartullo." She extended a hand. "I'm with Keller Williams here in town. I'd give you a card, but I know for a fact all I have are graham crackers." She let go an easy laugh. She looked like any suburban mom in leggings and a sweatshirt, her hair swept into a slightly disheveled ponytail. "Who's your dad? Would I know the name?"

She was perfectly pleasant, but the question caught Cassie off guard. Even with her worry over Andrew, she'd been energized by her run, reluctantly charmed by the town's tasteful storefronts and pristine sidewalks. Appealing in a quiet way. Despite her love of New York, some days it was a battle just to walk out the door. New York was not easy. You had to fight for your scrap of sidewalk, shoulder your way onto the subway with eight million other people, and hope the train wasn't delayed. And horrifyingly, the rats were making a comeback. You saw them even during the day, darting behind piles of garbage or scurrying under parked cars. At times, especially lately, it all felt exhausting.

But no one asked if they knew your father in New York. She considered ignoring the question, but Beth was smiling expectantly and Cassie couldn't bring herself to be rude.

"Sorry, I'm Cassie Linden. My father is Stuart Linden."

"You're the Linden property?" Beth's eyes opened up. "That's right next door."

"Yes, I know."

"What's your dad going to do?"

"About what?"

"Rumor has it Weber is after his property too. They want to build another ten homes."

Her father had said nothing. Did he even remember? In his day, her dad had been one of the sharpest attorneys around. A partner in Linden, Soule and Harrison, one of Fairfield County's most well-connected firms. Her dad had always known who was buying and selling. Who had a deal in the works. "I ah...just got here," Cassie said, slightly embarrassed. "He hasn't mentioned it."

Beth swung the little boy to her other hip. "Don't let him sell to Weber. If he's looking to sell, have him give me a call." She lowered her voice, which carried even in the crowded coffee shop. "Seriously. Forty houses is bad, but fifty would be a disaster. I'm sure your dad knows what's going on. You ask him."

"I will," Cassie assured her, although she had no faith she would get any kind of answer.

• • •

Her father was out in the field tinkering with his hives when she got home. They used to be sky blue but had bleached out over the years and were now the milky hue of a cloudy day. Two of them, three boxes each, one stacked on top of the other. Cassie wandered out to join him, keeping a wary eye on a couple of stray bees. Her parents' field was an untamed thing—it started out as lawn near the house but soon abandoned any pretense of cultivation. Her dad had the field mowed spring and fall so it wouldn't revert to woods. And now, after a long winter, the grass was just starting to grow.

"Do you know about this?" She handed him the *Tribune.* "They want to build forty houses on the Kingsley property." They'd always called it the Kingsley property because it had originally belonged to a family named Kingsley. No one knew anything about them, except they were from England. They'd never seen any Kingsleys, and the property had been wild for so long, they'd assumed the family had gone back where they came from and forgotten all about it.

Until now.

Her father squinted at the newspaper. "I might've heard something."

"Didn't you see the sign?"

"What sign?"

"On the way to town. A woman at the coffee shop told me the developer is interested in this property too. Has anyone called or sent a letter?"

"This property? Why would I want to sell the house?"

"I'm not saying you do. I'm just asking." It struck her how easily someone could take advantage of him. The elderly mother of a colleague had nearly lost her life savings when a scammer got her on the phone and convinced her to hand over her bank password. Only by chance the woman's son happened to drop by and made her hang up. But they had to close all her accounts, and her mother wasn't permitted to go online after that. The colleague, one of Cassie's friends, was heartbroken at how quickly her mother had lost all sense. Before any of them realized what was happening.

"I'm not interested," he said. But underneath his dismissal, there was the slightest hesitation that he might have missed something. He handed back the paper. "Here, why don't you give me a hand?"

"Me?"

"There's no one else around."

She swallowed, but that's what she was here for, to help.

Her mother would have adored all this. She'd loved the idea of bees. The seed had taken root on her parents' honeymoon in Greece where, to hear them tell it, they'd tramped through dusty olive groves and tasted honey straight from the comb. They'd come home enchanted with the idea of one day planting a few olive trees and raising bees on their acreage in Connecticut. The climate was wrong for olives, but they reminisced about Greece and those sunny hives.

But her mom had run out of time. So her father picked up the torch and carried it, faithfully tending the hives his Maggie had dreamed about but never got to see. His passion for the bees wrapped up in his love for her, until finally, there was no difference between them.

With a grunt, he lowered himself to one knee and began stuffing leaves and bits of sticks into a small can that gave off a faint aroma of wood smoke. "Having trouble getting this thing lit," he grumbled. He struck a match, but the flame faltered in the breeze.

"Shouldn't you be wearing your veil?" Cassie said.

He wasn't wearing any protective gear, not even a baseball cap, and bees had started drifting around. "If I could get this damn smoker started, they'd calm down. They don't like it when you open the hive."

She flinched as a bee careened past her nose. "Then why did you?"

Her dad looked up. "Why did I what?"

"Open it."

"Here." He handed her the box of kitchen matches. "See if you can get this going." The smoker reminded Cassie of the oil can from *The Wizard of Oz* with a tiny bellows in back. She didn't particularly like the idea of hanging around open bee hives, but she squatted next to him and struck a match, shielding the flame from the breeze. This time it caught, and the tinder sparked, sending up a satisfying flame. She smiled up at him, pleased she could help. "Now what?"

"Close it," he instructed.

She quickly closed the top and pumped the bellows until white smoke issued forth like a signal to surrender. Her dad took the bellows and lumbered to his feet, puffing smoke in the general direction of the hive. Bees were everywhere, crawling all over the open box, with more flying around.

"So what are you doing?" she asked, stepping back to avoid getting a lungful of smoke.

Her dad pumped vigorously. "Need to see what's going on in there."

"Don't they just do their thing?"

"I always open them up this time of year. Need to see how they came through the winter. It's April, right?"

"Yes, it's April," she said, her heart catching that he didn't know.

"Give me a little more smoke," he said. He was attempting to lift one of the frames from the open box, which agitated the bees even more. Dozens of them boiled around his head.

She puffed the smoker, which cleared some of them, but her father was still having trouble freeing the frame. "I need that tool."

"Which tool?" Cassie scanned the ground to see if he might have dropped it on the grass.

"That flat thing, you know…" He waved her off impatiently then gave the frame a yank and managed to pull it free. But he lost his grip, and the whole thing, black with bees, dropped into the box with a sickening thud.

"Look out. They're all over you!" Cassie steered him to a safer distance, her heart clamoring as she puffed smoke at a posse of pursuing bees.

Her dad seemed shaken too. He looked old, without the vigor she remembered. His hair thinner, the skin on his face and neck gone slack. Miraculously, neither of them had been stung.

"Maybe I'll leave it for tomorrow," he said. "They're too riled up now."

She heaved a sigh of relief. "That's a good idea."

•   •   •

She regrouped on the porch steps after her father went inside to rest. The house was a classic white colonial. Black shutters. Red door. Back in the day, painting the front door red had been a stroke of daring. Her mother, of course, was the instigator. She loved color, wrapped herself in flamboyant shades of orange and electric blue, blazing through their staid Connecticut town like a meteorite. Always nudging her buttoned up husband to step out. He'd repainted the door over the years, but like the hives, it was now a washed-out version of itself. The whole house needed a good going over. Bits of paint were flaking off, and moss crept along the siding, giving the wood a greenish cast.

She turned her face to the sun, which was surprisingly warm for April. Her dad needed more help, but he wouldn't accept it. Especially as an edict from her. She wasn't sure why it had always been so difficult between them. From the time she was small, she'd chafed at his decrees, even when it would have been easier to go along. Even when she secretly thought he was right. He'd urged her to consider Columbia, but she refused. He insisted she see the campus anyway, pulling alumni connections to get her an interview. "You love New York," he said, "and you have the grades. It's the perfect place for you." She was taken with the campus and its heady urban feel but stubbornly wouldn't say so. It was too close to home and an even bigger strike—her father's alma mater. Her mother, fumbling in her own mist of confusion, couldn't see Cassie was wavering. She might have accepted Columbia with a little nudge, but her father was a bulldozer, and she wouldn't give him the satisfaction. She went to Boston University instead. A reputable school, but not Columbia.

Her father drove her up to Boston on move-in day, but she was spoiling for a fight and took offense at what he didn't say. Her mom, riding along with them, cried and clung when it was time to say goodbye, like Cassie was the parent and her mother the child.

Her mom had been gone more than twenty-five years, but Cassie missed her every day.

She was about to get up and see what her dad was doing when a postal truck turned up the driveway, spitting stones as it came.

The driver retrieved a white wooden box from the back and set it gingerly on the ground. "I need someone to sign for this," he said.

"What is it?" The box was about two feet wide and a foot high with screened holes on either side. A suspicious buzzing came from inside.

"Bees. Can you sign?"

"Bees! He ordered more bees?"

The driver consulted his manifest. "Linden, right?"

"Yes, that's us. But I don't think he meant—"

"Ma'am?" The driver handed her a pen. "If you could please just sign."

She sighed. "Yes, of course." She signed then left the box and went to find her dad.

"My bees!" he said, hurrying out after her. "I forgot they were coming. I meant to order another hive. Now I have nowhere to put them." He squatted next to the box, peering through one of the small, screened openings.

Cassie squatted next to him, even though the buzzing made her skin prickle. "Can't you just put them in with the other bees?"

"No." Her father looked horrified. "There's a queen. They need their own hive." He sounded definite about this part. Cassie supposed it was like asking a mother and her kids to move into some other woman's house. No way was that going to work out.

"Can't they stay in here for a while?" They were just bees in a box. It looked pretty much like a hive, just a little smaller. She couldn't imagine why he needed another hive.

"No, they can't stay in here. They'll die. They need to be in a hive."

"Well, what are you going to do with them?" She knew she sounded cross but couldn't help it. He'd ordered bees he didn't remember and now had nowhere to put them.

He lowered himself to the front step. "Give me a minute. I need to think. I don't need you nattering at me."

The defeat in his voice stopped her. Her mother had begun with incidents like this. Not bees, of course, but the inability to follow through. She would find a recipe then couldn't make sense of it. Or start telling a story then lose track in the middle. Who knew if her father had Alzheimer's or run-of-the-mill dementia. It didn't matter. What mattered was he was losing the ability to think sequentially. He'd seemed almost his old self when he bustled out of the house, excited about the bees. But now he was sitting here dejected, unsure what to do next.

The hives would have to go, that was obvious. He couldn't take care of bees anymore. But she would need to talk him into it. The bees meant the world to him, a fraying but unshakeable link to her mother.

She touched his arm. "We'll figure it out." She'd been planning to look at flights to New Orleans even though Andrew had told her not to come. He needed her, but at the moment her father needed her more. And maybe she should give Andrew a chance to handle this.

Right now, she had to find a hive, or somewhere to put these bees. But even if she managed to get a hive delivered before the bees died, would her father know what to do? She wasn't going to be much help.

She pulled out her phone and typed in *bees*. No. That wasn't it. She needed someone in a white suit who knew what the hell he was doing. Someone who could transfer the bees or whatever needed to be done. Who could give her father a hand until she could convince him to get rid of them.

A beekeeper. That's what she needed.

Chapter Three

Glenn was elbow deep in a customer's hive when the woman called. He didn't usually answer his phone when he was working bees, but he'd told Lilah to let him know when she got home. Made her promise. He liked to be around for her on the weekends, but it had been one crisis after another. A customer in Ridgefield whose colony had swarmed, and now Mr. Conte, new to beekeeping, who'd opened up his hive for the first time this spring and found very few bees left. People didn't realize they had to leave their bees honey over the winter. You couldn't harvest every drop in the fall and expect them to survive. Conte had called in a panic, and Glenn couldn't say no.

He set the frame down gently so he didn't crush any of the bees crawling on top. Mr. Conte hovered like an expectant father. "So what do I do now?" he said.

"First of all, we'll take a look and see if your queen survived." The guy should have had enough sense to keep his bees alive, but all kinds of people got into beekeeping. Most just liked the idea of honey and had no clue what was involved. Glenn lifted out another frame from the middle of the box, a likely place for the queen. "Strong hive can re-queen itself, but a weak hive like this, you'll probably have to order one. Frames and worker bees too." He didn't see a queen, or any brood for that matter, which didn't bode well.

When his phone buzzed a second time, he lowered the frame back into the box. "Excuse me a minute," he said. He instructed Conte to pull out a couple more frames and keep looking for the queen. "You'll see her if you look carefully. She's bigger than the workers." He walked off a couple of yards. When you weren't working bees it was better to give them some room. They didn't like people hanging around the hive. Couldn't blame them. He wouldn't want some stranger loitering around his house either.

He'd helped Conte site the hives last summer, a yard in North Stamford with good southeast exposure where they got morning sun. Plenty of room, with woods edging the property and forage for the bees. And no pesticides. He wouldn't work bees for people who sprayed. Period.

He waited until Conte had successfully extracted a frame, then pulled out his phone.

Not Lilah.

He rubbed the stiffness in his neck. She should be home by now. He was a little uneasy about this new friend of hers. He didn't know the family and even though Lilah had assured him the mom was going to be home, he had his doubts. Not that Lilah actually lied, she just conveniently forgot. Like the time he went to pick her up at the movies, and she'd gone off with a friend to get ice cream. "I didn't know you were coming," she'd said. "I thought I was supposed to call." He was about to try her now when his phone lit up again.

The same number. Who *was* this? He felt a prickle of worry. The hospital. The police. A million things could happen to a twelve-year-old girl.

"Glenn Marsden," he said curtly, his heart suspended. Lilah was his everything. There would be no world without her.

"I'm so glad I reached you." The woman sounded out of breath. "I'm looking for help with some bees. For my father, actually. He's the one with the bees. We have a bit of an emergency."

"What kind of emergency?" His heart rate began to settle. It wasn't about Lilah. Just some homeowner with what they thought was an emergency. "Bees get into the house?" That was it ninety percent of the time.

"Oh God, no! I mean I hope not, there's no sign of that. I haven't seen any inside the house."

He glanced over at Conte, who was trying to replace a frame. He'd stirred up the hive, what was left of it, and a bunch of bees were flying around his head. It wouldn't take long before one found its way up his pant leg or under his veil.

"So what's the problem?" He didn't have time for a long conversation, he needed to make sure Lilah was home where she was supposed to be. It was easier when the babysitter used to come, but now, in seventh grade that was a nonstarter. Last week, he'd made the mistake of yelling at her when she went to a friend's and didn't tell him, which sent her into a funk for two days. God help him, he had no road map for parenting a preteen girl.

"The problem is my dad ordered a box of bees and has nowhere to put them. They're here right now and—"

"Well, he'll need a hive for starters." This was no emergency, just someone who'd failed to plan. He had no time for this.

"He has a couple of hives, but they already have bees in them. Look, he's ah…" She dropped her voice. "He's eighty-five and having memory issues. He needs help. Is there any way you can stop by?"

"So he has bees now?" Across the yard, Conte was struggling with another frame. They must be stuck together with propolis. Bees would glue together every crack if you let them. "Can you put him on? It would be helpful if I could talk to him." He needed to wrap this up, deal with Conte and get home.

"He ah…doesn't know I'm calling. It would be better if you could just come by."

"He doesn't know you're calling?" He had no patience for people who weren't transparent. He'd had enough of that with Sophie. "Why don't you talk it over with your dad. If he's interested, he can give me a call. I'm sorry, I have to go."

"Wait. What do I do with these bees? My dad's been keeping bees for years, but it's too much for him now. I'm just here for a few days, and I need to get him some help. Please. I don't even know if he should be living on his own anymore, much less handling bees." She said this last almost like she was talking to herself, like she'd forgotten he was on the phone.

"Is it a package of bees or is there a queen? If there's no queen, he can introduce them into one of his other hives." He still hoped he could get her off the phone without committing himself, but he did feel bad for the old man. If he did have memory problems, handling bees would be tough. You had to know what you were doing and what you did the day before.

"I believe there's a queen, yes he said so. But he can't even manage the boxes anymore. He nearly dropped one yesterday."

Glenn sighed. "Where do you live? I might be able to swing by later this afternoon. But if your dad's not on board, it's not going to work."

"He'll be on board! I promise." She sounded immensely relieved. "Thank you so much."

"Don't thank me yet," he muttered. "I haven't done anything."

• • •

Lilah was already home when he got there, curled up on the couch with her phone like nothing in the world was the matter. The dog jumped down guiltily, but Lilah barely glanced up.

"When did you get home?" Glenn said. "You didn't answer your phone."

"Oh yeah, sorry. I meant to call you back."

He took a breath. He was sweaty from wrestling with Conte's hives and had gotten stung on the neck for his trouble. Stings didn't usually bother him, but he hadn't gotten the stinger out in time and this one was starting to swell, adding to his aggravation.

"Lilah, we need to talk." He sat on the couch, which the dog took as an invitation. Wriggling, he banged Glenn's leg with his stuffed hippo. "No Charlie!" he said crossly.

"Why can't he be on here? He's not hurting anything." Lilah looked mutinous at this affront.

"Oh fine, let him." He moved over and Charlie jumped up obligingly. He didn't want an argument over whether the dog could sit on the couch.

"Lilah, put the phone down please."

She clicked out from whatever site she was on with a barely suppressed sigh.

"All the way down, so it's not in your hand." He waited until she set it on the coffee table. "Thank you."

"What? I did it."

"And I'm saying thank you."

She started an eye roll, then thought better of it. He knew she was just posturing, but it got under his skin. Too much girl drama. He let her sit and stew a minute.

"What did you want to talk about?" She'd lost the bravado and sounded like a kid. A little anxious. Eight years since Sophie left and Lilah was still struggling. Glenn didn't give a rat's ass about Sophie anymore, but it killed him the way Lilah still suffered. No tears, at least not that he saw, just this vague resentment of him she wasn't even aware of. The parent who stayed. It had been so much easier when she was little and he could just swing her into his lap.

He took a breath. "I get that you don't want to be treated like a little kid, but I've got to know where you are. That's why I got you a phone."

"It's seventh grade, Dad. Everyone has a phone."

"And you need to use it the way we talked about. When you get home I want to know. If you want to go to a friend's, you need to ask."

"Why don't you just attach a leash to me like Charlie?"

"Dammit, Lilah, you're twelve, not twenty!" His voice startled the dog, who gave him an anxious look. Glenn ran a hand across his beard, lowered his voice. "I love you, and I want to keep you safe. That's all this is about." He waited until she made eye contact. "All right?"

For a moment she looked like she might cry, which took him aback. Had he been that hard? He hadn't meant to yell.

"All right," she said.

He squeezed her shoulder. "Want a snack? I'm starved."

She disentangled herself from the couch. "I could eat something."

He rummaged through the fridge, settling on peanut butter and honey sandwiches. When all else failed, he always had honey in the house. His own honey. Lilah, who'd always been artistic, had designed the label for him when she was six. A whimsical drawing of a bee on a flower. He loved it and wouldn't hear of changing it, even though she was after him to let her do something better. He sold a lot of honey at craft shows and farmer's markets, and people always commented on his label.

He found some oranges and brought it all to the table, with Charlie trotting along behind. He'd slathered extra honey on Lilah's sandwich, the way she liked it. He felt bad about coming down on her, but he needed to be firm. He remembered what it was like to be a teenager. He and his brothers had gotten into plenty of trouble. And that was with two parents at home.

"I thought you were hungry," he said. She was picking at her sandwich, not really eating.

She shrugged. "I guess not that much."

The shrug reminded him of Sophie, the casual way she used to dismiss him with the bored hike of a shoulder. It made him nervous on a level he could barely acknowledge. That fear, never far from the surface, that Lilah might grow up, and like her mother, find him lacking. She looked so much like Sophie, the blond hair and delicate features. She was going to be tall like her mother too. Right now she was gangly, but she'd grow into it.

He tore off a piece of his own sandwich and fed it to Charlie, a peace offering, even though he had a rule about not feeding the dog from the table. He had a lot of rules. Maybe that was why Lilah was starting to chafe.

"I saw that," Lilah said with the hint of a smile.

"Yeah, I know." He smiled back. "He's such a beggar."

"He rolled in something when I let him out before."

He sniffed in Charlie's general direction. "Ah jeez, that's what I smell. Where'd he go, the swamp?" They joked that it was a swamp, but the yard actually sloped down to a wetland. Skunk cabbage and milkweed. Marsh marigolds, with their riot of yellow flowers that were early forage for bees. When a tree fell, it rotted where it lay, no one came to chip it up. Not everyone wanted a wetland in their backyard, but he treasured it. That was why he'd bought the house a decade ago. A wooded neighborhood in an older modest section of Laurelton, a quiet place to raise bees and a family. At the time, Sophie was still on board, although he should have seen signs of her discontent.

Lilah got up with her plate. "I don't want any more," she said, tipping the remnants of her sandwich in the dog's bowl, which brought Charlie skidding across the kitchen. Charlie was a rescue—part lab, part shepherd. Maybe a little something else thrown in. Good natured and smart enough to know where he'd landed. Glenn hadn't been keen on getting a dog—he had enough to do—but when did he ever say no to Lilah?

Charlie had been advertised as housebroken but wasn't even close. If he had an accident, and there were plenty, he always managed to hit the rug instead of the floor. Lilah wouldn't hear of locking him in a crate when they left the house, so Glenn papered the kitchen and hoped for the best. Charlie was a terror, but a lovable one. As a puppy, he'd chewed up any shoe he could find and still surfed the counter for food the minute they left the room. He was always overjoyed to see them whether it had been fifteen minutes or five hours, greeting them at the door with his hippo, his whole body vibrating with excitement. Lilah had become moody but Charlie never wavered, always thrilled to chase a squirrel or roll in whatever disgusting thing he could find. Charlie was the great leveler. Even when they couldn't laugh at much, they still laughed at Charlie.

"Do you have any homework this weekend?" Glenn asked as he rinsed the plates.

"Just some math, which I already did. And we have a project for social studies."

"Oh yeah? What's it on?"

"We can choose. Either the causes of the Civil War or Reconstruction, you know, after the war."

"So what are you thinking about?"

She shrugged. "I haven't thought about it much yet." She was drifting back toward the family room, but he didn't want her on the couch all afternoon.

"When's it due?"

"Don't worry. I have plenty of time."

"I'm not worried, just trying to stay on top of things. That's all."

"It's my project. You don't need to stay on top of it."

"Hey!" He cut her a look. "There's no call to speak like that."

Out of nowhere she crumpled.

"Peanut, what's the matter?" He smoothed her hair, a hard pit in his stomach as she sobbed into his sweatshirt. "Is it the project? I'm happy to help, or if you don't want help, that's okay too. I know I need to give you more space. I get that. I'm sorry." Somehow he always managed to step in it.

"It's not you."

"Tell me then." He could take pretty much anything except Lilah crying. That eviscerated him.

"I called Mom the other day, but she never called back. I even left her a message." She buried her face in his chest and wouldn't look at him.

So that was it. Goddamn Sophie. What kind of mother wouldn't even pick up the phone? She didn't deserve a child in this life or any other. He took a breath. Even when Sophie was being a shit, he tried not to badmouth her. The child psychologist had made a point of telling him that he needed to support Lilah's relationship with her mother. Whatever shape it took. So he buttoned it up even when he wanted to wring Sophie's neck.

"She's probably just busy," he said, rubbing Lilah's back in small circles. "I'm sure she'll call when she gets a chance." He was so fucking sick of making excuses for Sophie, but how did you tell a kid her mother was a self-centered jerk who was never going to change? It would have been better if Sophie had dropped dead.

The one time Lilah went to Colorado to see her mother had been a disaster. Lilah had been eight, tentative about seeing the mother she hardly knew, but still young enough to be hopeful. Glenn was wary but couldn't think of a way to say no. Right from the beginning, Lilah was homesick, calling to ask what Charlie was doing, inquiring about the bees. There was a boyfriend in the house, which Glenn didn't like. Some other man around his daughter. Sophie, newly enamored with the idea of motherhood, bought books and toys for a younger child, then from what Glenn could tell got frustrated when Lilah didn't use them. She paraded Lilah around town, introducing her to friends but forgot a child needs lunch. She sounded relieved when Lilah asked to come home early.

Lilah put a gloss on the visit once she got back, talking about Colorado and what they'd done, but Sophie didn't return her calls, and Lilah wilted a little more each day, which made Glenn furious. It was one thing to trifle with him, unpardonable to hurt his daughter.

Lilah pulled back, eyes wet. "Maybe she's backpacking and doesn't have service. That happened before, remember?"

"Yeah, that's probably it. You know how bad the service is there." He kissed her forehead, hoping she couldn't see what he really thought. Her optimism slayed him, how she found reasons to believe. Doubtful that Sophie was backpacking in April, with the kind of snow they got in the mountains, but he wouldn't lay bare the truth, that she just didn't give a damn. Sophie had never wanted to be a parent. Glenn was the one who'd urged her, said it would bring them closer. Too young and naïve to recognize they were never going to make it.

"Whatever." Lilah swiped at an eye, ready to move on. Her mood changes were so quick he could never keep up.

"Hey, I've got to see a guy who's having trouble with some bees. Why don't you come with me? Shouldn't take long. We can pick up Thai food on the way home from that place you like on Chestnut."

"Maybe I'll just stay here."

"And do what, sit on your phone all afternoon? I doubt you're going to start that social studies project this minute. Come with me; it's a nice day. We can bring Charlie too."

"Bring Charlie to some bee guy's house? You never do that." She looked skeptical, but he could tell she was wavering.

"We'll leave him in the car with the windows open. He'll think it's great just to get out of the house."

She smiled. "Yeah, he doesn't care where he goes."

"What do you say?"

She chewed a nail. "I don't know…"

"Aw, come on. We'll get ice cream too."

"Sunny Daes?"

"Whatever you want."

She brightened. Sunny Daes had sealed the deal. "All right, let me get his leash."

Glenn took hold of the dog's collar. "We better hose him down first."

They rinsed the dog, who shook all over them, but at least was now semi-clean. They got in the truck with Charlie dripping in the back seat, and Glenn leaned over and mussed Lilah's hair.

"What's that for?" she said.

"Because I've got my daughter with me, and we're going for Thai food and ice cream. Sounds like a pretty good afternoon to me."

She rolled her eyes but she was smiling, which he counted as a win.

Chapter Four

The beekeeper drove up in a truck with a girl in the passenger seat and a black dog hanging out the back window. If it weren't for the name, *Marsden Apiaries,* Cassie might have assumed he'd blundered up the driveway by mistake. She wondered briefly if he always carted around the whole family, but it didn't matter. At least he'd come.

He didn't exit his truck immediately. He stayed put for a minute, talking to the girl, who Cassie assumed was his daughter. Pretty, with white-blond hair, maybe eleven or twelve.

"Don't know why you had to bring someone out," her dad groused. He'd been babysitting the bees all afternoon, spraying them with sugar water and moving them into deeper shade when the sun hit the front of the house. "All I need is another hive. I could've called a few people. I don't need this guy telling me how to run my bees."

"Well he's here now, so let's just see what he has to say. You don't have to do anything you don't want to." She gently nudged her father off the porch as the beekeeper got out of his truck.

"Glenn Marsden," he said, extending a hand. "I guess I talked to you earlier."

"Thanks so much for coming." Cassie shook his hand. "This is my father, Stuart Linden." She'd imagined someone older, a little fusty, with a pot belly, who puttered around the yard puffing smoke and whispering to the bees.

Glenn Marsden was not the least bit fusty. He appeared about her age, maybe a few years younger. And fit. Like he worked outside for a living, which come to think of it, he did. Although beekeeping didn't seem rigorous enough to look the way he did. Then again, hefting all those hives was hard work. He was good-looking in an unselfconscious way. Jeans and work boots, hair that might once have been light like his daughter's but was starting to gray. She was used to Phil and the lawyers she worked with, pasty all of them, with bellies gone soft from too many lunches out. Glenn Marsden didn't look like he had much use for fancy lunches. He probably grabbed a sandwich on the run.

"We've been—" she began, but he stepped past her to squat next to the box of bees.

"How long have they been here?"

"Oh, a couple of hours," her dad said.

"More than a couple," Cassie put in, vaguely annoyed Marsden had cut her off. If he was one of those men who didn't listen to women they were going to have problems. "They came this morning, remember Dad?"

Marsden ran a finger along the rim of the box. "You give them any food?"

"Sugar water." Her dad seemed relieved to recall this.

Marsden got up, frowning. "That's okay for now, but they need honey. Sugar doesn't have any nutrients."

"I know that." Her dad bridled. "I've been keeping bees for years. My daughter, here, she's the one who got panicky."

"Didn't mean to offend," Marsden said, "but you'd be surprised how many people feed sugar or corn syrup when the honey's a little light. Not faulting you, a lot of commercial beekeepers do it too." He cast a glance down the driveway. "I saw your hives on the way in, you've got them in a good south-facing spot."

"Sited them myself," her dad said, but Cassie could tell he was still ruffled.

"What kind of bees do you keep?"

"Italians."

Marsden nodded. "They don't usually give much trouble. Should we take a look, see what's going on? Then we can figure out where to go from here." He had a nice respectful tone with her dad, which would go a long way. Still, her father had that stubborn look. This wasn't his idea, and he was going to fight it.

"Your daughter is welcome to get out of the car," Cassie said. "It's cooler on the porch." The windows were open, but it didn't seem right to make the girl sit in the car on a warm day.

"Want to get out, Lilah?" Marsden said.

She shrugged. "I'm okay."

"Why don't you come down and give us a hand?" His voice was mild, but it wasn't really a question. The girl sighed extravagantly, and Cassie thought she might be about to argue, but she disengaged from the passenger seat. "Can Charlie get out?"

"No," Marsden said. "Let him stay in the car."

"It's okay if you want to let him out," Cassie said. "There's plenty of room for him to run around."

Marsden shot her an irritated look. "Thank you, but he's fine. The windows are open."

Lilah gave her father a sidelong glance. "She said he can get out." The girl wasn't letting it go, and Cassie realized she'd unwittingly stirred something up, or maybe it was already stirred and she'd just stepped in it.

"Oh, all right," Marsden said. "You can let him out. But leave the phone."

The girl opened the back door and the dog shot out like he'd been imprisoned for a decade. He did a couple of quick circles, then came to sniff at Cassie and her father. After he was satisfied, he gave a wag and ambled off toward the field.

"Keep an eye on him," Marsden told the girl.

They all trooped through the field down to the hives, following the path her father had worn over the years. Even in spring, when the grass grew tall, it never entirely disappeared. Always the whisper of a track from the house to the hives. And past the hives, an old stone wall that bordered the woods. The trees were still bare but had started to soften with a hint of green. Only a matter of days until the woods were lush with leaves.

Cassie kept a wary eye out as they approached the hives. She'd had a vehement dislike of bees ever since fourth grade when her best friend,

Marianne McKenzie, nearly died of a bee sting. Within minutes of getting stung on the softball field, Marianne had gone clammy and was wheezing for breath, her tongue swollen to twice its normal size. There were no EpiPens in those days, so the gym teacher bundled her into his car and rushed her to the hospital. Marianne recovered, but forty years later, the sight of a bee still made Cassie sweat.

"Have you opened them up yet this year?" Marsden asked.

"He tried yesterday," Cassie said, "but ran into trouble."

"Didn't have any trouble," her father said irritably. "The wind came up, that's all. Will you let me talk to the man?"

"Sorry." The rebuke made her feel foolish, but she hated to see her dad flounder, especially in front of a stranger. She had a hard time knowing when to step in and when to shut up. One minute he seemed lost and the next he was almost his old overbearing self. She tried to see it his way. She'd come traipsing in yesterday, and now here was a guy telling him what to do with his bees. She needed to give him some time to get used to it.

The hives were set on top of platforms her dad had built to keep them off the ground, which made them about chest height. This time, her dad managed to get the smoker started and after a few good puffs, wriggled the outer lid free on the first hive, releasing a few more bees. He'd put on his veil up at the house but wasn't wearing gloves or any other protective gear. But Cassie wasn't going to mention that now. The beekeeper didn't have on any gear at all, not even a veil, although he'd brought one with him.

With the lid successfully removed, her dad went to lift off the top box but couldn't get a grip on it.

"Can I give you a hand?" Marsden said.

"I've got it." Cassie's dad huffed, but the box wasn't budging.

"Here." Marsden handed him a flat metal bar with a hooked end. "Try this."

Her dad inserted the tool between the top box and the one beneath. He wiggled it a little but still couldn't manage to work the box free. "Got a hundred-fifty pounds of honey out of these hives last year," he said, stopping to catch his breath.

"Oh yeah? That's not bad." Marsden had produced another hive tool and without waiting to be asked, neatly popped the top box, lifted it off and set it on the ground. "What'd you do with it all? Sell any of it?"

"Ate some," he said, "gave away the rest. I might still have a couple of jars left."

Cassie had been through the cupboards and hadn't seen any honey, but she didn't mention it.

"When I can get her to help, Lilah's pretty good with extracting," Marsden said, smiling at the girl, who'd wandered over with Charlie. "Not so good with the cleanup though."

"What do you mean?" she protested. "I always help clean up."

He gave her a good-natured look. "That's debatable."

He was probably divorced, his weekend to have her. Cassie had never thought much about the logistics of divorced families, but now she noticed this kind of thing. Andrew wasn't a child anymore, but she knew he was hurting, especially with Phil getting remarried. A woman with young kids, a do-over family. Andrew had to wonder where that left him.

"Let's take a look." Marsden lifted out a frame from the open box and propped it against the hive. Bees crawled all over the top and sides of a thin wax foundation.

Cassie took a step back. Jesus, so many bees. She didn't think she'd said it aloud, but Marsden turned the frame over, frowning. "Not that many. Should be more."

Her dad pried free another frame. This too was thick with bees, at least to Cassie's eye, but Marsden looked displeased. He scraped at a section with his hive tool. "See this?"

Her dad leaned in.

"You've got varroa. And if they're in here, they're in the other hive too."

"Varroa?" Her dad stood blinking, the breeze lifting his thin hair.

"Mites." Marsden looked surprised her dad didn't recognize the problem. "They're parasites." He pointed with the edge of the hive tool. "See that reddish spot?" Cassie stepped closer. In the section he'd scraped clear, she spotted a tiny reddish fleck in one of the hexagonal cells. "The mites get into the brood and weaken the larvae. They can attack the adults too, but you mainly see it in the brood. When the bees hatch they're malformed and have all kinds of issues. Sometimes they can't even fly." He carefully slid the frame back into the box. "Varroa's bad. It can destroy your colony."

Her father said nothing. He seemed stunned.

"What causes it?" Cassie asked.

Marsden hiked a shoulder. "Colonies get stressed, maybe they went into winter without enough food. Pesticides are a big problem. They kill the bees that are out foraging, which weakens the hive. A weak hive is susceptible to pests."

"I don't use pesticides," her dad said.

"What about the gardeners, Dad?"

Her dad opened his mouth then closed it again.

"Don't beat yourself up," Marsden said as he helped her father lower the top box of the other hive to the ground. "Pesticides are everywhere—the golf course, your neighbors. Bees can forage up to three miles. There's no telling what they get into."

"Three miles?" Cassie said. "That's all the way downtown. How do they find their way back?"

"Mental mapping. They have a kind of internal GPS. They use the sun to navigate so they know exactly where to come back to. In fact, if you move the hive three feet, they'll fly around confused. When they return, the foragers do a kind of dance to let the others know where the food source is." He stopped, looking embarrassed he'd said so much. "Anyway, that's how they find their way back."

"That's amazing how they don't get lost." Cassie felt a surprising tug of admiration for the bees. So determined to get home. Better than she'd been.

"They have to get back before dark though," Lilah put in. "They don't fly at night."

Cassie's dad gave the girl an approving look. "There's a young lady who knows a thing or two about bees."

Lilah tossed a stick, which sent Charlie scrambling. "Not really, I've just hung around my dad a lot."

"So is there any way to get rid of the mites?" Cassie asked.

"Chemicals," Marsden said, "but I don't believe in treating. There are other options, but depending on how bad the infestation is they don't always work. Sometimes you lose the colony and have to start over. But you can breed for bees that are stronger, then if you get a few mites it won't wipe out the hive. Would help if they could forage without bringing back toxins." He glanced toward the Kingsley property. "It's a shame they're trying to develop that land next to yours. It's the last open space we have in Laurelton."

"They want to develop that property?" Her dad looked shocked. He'd apparently forgotten their conversation from the day before.

"Some developer bought it, but they don't have zoning approval yet," Marsden said. "The town could tie it up for a while. At least that's what I've heard."

Her dad scowled. "We like this area the way it is, that's why we bought this house." *We.* The way he said it gave Cassie a pang. He spoke about her mother as though she were still alive and they were navigating life together. Her father had been alone a quarter century, but his marriage was still fresh in his mind.

"So," she said. "What about those new bees? If my dad puts another hive in here, will they get sick?"

Marsden gently nudged a bee off his arm. "I don't recommend putting in a new hive when you have varroa. You'll likely lose that one too."

Cassie glanced at her dad, who was busy inspecting another frame. She lowered her voice. "Look, I'm sure you can tell we need help."

Marsden nodded thoughtfully. "I can see that."

"Can you manage the hives? Do you do that kind of thing?"

"I can do as much or as little as you want, as long as he's okay with it. I can't come in here and strong arm him. That'll never work."

They stood for a moment looking at her dad, who was trying to slot the frame back into the box. This one too, was infested with mites. There didn't seem much point in looking at any more frames, so Marsden helped her dad put the boxes back together and seal up the hives.

"Dad," Cassie said, "with the mites and all it doesn't sound like a good idea to keep these new bees. Mr. Marsden might be able to find someone to take them."

Her dad removed his veil. His face was set. "I'm not giving away my bees."

Cassie glanced at Marsden, who rubbed the back of his neck.

"Mr. Linden, the arboretum might let you keep your bees over there, the new ones that aren't infected. I have an empty hive we could put them in. That way you could work them whenever you wanted."

"I'm not working my bees somewhere else. I want them here. Don't want to drive to see them."

Cassie felt a small ping of alarm. Driving to see his bees definitely wouldn't work. He needed to be driving less, not more. But the bees meant the world to him. What would he do if he didn't have his bees?

She glanced at the box, which Marsden had left in the shade of the truck. They were back to square one with a box of bees and nowhere to put them. "I don't know how we can put these near other bees," she said. "You understand the hives are infected, right?"

"Of course I understand," her father snapped.

Marsden stowed his hive tool in his pocket. He looked ready to be gone. "Why don't you think it over? You can let me know any time. If you find something else, that's fine, just be sure to get those bees situated in the next day or two."

"Wait," Cassie said. She was near panic at the thought of letting him get in his truck and leave. "Would you, I mean I know it's not ideal with the mites and all, but could you bring that empty hive over here?"

Marsden looked dubious. "I guess I could. You run the risk of the infestation spreading though." He looked at her dad. "If you're willing, we could try a couple of things with those infected hives."

"How about we let Mr. Marsden give us a hand?" Cassie said, willing her dad to be amenable.

"*Us?*" Her dad scoffed. "Since when do you have anything to do with the bees?"

She tried not to bristle at his tone. She'd like to chalk it up to the frustration of dementia, but the truth was, he'd always been imperious. Making pronouncements, expecting everyone to fall in line.

"Dad." She couldn't quite keep the frustration from her voice. "You're right, I'm not much of an assistant, and I'm not going to be here long anyway. You need a professional."

Her dad was quiet for a minute.

"Fine," he said finally. "He can bring over the extra hive, but I'm not turning over my bees to someone else." He glowered at the two of them, as if they'd cooked up some conspiracy. "I can manage them myself," he said and began stumping back to the house.

"I'll bring the hive over first thing Monday," Marsden said, then surprised her by adding quietly, "I've seen this happen before. People get to an age when they can't handle it, but it's hard to let go."

She smiled ruefully. "You don't want to sneak over in the middle of the night and steal them, do you?"

He shook his head. Under the right circumstances, he looked like he could have a nice smile. "Sorry."

She waved him off from the top of the driveway to be polite. She'd been here twenty-four hours and had accomplished exactly nothing. It had been one crisis after another—the bees, Andrew.

Five o'clock. She thought about pouring herself a glass of wine but laced up her shoes instead.

Four or five miles would help.

Chapter Five

Meyer's Toys in downtown Laurelton was just the way Cassie remembered, a treasure trove of Legos and paint sets and battery-operated cars. Cassie half expected Mr. Meyer himself to be at the register but it was a teenager she didn't know, and she realized if Meyer were still alive, he would be her dad's age.

She'd stopped in to look for a puzzle, something her dad might enjoy that they could do together. With his sense of order he'd always been a big puzzle person and they'd spent many family nights around the coffee table. She rifled through the ones on the shelf, but most were way too complicated, a thousand pieces or more. He would never be able to manage that. Her heart ached with how diminished he'd become. His decline was so uneven. He hadn't yet lost the force of his personality and still spoke with conviction, even if he didn't always know what he was talking about. But after three days, she'd begun to hear the repetition, the "loop" was the way she thought of it. He came back to chew on certain subjects, like the bees, that were top of mind.

Maybe a bee puzzle. He might like that. But she couldn't find any and finally settled on a hundred-piece dinosaur puzzle. Was that too childish? She didn't want to offend him either. Such a fine line to walk.

She was on her way to the register when a little girl skipped by with a doll Cassie had loved as a child, an iconic doll that had been around forever. Blond and curvy and definitely not PC anymore. *What was it called?* A flush of fear crawled up her throat. Everyone in the world knew this doll. Why couldn't she think of it? This happened more lately, these sinkholes that swallowed her memory. No telling why or when it might happen. One minute she was perfectly fine and the next she couldn't remember a goddamn *doll.*

She squeezed her eyes shut right there in the store, trembling with the effort. It was right on the tip of her tongue. Something with a *B.* Why couldn't she *remember?*

It came to her all at once. *Barbie.* Of course. They'd even made a movie.

She let go a shaky breath. Stress could do this, right? She was under a lot of stress. The divorce. Her dad. And now Andrew.

But Jesus. *Barbie.*

She had a way to deal with this. This raw terror of forgetting.

She felt for her purse. She knew exactly where the paper was—zipped into a side compartment of her wallet. The name of the genetic counselor Shelly had found. Her sister had located someone in New York and insisted Cassie write it down. But every time Cassie thought about making the call her heart balled up into a tiny fist.

What if the news was bad? How would she go on with her life?

She'd almost tossed the paper a couple of times, but at the last minute something always stopped her. A grim insurance policy of sorts. If she wanted to know, all she had to do was make an appointment.

She was paying for the puzzle, still rattled by the Barbie incident, when her phone lit up.

"What's going on there?" Phil said without preamble. "How's your dad?"

"You want the long version or the short one?" She still found it easy to talk to Phil, but it often left her with a lingering sense of loss. Not so much for him, but for her former life, when she had a partner to share things with. Maybe that was why she'd missed the signs he was checking out, because they'd always been cordial. Touching base about their day, conferring about Andrew. Their emotional connection fraying so gradually she never noticed until it was gone. Now, she was left trying to figure out what was next. Friends urged her to try one of those dating sites, but she couldn't imagine posting her picture online and hoping somebody swiped. What was she supposed to say about herself? *Almost fifty. Might forget my name in a few years.*

"There's a long version?" Phil said. "That doesn't sound good."

"Shelly was right, he's slipping. And crankier than ever. I'm trying to get him help with those bees, but you know my dad. I've got a beekeeper coming over today." She felt a sudden, surprising warmth at the thought of seeing Marsden, which she quickly tamped down. This was no time for a silly crush. "Anyway, I'm going to have to stay a week or two to get things sorted out. I'll work from here and go in if I have a meeting."

"Have you talked to Andrew?"

Her stomach immediately cinched with worry. "Not since Saturday. I tried a couple of times yesterday but couldn't get him. Have you?"

"Yes, and it's not good. He called me earlier. I wish you'd told me about this over the weekend. I thought we were going to stay connected about anything to do with Andrew." His irritated voice.

"I thought you should hear it from him. He said he was going to call as soon as he got off the phone with me."

"Well he didn't, not until this morning. But it doesn't matter now. What matters is that the university is convening a review board to look into what happened."

"Oh God." She stepped onto the sidewalk with her package. In the time she'd been inside, it had become cloudy and the raw morning crept through her clothes. "How's the boy, do you know?"

"Apparently still in the hospital."

"How did Andrew sound?"

"Scared, as he should be. This is serious, Cassie."

"I realize it's serious." Phil could be so condescending; she didn't miss that. Big Law hubris. She took a fortifying breath. No point arguing with him. "So what's happening?"

"The frat is on probation, and this review board is going to be looking for someone to blame."

"When's the hearing, should one of us be there?"

"The twenty-third. I already called, and they won't allow parents to attend. He has to appear alone."

She thought with dismay of Andrew trying to hold it together. "He's going to be a wreck. You know how he is. Maybe I should fly down for moral support. I hate him dealing with this all alone." Yes, Andrew had told her not to come, but what did a nineteen-year-old know? He was in trouble and she was his mother.

"Don't go. It'll make him feel like we think he can't handle it."

"He *can't* handle it. Where was his judgment the other night? You wink at all this drinking, but now look what's happened."

"For God's sake, Cassie. You make it sound like I condone this. I'm as concerned as you are."

For years, she and Phil had been on the same page when it came to Andrew. Phil, absent so much, had deferred to her. But college, and maybe divorce, had shifted the dynamic and now in ways big and small Phil constantly undermined her.

"I wish he'd get out of that frat house. I want him to find somewhere else to live in the fall." She knew this was a losing battle. He'd pledged the same fraternity as Phil, and the two of them had formed an unholy bond over it.

"Let's take it one step at a time. Right now, he needs to get through this hearing."

"Is he allowed any kind of counsel, at least?"

"No. It's not a legal proceeding. He just needs to go in there, tell the truth and show remorse. He's never been in any trouble, so hopefully they'll let him off with a warning."

"What if they don't?" She still had an uneasy feeling Andrew hadn't told her everything. But she didn't want to prod him and make him defensive. She'd never get anything out of him that way.

"Don't get ahead of yourself." Phil was beginning to sound impatient. He wasn't one to worry endlessly, he was a fixer. Identify the problem and take care of it. But she knew from experience that some things weren't fixable. "It's not going to do Andrew any good if you're a mess," he said. "That's probably why he's not answering his phone."

"I'm *not* a mess. You just said they're looking for someone to blame. What if he gets expelled?"

Phil exhaled into the phone. "If he's smart that won't happen."

"Since when are nineteen-year-olds smart?" She adored her son, but no college kid had any judgment. At that age, she'd plunged into one relationship after another, numbing herself with parties and boys to avoid thinking about what was happening at home. Too painful to hear her mom's silence on the phone, already hard for her to follow a conversation with someone she couldn't see. Her dad tried to cover, but her mother's silence swallowed every word. At least Andrew had two functioning parents. For the time being, at least.

"I have a meeting in ten," Phil said. "I'll call if I hear from him." He hung up, which made her feel cheated. At least he could have said goodbye.

She tried Andrew again, but of course he didn't pick up. He was on Mom Alert now. He would never answer.

•   •   •

Her father was parked in his usual spot in front of the TV when she got home.

"So I thought we could do this together," she said, showing him the puzzle. She expected him to scoff, but he looked it over carefully.

A memory rose up, fully formed. Heartbreaking in its specificity. "Remember, Mom used to make popcorn when we did puzzles. I always wanted extra butter, but Shelly only liked salt. We had to have separate bowls."

A smile came to him. "I remember. Your mother spoiled you girls."

"I miss her," Cassie said.

His voice was quiet. "Me too."

She drew up a chair and set a tentative hand on his. His skin was paper thin, almost translucent with delicate blue veins showing through. "I'm sorry that I haven't been very good about coming home."

He inclined his shoulder slightly. "You have your work, you're busy."

"No. I live close by. I should have been better about visiting." Something unexpected welled up inside her. "I'm going to be better from now on, okay?"

He was silent and she felt a sinking despair. It was too late, she'd squandered the chance to repair their relationship. All these years when she could have come and didn't. She hadn't even called very often. It would have taken so little.

Then, his hand closed around hers and the gentle pressure brought tears to her eyes. Her mother was gone, but her father had been here all these years. Sitting in this same chair, his hands smooth and warm and reassuring. She could have come any time, and he would have been happy to see her. In spite of everything he was happy to see her now.

They sat this way for a minute, and when he released her hand she felt a sudden loss. "Did you have a snack while I was out?" She collected an empty cereal bowl from the coffee table, swallowing the lump that had formed in her throat.

"Hmm?" He'd turned back to the TV and was absorbed in the news again.

She set down the bowl. "Dad?"

"What's that?" He lowered the volume a little.

"We need to find another housekeeper now that Elena's not coming anymore."

"Who said she's not coming?"

"You did." As she'd suspected Elena did not have a sister, at least not one who was coming to clean. "Someone who can do a little cooking too, the way Elena did." Cassie's secret plan, cooked up with Shelly, was to find someone who could transition into a caregiver as their father began to need daily help. Do the shopping and drive him around. Who was she kidding, he was almost at that point now.

"Doing fine," he said. That seemed to be his mantra. "I don't need any help."

"Not help in a big way. Just someone to keep the place tidy." She shouldn't have used the word *help*. Help with the house, help with the bees. She couldn't blame him for being resistant. He undoubtedly felt he was losing control of everything. "We can talk more about it later." Best to retreat for now. "The beekeeper is going to be here soon with that hive."

"The beekeeper?" He switched off the TV. "I'd better get ready."

•   •   •

The beekeeper's white truck bumped up the driveway, pulling over where it widened into a cut out, the gravel thinning to dirt. He had the hive bungeed into the truck bed so it wouldn't bang around.

Cassie went down to meet him, and Marsden killed the engine and got out. "How's your dad today?" he said by way of greeting.

"He remembered you were coming, at least."

He smiled. He did, in fact, have a nice smile. "That's encouraging." He glanced at the sky. "It's chillier than I'd hoped. We lost the sun. The bees don't like it much when it's cool like this; they tend to hunker down."

She looked worriedly at the empty hive. "Will we be able to get them in there?" Her dad was still adamant about managing the bees himself. She'd broached the subject again last night, hoping he'd softened, but he was still dug in. "Piece of cake," he'd said about transferring the new bees. Somehow, she doubted that. Nothing with bees was a piece of cake.

"Should be okay," Marsden said. "Might just take some doing, is all. I'm happy to help if your dad wants me to."

"We'll see," she said dubiously. Her father was waiting on the porch with the box of bees, already dressed in his bee suit and veil. Cassie hopped into the truck so they could collect him.

"Did he feed them again yesterday?" Marsden said.

"Oh yeah, he's been busy with the sugar water." She glanced at him, curious. "So how do you happen to have an extra hive?" He'd mentioned bottling honey, but she had no idea what he did besides making house calls. How many bees did a beekeeper keep?

"I always have a few extra hives lying around."

"Do you have a lot of bees?"

"About three hundred fifty hives, not that many."

She turned to see if he was kidding, but he was serious. "Three hundred and fifty! That sounds like a lot to me. How do you have time to deal with your own bees when you're taking care of other people's?"

He slid her a look, not impatient exactly, more like he wanted to be sure she wasn't trifling with him. "They're pollinators. I rent them out to farmers during the growing season. Apples and peaches. Pears. Some apricots."

"You can't possibly truck all those hives around in this."

He looked amused. "Not hardly. If I have to haul a lot of hives I rent a flatbed."

"Do they mind being transported?"

He actually laughed at this, which softened his face in an appealing way and made her smile too. It was nice to hear a man laugh, even if she'd said something ridiculous.

"They don't have much choice. And no, they don't mind. It's fine, it doesn't hurt them and the forage is good. I only deal with organic farms."

"How far do you take them?" She couldn't remember seeing any farms in this part of Fairfield County, but she'd never paid much attention. She was always in a rush to get back to the city. Here was a life she knew nothing about.

"Up to Easton and Glastonbury. Southington. It's a bit of a trip but not as far as some guys who truck their bees all the way out to California for the almond farms every year. I won't do that."

"Oh, that's much too far."

"Even if I lived out there I wouldn't do it. Those big operations are factories. It's all monoculture—just almonds. And the bees get stressed with the pesticides. I know several beekeepers whose colonies have collapsed."

She'd heard more about bees in the last three days than she'd ever hoped to, but his enthusiasm was refreshing. As much as Cassie liked her job, it wasn't a calling like bees apparently were for him.

She snuck another look at him. She'd expected someone more along the lines of a plumber, a handyman type who happened to be good with insects, who did his job, went home and had a beer. But Marsden seemed more complicated than that, concerned about pesticides and the environment. Even though she tried to eat organic, she'd never given much thought to how bees were connected to the food supply.

When they got to the house her father handed Marsden the box of bees, watching closely as he strapped them into the truck bed next to the empty hive.

"Why don't I sit back there and hold them?" her dad said.

"No need, they'll be fine," Marsden assured him. "You can sit up here." Cassie could just picture her father bouncing around in the back of the pickup with his bees.

Her dad lifted himself into the passenger seat, angling a shoulder to keep an eye on the bees.

Marsden looked at Cassie. "You coming?"

"I'll walk down," she said. Marsden had a nice way with her dad, seemed better able to defuse him than she could. Probably because they had no history.

Marsden bumped across the field and had the truck bed open by the time she made her way down the driveway. He paused before lifting out the box of bees. "Before we do this," he said to her dad, "I just want to make sure you understand there's a risk these new bees will get infected too."

"They might not."

Marsden raised an eyebrow. "Just so you're clear. We can go ahead if it's what you want."

"That's what I want." Her father's mouth was set.

"Understood." Marsden lifted out the box of bees then unloaded the empty hive. "Do you have a stand for this one?"

"A stand?"

"Like the others, to keep the boxes off the ground. Keeps them dry." Marsden said this neutrally, like it was the most reasonable thing in the world her dad wouldn't remember he had his other hives on concrete blocks. "No matter," he said lightly. "You can always add one later."

Her father had forgotten his smoker, so Marsden produced one and pulled out a wad of burlap from his pocket. He had on a fleece vest over his jeans and looked like he was ready to go hiking. No bee suit, just a veil he'd grabbed from the truck but hadn't yet put on.

When she'd googled beekeepers, most of the pictures that came up were people encased in white hazmat suits so you couldn't tell what they looked like. Marsden seemed unconcerned with the risk. He looked like someone you'd run into on a trail with a fifty-pound pack on his back and a cannister of bear spray. A man who could handle whatever came his way.

"You don't wear a bee suit," she observed.

"I do." He was puffing smoke at the bees, which made them retreat from the screen to the interior of the box. "When I'm working a lot of hives I put it on. I've been stung plenty of times, believe me. It's just that it's easier to work without one, so for small jobs like this I don't always bother."

"No gloves either?" She couldn't imagine picking up a frame of bees with bare hands.

"They're in the truck." He turned to her dad. "Ready?"

Her father shuffled over. He didn't move as well as he used to, and the bee suit made it even more awkward. It would probably take Marsden all of five minutes to transfer the bees, but he stood back, letting her dad take the lead.

Her father lifted the cover off the new hive and set it on the grass. It looked like an empty condo, scrubbed clean by the previous owner. He squatted to get his arms around the box of bees but the suit made everything difficult, and he managed only to hoist the box a couple of feet before it toppled to the ground. The bees, which had been stupefied by the smoke, began to stir restlessly.

"Give them more smoke," her dad barked.

Marsden obligingly puffed the smoker a couple of times and the bees quieted. Cassie wished he would take over, but her dad had made it clear he wanted to go it alone.

She didn't see exactly how it happened, whether dropping the box loosened the screen and allowed a rogue bee to escape, or whether the attacker came from one of the other hives, drawn by the commotion.

One minute her father was trying to get a better grip on the box, the next he'd launched himself into the air and was batting frantically at his veil.

"Got a bee in here!"

"Don't move," Marsden said. "I'll get it."

But her dad swung his head like an enraged bull, pawing at the veil as though he could dislodge the bee from the outside.

"Dad, hold still!" Cassie cried.

Marsden tried to unzip the veil, but her dad shook him off with the panic of someone who had a stinger an inch from his eye. "Get it out of here!" he bellowed.

"Crap," Marsden grunted. "The zipper's stuck."

"What do you mean, it's stuck?" her dad snapped.

Marsden still had a grip on the veil as her dad thrashed. "If you hold still," Marsden said through gritted teeth, "maybe I can pinch it through the mesh."

"Pinch it? You can't pinch it!" Her dad tugged furiously at the zipper. The bee was agitated, pinging off the veil, finally settling on his cheek. "I need to get this thing off!"

Cassie watched in horror as the bee crept toward her father's eye. "Daddy, hold still! He'll get it." She didn't see how Marsden was going to pluck the bee from her father's face through the veil, especially the way her dad was flailing around.

Marsden managed to get hold of him again, but her father pushed him off with surprising strength, stumbling toward the woods, swatting at his head.

"Don't run!" Cassie shouted, rushing after him. They would have to tackle her father to the ground at this rate. She could just picture it—taking down an eighty-five-year-old whose heart rate had probably shot through the roof. Never mind a bee sting, he'd be lucky if he came through this without breaking a hip or suffering a heart attack.

He made it a couple of yards before tripping. A soft spot on the ground, not even a hole, just a slight depression where the earth took a little dip. He went down with a howl of pain.

Marsden reached him in an instant, whipping out a pocketknife and expertly slicing open the veil. He yanked it off as her father sat dazed, breathing hard, his injured ankle splayed awkwardly in front of him. "Too late," he mumbled.

The bee had gotten him in the soft tissue of his lower lid, and the eye had already begun to swell. Cassie shook out the veil, jumping back when the bee fell out.

"It's dead," Marsden said. "They only have one sting."

She knelt in front of her father to assess his face. "This one's a doozy." The eye was puffing up fast, and the rest of his skin had a pasty color she didn't like.

"Are you dizzy?" she asked. "How do you feel?"

Her father glared at her. "How do you think I feel? I got stung on my eye, and my goddamn ankle hurts."

Marsden helped him gently to his feet. "Let's get some ice on the eye and that ankle too." They made their way to the truck, her dad grudgingly allowing Marsden to support him.

"What about the bees?" Her father cast a look at the box, which had toppled onto its side.

"Can you right it?" Marsden asked her.

"Me?" Cassie's mouth went dry.

"It's not hard," Marsden said. "Just take it by the edges and set it upright."

"Easy for you to say," she muttered. But there was no one else to do it, and she couldn't leave the bees sideways like that. Her heart skittered as she lifted the box, careful to keep her fingers away from the screen. The bees were riled up, banging around unhappily. She gently set the box upright and stepped back.

"They'll be fine," Marsden assured her dad. "It's cool today."

Once inside, they got her father settled in his wingback chair with his foot propped on the ottoman. Frozen peas on his eye and a package of assorted vegetables around the ankle.

"That's going to need an X-ray," Cassie said.

He glowered at her around the peas. "It's not broken. Look." He tried flexing his foot but winced in pain.

"We're going for an X-ray. No argument."

Her dad leaned back and closed his good eye. He looked utterly defeated.

She kissed the top of his head, which was matted with sweat. "Why don't you rest now, we can go later." She tucked the vegetables more tightly around his ankle. Her dad had always been a big believer in frozen vegetables. When she sprained her ankle playing dodgeball in sixth grade, he'd packed it with a pound of frozen Birds Eye, and they played Scrabble to take her mind off the pain. There was something comforting about frozen vegetables, a vestige of childhood when her dad could still make everything right. To this day, she kept a package of peas in the freezer.

Her dad opened his good eye and fixed it on Marsden. "Can you do it, move those bees?"

Marsden, who'd been standing near the door, stepped forward. "Of course. Don't worry about a thing, I'll take care of it right now."

Her dad struggled up and the peas slid off his face. "I'm going to be laid up for a while with this, this—" He looked down at his ankle but couldn't come up with the word. Marsden waited quietly. "This trouble," her dad said finally. "Might need some help till I'm back on my feet."

"I'd be happy to help," Marsden said. "Maybe we can discuss things in a day or two, so I know what you're thinking. I might have some ideas about those mites."

Her dad nodded, exhausted. He picked up the peas and closed his eyes again. Cassie knew what it cost him to ask for help, the man who'd always managed everything. Who'd been opinionated and overbearing but believed in his heart he was doing right for his family. He'd been reluctant to accept help even with her mom, allowing someone in only so he could go to work. Insisting he knew best what she needed. It had to be humiliating to bump up against his own frailty.

"Thank you," Cassie said as she walked Marsden outside. "I'm sure you didn't bargain for all this."

"I'm glad it wasn't worse." Now that the crisis was over, he seemed uncomfortable, rubbing his thighs and looking off toward the field. "I'll just go move those bees."

"Can I see how you do it?"

He looked surprised but pleased. "Sure, it's pretty simple."

Back at the field, the bees chafed in their box, ready to be released. She wasn't sure why she'd asked to come along when it would have been easier to let him handle it.

"I don't have a veil," she remembered.

"Don't worry, you'll be fine. Just keep back a way. They'll start flying around when I open it up." He squirted sugar water through the screen. "Occupies them a little, so they don't all rush out at once."

Controlled release. That seemed like a good plan, although Cassie couldn't blame them for wanting to get out of that box. It had been three days.

"How'd you get interested in bees?" she asked.

"My grandfather kept bees. Had a farm up in Easton. He used to let us suit up and help once in a while. My brothers weren't interested but I loved it; anytime we went to his place I wanted to see the bees. He grew lavender, made the best honey I've ever tasted." He produced a hive tool and pried open the round wooden cover on top of the box. "Why don't you take out a couple of frames from the middle of that empty hive. Just set them on the ground next to it."

Cassie did as he said, stepping back as a handful of bees arrowed out of the open box. Marsden bumped the box twice on the ground and most of the remaining bees fell to the bottom.

"You just dropped them on their heads!"

He smiled. "They're okay. Gives me a minute to get the queen out. Here, take a look."

She leaned in warily as he removed a tiny wooden cage with a couple of bees clinging to the top. "What are those bees doing?"

"Her entourage. There's always workers around the queen. They feed and groom her. They all have jobs."

"Every bee has a job?"

"And what they do changes during their life cycle. They're programmed that way."

A miniature workforce where everyone knew their role. No midlife crisis or angst about finding a meaningful career. When they finished one job they moved on to the next. "They just get to it, don't they?"

"They do." With his hive tool he flicked out a cork stopper from one end of the cage. "They'll eat this little piece of candy and free the queen in a few days. Gives everyone a chance to get used to the new surroundings and accept her."

He stapled the queen's box to a frame in the new hive, then in one quick motion shook the box of bees upside down over the empty hive.

Cassie laughed as the bees tumbled out like peppercorns. "What about the rest?" A good number had clung stubbornly to the box.

Marsden set the half empty box next to the hive. "They'll find their way in. Some just take a little longer." He glanced at her with a hint of amusement. "I thought you'd be over in the next county by now."

Cassie realized with a start she was close enough to see bees crawling up the frames inside the hive. She took a step back.

"Want to close it up? The rest can get in through the front entrance."

She swallowed. "Maybe not."

He gave her a moment, then gently set the cover on top of the hive. "That's all right, you got to see how it's done. Like I said, pretty straightforward. When the box is empty you can toss it or save it, whatever you want."

More bees were finding their way out of the box, some congregating at the hive's entrance like neighbors visiting on the front porch. Others were airborne, getting the lay of the land.

A couple of stray bees tagged along as she walked Marsden to his truck, then banked off in another direction. She glanced back at the hives, the new one sharply white against the gunmetal sky.

It had been quite a day, and it wasn't even lunch time yet.

Chapter Six

Laurelton's official business took place at Town Hall, a nineteenth century farmhouse that had been expanded over the years but still had the cramped feel of an earlier era with low ceilings and a few original scarred beams. The meeting room was packed by the time Glenn got there, and he squeezed down a row to an empty seat.

Zoning meetings were usually a snooze unless something controversial was on the agenda.

Like the Weber development.

The zoning board was the first hurdle. If they green lighted the project, the town council was likely to approve it. The thought left an unhappy knot in his stomach. He didn't like public meetings, but this was the last undeveloped tract of land in town. Untouched habitat for animals and birds, healthy forage for pollinators. He even kept fifty of his own hives there. A nice sunny clearing at the edge of the woods. His bee yard was getting crowded, and the honey from this second location was exquisite. But this wasn't just about his own hives. This issue was too important not to be here.

An older man in the next seat looked him over. "You here about that project?" Early seventies, with a head of silver hair, clothes rumpled but expensive. A lot of finance types up here, you never knew who you were talking to.

"Thought I'd see what was going on," Glenn said evenly.

"You have a horse in the race?"

"Just interested." Something about the guy's tone set him on edge. The presumption that Glenn, in jeans and work boots, couldn't have a stake here. "Actually, it'd be a shame to see that property developed."

"I'm guessing you don't pay taxes here in town."

"As a matter of fact, I do," Glenn said. This was what he disliked about Laurelton, the frank dismissal if you weren't a money guy from Wall Street. How someone like him could possibly have anything to say.

"If you live here," Wall Street said, "you ought to know what forty homes will do for the tax base in this town. Ever think of that?"

"What the tax base needs is more business downtown, not a bunch of new homes that are going to stress the schools. You have kids in public school?" Glenn knew the man didn't. Grandkids maybe, but he'd bet they went to private.

A few heads turned now, curious.

A woman to Glenn's left whispered, "Did you sign up to speak? You ought to; we need everyone we can get."

He shifted uncomfortably in his seat. "I'm not much for public speaking."

"I heard what you said. You totally made a good point about the schools." She tipped her chin toward the back of the room. "The sign-up sheet's by the door."

"Thanks," he said, although he hadn't intended to speak, just listen. He'd rather open a hive of stressed bees than stand in front of a room full of people. Bees weren't always forgiving. They could chase you fifty yards if they thought you were a threat, but they weren't duplicitous. They didn't promise one thing and do another. The only heartache was when you couldn't keep them alive.

"I'll save your seat if you want to sign up," the woman offered.

"Um, sure," he said reluctantly. She was right. Even though it made him uncomfortable as hell, he needed to speak.

First the board took up other zoning matters—a variance to widen a residential street, a homeowner who wanted to operate a hair salon out of her garage. By the time they got to the Weber development it was eight o'clock, but not a soul had left.

The developer, Chuck Weber, gave a smooth presentation. He was late thirties, in black jeans and a blue blazer with the polished look of a salesman. "Of course there are concerns about any development," he said, "but at the Weber Group we understand that a home is not just a place to live, it's where families and memories are built." He'd been facing the dais but glanced warmly over his shoulder at the audience. "These will be exceptional homes, with every amenity, that encompass elegance and technological innovation for the most discerning buyers. Starting at about three and a half million."

A murmur ran through the crowd. Weber let the room settle. He'd clearly anticipated a reaction. "This caliber of development will provide a secure underpinning for your tax base and favorably impact your own property values. Even more important, the families who move here will be your neighbors, part of your community."

Glenn's leg twitched. What a load of crap.

The rest of the speakers were divided. The woman next to Glenn spoke about the traffic a big development would bring. A local real estate agent urged the zoning board to approve. "He'll go to Darien or Greenwich if we don't jump on this. Woods are nice, but we have plenty."

The Wall Street guy clapped pointedly, and Glenn shot him an irritated glance.

When they finally called his name, Glenn's mouth went dry. The woman who'd urged him to talk gave an encouraging nod. "I think their minds are still open, just say what you said before."

At the podium, Glenn cleared his throat, heat riding up his neck at the thought of all those people behind him. He hadn't written anything down since he'd never planned to speak. All he could say was what was burning a hole in his heart.

"Twenty acres of woods and open space. It's not much in the scheme of things," he began. "Connecticut has thousands of acres of parkland and state forest for recreation and public use, and New York State has many more thousands. So why should we care about an insignificant twenty acres here in Laurelton?" He felt himself winding up, his chest expand. "We should care because it's the last open space in town and once it's gone, it's gone for good."

The zoning board chair was on his phone, but a couple of committee members appeared to be paying attention.

"I'm a beekeeper here in town, and I see firsthand what's happening to our pollinators. They're stressed by pesticides and acres of manicured lawns, which are an environmental desert. There's good healthy forage for bees and other pollinators on that property. If we don't save this piece of pristine land, what does that say for our future? Not just for us here in Laurelton, but the bigger picture? That we're so concerned about property values we're unwilling to say no to one luxury development? What message does that send to our kids and our grandkids?"

He risked a glance at the audience. Several people were nodding. "This is bigger than twenty acres," he plowed on. "It's who we want to be as a society. What kind of world we want to leave for our kids." Embarrassingly, his voice caught. "We won't get another chance here. I'm asking you to do the right thing."

He stopped, stunned he'd said all that, that it had just poured out of him. "That's all I have to say." Scattered applause greeted him as he made his way back to his seat, but when he got to his row he kept going. He was too keyed up to sit, especially next to that Wall Street asshole.

"Nice job," a woman said when he reached the back of the room. "Very heartfelt."

He turned to look, still buzzing with adrenaline. Cassie. The Linden woman.

"Oh hey." He felt disoriented seeing her here. "I...uh didn't know you were coming."

"I wanted to see what's going on since it's right next door." She gave him a thoughtful look. "You made some good points."

"I couldn't tell what they thought." His hands were sweaty, but he didn't want to wipe them on his pants in front of her.

"I saw those bees when I was out for a run the other day. Didn't know they were yours." The next speaker had started, so they edged closer to the door. "How do you think they'll vote?" she said.

"Hard to say. A couple of them might have been leaning against it, but Weber was persuasive. I'm sure they like his grand vision. And it's tough to vote against growing the tax base."

She smiled. "For what it's worth, you were persuasive too."

She was wearing jeans and a gray sweater that fit just right, and he didn't quite know where to look. "I never do this kind of thing. Honestly, I was nervous as hell."

"Could have fooled me."

"How's your dad's ankle?" he said to change the subject. "Did you take him for an X-ray?"

"Luckily just a sprain. Could have been worse." She smiled ruefully. "Things can always be worse, right?"

He relaxed fractionally. She had that right. "Is he ready for me to give him a call?"

"It's easier if you just stop by. Mornings are best. He's sharper then." She hiked a shoulder. "Although sharper is a relative term. You saw him the other day, that's about as good as it gets."

"Will he uh remember what happened?" He didn't know exactly what the diagnosis was, but Mr. Linden clearly had memory issues. Cassie had said she was only staying a few days, but here it was going on a week. She hadn't mentioned what she did, but he pegged her for something professional. The way she carried herself. Although he didn't detect a big ego. There was something careful about her, a little dented, like maybe life hadn't turned out exactly the way she wanted either.

"Oh yeah, he'll remember. He's got his foot in a boot to remind him. I told him I was going grocery shopping tonight, otherwise he would have wanted to come. I didn't think that was such a good idea with his ankle and all."

"So do you have to pick up groceries now?"

She laughed. Away from her dad and all the bee drama, she was easy to talk to.

"I suppose I should. Sometimes he surprises me with what he remembers and other times..." Her voice trailed off in a dispirited way.

Glenn felt a pinch of anxiety, like when he said the wrong thing with Lilah. Which was pretty much all the time. "Sorry. I didn't mean to make light of it, his situation."

"It's fine. If I didn't laugh, I'd cry. We lost my mom to Alzheimer's, but I never thought it would happen to my dad. He was always the one in control. I don't know if it's Alzheimer's but you know, dementia. It's hard to see."

His phone buzzed but he ignored it. He didn't want to be rude when she'd just shared something so personal. "I'm sorry about your dad, I mean the dementia and all." He didn't know what else to say. She was open in a way he wasn't used to. Sophie had never lifted the lid on what she was feeling. When he was in college, the mystery excited him. A beautiful woman, the tantalizing possibility of unseen depths. He spent years trying to fathom her, tease out what she was withholding, but eventually realized what he'd mistaken for introspection was just self-absorption. It was always about her.

"Isn't there some kind of medication to slow it down?"

"Not really, and he's still at the point where he doesn't want to admit he has a problem. He's still sharp enough to give me a hard time. That hasn't changed."

When his phone buzzed again he looked at it.

Sophie. His stomach tightened. What the hell did she want? He shoved the phone back in his pocket. She only ever called when she wanted something. It couldn't be good.

"Everything okay?" Cassie said.

"Excuse me," he said. "I have to make a call." He shouldered off through the crowd, his mind churning. He should take a breath and call her tomorrow. He knew better than to plunge unprepared into a conversation with Sophie. But if he didn't call her back he would spin all night, inventing anxious scenarios about what she was up to.

He ducked out a side door, a small measure of calm returning in the cool of the evening. Dusk had fallen and a late bird dipped into the trees at the edge of the parking lot. He headed without plan to the enveloping quiet of the wood, away from the lit busyness of the building. Even after all this time, no one could wind him up him like Sophie.

She picked up on the first ring, which increased his uneasiness. "I saw you called," he said. It often took Lilah a week to get her, but suddenly she wanted to talk.

"Hiya," she said. "It's been a while. Everything good there?" Her chummy voice, which used to make him feel like she was letting him in on a delicious secret, now just annoyed him.

"We're fine, Lilah's fine." It pissed him off all over again how she could go so long without calling her daughter.

"It's so beautiful here right now. We had snow last week but it's melting. Brad and I are going to do some backpacking in a couple of weeks."

"Listen, I'm at a meeting. What do you need?"

"Oh okay. Well this is exciting! One of my pieces was accepted into the Stowe Art Festival, and it's up for a nice cash prize." She waited for him to congratulate her but when he didn't she kept going. "Anyway, I figured I'd fly out and collect the prize and see my mom while I'm there. And I thought, you know what, I'll swing by Connecticut for a day or two on the way."

The sky was almost purple black now. He couldn't make out individual trees, just the swallowing denseness of the woods. It took him a second to realize what she was saying. "You're coming here?"

"I haven't seen Lilah in a while."

"Four years."

"Has it been that long? It feels like she came out a couple of years ago."

"When she was eight. Now she's twelve. You can't even be bothered to call her back when she wants to talk to you." He found his voice in a rush of anger. "Now all of a sudden you're coming to visit?"

She let out an exasperated sound that he knew well. "I'm coming and I want to see her. I thought I'd stay with you if that's okay."

"What?" His stomach made a hard landing. "Not a good idea."

"I'm not bringing Brad, it's just me. I guess I could get an Airbnb if it bothers you that much."

"I don't give a damn. It's Lilah I'm thinking about. She hasn't seen you in four years and now you just want to pop in?"

"I'll only stay a couple of days, then I'll be out of your hair. I thought maybe I'd take her to Vermont to see her grandmother."

"No. Lilah's not going to Vermont." The words were out of his mouth before he could stop them. He didn't know if the idea had just occurred to Sophie or if she'd planned it all along, but this was what he'd always feared, that one day she would remember she had a daughter and invade their lives like a robber bee, trying to snatch what wasn't hers.

"Why not?" An unexpected challenge in her voice. "She hasn't seen her grandmother in years. You know I have the right to take her for vacations."

A cold sweat crept along his neck. Sophie did have visitation rights. In theory, Lilah could be made to spend summers and some holidays with her mother, but Sophie had never pressed it.

"I don't want you staying at the house." The prospect of Sophie under his roof filled him with a stewing dread. Not that he might fall back under her sway; he worried about Lilah. The sudden, gratifying attention of a mother. Even a mother as unreliable as Sophie. What famished twelve-year-old girl wouldn't be seduced?

"Why not? Oh wait—" A note of amusement in her voice. "Do you have a lady friend these days? Is that the problem?"

He glanced toward the building, his face suddenly warm. "Whether I do or don't has nothing to do with it. I just don't think it's a great idea."

"Tell her not to worry, I'll sleep in the extra bedroom. Unless you've filled it with bee stuff."

"There's no bee stuff in there," he growled. "I have a shed."

"Then what's the problem?" She sounded like she honestly didn't know. That was Sophie, so caught up in her own drama she couldn't imagine what it might be like for him if she suddenly reappeared.

He took a breath. "The problem is that we're no longer married and you no longer live here and it would be better for all of us if you stayed somewhere else while you're in town."

"Better for Lilah?"

The question hung in the air like a fine mist. Was he being unreasonable? *Was* it better for Lilah to have her mother stay with them? It made him crazy uncomfortable, but maybe he was being unfair to Lilah. How would she feel if he wouldn't allow Sophie in the house?

"When are you coming?" he said flatly.

"A week from Monday. I'm going to fly into JFK and rent a car."

"It's not school vacation."

"It'll just be a long weekend so she won't miss much."

"You've got it all figured out, don't you?" He couldn't keep the bitterness from his voice. How she'd inserted herself, just like that.

"Glenn." She softened her voice. "I know it's a little awkward but it's only a few days and it would be nice to stay at the house with Lilah. Can't we do that?"

He shut his eyes briefly. Then opened them. But he was still having this conversation. "I'll think about it."

"Okay then!" she said as if he'd given a wholehearted yes. "See you next Monday. I get in late so don't bother waiting dinner but if you could you pick up some salad stuff that would be great."

"Wait. I didn't say—"

But she rang off, leaving him shaking. Who the hell did she think she was dropping in to play Mom after all this time? Wanting to take Lilah out of state. And the thing that filled him with a panic he could hardly name—*what if she didn't bring her back*? He couldn't even go down that road.

It was full on dark now, the meeting room a blazing rectangle of light, jammed with people and their passions. He didn't have the stomach for it anymore. The housing project or anything else. He should find Cassie and apologize for leaving so abruptly, but he couldn't manage it.

Sophie was coming. It felt like a freight train headed right at him.

Chapter Seven

The home care service had assured Cassie that Mrs. Macuja was just what she needed. Patient, kind and willing to do some housekeeping. The elderly woman she'd been caring for had passed, and she was available full time, even live-in if Cassie wanted.

"Let's start with three days a week," Cassie said. "Provided it's a good fit." She'd checked Mrs. Macuja's references, which were excellent, had a lovely conversation with her over coffee and scheduled a visit to the house. That would be the real test. If her father threw a fit, it wouldn't work.

But on Tuesday when Mrs. Macuja showed up at the door, neatly dressed in gray slacks and sensible shoes, Cassie blinked in surprise. "Mrs. Macuja, I thought you were coming tomorrow."

"You say Tuesday, right?"

"Tuesday?" Had Mrs. Macuja gotten it wrong? Had *she*? Cassie's stomach did a slow slide. Mrs. Macuja was right. The appointment was for today. She'd forgotten all about it.

"Yes, yes. Of course today is Tuesday," Cassie said, ushering her in. She'd been planning this visit for a week. *How had she completely spaced?* She'd put it on both calendars, she'd even prepped her dad, who hadn't been enthusiastic but hadn't said no either. A finger of dread wormed its way into her gut. Yes, she was waiting for Andrew to call, but how did you forget something this important?

Mrs. Macuja took in the entry. Years ago there'd been a vase with dried flowers in the corner and a small table with a bowl where her mother kept fresh oranges. The table was still there, but these days her dad stowed his mud shoes underneath. Cassie caught a glimpse of herself in the mirror. Hair a mess, still hadn't showered after her run. What a way to greet someone. She had another worrisome thought: what if Glenn came to see about the bees? She'd told him just to stop by, although that was five days ago and he still hadn't shown. Maybe she'd scared him off with all the talk of dementia. She usually didn't share that kind of thing with people she didn't know well but he seemed trustworthy and it had just slipped out.

She gave up on her hair and showed Mrs. Macuja into the kitchen. She was a small, pleasant-looking woman, a widow with three grown daughters and a number of grandchildren. "Just so you know," she'd told Cassie during the interview, "I not afraid to change diapers. Babies or old ones."

"Oh, he's not at that point yet," Cassie had assured her but just thinking about it brought on a feeling of dismay. Dementia was so unpredictable, the slide so erratic. One day her father seemed fairly lucid, the next he didn't know what month it was.

Her dad was at the kitchen table, studying the newspaper. He had trouble making sense of the articles now, but he labored over them every morning anyway. Breakfast leftovers were still scattered about, even though he'd finished an hour ago. When she first arrived, Cassie had scooped up his dirty dishes right away but that upset him. Now she left him alone in the morning, even though the mess made her twitch. Better for him to be unruffled.

"Dad, this is Mrs. Macuja. She's going to help around the house. This is my father, Mr. Linden."

Her dad looked up from his paper. "Who?"

"How do you do?" Mrs. Macuja crossed the kitchen briskly, holding out a hand.

Cassie's dad took it grudgingly. "What's all this about?"

"I need some help with the housework," Cassie said. "Bathrooms, floors, everything's getting away from me." Shelly had suggested going about it this way, couching it as cleaning help. "He'll never do it if you say he needs looking after," Shelly said. "Trust me."

He rustled the newspaper unhappily. "I told you, I can do all that. Been doing it for years just fine."

"You had Elena, Dad, remember? She's not coming anymore."

"Hmmpf." He looked suspiciously between Cassie and Mrs. Macuja, who'd bustled right into the kitchen.

"Would you like a little more coffee?" she said.

"No, I don't want any more coffee."

She appeared with the pot anyway. "How you take it?"

He looked confused. "What do you mean?"

"Oh, he drinks it black," Cassie said.

"If I want more coffee I'll get up and get it. I don't need someone following me around with the pot." Her father snapped the newspaper closed and pushed away from the table. If he thought he was being managed, he would dig in. Just like Andrew when he was little, always suspicious of anything new. He used to hang back even when Cassie brought him to play with other kids. She'd worried he would be a friendless, solitary child, but Phil scoffed, predicting he'd grow out of it. And he had. Too well, judging by the trouble he was in at school. She checked her watch. Ten-thirty already and the hearing was at ten. How long could these things go? If she didn't hear from him in half an hour, she would call.

"What you do to your foot?" Mrs. Macuja asked as her dad shuffled toward the den. Cassie hadn't said anything about the sprained ankle. Or the bees.

Her dad didn't answer, just flapped his hand like he was swatting them away.

"So," Cassie said brightly as he stalked off, "want to see the rest of the house?"

She showed Mrs. Macuja the laundry and explained what her father liked to eat. "Roast chicken is always good," she said. "He'll complain about whatever you make, but he'll eat it." With surprisingly little pushback from her dad, Cassie had taken over the grocery shopping along with the cooking and cleaning. But she'd been here nearly two weeks and her own life, whatever that looked like now, was receding. She missed the give and take of the office. She missed her running club. They met in Central Park on Saturday mornings and lingered over coffee afterward. She'd made good friends in that group; Phil had even liked some of the husbands. She missed her weekly yoga class, although she supposed she could find yoga in Connecticut. The thing was, she felt like she'd been pulled up by the roots and left dangling.

"You want me sit with him while he watch TV?" Mrs. Macuja asked when they finished the tour.

"Probably not, best to give him some space unless he wants company. But once he's out of that boot, maybe you can get him out for a walk in the afternoons. I don't like him sitting in front of the TV all day."

"I clean up kitchen," Mrs. Macuja said, pulling on rubber gloves, "then make lunch. He like an early lunch?"

"Noon is good. Let's give him time to recover from breakfast."

•　　•　　•

Cassie settled herself at the desk in her old bedroom with its lilac walls and boy band posters from high school. Her ancient stuffed dog, Frederick, one ear chewed off by their real dog decades ago, slumped on the bed. She opened the lease she'd been working on. A redevelopment project, converting an old factory in Brooklyn into affordable housing. The neighbors disliked the factory but didn't want low-income housing either. Always a fuss over change. Her childhood desk was narrow and the Wi-Fi spotty upstairs. Hard to work here.

She checked her watch again. Ten forty-five. Andrew was surely done. She swiped open her phone, then thought better of it. She should give him a chance to call. She needed to work on letting him be an adult. But the not knowing was killing her. She stared at the screen, unable to concentrate, thinking of Andrew and the fact that she'd completely blanked on Mrs. Macuja.

She shut her computer, heart pounding. She had no confusion. She knew the day of the week for God's sake. Just sometimes lately she forgot things. She was under stress. It could happen to anyone. She dropped her head into her hands, and a small, choked sound escaped her.

But she wasn't just anyone. Not with her history.

She fished the paper from her wallet. *Jeanette Torrington, Mount Sinai Hospital.* The sight of it sent a spike of fear through her. If she didn't have the mutation, it didn't mean she would never get Alzheimer's, but her chances were substantially lower—like a normal person's.

But if she did have it, she would definitely develop early onset. One hundred percent.

And if she had the mutation, Andrew might have it too. Did she owe it to Andrew to get tested? If she was negative, Andrew had no elevated risk. He could live his life without worry. She needed at least to explain all this to him. He knew none of it.

A clammy sweat sprang up under her arms and between her breasts. She couldn't live this way, terrified every time she forgot something, wondering if the end was starting. If the test came up clean, she could get on with her life and chalk all this up to stress.

If not, at least she'd know what she was dealing with, and Andrew could decide what he wanted to do. There would be time to put things in order. However you did that.

She ignored the thundering in her chest and picked up the phone.

Shelly was right. She needed to know.

•   •   •

She leaned back in the small chair, wrung out after making the appointment. The raw fear had given way to a depleted feeling, like she'd run eight miles and hadn't eaten. This wasn't something she could remedy with a granola bar, but at least she'd set things in motion.

She texted Shelly, who sent back a heart. `I'll fly out and go with you.`

`It's not for six weeks.`

`Ugh so long?`

`First one she had.`

Cassie was about to give her sister a call just to hear her voice when her phone rang.

Andrew. *Finally.*

"Sweetie!" she said. "How'd it go?"

"Grandpa FaceTimed me in the middle!"

"What! He doesn't even know how to FaceTime." This didn't compute. Her father had a cell phone but barely used it. He sort of knew how to text, but she doubted he knew what FaceTime was.

"Well he did," he moaned, "and I forgot to turn off my phone."

"Oh Andrew."

"It went off in my pocket. One of the deans got pissed and yelled at me for like a whole minute on how I was disrespectful. I *wasn't* being disrespectful, I just forgot."

Her stomach swooned with anxiety. "So what happened?"

"I think they were going to let me off with a warning. That one dean was an asshole, but the other two were nice. They asked me what happened and if I knew I made a mistake. I said I did, and I wore the blazer like you said and—"

"Miss Cassie?" Mrs. Macuja stuck her head in the door. "I need to ask—"

Cassie waved her off. "Not now."

"What?" Andrew said.

"Not you, sweetie!" She motioned to Mrs. Macuja to close the door. She couldn't believe the woman had barged right in! Wait. What if there was an emergency? "Hang on, honey." She set down the phone and dashed after Mrs. Macuja, who was already on her way downstairs.

"I'm on the phone with my son. What's the matter?"

"You out of Mr. Clean. Okay to use vinegar on the floor?"

"Oh, my God. That's all? Yes, vinegar's fine." She hurried back to the bedroom. "Mix it with water," she called. CNN was blaring on the TV downstairs, and a throbbing had started behind her left eye.

"I'm sorry, honey, someone's here to help with Grandpa. Tell me what happened."

"They suspended me," he said glumly. "For a week."

"Oh no." This was what she'd feared, that the school would want to make an example of them. Phil had been way too sanguine about this. "What about the other kids, were they suspended too?"

"They haven't had their hearings yet. They're calling us in separately."

Outside the window, a striking yellow bird with black wings tucked into the safety of the red maple. A goldfinch maybe. She didn't know her birds. In the city you mostly saw pigeons. Utilitarian birds that knew how to survive. "And your friend, is he still in the hospital?" Her heart ached for this boy, whose life might be forever altered.

"His name is Jack. His parents flew him home to Dallas. I tried calling, but his mom wouldn't let me talk to him." Andrew sounded like he was on the verge of tears. "I just wanted to see how he was doing."

"Of course you did." She still felt an undertow of unease about how a boy could fall and hit his head like that. What Andrew wasn't saying. Not surprising that the mother wouldn't let Andrew talk to him. She'd be outraged too if her son was lying in the hospital and the other kids had walked away. "Why don't you fly home? I'm at Grandpa's, you could come here."

"And do what?"

"You can't go to class for a week. What are you going to do there?"

He was quiet for a moment, thinking about this. Andrew came to things slowly, it didn't do any good to push him. "I still have to study. I have finals in three weeks."

"You can work here. I am."

"I don't know. Maybe I'll just stay here."

"Andrew, I don't want you holed up in that frat house for a week with nothing to do; it's not a good idea."

"I live here." His voice brought her up. The way he sounded like Phil.

She took a breath. She'd been trying hard to give him space, and here she was ordering him around like he was twelve. But he'd been foolish, more than foolish. Irresponsible. And now a boy was hurt. How had things come to this? Had she failed somehow as a parent? She'd tried her best, but something awful and unforeseen had happened anyway. Could she have set another course five or ten or twenty years ago? Maybe this terrible thing could have been avoided if she'd put her foot down about joining the frat. Or forbidden him from going to Tulane in the first place. But couldn't something bad have happened somewhere else? Maybe not this particular thing but another misfortune. Life was a series of pitfalls, some small, some catastrophic. She knew that all too well.

She began again. "All I'm saying is it might be better to get out of there for a week. And you haven't seen Grandpa since Christmas. It would be nice to spend a few days with him."

From the window, she saw Glenn's white truck turn up the driveway, and in spite of everything, her heart lifted. He hadn't forgotten.

"Okay. I'll come, but I'm not going to Connecticut for the whole time. I'll stay in the city with Dad." He was pushing back, angry and upset at what had happened, choosing his father because he knew it would hurt her. It did hurt, a little. From what she could tell, Phil had pretty much moved into the fiancée's place. She hoped he'd have the sense to carve out some time for Andrew.

"That's fine, just come here for a couple of nights."

"All right," he relented. "I'll take the train up. I'd like to see Grandpa too."

"He'd love that." She didn't add that she would love it too. No sense pushing her luck.

•   •   •

She met Glenn outside as he was getting out of his truck. Even though the day was cool with a sharp breeze, he was wearing shorts and a fleece vest, and she couldn't help noticing he had nice legs. She quickly averted her gaze. Jesus, her world was falling apart, and here she was gawking at the man's legs.

"My dad fell asleep on the couch," she said, her face warm. "I don't know how he sleeps with the news on so loud."

"I can come back. I just stopped by to talk about a management plan for the bees. Maybe we can get a handle on that varroa."

"No, don't leave. I'll get him up. Otherwise, he'll be unhappy he missed you." The thought of him leaving right away discouraged her. It was everything—Andrew, the memory lapse. Her looming appointment with the genetic counselor. The day had gone from bad to worse in a hurry.

"I uh...didn't mean to be rude the other night, when I took off like that." He shifted from one foot to the other, and she had the sense that whatever happened that night had upset him. He was a hard man to read, unlike Phil, who had no problem letting you know what he was thinking. She'd appreciated that transparency at first, but somewhere along the way what Phil was thinking had become less interesting. Less conversation and more monologue. Maybe the new wife would be enthralled.

She had a sudden troubling thought. "Is everything okay with your daughter?"

"Oh yeah. She's fine, thanks."

"I saw in the paper that the zoning board approved the project." She hadn't stayed for the whole meeting. When she'd left at ten people were still lined up to talk. God knew how long it went.

"No surprise there." His expression darkened. "Pretty much a foregone conclusion."

"At least they mandated some below market units, which seems fair."

"Below market around here is still out of reach for most people. And bottom line, they're going to plow it under." He regarded her suspiciously. "You're not in real estate, are you?"

She smiled. "You make it sound like the mafia. No, I'm not in real estate. I do economic development for the city of New York. I'm a lawyer in their legal department." She glanced toward the Kingsley property. "How did you end up keeping bees there? Do you know the family?"

"Not personally, just made some calls. It seemed like a good spot to keep a few hives."

"More than a few."

"With bees one thing always leads to another."

"Your daughter seems to know something about bees." Cassie glanced at the truck, on the off chance Lilah was inside. "She seems like a sweet girl. What is she, about eleven?"

"Twelve. Going on twenty."

Cassie laughed. "I remember being that age, so much drama. So you see her on the weekends?"

Something softened in his face. "I have her all the time. Her mom's not in the picture."

"Oh." She hadn't expected that, a single dad raising a preteen daughter on his own. "That's got to be challenging."

He rubbed his jaw. When she'd first met him she'd assumed he needed a shave, then realized he probably kept it that way. She didn't see a lot of scruff in her world. "Challenging is an understatement," he said.

"I'm a single parent now too, although it's easier since my son's off at college." She frowned. "Sort of easier. He just got suspended. You have to go out of your way to make that happen."

He laughed, which eased the hard, knotty thing inside her.

"How long have you been divorced?" she asked.

"Eight years now." He ground one of the small stones under his boot. They both looked at it.

"Lilah was little."

"Four."

"I'm coming up on a year," she said. "Next month."

"Sorry to hear that."

She shrugged. "It's okay. Some days I'm fine with it, other days I don't know what I'm going to do with the rest of my life. He's about to get remarried."

"Ouch." He looked genuinely pained for her.

"Does it get easier, the whole being single thing?"

"Um…" He glanced up at the house, which she realized was her cue to get her dad. She'd gone and made him uncomfortable.

"Sorry, I didn't mean to pry. It's just that I'm new to all this, and I don't seem to be doing it very well. The single parenting thing anyway."

"That part's hard," he agreed.

"Is there an easy part?"

He smiled. "I'll let you know."

She turned toward the house. "Sorry to unload on you. Let me get my dad."

"Do you like honey?" he said.

"Honey? Yeah sure."

"I'll bring you some. I've got a few jars left over from last summer. It was a good year."

"I'd like that," she said. They stood awkwardly for a moment, neither of them quite sure where to go with this.

"Okay then." He shoved his hands in his pockets.

"Okay. Well, thanks." She headed up to the house with an unexpected lightness in her step.

She had a feeling Glenn Marsden made very good honey.

Chapter Eight

Lilah put fresh sheets on the bed in the spare room and snipped a few daffodils that appeared each spring at the edge of the woods, arranging them in a glass jar since they didn't have a vase. She set the jar on the nightstand then moved it to the dresser, then back to the nightstand.

"It's fine," Glenn said. Sophie wasn't even here yet and already she was turning their lives upside down. "Go to bed."

"Wake me up when she gets here," Lilah begged, but Glenn had no intention. Lilah could see her mother in the morning before school. If Sophie was even up. She was a notoriously late sleeper; he didn't imagine that had changed. Lilah told him that when she was in Colorado Sophie slept until almost ten every day. Lilah had watched his face for reaction, but he was careful not to show it.

Careful, that was what he always was. Careful not to badmouth Sophie. Careful to nurture memories of the three of them before she left. So damn careful, and where had it gotten him? A wife he hadn't been able to please and a daughter who would forever suffer the fallout.

After Lilah went to bed, he tried to read but kept getting up to check the front window. Too antsy to sit still, way too keyed up to concentrate. When the lights of Sophie's rental finally swung up the driveway close to midnight, he was wrung out. Why on earth had he agreed to this? He should have held firm and insisted she stay somewhere else.

In a small act of resistance, he hadn't changed out of the jeans he'd worn all day but couldn't help tossing a couch pillow back in place on his way to the door. Not much had changed around here since she left, but the couch was new. He and Lilah had picked it out at Macy's. Lilah thrilled to be consulted, Glenn relieved to be rid of one more thing that had come with Sophie.

He stepped out the front door, the asphalt gritty on his bare feet, his heart beating fitfully. Sophie was on her phone and didn't see him at first. The boyfriend, no doubt. For an instant, jealousy sparked—then fizzled.

She hadn't opened the car door, and all he could see was the fall of her hair in the darkened interior and the artificial brightness of the phone. It made him feel like he was spying, so he released Charlie's collar and the dog bounded over.

Sophie looked up and gave him a wave, then without hurry stowed the phone. He recalled that she never hurried; that had been one of her great attractions. The unrushed, almost languid way she moved through the world, which drew every eye, including his own. In the beginning he was gratified by all that male attention, but she shrugged it off, insisting she was hardly aware. He didn't believe her, but what did it matter? Let them look. She was his.

He stood back, waiting for her to get out of the car, hands in his pockets, his stomach on spin cycle. Once he would have been falling all over himself like Charlie. But now he just felt irritated.

"Well, look at you," she said as she unfolded herself from the driver's seat. "You've gone a little gray."

Reflexively, he ran a hand through his hair. He wasn't *that* gray. "How was your flight?" he said, ignoring the comment.

"Fine. I slept through most of it." She popped the trunk, and he couldn't let her manhandle the suitcase herself, so he got it. The one-inch heel on her cowboy boots brought her nearly to his height. He'd forgotten how tall she was. She accidentally brushed his shoulder as she reached for her carry-on and he drew back, which made her laugh.

"Oh my God, Glenn. I'm not going to bite." Charlie had wedged himself between them and was sniffing at the contents of the trunk. "Who's this?" she said, ruffling his head.

"Charlie."

She slung her purse over her shoulder and locked the car, the beep shrill in the quiet. "I don't remember you wanting a dog."

"Lilah wanted one."

"Ah, well that explains it."

He carried her bags up the steps, keeping an eye on Charlie to avoid tripping. Acutely aware of Sophie just behind him, though he dared not look.

"Lilah's asleep," he said as he set the bags down in the entry.

"Oh, too bad." Sophie sounded disappointed. "I was hoping to see her tonight."

He had no choice. Here in the house, in the light, he had to look at her. At forty-two she was still beautiful. Her face beginning to line in a delicate way, the hair still blond, but not the wild, white blond of youth. She was still in shape, of course. He hadn't expected anything less. All that hiking and whatever else she did. She would turn heads at sixty.

He shoved his hands in his pockets. The entry, which had never before seemed cramped, suddenly closed in. "You hungry? There's grilled chicken if you want something."

"Nah, not that hungry. I had something on the plane, but thanks." She squatted nose to nose with Charlie, who'd presented her with his stuffed hippo. She rubbed him behind the ears, which made him squirm deliriously. "Does he have some shepherd in him?"

"He's half shepherd." Charlie was on his back now, getting a stomach rub. The dog had no shame.

"I've got a girl at home who'd like you," Sophie cooed. "Only she's fixed so you wouldn't get very far." She stood, brushing off her jeans.

"He's fixed too," Glenn said stiffly.

"I had no doubt." She gave Charlie a last pat. "Your daddy was always very responsible."

"Someone had to be," he muttered. It was beyond strange to have her here, showing up like a rodeo star in those cowboy boots. Who wore cowboy boots anyway? And Lilah was going to be all over those silver bangles. He wondered sourly whether Sophie had decked herself out that way on purpose to reel Lilah in. But Sophie had never been conniving, just self-absorbed.

"Come on." He picked up the bags, aware she was studying him, an anxious thrumming beginning in his gut. He didn't want to be dissected, especially by her. "Let's get this stuff to your room."

"The place looks good," she said. "You painted. The yellow lightens it up."

"Thanks."

"Did you refinish the floors too?"

"Nope, they're the same."

"Still can't get two words out of you." Her amused tone of voice, which annoyed him.

"This was your idea, not mine." He set her suitcase down in the spare room, which served as his office too. Besides a desk it had a full-size bed and a chest of drawers he'd picked up at a tag sale. Enough space for someone to put a few things away. Not that he had a lot of guests.

She tipped her head, appraising him. "You look good." She rubbed her face, miming his beard. "I like the scruff. It suits you."

He took a step back, the small rush of pleasure that she still found him attractive immediately hardening into wariness. Then a wash of relief that he no longer felt the powerful tug that made men chase her like besotted drones. He'd been one of them, so desperate to keep her he'd ended up driving her away. So devastated when she left that his mother had to move in to help with Lilah until he could put one foot in front of the other.

Now all he felt was irritation that he'd let himself be talked into this. "It's late," he said. "I'm tired and I'm sure you are too."

She plopped onto the bed. "It's only ten for me. How about a glass of wine?"

"There's some in the fridge. Help yourself." He was too wound up to be tired, but he had no intention of having a glass of wine with her. He'd opened his home for Lilah's sake, but that was it. He wasn't about to get chummy with Sophie like they were old friends. Because they weren't.

She tugged off a boot, groaning in relief.

He eyed the boots narrowly. "Why do you wear those things if they're so uncomfortable?"

She laughed. "I live in Colorado. People wear cowboy boots." She massaged her foot, and he looked away. "Oh have a glass of wine with me, Glenn. I haven't seen you in ages, and it'd be nice to hear what Lilah's up to."

His anger flared like a struck match. "You could talk to her on the phone once in a while and find out for yourself."

She sighed. "I know I'm not going to win any awards for motherhood. I get that. But I do think about her. She sent me a little video of her talking about school and stuff. She was so cute."

He kept his face expressionless, but a seed of worry took root in his gut. Lilah hadn't said anything about a video. What else hadn't she told him?

Sophie reached for something in her bag and her bracelets jangled. "What's with those?" he muttered. They seemed to have a life of their own, clattering up and down her arm depending on how she moved.

"These? I got them at a flea market. What's the matter with them?"

"Nothing. Forget it." He didn't give a damn about the bracelets; what he disliked was the way she had shimmied into their lives. A place to land on the way to visit her mother, and oh yeah, try to convince Lilah to go along. An impressionable twelve-year-old who would find everything about her mother intoxicating.

"I need to get to bed," he said. "There's clean towels in the hall bathroom."

"Hey, I know this is weird. I do."

He turned to look at her. "Do you? I don't even get why you're here."

She patted the spot next to her on the bed like she was inviting the dog. "If you won't have a glass of wine with me, at least sit for a minute." When he hesitated she rolled her eyes. "Whoever your lady friend is, she's got you on a short leash. Believe me, I'm not that alluring after eight hours of travel."

He sat reluctantly, worried her proximity might dredge up some dormant desire, but he felt only a mild surprise that he'd once been married to this person. How did you share your life with someone—have a child together!—then end up strangers?

"Why are you here?" he said. "Don't tell me you haven't seen your mother in eight years."

"She's been out to Colorado a few times, but I haven't been back. I meant to, but one thing or another...she's actually not doing that great."

"I'm sorry to hear that," he said grudgingly. "What's the matter?"

"Breast cancer. She's in treatment. She says it's going okay, but you know...it seemed like a good time to come."

He hadn't known her mom well. To hear Sophie tell it she'd been a hands-off parent who left Sophie and her sister to fend for themselves. Her parents had divorced early, and her dad was hardly in the picture. No wonder Sophie had missed the maternal gene. But that was too generous. People made their own choices no matter what kind of childhood they were handed. He would crawl through fire for Lilah. He could never forgive Sophie for walking away.

She rubbed her other foot, which she'd freed from the boot. "My mom being sick got me thinking I should spend more time with Lilah."

"What do you mean?" he said warily. "How much more time?"

"I shouldn't have let four years go by, I still can't believe it's been that long. I want to see her more. I do."

"Lilah's on an even keel right now," he said, choosing his words. "She's doing well in school, she has friends. I don't want to disrupt that." Colorado had been a whipsaw of emotion for Lilah. After four long years, her mother wanted her. Then she didn't. It had killed him to see it. He took Lilah back to the therapist after that, but every appointment became a struggle and eventually he let it go.

Sophie shot him an offended look. "I'm not talking about disrupting anything. I'm her mother and I want to see her."

"Today you do." As soon as he said it, he knew he'd made a mistake. Backing Sophie into a corner never worked.

"It's not up to you." A tone in her voice he didn't recognize. He was used to her apathy, at least when it came to him and Lilah. This was something new and vaguely threatening.

"No one's saying you can't see her," he backpedaled. "You're here, aren't you? I'm just saying she's had enough disappointment."

"Don't lecture me, Glenn. It didn't work when we were married, and it won't work now."

He inhaled deeply. Lilah's therapist had gently suggested he might want to talk to someone too, but he'd never done it. What was he going to do, spill his guts to a stranger? *My wife left and I'm miserable.* No shit. Who wouldn't be miserable? "I just want to know what you have in mind."

She shrugged. "I just got here. I don't know what I have in mind. Why does everything have to be mapped out a year in advance?"

He pushed off the bed, done with her. "Because a kid needs to know her parent isn't going to up and leave. That's why. You have no idea what Lilah's been through, how long she cried after you left, asking every night when you were coming back. How it's been for her in school without a mother. You've never given a damn about any of it. Now she's half-grown and it sounds fun. Sure, why not. You can go shopping or some crap like that. But what about when she's in a mood and smarts off? Or won't get off her phone and do her homework?" He knew he should back off, but eight years of heartache and struggle came roaring back. "Any bright ideas about parenting, Sophie? I'd love to hear them."

"I'm sorry you're so bitter, Glenn." She gave him a disappointed look. "I wish for your sake you'd been able to move on."

"Fuck you. I'm not bitter." He glared at her from the doorway. "I'm *here.* That's what I am. I'm here."

She regarded him calmly, which infuriated him even more. He hated that Zen crap.

"She's on the bus at seven-thirty if you want to catch her before school," he said as he stalked out of the room.

"That early?" She sounded slightly stunned.

"Yep. We don't sleep all day."

Upstairs, he stuck his head cautiously in Lilah's room, but to his great relief she was still asleep. The only saving grace of this whole fucked up evening was that Lilah had slept through it.

•   •   •

To his surprise, Sophie got up in the morning. She floated into the kitchen a few minutes after seven in leggings and a sweatshirt, hair tucked into a sloppy knot. He still felt raw from the night before. He hadn't been able to sleep and had a parched hungover feeling even though he hadn't had a drop to drink. Within half an hour he'd let her get to him, and she hadn't even been trying.

She went unerringly to the right cabinet for a coffee mug, which annoyed him. He should have moved things around so he didn't seem so predictable. Sure, he'd painted a few walls, but eight years later she still knew where to find a mug.

"We got off to a bad start last night." She let the coffee steam her face like some sort of spa treatment. "Can we reset?"

He took a swallow of his own coffee. "Sure." It was still beyond strange to have her here, but at least in the light of day, he felt more in control. "Lilah should be down in a minute."

He reached past her to set out Lilah's Frosted Mini-Wheats and poured a glass of orange juice. Her lunch was already made. He did that the night before—a peanut butter and honey sandwich and an apple. A box of raisins. She still liked him to pack it, but he knew the time was coming when she wouldn't. When she wouldn't need him for much of anything.

He slid the bagged lunch into Lilah's backpack, taking a small pleasure in doing this in front of Sophie. She knew nothing of their routine, the thousands of lunches he'd packed. The dinners he'd made, the homework he'd supervised. That heart-stopping moment in second grade when the school nurse called and told him Lilah had fallen off the play equipment. Thank God it had only been a broken wrist. Only a parent felt that kind of fear. *He* was the parent. Like he'd told Sophie last night, *he* was here.

Motherhood had been difficult for Sophie. The baby left her tired and cranky and frustrated that she had no energy for her art. Glenn did as much as he could, rushing home from work to make dinner and bathe Lilah so Sophie could escape to her studio in the garage. He was smitten with Lilah, the baby was all he could think about, but Sophie seemed joyless.

"Give it time," his mother had said. "It doesn't come easy for some women." But he could tell his mom was concerned too.

They hired a babysitter to give Sophie a break and made time for date night once a week. But she was remote, and her discontent ate at him.

"What do you want?" he asked at dinner one night. An expensive restaurant, a splurge for their fifth anniversary. Lilah a year now, pulling herself up. She'd be walking soon.

"There's no mountains here," Sophie said. "It's just a wall of green. Everything looks the same."

"We could take a weekend and go to Vermont, see your mom." He felt her slipping away. They hardly touched anymore. He didn't remember the last time they'd laughed together.

"It's not just that. I feel hemmed in."

His heart stalled. "What do you mean, hemmed in?"

"I don't know." She shrugged it away. "Maybe if I sell a piece I'll feel better."

Sophie was accepted into a show in a local gallery, and he put a deck on the house so she could paint outside. But she was still disengaged. Uninterested in Lilah's new tooth, impatient when the baby fussed. She flew to Colorado to visit a college friend and came back gushing about how beautiful the mountains were.

"I missed you," he said, reaching for her. The house had been too quiet, and she hadn't called once. She said she was beat and bought him off with a kiss on the cheek.

Awake in bed, he wondered if she'd slept with someone else. If she would.

She stayed for Lilah's fourth birthday, but by then she'd already checked out. They were sitting on the deck when she told him. End of August, the days shortening. Lilah stuffed with cake, already asleep.

"I can't do it anymore," Sophie said.

"What do you mean?" But he knew with a sickening certainty what she meant. "What about Lilah?"

"You're so much better with her than I am."

"We'll get you more help. A nanny. Whatever you need. I know we've hit a rough spot, but we've been married nine years. You have a four-year-old. How can you just leave?" He heard himself pleading, the futility of it. He would have opened a vein to get her to stay.

In the near dark, a lone firefly floated up from the grass. Fewer of them now in the waning days of summer. "I'm going to Colorado. I'll stay with Jenny for a while, then we'll see."

"We'll *see?*" His wife was leaving. The mother of his child. The woman he'd loved for better or worse all of his adult life. "That's all you can say, we'll see?"

She finally turned to look at him. "It's not working, Glenn. It hasn't worked for a long time. I know you see it."

She gave his shoulder a squeeze as she went inside but he wasn't quick enough to shake her off, and he burned with shame that his body still leaped at her touch.

Now, he tossed back the rest of his coffee as Lilah pelted down the stairs, hair flying, shoes in hand. She came to a dead stop when she saw her mother.

Sophie took a step forward, then appeared unsure what to do next. "Oh my God, you're so big. I never imagined you'd be so big."

"Hey Mom." Lilah's face had done something complicated, rearranging itself into a mixture of wariness and unfiltered hope. "I tried to wait up." She shot Glenn an accusing look, still miffed he hadn't let her.

He'd forgotten how much Lilah looked like Sophie, or hadn't wanted to see. But he couldn't miss it with the two of them together. Lilah was still all arms and legs, but the face was Sophie's. The bone structure, the delicate nose. Lilah had resembled him more when she was young but now she was all Sophie. Except for the eyes. At least she had his eyes. Not Sophie's dazzling blue. His and Lilah's were a sturdy gray.

Sophie opened her arms. "Can I give you a hug?"

Lilah nodded but when Sophie enfolded her, she stiffened, unwilling or unable to put her arms around her mother. When she squirmed away, Glenn felt a small swell of satisfaction, which quickly curdled to shame. This wasn't some competition; it was Lilah they were talking about.

"How long are you here for?" Lilah hadn't touched her cereal, she couldn't tear her eyes from her mother. She ate up Sophie the way you'd devour birthday cake.

"A few days. I'm heading to Vermont to see your grandmother and thought you might want to come." Sophie said this comfortably, like it was the most natural thing in the world to show up after eight years and whisk your daughter away.

"Grandma?" For a moment, Lilah looked confused.

"Your other grandmother," Glenn said.

"Um, I don't know." Lilah glanced uncertainly at Glenn. He tried to keep his face neutral, but Lilah could read him.

"We can talk about it later," Sophie said easily.

Lilah looked between them, a sudden worry creasing her face. "I have to catch the bus, but I'll see you after school. You'll be around right?"

"Absolutely." Sophie beamed. "We'll catch up then."

"Here." Glenn tucked a foil wrapped bagel into Lilah's bag. "You didn't eat any breakfast. Take this."

"Thanks." Lilah surprised him with a kiss on the cheek, then dashed out the door.

"She's really something," Sophie said softly.

"Yeah, she is." He was still warmed by the fact that Lilah had kissed him all on her own without any prompting. In front of her mother. That had to mean something.

To his relief, Sophie went back to bed after Lilah left, and he decided against a second cup of coffee. The only thing that would settle him now was his bees.

Chapter Nine

When Lilah got home from school Glenn was still busy with his hives. The careful work of opening up each hive, checking for a queen and assessing overall health. Bee season began with a bang as soon as the weather warmed up and the bees became active, but he could hardly find time for his own bees in the spring when every client was calling. He never had enough time.

"Where's Mom?" Lilah surged through the gate, fending off Charlie, who wriggled with delight. She shed her backpack and plopped onto the grass next to an open hive, careful not to put herself directly in the bees' flight path. "She said she'd be here after school."

Glenn set down the cover of the box he'd just opened. He'd situated the hives far enough from the house that they wouldn't cause trouble, but close enough where he could keep an eye on them. A good, dry spot at the edge of the woods that got morning sun and dappled shade in the afternoon. A fresh water source from the stream that trickled through the wetland and never entirely dried up, even in summer. The top of the hive was alive with bees, a good sign. He gave them a puff of smoke so they'd retreat. "She's having lunch with a friend, said she'd be back around three." Of course Sophie was late, when did she not disappoint?

Lilah ran a hand up and down along Charlie's back, standing his hair on end. Back and forth until the dog turned in puzzlement to lick her. She was quiet, but Glenn felt the sharp edge of her disappointment.

"Hey," he said, "hand me that bee brush, will you. It's on the ground over there." His stomach had been in a knot since breakfast, remembering the way Lilah had looked at Sophie. The frank longing. No matter what he did or how long he lived, he would never be enough. Lilah would always yearn for her mother.

She retrieved the brush, but instead of handing it over, she began gently coaxing the bees off the top of the open box so he could lift out the frames.

"Want a veil?" he said. He hadn't put one on since most of the bees were out foraging, but he had one at hand in case they got testy. You never knew.

"I'm okay right now."

He stepped back to get out of her way. She was good with the bees, had a nice, quiet way about her. Bees got agitated when people were jumpy. "She'll be back," he said. "She wants to spend time with you. That's why she's here." It pained him to say this, but it was true. And Lilah needed to hear it.

"I know." She didn't look up but her shoulders unbunched a little.

"Why don't you go ahead and lift out a frame."

She carefully lifted the corners of the outermost frame, drawing it straight up and out to avoid crushing any bees. "This one looks good." She held it up high with the sun to her back like he'd taught her so they could get a look.

"Plenty of brood, that's what we like to see. Looks like we've got ourselves a queen in this one." With his hive tool, Glenn carefully scraped off the burr comb along the top of the frame that would gum things up if he left it. The bees would fill every space if you let them.

Lilah leaned the frame against the outer box, and together they inspected the rest. "A little light on honey," he concluded, "but that's okay. Now that the pollen flow's started they'll be fine." He never got over the industry of this all-female work force. The drones, good only for mating, didn't lift a finger around the hive. In fact, the female worker bees kicked them out in the fall. Shiftless males who would just take up space over the winter and gorge on honey.

He smiled to himself remembering how horrified Lilah had been when she learned that. "That's so harsh! They just leave them to freeze to death out there?"

"They pretty much die of starvation first," he conceded.

That was a few years ago. She was less sentimental now, which was a good thing. You couldn't let your emotions get in the way with bees. Not every colony thrived. You had to sweep up the dead bees and go on.

He pierced a capped cell with his hive tool, and a drop of golden liquid oozed out. He held out the frame. "Go ahead and taste it."

Lilah swiped a finger and brought it to her mouth. "Mmhm." She smiled, and his heart eased a little that something so simple could still make her happy. He'd crack open every comb to get a smile like that. "You going to help me bottle again this year?"

"I always do."

"Just checking."

Charlie heard it first, the crunch of Sophie's car turning up the driveway. He heaved himself up and trotted to the gate.

Lilah hesitated. "Do you mind if I go?"

Glenn waved her off. "Go on. She's here."

The bees had recovered from the smoke and were beginning to reemerge from the box. A few had become irritated and were buzzing around their heads. He needed to close this one up and get on with it.

Lilah toyed with the zipper on her backpack. "I mean to Vermont, like Mom said. Do you mind?"

He slid in the last frame and sealed up the hive. Of course he minded. He hated the hell out of it. He hated that Sophie had come in the first place. He didn't trust her and never would. Showing up with her cowboy boots and silver bracelets, dangling her affection like a gaudy prize. What motherless girl could resist?

He squeezed Lilah's shoulder, comforted that he was looking into his own eyes. "Go if you want. Spend time with your mom, see your grandmother. It's okay."

"You sure?" She still looked torn. "I won't go if you don't want me to."

"Of course I'm sure. You don't think I can manage to feed Charlie for a few days?"

She laughed and gave him a quick hug, then skipped off to see her mother.

•   •   •

They left for Vermont the next afternoon.

"Have her back by dinnertime Sunday," Glenn said as he walked them to the car. "She's already missing two days of school."

"Don't worry." Sophie had on the cowboy boots and a suede jacket with fringe. God knew where she thought she was going.

Glenn folded Lilah in a hug. "Text me when you get there."

"I will." She gave him a kiss, but her eyes were on the jacket, the way the fringe swung when her mother moved.

"I packed you some snacks for the road." He handed her a bag with peanut butter sandwiches and some apples. "There's enough for your mom too."

"We're not going into the outback," Sophie said, "but thank you."

He waved them off, his heart a tight fist in his chest. Four days without her. Lilah was older and warier than when she went to Colorado, but he could see her need to believe in her mother. The way she'd tumbled off the bus, ready to go. Her bag already packed. Maybe it would be different this time. For her sake, he hoped so.

He ate Mini-Wheats for dinner and washed the cereal down with a beer. Turned on the TV but couldn't find anything to watch. The house was too quiet, and he finally turned it off and went to bed. Sleepless, he listened to the dog's soft snoring and spun anxious scenarios.

What if Sophie didn't bring her back? He had custody, but noncustodial parents ran off with kids all the time. He would have to get a lawyer, go to court. He sat up, heart pounding. Or what if Lilah decided she wanted to live in Colorado? She was twelve, almost thirteen. Kids that age could have a say. If given a chance, would she choose her mother over him?

He gave up on sleep and made a pot of coffee. Almost morning anyway, the sky just beginning to lighten, the birds setting up a racket. Outside the kitchen window, a smudge of orange singed the horizon.

He kept busy while they were gone. He drove to Wallingford to talk to an apple farmer about pollination and spent time with a client who'd bought top of the line equipment but didn't know the first thing about using it. He had to show the guy the basics, even how to securely fasten his veil. He didn't mind; he enjoyed beginners with their enthusiasm. Poor Mr. Linden was at the other end—knew a lot but was frustrated he couldn't handle it anymore.

Sunday afternoon he started watching the clock. He made meatballs, heavy on the cheese the way Lilah liked and put up a sauce to simmer. At four, he turned it off. Way too early. He'd said dinner time. That could be anywhere between five and seven. Even seven-thirty. Knowing Sophie, she'd push it.

By five, he had to get out of the house. He went out to the shed and reorganized a couple of shelves, even though everything was already where it should be. Vermont was a five-hour drive. There might be traffic, an accident on the highway. Should he text Lilah? No, better to give them their time together. But his stomach was wound tight, and at five-thirty he turned the sauce on to warm again. Lilah would be hungry; he should be ready.

When the rental turned up the driveway at six o'clock, his heart flew up in relief. He and Charlie banged out the door, and he swung Lilah into a hug so huge her feet left the ground.

"Have a good time?" he said as he set her down.

"It was great! Grandma Nora's house is really cool. It has a laundry chute from the second floor all the way to the basement and we went shopping in Stowe and Mom got me this jacket." She twirled to show off a miniature version of Sophie's jacket. Suede minus the fringe.

"Very nice." He caught Sophie's eye. "Thank you for getting her home on time."

"Ye of little faith."

"Has Charlie had dinner?" Lilah said. "He's got his nose in my bag."

"Not yet. You can feed him."

Lilah disappeared into the house with Charlie on her heels, having heard the word dinner.

"When's your flight?" Glenn said.

"Tomorrow morning but I'll get a room near the airport."

He was ready to have her gone, more than ready. But she'd stepped up and brought Lilah back on time, and Lilah would be thrilled to have her mother one more night. "Why don't you just stay here tonight," he said.

"Are you sure? I don't want to wear out my welcome."

He hefted her bag. "It's fine. Lilah will like it." Just one more night. He could do that.

"Thank you. That would be nice. I know you were worried about me taking her."

"A little," he admitted. More than a little, but she didn't need to hear that. The main thing was she'd brought Lilah home when she said she would.

"I made meatballs," he said, ushering her into the house, "but if you don't want that, there's salad."

Chapter Ten

On Sunday, Cassie and her father went to meet Andrew at the Stamford train station. She hadn't said anything about the suspension, and her dad hadn't questioned the sudden visit near the end of the term—she doubted he had a sense of the school calendar—but he'd been in high spirits ever since Andrew called and said he would come up Wednesday morning. When she came back from her run, her dad was already dressed and ready to go, even though the train didn't get in for hours.

Now he was anxiously scanning the tracks. "You said he'd be here at eleven-fifty. It's eleven fifty-four now."

She smiled at his impatience. "Should be here any minute." Shelly had two girls, who he dutifully loved, but Andrew held his heart. Andrew, with his grandfather's deliberate view of the world, who could discuss cars for hours on end or huddle with him over his workbench, painstakingly taking apart an old clock radio. Even when Cassie couldn't bring herself to come home, she would bundle Andrew on the train to Connecticut for summer camp with Grandpa. Her father would take off a couple of weeks and the two of them played mini golf, went to the beach and tinkered in the garage. Andrew was still good about calling her father but had confided lately that conversations with Grandpa had become difficult. A lot of the same questions and last time he'd forgotten where Andrew went to school. "I told him Tulane," Andrew said, "but he asked me again five minutes later."

When the train lumbered into the station her dad heaved himself out of the car. "There he is!" He waved heartily to Andrew, who was making his way down the platform with a clutch of other commuters.

Andrew raised a hand in greeting but even from a distance Cassie could tell he was down. He stowed his bag in the trunk and gave them both a hug, but in the back seat he stared out the window with a tightness in his jaw. He had Phil's dark hair and fair skin, but looked peakier than usual, like all the sunshine had been drained out of him.

"Grandpa wanted to go to Bobby's," Cassie said. "Is that okay?"

"Bobby's is fine," he said without much enthusiasm.

Bobby's was her father's favorite place, a no-frills diner on Laurelton's main street, where he used to take Andrew for hamburgers and orange soda. It had been their go-to place for ages, long after nicer, trendier restaurants opened up. Bobby's was frozen in time, run by the same family for decades. The name scrawled in neon, the blue awning faded. No restaurant would be allowed a neon sign in Laurelton these days, but Bobby's was a relic. So out of date no one would hear of changing it. The tables were Formica, the menus plastic, but people called ahead for the meatloaf and pies. Her dad loved Bobby's with an unwavering devotion, and whenever he took Andrew out for a treat, they always went there.

They settled into a vinyl booth and her dad ordered two orange sodas. "For me and my grandson," he told the waitress.

Andrew hadn't said much since he got off the train, which wasn't like him. He was usually a talker, at least when it came to friends and school and the latest car he found interesting. He could talk up a storm about that kind of thing. Not so much his feelings. But now he was quiet, which Cassie didn't like. And he had dark circles under his eyes too.

"How were things at Dad's?" she ventured. She'd been a little surprised he'd only stayed three nights.

"Okay." Andrew fiddled with the saltshaker like he used to do when he was little. "We went for sushi one night, then the next day he had to work late, so I just hung out. Last night we had dinner with Natalie and her kids."

"Who's Natalie?" her father said.

"Phil's fiancée, Dad." The word *fiancée* sounded ridiculously fluffy. It conjured up bridesmaids and rehearsal dinners. The man was fifty, for God's sake. And honestly, with everything going on with Andrew, Phil could have spent a couple of nights alone with him without dragging Natalie and the kids along. "How was that?" she said, hoping to sound noncommittal.

Andrew shrugged. "They're kind of annoying. They're like five and seven. The little one, Kyle, kept having to go to the bathroom."

"Phil's getting married?" her father said. "You didn't tell me that."

Cassie nodded wearily. "I did, Dad."

"When?" He frowned at her like the whole thing was her fault. Which maybe it was. She'd been inattentive to her marriage, she realized that now. She and Phil had started out with such high hopes, newly minted lawyers ready to conquer New York. It took two to do daily battle in Manhattan, and they were a well-oiled machine. Even after she dialed back her career to work for the city, they still had it figured out. He researched private schools; she remembered the doorman at Christmas. They'd always been good partners, but somewhere along the way that's what it became—a partnership. Sure, they had sex every so often, but it had been years since they'd strolled along the river holding hands. She should have carved out time, insisted they get off the treadmill once in a while. Phil's hours were impossible, at the beck and call of clients. And even her job demanded she work late sometimes. Maybe no one's marriage could prosper in a place as ravenous as New York. Hers certainly hadn't.

"The wedding's in October," she said.

Andrew twirled the salt, knocking it over this time. "I meant to tell you...Dad asked me to be his best man."

Her heart, which she'd thought was immune at this point, cracked open just a little bit more. Of course Andrew would be in the wedding. It would have been unthinkable of Phil to leave him out. But still. The thought of her son standing up in a tux, toasting Phil and his new bride made something wilt inside her. She summoned a smile. "Where are they having it?"

"The Pierre." He scowled. "But I told him I didn't want to."

"You did? What did he say?"

"Doesn't matter. I'm not doing it."

"Andrew, I think you ought to. He's your father."

"The Pierre?" Her dad, who'd been studying the menu even though he always got the same thing, tuned back in. "Your mother and I went dancing there once. They had a good piano player. I remember that."

Andrew looked confused. "You and Mom?"

"Your grandmother." Even with her worry over Andrew, Cassie couldn't help smiling. "On your anniversary, right?" She'd heard the story before, only they'd gone to the Waldorf, not the Pierre. But she wasn't going to correct him; at least he remembered the dancing. "I think it was your twentieth. Mom wore that fabulous blue dress."

"I liked that dress." Her father smiled mistily, then his smile faded. "Where is that dress? I haven't seen it in a while."

"I don't know." Likely donated years ago, but no point going there.

"I need to find it."

"I tell you what, when we get home, I'll help you look. Okay?"

He twisted his napkin. "That was her favorite."

Cassie stroked his hand, which seemed to calm him. "I'm sure we'll find it. It's got to be in a closet somewhere." Sometimes a memory sparked like this, briefly intense before it flamed out. He would likely forget about the dress by the time they got home.

She felt a twinge of apprehension. Her appointment with the genetic counselor was four weeks away. In a month she would know one way or the other. She hadn't said anything to Andrew yet, too hard to have this conversation over the phone. But he was here now. They needed to talk.

She was relieved when the waitress arrived with her pad. "Let's order," she said.

Andrew and her father ordered hamburgers, and Cassie got a Caesar salad. "And two orders of fries," her dad said. Thankfully, he'd already forgotten about the dress.

"So how's school?" he asked Andrew once the food arrived. He'd divvied up the fries so each of them had the same amount, even though Cassie protested she'd never eat that many.

Andrew took a drink of soda. He looked worn out. That horrible accident and then the suspension and now whatever was going on with his father. It seemed like every word, every bite of burger was an effort. She would run him over to Dr. Milburn. That was what she'd do. She wouldn't let him talk her out of it.

"School's okay." Andrew gave her a despairing glance, but her father, removing the pickle from his burger, didn't notice.

"I don't like these." Her dad set the pickle aside. "Why do they put them on?"

"Some people like pickles, Dad."

"What are you studying?" her father said.

"Um…just regular stuff, a philosophy class this semester…"

"Philosophy." Her dad brightened. "That's a good foundation for law school. Are you thinking of law?"

"Dad, he's only a sophomore."

"Never too early to think of the future. I got through college in three years."

Andrew toyed unhappily with his fries.

"It was the fifties," Cassie said. "Things were different in those days." She hoped her dad wasn't going to start on his "loop." What he'd studied in college, where he'd worked after law school, how much money he'd made. All that stuff was buried deep.

"Andrew's smarter than I was at his age." He beamed at Andrew approvingly. "He could finish in three years."

"I'm not that smart," Andrew mumbled.

"Sure, you are."

"There's no reason to rush through college," Cassie said. Andrew looked like he wanted to crawl under the table. This definitely wasn't the time to grill him about school.

"I need to urinate," her dad announced.

"Do you want Andrew to show you where the restroom is?"

Her father gave her an irritated look as he maneuvered his boot out from under the table. "I know where the damned bathroom is."

"Go with him," Cassie mouthed, but her dad was already clomping off on his own. She was about to urge Andrew to follow anyway, but something in his face stopped her.

"What is it, sweetie?"

"I need to tell you something."

"Okay." She felt a rising dread. She'd had a feeling there was more, but what else could it be? What they knew was bad enough.

Her father had made it halfway across the restaurant then gotten confused and now was hovering near the coffee pots. She should go help, but across the table something was happening to Andrew. In the space of thirty seconds, his face had crumbled.

"I'm not going back to school," he said in a rush. "Don't try to convince me. I can't do it."

She blinked. "But finals are next week. You're almost done with the year."

"I keep thinking about what happened. Jack might have brain damage. They don't know."

"Oh, that poor boy." A life ruined. For nothing, a stupid frat party. And Andrew was a casualty as well. Not in a physical way, of course, but so traumatized he couldn't bear the thought of returning to school. "Sweetie, not going back doesn't help him. I agree it's not a good idea to be in the frat house, but we can get you a hotel room or an Airbnb for the last couple of weeks. You've worked so hard all semester, you can't just walk away."

"I can't!" He gave her an anguished look. "I just can't do it."

"Andrew." She lowered her voice. "Exactly what *happened* that night?"

"I told you."

"The whole thing?"

He swiped fiercely at his eyes but couldn't quite look at her.

She waited, but he didn't say anything more. "Have you told Dad?" she said finally.

"Dad won't fucking listen."

Her eyes opened up at his language, but she had no time to respond because her father was making his way back to the table.

"He's looking for the restroom," Cassie said when a waitress intercepted him. He let the waitress take a gentle hold of his elbow. Maybe they needed someone like that at home instead of Mrs. Macuja, who was turning out to be something of a drill sergeant.

Andrew was breathing in shaky gulps, trying to pull himself together. "I've been having nightmares. Where Jack gets up and his head is all bloody but he doesn't know it. And everyone's staring at him. Or he's walking around campus like that and I'm the only one who sees it. No one else even knows anything's wrong."

"Oh sweetie." She scooted around to his side of the booth and wrapped him in a hug. He resisted at first, then gave in with a small shudder. She pressed him to her, breathing in the sweet, peppery smell of him, a little sweaty from the train. "I can't make you go back, but you have to at least take incompletes. Otherwise, we'll lose the tuition. It's a lot of money." She rubbed his back, something that had always soothed him as a baby. She felt the sharpness of his shoulders, the half-grown angles of him. Whatever had happened, he was her son.

"How about talking to somebody?" she said. "That might help."

"I don't know," he moaned. "All I know is I can't go back."

"All right, we'll figure it out." But her heart was breaking. For him. For the other boy.

For the way life could change in an instant.

•   •   •

Her father still had a landline, so she shouldn't have been surprised that Chuck Weber from Weber Properties contacted them. Tuesday morning, her dad already back in front of the TV after breakfast, Andrew still sleeping. That was pretty much all he'd been doing. Ten, eleven hours a night. Tucked into Shelly's old room with her ancient comforter, frayed but still serviceable. That summed up the whole house. Barely holding together with rot around the edges and Lord knew what was happening in the basement. So she'd been astounded when Weber came right out with a very large number.

"You haven't even seen the house," she said before remembering they wanted to tear it down.

"We're looking to create a special community in Laurelton," he said, launching into the same speech he'd made at the zoning board meeting. "As you know, your property is adjacent to the larger parcel, and we believe it would complete the development. We'd like to discuss it with you."

She asked him to repeat the offer, not sure she'd heard correctly the first time.

"Is there a time I could stop by to speak with Mr. Linden?" Weber asked. He was a little pushy, but she'd never dealt with a developer who wasn't.

"My father's not looking to sell," she said. But the number ricocheted around in her head, making it hard to think about anything else.

"There might be some wiggle room there. How about I stop by and chat with you and your dad?"

He was smart, playing to her as well.

She got him off the phone with a vague promise to talk to her dad, then slipped out to the sunporch to clear her head. The porch was still in winter mode, the patio furniture stacked in the corner, windows and screens that needed a good washing. They used to eat out there every night when the weather was warm.

Her father was rattling around in this big old house by himself. Mrs. Macuja or someone else was only a temporary fix. How long could he manage? She pulled out a chair and sank onto a damp cushion. She'd always known that eventually the house would have to be sold, but maybe the time was now with a substantial offer on the table. Yes, it would be sad to see the property cut up instead of sold to another family, but you couldn't help what happened to a house after you let it go. No point being sentimental. Her dad had turned himself inside out to keep her mother here, even after she didn't know where she was, but how would she and Shelly manage? They both had their own lives, and Shelly was on the other coast.

The time had come. She just needed to convince her father.

·　　·　　·

Out front, a car door slammed. Glenn! She'd lost track of time.

"Dad." She stuck her head into the den. Her father had on the headphones she'd given him, and she had to wave to get his attention.

He removed them reluctantly.

"Glenn's here."

He gave her a blank look.

"The beekeeper. He's going to help with those mites, remember?"

He nodded, pushing himself out of his chair, wobbling in the boot until he regained his balance. She'd bought him a cane at a medical supply store, but of course he refused to use it.

"I thought we could try a couple of things to start," Glenn said after he shook hands with her father. He looked like he was about to offer to shake her hand too, then hesitated. "Good to see you," he said, shoving his hands in his pockets.

"You too." An embarrassing warmth crept up her neck. She wished she'd had time for a shower. He would run the other way if he knew how much she'd been looking forward to his visit. Even with everything going on. Maybe because of it. How sad was that? A guy she hardly knew. A beekeeper of all things. But he was attractive and smart. And not full of himself. There was something reticent in the way he held back, listening to her father now. Her dad had gotten confused about the mites and kept calling them termites. Glenn nodded respectfully, letting him speak. He'd be appalled if he knew she'd been talking to Weber Properties.

And he was wearing those shorts again.

She looked up guiltily, but he was busy showing her dad a bag of powdered sugar.

"So we can sprinkle it on the bees," he was saying. "It doesn't hurt them and it might work."

Her dad dipped a finger in the bag. "It's sweet," he said.

"Yup. They'll groom each other to remove the sugar and that gets rid of the mites." Glenn dug out a screened frame from the back of his truck. "Then if we put in these bottom boards with a sticky mat underneath, the mites fall through and can't get back up."

"That's clever," Cassie said. Beekeeping seemed to involve a lot of ingenious fixes.

Glenn leaned the frame against the truck. "It's not a perfect solution though. The sugar only gets rid of mites on the adults. The real problem is in the brood. That's harder to deal with."

Cassie was about to ask what they should do for that when Andrew petered out the front door, wearing pajama bottoms and a t-shirt, his hair wild from sleep. He blinked in the sun. He'd hardly been outside since he'd been home, and she was relieved to see him set foot out the door, even if he was still in his pajamas.

"Hey," he mumbled. "What's going on?"

"This is Glenn Marsden, he's helping Grandpa with the bees. This is my son, Andrew."

They shook hands, and Cassie was struck by how fragile Andrew looked. Five days of rest hadn't done much for him. If anything, he looked more wrung out than ever. She would make chicken soup tonight the way he liked with bits of potato. She was still hoping she could convince him to go back to school, but time was running out. His flight was on Wednesday.

Phil, of course, had hit the roof when she told him Andrew didn't want to go back. "He has to go back," he'd said. "No discussion. He's four finals away from the end of the semester."

"He's in a bad place, Phil." She was whispering in her old room upstairs so Andrew, across the hall, couldn't hear.

"He didn't say anything to me. How did this suddenly come up?"

"It didn't just suddenly come up. If you'd spent more than ten minutes with him he might have told you."

"What's that supposed to mean? He was here for three days."

"And I'm sure you were working most of it." She didn't add the part about Natalie and the kids. Provoking Phil wouldn't solve anything. What leverage did they have anyway if Andrew refused to go back to school? She hated the thought of him walking away right before finals, but he was on the edge. Even getting out of bed was an effort. At least she'd made him an appointment with Dr. Milburn.

Glenn helped her dad into the truck, then handed him the bag of powdered sugar.

Cassie smiled. "I have to see this."

"Powdered sugar?" Andrew said but ambled down the driveway with her. "Does this bee guy know what he's doing?"

"More than I do. Actually, he's been a lifesaver."

Her father, who thankfully had put on a veil, was given the job of holding the frames flat as Glenn sprinkled the bees with sugar. They immediately went into motion, hurrying away like animated white raisins, a few lifting off in a powdery haze.

"Let's do this quick," Glenn said, sliding in the first frame and removing another. "Before they get too annoyed."

Andrew, blinking in surprise, leaned in for a look.

Glenn offered him the sugar. "Want to try?"

"Um, sure."

Cassie was about to protest that Andrew wasn't wearing a veil, but she had to smile at the sight of him in his pajamas sprinkling sugar over the tray of bees, like a kid making Christmas cookies.

Glenn handed her father another frame and Andrew dusted sugar over that one too, laughing as the bees turned white. "Mom, you should try."

"Me?" Her stomach seized at the thought of cozying up to a frame full of bees.

Glenn raised an eyebrow, another frame at the ready.

"Um...I really don't..."

"Oh, come on. It's fun." Andrew handed her the sugar, looking happier than he had in days.

She took the bag, eyeing the bees apprehensively. They oozed over the wooden frame, a wiggling black mass of movement. A few lifted off right in front of her nose, and it was all she could do not to jump back. She crept closer and sprinkled a little sugar on top.

"Look close," Glenn said, "you can see them grooming each other."

Andrew's eyes went big. "I see them!"

"Oh, my goodness." Cassie let go a laugh. "I see them too. It's like a little salon. One right on top of the other."

Andrew laughed, a real laugh, which was the best sound she'd heard all week.

Once the bees were dusted, Glenn replaced the bottom boards with the screened frames and attached a sticky mat beneath each one. The bees were wound up now, zooming around their heads. Wait. What was that? *Oh my God, she had one in her hair!*

She let out a shriek, swatting at her head the way you weren't supposed to.

"Stand still," Glenn said. "They don't notice you unless you're moving."

"It's already noticed me!" She made herself stand still, but every nerve ending was vibrating. "It's walking around," she said through gritted teeth. "What do I do now?"

"Give it a sec, it'll probably decide there's nothing worthwhile up there."

She squeezed her eyes shut, her skin crawling with the horrible sensation of little insect feet roaming through her hair. Six little feet! Wasn't that what bees had? And a stinger on the end! Oh, why had she come down here?

"Don't let it near your eye," her father advised.

"Hang on, Mom," Andrew said. "It looks like it's about to take off."

"How can you tell?" she muttered. She took a deep breath, willing herself to stay calm. The worst thing that could happen was she would get stung. She wasn't allergic; she would survive. The bee probably didn't want to be caught up in that mess either.

She took another breath, trying to ignore the tiny tickling sensation on her scalp. In about three seconds she would scream.

"There you go," Glenn said with a touch of laughter in his voice. "It's gone."

She opened one eye, then the other to see the bee wobbling off in the direction of the hive.

Andrew gave her an approving look. "You were really chill, Mom."

"Not everyone can hold still with a bee in their hair," Glenn agreed.

Her knees were a little wobbly, but at least she hadn't made an idiot of herself by running and screaming. And she hadn't been stung like her poor dad.

Glenn offered to drive her father back to the house, but her dad, who appeared invigorated by the goings on, wanted to walk.

"I'll walk up with him," Andrew offered.

Cassie handed her dad the cane, which she'd brought along just in case, but he waved it off.

"Well, that was exciting," she said as Glenn stowed the rest of the powdered sugar in the truck. She was surprised they hadn't used it all. There'd seemed to be clouds of it in the air.

"Hopefully it'll slow down the mites. At least we'll be able to see how many end up on the sticky mat."

The bees had settled somewhat, but dozens were still flying around. She couldn't help admiring them. Such fearless creatures. Scrambling like fighter jets when the hive was opened, ready to defend their home. She didn't like them in her hair, not one bit. But they were heroic, going about their business even in the face of adversity. Half of their brood had been wiped out by mites, but they still got up in the morning.

"What other remedies do you have, anything with chocolate?" She needed to take a shower and get to work, but the morning was warming up and she had the irresponsible urge to shuck off her shoes and sit in the sun on the stone wall.

He laughed. "No chocolate, it's pretty much all about honey in my house. Oh, I almost forgot, I brought you some." He reached through the open passenger window and retrieved a glass jar filled with a thick amber liquid. "Lilah designed the label for me," he added almost shyly.

"It's adorable." The jar had a whimsical bee on the front and was warm from sitting in the truck. She tipped it up to the light. A wedge of comb floated inside. "Do you eat the honeycomb?"

"Sure, you can. A lot of people like it."

She unscrewed the lid and dipped a finger into the jar. The honey clung luxuriously, unspooling in a languid stream from her finger. Thick and slow and decadent. She gave up on propriety and licked it off. "Mmmm..." A bit more was about to drip so she licked that too. "It's delicious. Much better than supermarket honey." She looked up, embarrassed to find him leaning against the truck, watching her with amusement.

"Glad you like it."

She screwed the lid back on, but her fingers were still sticky so she had to lick them again. "Don't look. I'm a mess."

He reached in the open window. "Want a paper towel?"

"No." She laughed. "I'd rather make a fool of myself licking my fingers." She inspected her hands. "Anyway, they're clean now." She turned the jar over again, admiring the label. "Lilah's very artistic."

"Yeah, she's talented." His face lit. "I think I've kept every drawing she's ever done."

"Let me guess, they're all over the fridge, right?"

He laughed sheepishly. "Pretty much and everywhere else too."

"She must like that."

"It's mainly for me. I get an eye roll for everything I do these days."

"Andrew was horrified by having parents at that age. I think he preferred to believe he sprung from a rock."

Glenn chuckled. "He seems like a good kid now."

She looked toward the house, where Andrew and her father had gained the porch. "He is a good kid, just in some trouble at the moment."

"You mentioned he got suspended," Glenn said cautiously.

She sighed, debating how much to say. "A friend of his got badly hurt at a frat party. Fell and hit his head. They were all drinking, of course. Andrew's pretty shaken up, as he should be. But now he doesn't want to go back to school." Besides Phil, she hadn't told anyone about this yet, not even Shelly. She wasn't sure why she was confiding in Glenn, except he had a calm, nonjudgmental way about him.

"What are you going to do?"

"I'm not sure what I can do, but I worry about him leaving school."

"Maybe it's better if he takes some time, gets his head straight."

"You might be right."

"I'm not looking forward to the teenage years," he admitted.

"They'll be here before you know it." She gave him an encouraging smile. "You'll be fine. You seem like a good dad."

"I don't know, I hope so.

"I just meant, you know, you light up when you talk about her." She was making it worse; he was practically fidgeting. But it was true. He was clearly devoted to Lilah.

His face clouded. "Her mom just had her for four days."

"Oh. I thought her mom wasn't in the picture."

"She isn't, I mean she wasn't." He fiddled with the roll of paper towels he was still holding. "She took Lilah to Vermont to see her mother, Lilah's grandmother."

"That sounds sudden."

He looked deeply unhappy. "She reappeared after four years, but that's how she is."

"Four years is a long time." She tried not to show her shock. But *four* years. "How did Lilah feel about it," she couldn't help asking, "her showing up after all that time?"

He shrugged. "It's her mom. She wanted to go, but I worry she's going to get hurt if Sophie flakes out again."

Sophie. So that was the ex's name. Probably drop-dead gorgeous judging by the daughter. She wondered if Glenn was still a little in love with her. "You make flaking out sound like a sure thing."

"I hope not for Lilah's sake, but her mother doesn't have a good track record."

She felt sorry the way he said it, how things must be for Lilah. A twelve-year-old girl with a truant for a mother. "Must have been pretty quiet around your house the last few days."

"You could say that. At least she's back now." The relief in his voice was unmistakable. "Anyway, I didn't mean to go on." He looked like he wanted to change the subject. "I better get going."

She felt a twinge of disappointment. This was the most he'd spoken since she met him, and she wanted to keep him there talking. Find out what happened with his marriage and everything else about him. He was a reserved guy, but she sensed something solid underneath. And it didn't hurt that he was nice to look at too. But she had a meeting in an hour, and he was talked out anyway.

"Thanks again for the honey," she said.

"Anytime. I'll come by later this week and check on those mites."

"Okay great." Then to her astonishment, she blurted, "Hey, want to grab dinner some time? I mean just something casual." Her face went hot. Oh God, did she just ask him on a date? It had just come out of her mouth.

She liked him and he was alone too, and oh Christ. Now she'd gone and embarrassed them both.

For a second he looked stunned, then smiled uncertainly. "Sure. I guess so."

"Listen, I didn't mean it like that. Not like a *date* date. I haven't gone on a date in twenty-three years. I just thought it'd be fun to get together, you know, get out of the house." Oh wait. That was all wrong. "Not that it's just a way to get out of the house," she amended. "I mean, it'd be nice to talk some more." She groaned and covered her face with her hands. "I'm sorry. I'm so rusty at this. You don't have to say yes."

"I'm pretty rusty too. And yes, I'd like to."

She peeked up at him. "You would? Ok, wow. I mean, that's great. When should we...is Thursday okay?" Her mind was already spinning with what to wear. She'd hardly brought anything with her, she'd been living in the same jeans and leggings since she got here. Would they drive together? Oh no, that would be awkward. One of them picking the other up. Best to meet him there. Wherever they were going.

"Thursday's good." He glanced up at the house. "Can you leave your dad?"

"For a few hours and my son might still be here anyway." She had a feeling Andrew was not heading back to school on Wednesday. Spending a little time with his grandfather might do them both good.

"Okay then." Glenn still looked slightly stunned. "Should we touch base later this week?"

She nodded, smiling, and gave him a wave as she started up the driveway, hoping he didn't notice her stumble on an uneven patch of pebbles.

She had a date with the beekeeper. Wait until she told Shelly.

Chapter Eleven

Lilah cast a critical eye at Glenn's shirt.

"What's wrong with it?" he said.

"Don't you have anything better?"

"Better? What do you mean *better?*" He never should have told Lilah he was going out with Cassie. Now she'd made it her mission to spiff him up. He considered the shirt, a blue and green plaid, one of his favorites. It looked all right. He and Cassie had agreed on casual, so what was wrong with jeans and a flannel?

Lilah rummaged through his closet. "Why do you still even have this?" she said, zeroing in on a fleece he happened to like. "I remember this from when I was little."

"It's comfortable." He plucked it out of her hand. No way he was getting rid of that. He'd owned it since college.

She gave him her most severe look. "Seriously Dad. It's ugly."

"Well I'm not wearing it tonight so don't worry about it." This whole thing had become nerve wracking. Why had he agreed to dinner? He'd been floored when Cassie came out and asked him, and okay, tickled too. He'd been thinking about her a lot but never would have mustered up the courage to ask her out. He would have puttered along, taking care of the bees, finding reasons to get over there once a week, hoping for a chance to talk to her. But he would have left it at that.

He jettisoned the offending shirt. He knew why he'd said yes. Besides the fact that she was a great looking woman, she had a contagious energy that made him feel like he'd kicked up the burner on the stove. He'd been simmering on low for so long he'd forgotten what it felt like to be around someone who bubbled along at a boil. He liked that about her. She had a lot on her plate, but she didn't let it knock her down.

And she'd been pretty damn cute with a bee in her hair. But what if they didn't have anything to talk about? All they had in common was her dad, and how far could that get them?

Lilah selected another shirt. "Try this one," she said, plopping onto his bed for a better view.

"It's flannel, like the other one. Only red."

"It's more up-to-date. Trust me, you'll look better."

He gave her his *are you kidding look*, which made her giggle. "Okay, as up-to-date as you can be."

"Hey," he said, trying for nonchalant. "Have you heard from your mom?"

"She texted before. Why are you asking that way?"

He held up his hands. "I wasn't asking any particular way, I just wanted to know if you heard from her."

"She's going to call Sunday."

"Okay. Good." He'd been relieved when Sophie returned Lilah on time from Vermont, almost had him believing things might change. But when Sophie didn't return her calls, Lilah's upbeat mood deflated. True to form, despite all that bullshit about doing better.

Lilah was edging toward the door, but he didn't want to leave it like that, especially with him going out. "Listen," he said. "It's great that you went on that trip with your mom. I'd love you to have a relationship with her. I really would." Deep down he wasn't sure if this was quite true, but he needed to say it. He dropped a kiss on her head. "I'm on your side, okay?"

She surprised him by wrapping her arms around him and burrowing into his chest. "Okay."

He held her close. *Goddamn Sophie.* He had no doubt she would disappoint again. How many more times until Lilah was too bitter to care? Until she grew into an adult who could trust no one.

Lilah squirmed away, ready to move on. "Wear that one," she said, tossing him the red shirt. "And don't tuck it in."

"Won't it look messy that way?"

"You don't want to look like you're trying too hard."

"Tucking in my shirt is trying too hard?" Could that be true? Maybe with the middle school set. He was starting to regret this. He had no hope of impressing Cassie. She was a lawyer who lived in New York. She probably pulled down three times what he did and undoubtedly knew her wines. He was who he was. A beekeeper who drove a pickup with his name on the side. A big night out in the Marsden house was bringing home Thai food and watching a movie on Netflix. No point trying to be something he wasn't.

But here he was trying on a bunch of shirts with his stomach all wound up. He hadn't been on a date in ages. He barely remembered how to talk to a woman. He'd gone out a little here and there over the years—a divorced mom from Lilah's school, then someone his brother fixed him up with. But no one he was very interested in. Anyway, Cassie had made it plain she was a short-timer. She'd be gone in a few weeks or a month at most.

Lilah gave the red flannel a thumbs up and whipped out her phone to take a picture. "You look good."

"What are you doing?" he said, alarmed. "Who are you sending that to?"

"Just Crystal. I told her you had a date."

"You better not post that anywhere," he warned as she skipped out of the room.

She giggled. "Don't worry."

"I won't be late," he called as he trooped downstairs. It felt beyond strange, heading out on a date with his twelve-year-old daughter waiting up at home.

He gave Charlie a rub and headed for the door. Then, glancing back to make sure Lilah was out of sight, tucked in his shirt again.

At least he would look like a grown up.

●　　　●　　　●

He and Cassie had agreed to meet at Pascuale's, a popular Italian place in town. Cassie was already there when he arrived, which made him feel right away that he'd started off badly. He'd wanted to be polite and arrive first, but there she was, waiting at the hostess stand wearing black pants and a pale blue sweater. Heels too. He'd never seen her in heels.

She gave him a friendly wave, and he felt a sudden rush of anxiety. Should he kiss her hello? Shaking hands seemed too formal. What was the protocol with someone you barely knew? And a client, to boot. Wait. Was she his client, or was it her dad?

She rescued him with a quick hug. "Hey, you look nice. I like the shirt."

He gave a sheepish laugh. "Lilah's doing. She basically told me I needed to step up my game."

Cassie laughed and his stomach unclenched a little. "She has good taste."

"She thinks I'm hopeless."

She tossed him a smile as they followed the hostess to their table. "Of course she does, you're her dad."

Pascuale's had a bistro feel with tables packed close and waitstaff dashing around, lighting candles. Exposed brick with black and white photos of Tuscany on the walls. The place was busy, and Glenn's stomach knotted up again as they waited for what seemed like a long time to order drinks. What if they ran out of things to say, and everything became slow and wrong. He was *so* not good at this.

But Cassie seemed unfazed. "I've never been here. It's charming. My dad's go-to place is Bobby's—burgers and fries and orange soda. The same thing every time." Her gaze lingered on the room, which was starting to fill. "These days he wouldn't know what to do with candles and white tablecloths." She sounded a bit wistful.

"Believe me, tablecloths are normally above my paygrade too," Glenn said, and her smile eased the tight feeling he'd been carrying around. She was beautiful across the table in the candlelight, her hair dark and full, the sweater just low enough to be distracting.

When the waiter finally appeared they both ordered a glass of wine, Chardonnay for her, Cab for him.

"I pegged you for a beer drinker," she said playfully.

He arched an eyebrow. "Do all the beekeepers you know drink beer?"

"No, of course not. I mean...I actually, um, don't know any other beekeepers." She reddened. "I'm sorry, that was silly of me to assume."

He gave her an amused smile. "Just so you know, I do like beer but I drink wine now and then. When I had my first business I actually drank a lot more wine. Client dinners and all that."

"What was your business?"

"Land use, sustainable projects."

She tipped her head, interested. "What kinds of projects?"

"We created a tree grid for the parking lot at the Elm Street shopping center and sited a greenhouse at the high school. That kind of thing. I only took on projects I believed in."

"Why'd you get out of it?"

"Lilah's mother had just left, and I needed to be a full-time dad. I couldn't handle it—employees, clients. Dinners out. All of that. It was the right time to sell." He shifted uncomfortably at the thought of getting into a long story about his marriage. He definitely did not want to go there.

Cassie gazed at him thoughtfully. "So why beekeeping? Was it because of your grandfather?"

He sat back, surprised she'd remembered. "He was definitely my mentor. I wouldn't have gotten interested in bees in the first place if not for him. He helped me set up a few hives when I bought the house but he was in his late eighties by then and ready to wind it down, so I took his bees. Your dad sort of reminds me of him," he said with a smile.

"How so?" she said softly.

"The way he's so devoted." Glenn chuckled. "Your dad would have climbed into the truck bed with that box of bees if I'd let him. My grandfather was that way. It used to kill him when he lost a colony after the winter. He always took it personally."

"I can see that. I actually feel bad about those mites, the way they can wipe out a hive."

"Are we turning you into a beekeeper?" He smiled.

"Oh no! Not me. I'll leave that for the professionals." She twinkled at him over her wine. "The first couple of times you came over I thought you didn't like me." She said this in a teasing way, but she might have been half serious. He couldn't tell. He had a sudden urge to blurt out the truth—that she was smart and beautiful and he looked forward more than he wanted to admit to seeing her. But he took a long sip of his wine instead.

"So what do you think now?" he said.

She glanced at him mischievously. "I think the waiter's coming."

They ordered what the people at the next table were having: fried calamari to start and a couple of pastas. Vodka penne for her and rigatoni with meat sauce for him. Over another glass of wine she confided that Andrew hadn't returned to school on Wednesday.

"So what's he going to do?"

She looked weary all of a sudden. "Stay here for the time being, I guess. I want him to talk to a therapist. I've never seen him like this, so depressed."

"The powdered sugar seemed to liven him up the other day."

"That's the only thing that got him out of the house all week. Something's going on with his dad too. Andrew doesn't want to be in the wedding."

"Do you care?"

"Not really, except they've always been close." She pushed a bit of lemon around the plate. "I'm just worried about him."

They were sharing the calamari at this point. At first, they'd politely tipped a few onto separate plates, but something had shifted, and now they were picking up bits of fried squid from the serving plate with their fingers, like they'd shared food together a dozen times.

"What about you? How long will you stay?" He hadn't meant to ask this. He dipped a calamari into the sauce so he wouldn't have to look at her. New York wasn't far, but the city was another world. Her world. He'd never see her once she left.

She sighed. "I was supposed to be back already. I never thought I'd be here this long. But now, I don't know. I need to get my dad settled, and I'm starting to think it's time to sell the house."

"Sell the house?" Something tightened in the pit of his stomach. "Didn't you find a lady to help out?"

"Yeah, but it's not going great. She's keeping the place clean, which is a plus. But he doesn't let her do anything else, even put away his laundry. He had a fit about that the other day."

"Would he agree to sell?" He couldn't picture Mr. Linden giving up the house and hives that easily.

"That's the thing, I don't know. My sister and I would have to convince him. But he can't live alone anymore."

"I can see why he's attached to it," he said carefully. "You and your sister grew up there, and it's a beautiful piece of property. There aren't many like it around." He thought uneasily of the rumor that Weber Properties had been sniffing around. They'd snap up the Linden place in a heartbeat, then bulldoze it for a dozen more houses. Obliterate the meadow.

"It's not just that we grew up there," she said, "it's all tied up with my mom for him. They moved here when they first married and always talked about keeping bees one day. But then she got Alzheimer's. He took care of her at home until the end."

Their dinners had arrived, but neither of them made a move to eat. "I don't know much about Alzheimer's," he said, "except I had a great-aunt with dementia, and she ended up in a facility. They tried to keep her at home, but eventually it became impossible."

"It *is* impossible. It's horrible, I don't know how my dad did it. And I wasn't any help. I couldn't deal. I went off to college and hardly came back. Even after she died, I didn't come home. My dad and I always hit heads; he liked to give orders and I didn't want to take them. And the house..." She raised a shoulder. "It reminds me so much of her. My dad hasn't changed a thing."

"You were a teenager when she got it?" He did some quick math. "She must have been pretty young."

"My age," she said bleakly. "Early onset. And now every time I forget my keys I think—this is it. It's starting." She laughed a little to try to lighten the mood, but he could tell this was a deep, unrelenting fear.

"Does it always run in families?" He thought he'd read something about that, but he hadn't paid a lot of attention to Alzheimer's.

"This kind does, yeah."

The group at the next table had opened another bottle of wine and cranked up the volume. He leaned forward, focusing on Cassie. She was beautiful and fragile and terrified. Who wouldn't be? "Is there a test," he said gently, "so at least you'd know?"

"There's genetic testing if you know what mutation your parent had, which we do. Because my mom had it, there's a fifty percent chance I inherited the mutation. If I do have it, I'll definitely get early onset. One hundred percent. They can't tell me exactly when, but it will happen."

He exhaled softly. All his concerns seemed trivial compared to this. His ongoing irritation at Sophie, his obsessing over which bees had mites or if they had enough honey for the winter. None of it compared. Cassie woke up every day afraid she might lose her mind.

"What are you going to do?" he said.

She sighed. "I was on the fence for a long time, but Shelly's been after me. I wasn't going to do it because there's no treatment at this point. Maybe some clinical trials down the line." She picked up her wine, then set it down. "But it's so hard not knowing, wondering whether I'm cranky because my personality is starting to change or if whatever word I forgot means it's starting. So I made an appointment with a genetic counselor. At least I'll know."

He touched her hand, which felt cold even though the restaurant was warm. "That takes a lot of courage," he said. "Either way."

"How do you mean?"

"Knowing and living with it or deciding you don't want to know. And living with that."

She looked directly into his eyes. "What would you do?"

He considered for a minute. "I don't know. I probably wouldn't get out of bed in the morning."

She let go a laugh and her face relaxed. "You have a sneaky sense of humor, you know that?"

"I do?" He wasn't sure if this was good or bad. "I've been called a lot of things, but not sneaky."

She took a bite of pasta, her mood lighter. "I mean you're funny, but it sneaks up on you. Most of the time, you're so serious."

"I'm not always that serious," he objected. He tried to think of a time when he'd been lighthearted but came up blank. "Lilah thinks I'm a goof," he offered lamely.

She laughed at this. "I'm sure Andrew thinks I'm ridiculous too. He says I worry too much, but there's a lot to worry about. He's leaving school right before finals. Tell me how I'm not supposed to worry about that!" She aimed her fork at him for emphasis.

"So does it get any easier? Being a parent, I mean." This was something he'd actually thought a lot about. Whether he'd worry the same when Lilah was twenty.

"It gets easier in some ways. I don't worry about the stuff I did when he was twelve, but girls are tougher. All that drama." She shuddered. "I remember how I was at that age. My mother must have been a saint."

Somewhere along the way, they'd finished their wine and ordered more. He was pleasantly buzzed. He leaned back in his chair, amused and enchanted. He could sit across from her all night. The way she tossed her hair when she spoke, not even realizing how it showed off her lovely neck. And her eyes, which changed in the light. At first he'd thought they were green, then decided hazel. "So what were you like when you were twelve?"

"Pretty much a brat. You wouldn't have wanted to know me." She narrowed her eyes. "How old are you anyway? I bet I could have babysat for you."

He grinned. "If I tell you, will you tell me?"

"Definitely not."

"So we're at an impasse."

She gave him a mock serious look. "So what do we do now that we're at an impasse?"

"Go for a walk?" He needed to get up and move. If he sat here any longer he would say something stupid.

He paid the bill, refusing to let her split it even though she protested that she'd asked him. "Next time's on me, then," she said.

His heart sang. Apparently, there would be a next time.

They strolled through the downtown, which had mostly closed up for the night. A couple of restaurants were still open, but the stores were dark. Any night of the week, Laurelton was pretty much done by nine.

"A little quieter than New York," he said. Laurelton was a backwater. Pricey, but a backwater. No wonder she couldn't wait to get back to the city.

"Way quieter, but nice. We probably would have been run over by a taxi by now in New York."

"Do you miss it?"

She was quiet for a moment. "Believe it or not, I miss going to the office. And the coffee shop down the street. I miss that a lot. And my friends, there's a group I run with every week. I don't miss the traffic and how expensive everything is."

He had a sudden, ridiculous hope she would give up on New York all together. Stay here and take over her father's house. It would be the perfect solution, except she'd probably go insane. They stopped at the corner and looked both ways, but no cars were coming.

"Anyway," she said, "I have to get my dad sorted out first."

They passed the bakery and the real estate office, then meandered off the main drag onto a side street that sloped downhill past a frame shop and a consignment store, petering out to a dry cleaner at the bottom. The utilitarian side of downtown. The evening had cooled and she'd forgotten a jacket. He put an arm around her and she leaned into him. "This is nice," she murmured.

"It *is* nice." He breathed in the scent of her hair, her skin. She used something lemony, which he liked. She felt intoxicatingly good. They stopped to look in the window of the consignment store, and he trailed a hand lightly down her shoulder. She moved closer with a small intake of breath that made his heart skip.

She looked up at him. "So now's the time to tell me if you're seeing anyone."

He laughed in surprise. "Does it look like I'm seeing anyone?"

"My ex said he wasn't, but he managed to find someone new in record time. So I suspect he was." Her voice was light, but the hurt was plain underneath.

He turned to face her. "I'm not seeing anyone. Just Lilah and Charlie."

She looked perplexed for a moment then broke into a smile. "Oh Charlie." She gave him that teasing smile he found so irresistible. "I don't know why you didn't want to let him out of the car that day."

She was standing close, and he didn't want to talk about Charlie. "Because I hadn't been there before, and I didn't know you."

She looked at him in a way that made him forget everything else except how much he wanted to kiss her. "What about now?" she said, toying with his shirt right above his wrist. She was touching his skin, and he was having trouble breathing.

"What *about* now?" he repeated dumbly.

"Do you know me now?"

He ran his hands up her arms. Her sweater was buttery, but her arms were firm underneath. His heart banged around his chest. "Not as well as I'd like." He dipped his head and brushed his lips against hers, and the jolt that went through him just about brought him to his knees.

He kissed her then, for real, in front of the consignment shop, and even in her heels she stood on tiptoe, which made him even more crazy for her. That she couldn't get enough of him either. They kissed for a long time and his hands were in her hair, and when they finally pulled apart they were both out of breath, but smiling.

She took a look around and straightened her sweater. "We probably look like a couple of kids."

He laced his fingers through hers. "That was way better than anything I did when I was a kid."

She leaned into him. "Me too."

They walked holding hands back to her car and he kissed her again, more chastely this time since there were people walking by.

"When can I see you?" he said.

"Soon. Call me."

He gave her a wave as she pulled out, then made his way in a daze back to his truck, which was parked a block over. He wasn't quite sure what had happened tonight. Somehow, during the course of the evening he'd fallen hard for Cassie Linden. A lawyer from New York. A beautiful, strong, resilient woman who'd likely be gone in a month.

But he couldn't help grinning as he fired up his truck. He wondered whether tomorrow was too soon to call.

Chapter Twelve

On Friday, Cassie drove to Manhattan to meet Phil at the apartment. She hadn't been back to the city in a whole month. When she'd left, the trees were just leafing out and now here it was May. She felt a sudden yearning for her old life as she headed south on the West Side Highway. To her right the Hudson frothed in the brisk breeze and cyclists flew along the river path. She missed the city's relentless energy, the spike of adrenaline the minute you set foot on pavement. The sheer immensity of it all. You had to be up for New York.

She exited the parkway at Seventy-ninth Street, hitting the brakes when a car cut in front of her. *That* she didn't miss. She tightened her grip on the wheel and kept her eyes peeled for a parking garage. She pulled into one on Seventy-seventh and had just handed over the keys when her phone lit up.

"So how was it?" Her sister launched right in. "Did you sleep with him?"

Cassie glanced around, but the attendant wasn't paying attention. "No I didn't sleep with him! It was our first date. We went to dinner. I had a nice time."

"*Nice*, that's it?"

Cassie laughed as she exited the garage into the bright sun. "Okay, more than nice." She still had a lovely fizzy feeling in her stomach from her date with Glenn. What had *happened* last night anyway? "He's great. Smart and considerate. Funny in a quiet sort of way." To tell the truth, she'd been thinking about him all day. His adorable confession that Lilah had picked out his shirt. The careful, respectful way he listened without telling her what she ought to do. She wished she hadn't babbled on about Alzheimer's, but telling him had felt safe. Like it was okay to be scared.

"What, not good-looking?"

"Oh, he is. Very. I don't think he realizes it though."

"Send me a picture."

"I don't have a picture." She smiled to herself, imagining the two of them taking selfies like a couple of kids. Oops. She swerved to avoid stepping in something unsavory. You had to watch your step in the city.

"Will you see him again?"

"I think so." Something fluttered in her stomach. "I hope so." She most definitely hoped so.

"What about when you move back to the city?" As usual, Shelly had zeroed in on the heart of the matter. If she hadn't been a photographer, she would have made a good lawyer.

"Oh Shel, I don't know. I can't think that far ahead. Right now, I'm meeting Phil and a real estate agent at the apartment. We're going to list it."

"Ugh, I'm sorry."

"It's okay. I'm ready. I mean I don't have a choice. Phil told me he can't carry half the mortgage anymore. I'd have to buy him out, which I can't afford."

Shelly sniffed. "I bet Natalie put him up to this."

"Whatever. She's got two kids, and what woman wants to move into the ex-wife's apartment anyway?"

"At least you have Glenn to distract you."

She *did* need a distraction, but was Glenn just a distraction? She had a good feeling about him, but it had only been one date. She couldn't factor him into her thinking. But the thought of him tugged at her. Their surprising connection. The way her body rose when he kissed her. And kissed her.

"Gotta run," she told Shelly. She was coming up on the apartment building now, a leafy street on the coveted Upper West Side that had once seemed so promising. Elegant stone façade, detailed moldings. A beautiful building. She gave the doorman a wave and rode the elevator up to the sixth floor. She felt a soothing familiarity in the plush stillness, the way the carpet gave as she walked down the hall. Each door marked by a discreet gold number. So different from her father's house where chaos ruled.

She unlocked the door, surprised to see Phil already there, making himself at home on the couch. *How did he still have a key?*

"My meeting got canceled," he said by way of greeting, "so I got here a little early."

"Hi to you too."

"Sorry." He looked up from his laptop. "Just finishing some email." It threw her to see him there, his suit jacket casually slung over a chair like he'd just popped home for lunch, although when had he ever done that. He hadn't set foot in the apartment since he moved out a year-and-a-half ago. She wasn't oblivious, she'd realized they weren't connecting but figured they could make it right once Andrew left for college. They would make time to talk, spend some lazy mornings in bed, and if their marriage had deflated surely it hadn't gone completely flat.

But a week after they dropped Andrew at Tulane—one week!—the apartment so empty and quiet, Phil announced he was leaving. She'd just stepped out of the shower, an ordinary weekday morning, but the way he met her eyes in the mirror stopped her.

"I've been thinking about something," he said, "but wanted to wait until Andrew left." He had the decency not to look away, to wait for her to take the gist of his meaning.

Normally she would have whisked off the towel to dry her hair, but she felt his words coming and couldn't bear to receive them naked.

"I'm going to get my own place." He finally turned to face her. Even in that terrible moment it struck her that he'd missed a bit of shaving cream. A tiny blot between his mouth and chin. "I'll pay half the mortgage as long as you want to stay. There's no rush to sell."

"Is there someone else?" In the overheated bathroom, she was starting to shiver.

"There's no one else. There's just no us anymore." He handed her a towel for her hair. "I'm forty-eight years old, Cassie. I'm tired of phoning it in. I want to be happy. When's the last time we were happy?"

"You've been phoning it in?" She was still holding the extra towel, couldn't quite manage to get it to her hair. "Why didn't you say something? People work on marriages, we can go to counseling. Now that Andrew's gone, it'll just be us." But she saw his eyes dart toward the bathroom door, looking for the exit.

"Counseling isn't going to help. You have to want to make it work to go to counseling."

"And you don't." Later, when she thought about it—how he didn't even want to try—she was flattened, but at that moment her hair was dripping down her back and all she felt was cold and numb. And unbelievably stupid for thinking they had time to fix it.

"There's nothing left to work on. We've run out of steam. What's the point of going to counseling just to wind up here a year from now? We're both young enough to start over."

She eyed him suspiciously. "Who is she?"

"Really, there's no one." But she never believed him because before she knew it Andrew reported Dad was seeing someone new. The someone turned out to be Natalie, predictably blonde and a dozen years younger, who was now busy planning their wedding.

She dropped her jacket and purse on a kitchen chair. She didn't want to revisit that old history. "Have you talked to Andrew?" she said. Aside from Phil's presence, the apartment looked the same, with its orderly bookshelves and clean contemporary furniture. She'd thought it would be reassuring to be home, but in some ways, it felt like stepping into someone else's pristine life.

Phil shut his laptop. "Let me tell you Andrew was a real smart ass to me this morning. I called to see what was going on, and he said he would figure it out. So I reminded him that he'd better figure it out fast because we're on the hook for $28,000 for this semester's tuition."

"I hope you weren't too hard on him."

Phil snorted. "I'd like to see a little responsibility on his end. He can't just walk away."

"He said he was going to file for incompletes."

"He needs to hurry up before he misses the deadline." Phil was in no mood to coddle him.

Cassie sighed. "I'll remind him. You know, you might cut him a little slack with everything that's happened. I think he's upset about the wedding too." Talking about the wedding gave her a tight unhappy feeling, but Phil needed to hear it. "He's probably wondering where it leaves him, you getting a new family and all."

"That's ridiculous. Nothing's going to change," Phil said, but he looked a little sheepish.

"Well, there it is."

"Anyway, I can't tell you what a mistake this is, him leaving school. He should have been on that plane Wednesday."

"He's hurting, Phil. I don't know if you realize that."

"Of course I realize it, but dropping out of school won't solve anything." He was wearing his most aggravated expression. "Why couldn't you talk some sense into him?"

"Why couldn't *I*? You had him for three days, why didn't you talk to him?" She wanted to add that if he hadn't been so busy dragging Andrew off to see Natalie and the kids they might have had more time together. But that would just antagonize him.

"What the hell's he doing up there anyway? How long is he going to stay with your dad?"

"I don't know. Right now he's sleeping a lot. I think he's depressed. I made him an appointment with Dr. Milburn so at least he can take a look at him." Maybe Dr. Milburn would get him to open up because she hadn't had any luck.

Phil rubbed the back of his head where his hair was thinning. He'd always been vain about his thick, wavy hair, and she couldn't help feeling a smidge of satisfaction that he was starting to lose it. "All right, but if he's not going to be in school, he needs an internship or something. I can make a few calls. He can't just wallow around up there. That's not healthy either."

"He's not wallowing, Phil." She lowered herself onto the ottoman. "It's only been a few days. His friend might have permanent brain damage. Did he tell you that?"

Phil let go a sigh. "Yeah, he told me. I can't even imagine." Their eyes met for a brief moment, wordlessly sharing the unthinkable. "I didn't tell him about the apartment," he said. "I thought we should meet first."

They sat silently for a minute, absorbing the finality of this. Andrew had been sad but resigned about the divorce, but the apartment was something else. The only place he'd ever lived. "I'll talk to him," she said.

"We should do all right selling. The market's up." Phil sounded relieved she was on board. What did he think, that she'd make a fuss, insist he continue paying for an apartment he didn't live in anymore? She needed to find a new place and get on with her life. But what exactly did that look like?

Phil glanced at his watch. "Joan should be here any minute. Liam says she's a ballbuster." Liam was a partner in Phil's firm, one of those supremely confident men who assumed the rest of the world was there to make things easy for them. He'd introduced Phil to Natalie, or his wife had at one of their parties.

"Well that's good to know," Cassie said dryly. "I'd hate to settle for competent."

"Don't be hostile. You want to sell this place, don't you?"

Did she want to sell? Andrew had grown up here and she loved the neighborhood—peaceful but still close to restaurants and Riverside Park. An easy subway ride downtown. But after the expanse of her father's house, it felt cramped. Instead of trees outside the window, they had a view of the apartment across the way where a couple lived with two young children and all their toys.

The doorman buzzed and Phil went to open the door for Joan, who was about four-ten with spiky gray hair. Mid-sixties, smartly dressed in leggings and a stylish sweater. One of those skinny older women who looked like they never ate. But she had a grip like stone. Maybe that was where the ballbuster part came in.

Joan swept through the apartment, with Phil and Cassie hurrying behind like kids trailing after the teacher on a field trip.

"Just the one bath?" Joan said.

"There's one in the primary bedroom too," Cassie said. "A small one."

"Good. Two bathrooms are a big selling point. Let's see the closet situation." Cassie cringed as Joan threw open her bedroom closet. A wardrobe of Manhattan work clothes—dresses, jackets, heels she hadn't worn in ages. Those black patent leather boots she'd splurged on last year. She stifled a smile at the thought of traipsing around her father's house in those.

Joan seem unfazed. "Decent space," she pronounced, which made Cassie feel like she'd narrowly passed some sort of test.

Andrew's bedroom still looked like he'd dashed out that morning and would be home any minute. His dresser was cluttered with mementos from childhood—the heavy silver piggy bank her father had given him for his fourth birthday, a Darth Vadar mask that used to delight him with its ghastly breathing.

Once the apartment was gone, where would Andrew call home? Whatever small space she found or his father's busy new house with Natalie and the steps? But the truth was she and Phil both needed to move on financially, and as familiar as the apartment was, every room echoed with her failed marriage.

Shelly had advised having a good cry after Phil left, but she wasn't a big crier. She hadn't even cried when the divorce went through. She'd been numb by then, just wanted it over. The only time she'd cried was on their anniversary, which fell two weeks after Phil moved out. She'd believed she was okay—went for a run, grabbed the subway to work like always. It hit her midday when Phil didn't text about their plans for the evening. When she realized with a sinking heart that she had no plans for that evening or any other. She'd envisioned all at once how the years would unfurl, how she would grow old alone. She would visit museums on a senior pass or meet a friend for an early dinner, then go home to an empty apartment. She didn't even have a cat to keep her company. She was just another middle-aged single woman in a city full of them. She'd stumbled to the ladies' room, locked herself in a stall and cried.

That was the low point. It got better or at least it got ordinary. She found she didn't miss Phil that much, what she missed was having someone to check in with. Someone who would notice if she tumbled onto the subway tracks and got flattened by a train. Who might ask once in a while if she wanted him to pick up takeout for dinner. The apartment wasn't that much quieter than before since Phil had hardly been there anyway. But still, she was lonely. Knowing he wasn't coming home, that she would go to bed alone and wake up alone. That she couldn't give him a quick call about something that happened at work. Who would she tell if she screwed up or got a promotion?

The world was coupled. How had she never noticed? Men and women. Men and men. Women and women. And singles like her, hurrying along with half a sandwich and their earbuds in and no one to talk to.

She caught up with Phil and Joan in the kitchen, where Joan was frowning at the fridge. "You might think of updating. This has got to be seven or eight years old."

"More like ten, I think." Phil looked chastened. "But it still runs fine, right?" He glanced at Cassie for confirmation.

"Totally fine." Cassie had a quick worrisome thought about what might be lurking inside. She'd cleaned out the perishables when she left but could have missed a stray piece of cheese.

Luckily Joan had moved on to the cabinets, which she described as adequate. "Not as modern as new construction, but the building's bones are good. That counts for a lot."

"So you think it'll sell?" Phil said anxiously.

"Oh, it'll sell. I just sold another unit in this building. More updated than this one, but on a lower floor." She glanced approvingly out the living room window. "You have good light."

Light was at a premium in New York. Some apartments had windows that faced other buildings so all you got was an eyeful of brick and no direct sunlight at all. And other units saw only a patch of sky. Cassie thought of her childhood bedroom in Connecticut, the way the sun splashed across the bed when she raised the blinds. She'd groused about that as a teenager—too much light too early, but now, all that sunlight felt like a gift.

But the city had its own beauty. The old stone churches. Pockets of meticulously tended gardens. That was the problem. She missed New York and she didn't. As difficult as things were with her dad, she was grateful to spend time with him. She hadn't been there for the day to day with her mom. She'd only returned home for short, distressing visits. But now she saw her dad's hesitancy every day, the way confusion slowed his step. His frustration that once simple activities had become so hard.

He needed her.

Joan had moved on to a checklist of what had to be done before they could list the apartment. "Paint everything white," she said. "Don't get cute with color. People don't want yellow walls." She eyed the living room, which happened to be a nice buttery yellow. Cassie had picked it out herself, but apparently color was out. "And you'll want to get rid of those drapes, much too heavy. And update that main bath. It's tired."

"The bathroom?" Phil looked a little stunned. Apparently paint and drapery would not be enough.

"Once you find what you like," Joan said, "I have a guy who can install. He's not cheap but he's good."

"Do we need to do all that?" Cassie ventured. "Can't we paint and call it a day?" She was coming to grips with selling, but now it appeared she and Phil would be joined at the hip with renovations. Phil, who was fidgeting with his phone, didn't look thrilled either.

"Do what you like," Joan said, "but you'll get a much better price if you put some money into it. I can recommend a designer if you need help." Were all real estate agents this bossy? For some reason, Cassie recalled Beth Tartullo, the young agent she'd met in the coffee shop in Laurelton. Too bad they couldn't have found someone like that, a little more human-sized. But this was Manhattan. Nothing was to scale.

They walked Joan to the door, assuring her they would get right on the renovations. "If you need help finding a new apartment, let me know," she said to Cassie. "I've got a gorgeous one bedroom in Gramercy Park. Doesn't need any work and it's a nice, quiet neighborhood."

A single woman on the downslope of life looking for a nice, quiet neighborhood. Was that what she was? She could move into the apartment in Gramercy Park and never leave. Andrew would find her there thirty years from now gumming her food. Or she would board the A train, forget where she was going and end up in the Rockaways.

She accepted Joan's card, relieved to show the woman out. She'd blown in like an evil wind, deviling her with choices that had to be made. Phil was wrong, she wasn't a ballbuster, she was a mosquito that wouldn't leave them alone.

"Well." Phil exhaled once the door was closed. "I guess we have work to do."

"I guess we do." The apartment with the two of them in it suddenly seemed claustrophobic. She couldn't wait to leave. "Feel free to get some quotes," she said, gathering up her purse.

"Um, I thought you might want to do that."

"Why don't you go ahead and get started." It felt good to toss the ball Phil's way. Let him choose new bathroom fixtures. He could hand it off to Natalie for all she cared. She was moving on.

Somewhere.

Chapter Thirteen

Cassie had begun to hope Mrs. Macuja might work out after all. She was a bit opinionated—only certain cleaning products would do and the very fact of her existence annoyed Cassie's father—but she was definitely a big help. Her dad grumped about someone else washing his clothes and deciding what he was going to eat, but he'd seemed resigned.

But now, at nine-thirty on Monday morning, when she had a call at ten, something had gone awry.

"Mrs. Macuja wants to talk to you," Andrew called upstairs.

"I have a meeting in a few," Cassie said. "Can I talk to her later?"

"She wants to talk to you now."

She clicked out of the memo she'd been reviewing. She should have spent more time preparing over the weekend, but between dinner with Glenn and the trip to the city and—

"Mom!"

"All right, I'm coming!"

Mrs. Macuja was halfway up the stairs, her face an alarming shade of red. "I try my best. I do everything you ask but your father no good."

"What do you mean, he's no good?" Yes, her father was difficult, but he'd been difficult all along. "Is it the laundry, is he giving you a hard time?"

"Not the laundry. He pinch me!"

"He *pinched* you? Like on your skin? Are you sure?"

"What you mean, am I sure?" Mrs. Macuja lifted her skirt to show a red mark on the soft skin of her inner thigh.

Cassie felt slightly sick. "He *did* that? He actually touched you there?"

"He don't touch. He pinch!"

"Oh dear, I'm so sorry. Did he, I mean, what did he—" She glanced downstairs to see Andrew gaping up at them. She lowered her voice. "—He put his *hand* up there?" Dementia could lower inhibitions. She'd heard of elderly patients who suddenly began groping their caregivers or came out with lascivious comments that were completely out of character. Sometimes they even ended up getting kicked out of their nursing homes. But her *father*? The man so full of decorum he used to wear pressed slacks even on the weekends.

Mrs. Macuja glared at her. "How you think he do it?"

Cassie squeezed her eyes shut for a brief second. "I am *so* sorry. Let's go talk to him right now." She glanced at her watch. Nine-thirty-five. She needed at least twenty minutes to go over that memo. But her father had pinched a woman. That couldn't wait.

In the family room, her dad was placidly watching TV with his headphones on.

"Dad," Cassie said. "Dad!" She muted the TV.

He tugged off the headphones. "What are you doing?"

"Did you pinch Mrs. Macuja?"

He stared at them blankly but not before the briefest look of cunning passed over his face. "Why would I do that?"

"Because I clean up the puzzle on coffee table." Mrs. Macuja gave Cassie an accusing look. "You don't tell me to leave it."

"Oh." She groaned. "That damn puzzle."

Mrs. Macuja drew herself up. "He old but that not right."

"No, no of course it's not...I'm so sorry. It won't happen again. I promise." Her father had *pinched* Mrs. Macuja. And not just anywhere, he'd put his hand up her skirt like a sleazy old pervert. "He's not usually like this. The puzzle got him upset. I mean, that's no excuse, but he's never done this before." She looked at her dad, who was still absorbed in the TV even without the sound. "Dad," she said severely, "you need to apologize."

Her father looked at them benignly.

Mrs. Macuja crossed her arms. "I already ask him."

"You did? What did he say?" Cassie felt like she'd swallowed a prune, pit and all.

"He say he don't do it."

"Dad." Cassie took a fortifying breath. "This is *not* okay. If you're upset you need to say something. You can't go around pinching people." The puzzle pieces that had been scattered on the coffee table were all now neatly stowed in the box, which was sitting on a stack of magazines. "How was Mrs. Macuja supposed to know you were working on it?"

Her dad looked mildly at Mrs. Macuja, who glowered at him and then Andrew, who'd crept to the doorway, looking horrified.

Her dad gazed at the rest of them serenely. "I didn't pinch her."

"He lying!" Mrs. Macuja rounded on Cassie. "You don't believe me?"

Cassie looked between her father and Mrs. Macuja, who was practically shaking she was so mad. "I believe you," she said quietly. Her dad—meticulous lawyer, devoted husband, opinionated but never malicious—had pinched a woman in a very private place because she aggravated him. And then denied it.

In his former life, he would have been aghast.

"I can't work here," Mrs. Macuja said.

Cassie dropped her voice. "He's old, he's got dementia. He doesn't realize what he did." She doubted this last part was true. She'd seen that sneaky look and so had Mrs. Macuja.

Mrs. Macuja narrowed her eyes. "He know what he do."

Cassie's shoulders slumped. Her father definitely knew. Whether he believed it to be wrong was another story. In his mixed-up mind, maybe a pinch was justified. "Is there anything I can do to get you to reconsider?" she asked without much hope. She didn't blame Mrs. Macuja. In some ways it would be easier if her dad needed to be bathed or have his food cut up. Depressing yes, but this in-between stage, where his inhibitions had skipped off along with his judgment—she had no idea what to do about this.

"I don't change my mind." Mrs. Macuja collected her purse and sweater from the kitchen. She cast a final glance at Cassie's dad, who'd put his headphones back on and resumed watching his show. "I have to tell agency why I quit," she said.

"Of course. I understand." She paid Mrs. Macuja for the rest of the week and saw her out, her stomach puckered with anxiety. The agency might file a sexual assault complaint. Social Services could get involved. This could be an utter nightmare.

In the family room, her dad had switched from CNN to MSNBC. "Is that woman gone?" he said when Cassie entered the room. With the headphones on, his voice was overly loud.

Cassie sank onto the couch. Her meeting was in ten minutes. She'd done absolutely nothing to prepare. Sometimes it felt like this was her full-time job and being a lawyer was incidental. "Yes, she's gone," she said wearily.

Her dad nodded and went back to the news, which was airing a business segment about electric cars. Who knew how much of it he actually followed.

She thought of Chuck Weber, who'd called again and left a message. She hadn't called back, but his offer rolled around in her head. A very big number that might even get through to her dad. He said he didn't want to sell, but what was the alternative? After this pinching incident they might be unable to find another caregiver and eventually her dad would need help at night too. He might stumble out of bed and forget where he was. Fall down the stairs. It happened to old people all the time. And the house needed work. Just the other day she'd noticed a woodpecker drilling near an upstairs window. Wasn't that a sign of rot? It was only a matter of time before something major, like the furnace, went. Who was going to handle that?

No, staying in the house was not a long-term solution. There was only one thing to do. And the time to do it was now when they had an offer on the table.

•　　•　　•

She arranged for Chuck Weber to come over at ten o'clock Wednesday morning. After her dad had relaxed over breakfast and the paper but before he started dozing in front of the TV. A short window of time when he was most lucid. Andrew had convinced him to start over on the dinosaur puzzle and they'd been working on it together, but Wednesday morning Andrew would not be around. He had his appointment with Dr. Milburn that day.

Weber arrived promptly at ten, which Cassie took as a good sign. Punctual people tended to be direct and to the point. That was what this conversation needed to be—pleasant and unemotional. A simple business proposition. She took a breath as she opened the door. Who was she kidding? Selling the house was the right thing to do—Shelly was on board too—but her stomach was still tied in knots. As ambivalent as she always felt about coming home, seeing the house torn down would be wrenching. Her mother still lived in every one of its rooms.

Weber was dressed like he'd been at the zoning board hearing in jeans and a blazer. He offered a firm, friendly handshake. She dropped a look at his card. Charles Weber, Jr. He'd probably grown up buying and selling property, putting up developments. This was just one more deal to him and his family.

"Coffee?" she said. She wasn't sure about the protocol for a visit like this, but she'd put on a fresh pot just in case. Coffee might make it feel like a neighborly chat instead of a sales pitch.

"No thanks, I'm good. Already had too much this morning." She saw him look around, take in the worn floorboards, her dad's muddy shoes under the hallway table. How shabby the house had become.

"Dad," she said, leading Weber into the family room. Her dad had settled in front of the TV a little sooner than she'd anticipated. She'd wanted to have this conversation in the kitchen where he wouldn't be distracted but asking him to move now would only irritate him.

"This is Chuck Weber from Weber Properties. He wants to talk to us. Can you turn off the TV?"

Her dad gave Weber a suspicious look and reluctantly clicked off the TV. "What's this about?" he said.

Weber set a business card on the coffee table and took a seat on the couch across from her father. "How are you today, Mr. Linden?"

"I'm fine." Her dad glanced at Cassie, who couldn't quite meet his eyes. She glanced out the window, where the trees were bursting with the incandescent green of early spring.

"Dad, Mr. Weber is developing the Kingsley property. You know, next to ours."

Weber gave her a puzzled look.

"That's what we've always called it," she said, a little embarrassed she'd used the family nickname. "It used to be owned by people named Kingsley."

"Ah, I see," Weber said. "Well, as you probably know, Mr. Linden, we're planning to build luxury homes there." He extended a glossy flyer, but Cassie's dad didn't take it. Weber set it next to his card. "Very tasteful," he went on, "in keeping with the character of the neighborhood. We've built a lot of homes in Laurelton, maybe you're familiar with the Running Brook development. That's one of ours."

Her dad looked at him blankly. "Never heard of it."

"Over on Cross Ridge, up near the New York line?" Weber looked at him expectantly, but her dad was beginning to seem bothered, like a bee was buzzing his head. "What does that have to do with me?"

Cassie swallowed. Andrew and her dad had made progress on the dinosaur puzzle. The volcano was mostly filled in and they'd started on the greenery, which gave it a promising look. Small activities with lots of help, that's what her dad could handle now. The less frustration the better. "They're interested in this property too," she said, her mouth dry.

Weber smoothed his jeans, taking this as his cue. "Mr. Linden, we envision extending the development to include your property. As I'm sure you're aware, it abuts the project and we'd like to be able to go all the way to Southington Road, which will allow us to include common space. Buyers appreciate that now. The zoning board has given us the go ahead and we anticipate the town council will approve as well. It's just a formality at this point."

Her dad looked bewildered. "What's he talking about?"

Cassie swallowed around the lump in her throat. "They want to buy the house, Dad."

"Mr. Linden." Weber leaned forward. "We're prepared to make you a very attractive offer."

"Sell the house?" Her dad looked at Cassie. "To who?"

Cassie felt a creeping shame that she'd put this in motion. But if not now, when? Her dad was still competent enough to make decisions but soon he might not be. "To Weber Properties, Dad. That's why Mr. Weber is here. Let's just listen to what he has to say."

"Mr. Linden, we can offer you three million dollars. That's substantially more than the house, even with five acres, would get on the market. It's a generous offer."

Her dad's face had gone blotchy. He tried to push himself off the chair, but his cane was out of reach. "This house isn't for sale. I don't know why you thought that."

"Dad, it's a lot of money," Cassie said. "We should at least think about it." She'd done some research. Three million was a very good price. Weber didn't want to fool around; he wanted the property.

"There might be some wiggle room in that offer." Weber didn't seem perturbed. "I could go to three-two."

Her dad glared at Weber. "Young man, we've lived in this house for...for—" He looked to Cassie for help.

"Fifty-five years," she sighed, "but you don't need this much house. Three-point-two million is a lot of money. You'd be very comfortable."

"I'm comfortable now." Her dad scowled at Weber then Cassie. "Did you invite him here?"

"I thought we could talk about it," she said miserably.

"There's nothing to talk about." Her dad managed to get hold of his cane and shoved out of the chair, swaying precariously until he regained his balance.

Weber stood too. "Nice meeting you, Mr. Linden. I hope you'll give it some thought." He held out a hand, but her father refused to shake. He looked old and fragile in his ancient green sweater and walking boot, and Cassie felt a rising misery that she'd upset him. She'd thought a big offer would impress him but inviting Weber over had been all wrong. She should have introduced the idea first, let her dad come to it slowly. Now his back was up, and it would be that much harder.

The truth was, they needed to sell the house. And Weber Properties was prepared to buy it as is. No sprucing it up or renovating bathrooms. They wouldn't get another offer like this. Yes, it made her sad to think of it being torn down. It would be nicer to imagine a family moving in and taking care of the place. But you had to be practical. And her dad would be resistant no matter who was buying.

Weber shook her hand as she showed him out. "I'll be in touch," he said.

When she came back inside, her dad was in the kitchen fixing himself a cup of coffee. His hands were shaking.

"I'm sorry," she said, pouring herself a cup. She would twitch all day after more caffeine, but the morning had already been a disaster. She added a little milk and sat down across from her father, who wouldn't look at her.

"I really am sorry," she said again. "I should have told you he was coming."

"I'm not selling."

"It's too much to keep up. You don't need all this space. You go from the kitchen to the family room."

"Don't tell me what I need. First you brought that lady in here, that busybody, trying to tell me what to do all day. At least she's gone," he said with satisfaction.

"Because you *pinched* her." Cassie felt a spike of worry. Someone from the agency had called yesterday, but she hadn't yet called back. "What happens when I'm gone and you slip and fall and nobody finds you for days. You can't live alone here anymore."

A flicker of uncertainty crossed his face, but only for a moment.

"It's not just me," she continued. "Shelly agrees it's not safe for you to be alone. It'd be one thing if you accepted help, but you don't want anyone."

He glared at her over his coffee. "I've lived in this house longer than you or your sister have been alive."

"Daddy." She touched his hand gently. The skin was soft and spotted, and his fingernails needed trimming. "I love you. You know that, right?"

He looked away but not before she saw the tears in his eyes.

"All I want is what's best for you," she said. He didn't answer, but she could tell he was listening.

She sighed and let go of his hand. "I know this is hard, and I'm not saying you have to decide right now. Just think about it. We might not get another offer like this."

"I hope not," he said and hobbled back to the TV.

Chapter Fourteen

Cassie knocked lightly on Andrew's door. He'd been home two weeks, and she still hadn't found time to have The Conversation with him. Well, that wasn't exactly true. There'd been plenty of chances but whenever she went to tell him, her stomach seized up with a fluttery panic. She kept promising herself she would do it the next day, but the next day always came and went and now her appointment with the genetic counselor was three weeks away. Even though it terrified her, Andrew needed to know what might be lurking in his family history.

She knocked again, more firmly this time.

"Whaat?" he said sleepily.

She stuck her head in. The room smelled like sweat and dirty clothes. She pulled up the shade and threw open a window.

"Aaahhh!" He buried his head in the pillow. "What are you doing? I was asleep."

"Time to get up. It's ten o'clock."

He opened one eye. "It's still early."

She wrestled open the other window too. Shelly had always complained that this one stuck. "You've been sleeping too much. It's not healthy."

He dragged himself up to sitting. "That's because I'm tired." He was wearing the same t-shirt he'd had on for the past two days. She needed to grab that for the wash. "Why'd you wake me?" he said.

"Here, have some orange juice." She handed him the glass she'd carried upstairs and watched him drink it. Andrew had always been a cheerful riser, jumping right out of bed in the morning. Had his backpack ready for school the next day, set his own alarm when he was old enough. Phil was usually long gone, but Cassie didn't mind. It gave her a few extra minutes alone with her son.

She set the empty glass on the dresser and sat on the edge of the bed, her stomach in free fall. Maybe first thing in the morning wasn't the right time to spring this on him. He was barely awake. And she needed to tell him about the apartment before Phil mentioned it. She couldn't possibly lay it on him all at once.

"So...Dad and I went to the apartment the other day." She would definitely find time for the family history talk tomorrow.

"Our apartment?" Andrew said.

"We met with a real estate agent. We're going to list it."

He pushed up in bed. "What? You're selling the apartment?"

"It doesn't make financial sense for us to keep it. Dad's been paying half the mortgage, but he doesn't live there anymore."

His face darkened. "So he's making you move?"

"He's not making me move or throwing me out in the street. I could keep it if I want, but it's an expensive place on just one income." Of all things, here she was defending Phil.

"When did you decide this? No one said anything to me." He threw off the covers. "What happens to my stuff?" The hitch in his voice caught her, how he sounded so young.

"Oh sweetie." She reached for him but he swung out of bed. "Your stuff will go with me; I'll always have a room for you. We'll box it up together, and you can decide what you want to keep."

He rummaged through a heap of clothes on the floor, then gave up and slumped back on the bed in his t-shirt and shorts. "Dad's such a jerk. This is obviously his idea."

"It's no one's idea. It's just the way things are. And you need to be in the wedding. He'll be hurt if you aren't, and you'll regret it. It might not feel that way right now but trust me. You will."

"I don't want to be his best man. I don't want to be in it at all."

"Andrew. He's your dad." It wouldn't do him any good to hate his father. It would only cause a lifetime of hurt. She'd butted heads with her dad so often over the years that she'd become wary of every encounter. Bristling had become her default reaction, even when he wasn't saying anything provocative at all. She didn't want that for Andrew. He might not like the fact that Phil was remarrying, but he would have to come to terms with it.

Andrew scrubbed his hands through his hair. A Phil mannerism. The same thick wavy hair. He was Phil's son too. "I'll think about it," he muttered.

"Want some breakfast?"

"I'm not hungry." He gave her a baleful look. "When's all this happening?"

"Not for a while. We have to do some updating first."

"Update what? The place is fine."

"I think it's fine too but the real estate agent has other ideas." She kissed his forehead. "You sure you don't want breakfast? I can make eggs."

He groaned and pulled the covers over his head. "I'm going back to sleep."

• • •

It had been a difficult week. Thankfully, Mrs. Macuja had declined to file a sexual assault complaint but the home care agency said given Mr. Linden's proclivity—*they'd used that exact word!*—for inappropriate behavior, they would not send over another candidate.

"We understand these things sometimes happen with elderly patients," the woman said, "but we have to protect our staff. We can't place someone in a home where there's physical or sexual abuse."

"No, of course not," Cassie agreed, her face flushed with embarrassment. Her childhood home was now flagged as a place where unsafe things might happen. Where there might be physical or sexual abuse. Her elderly father lying in wait! It was beyond mortifying.

Then that discouraging meeting with Weber and the wrenching conversation with Andrew about the apartment. And she still hadn't talked to him about the genetic counselor. It had all been too much for one week.

But today was Saturday. Today she was going hiking with Glenn.

They'd been texting all week, semi-flirty texts, which sent her heart skipping. At least she considered them semi-flirty, but she would have swooned over his grocery list. Just the sight of his name popping up on her screen gave her a giddy little rush.

Just yesterday he wrote, `Looking forward to our hike`, and she'd answered back, `Me too`. But was that enthusiastic enough? Maybe she should have used an exclamation point. `Me too!` Everyone used exclamation points these days. Why hadn't she done that? He would think she wasn't interested. Dating, if that's what they were doing, was such a minefield. Back when she was going out with Phil, no one texted. You called someone on the phone or you didn't. And of course they were in school with their own apartments, where anything could happen, and usually did.

She yanked her hair into a crisp ponytail. She and Glenn both had kids, and she was living with her dad and son at the moment. Not a lot of privacy there. Besides, she hardly knew him. They'd had one kiss. But her mind had become rambunctious, galloping off in all kinds of scandalous directions.

Let's face it. The man was very sexy.

She spied his truck from the bedroom window and ran downstairs to give Andrew a last word of instruction. "Is this the beekeeper guy?" he said, glancing up from a bowl of cereal.

"Yes. His name is Glenn. You've met him." This was so awkward, Glenn picking her up like they were in high school. Her nineteen-year-old son seeing her off.

"You'll stay here with Grandpa, right?" she confirmed.

"Yup." He tipped back his bowl to get at the milk.

"Okay. I won't be late. Maybe try one of the new puzzles." Andrew and her dad had finished the dinosaur puzzle, and she'd picked up a couple of new ones at Meyer's. Although she had a feeling he could start on the dinosaurs all over again, and it would be completely fresh. "Call if you need me," she said. "We aren't going far."

Glenn was waiting for her on the porch. He had on jeans and an olive green Henley and Cassie's heart flew up at the sight of him. Charlie was standing in the passenger seat, nose wedged through a slice of open window.

"I hate to leave him if I'm going hiking," Glenn said. "You don't mind, do you? I can always drop him home."

"Of course not. I'm delighted to see Charlie." She gave the dog a rub and nudged him into the back seat as she climbed into the truck, suddenly a little nervous. The wine had loosened them up the other night, but what if they couldn't find anything to talk about in the light of day? They were such different people, and a trek in the woods wasn't really her thing. She couldn't remember the last time she'd been hiking. Central Park probably didn't count.

"I made peanut butter cookies," she said, stowing the backpack she'd borrowed from Andrew under her feet.

Glenn chuckled. "And I made peanut butter sandwiches. Guess we should have coordinated."

"Oh well." She smiled. "You can never have too much peanut butter."

He started up the truck, and they fell into an easy conversation after all. Glenn was surprisingly talkative, telling her as they drove about a new client who against all advice had ordered an assertive strain of bee and now was having trouble getting into his hives.

"They're more protective than the Italian bees," he said. "You've got to smoke the heck out of them, and even then you don't have much time."

"Will they come after you?"

"Oh yeah, they get pretty annoyed that you're mucking around their house. And when one stings, it releases a chemical alerting the others there's danger. So they all pile on. It's not just this strain, they all do that."

"You can't blame them for defending themselves."

He shot her an amused look. "Says the woman who had a bee in her hair."

She laughed. "I'm feeling more charitable after the fact."

"You were a champ."

"I don't know about that. I was just this side of hysterical."

Now that it was May the trees had exploded in a torrent of green and they took the back roads from Connecticut into New York, eventually turning onto a narrow road that wound past stately homes with long driveways and modest houses hugging the road. She didn't see any hiking trails, but Glenn finally pulled over onto a gravel turnout next to a discreetly marked trailhead.

"It's part of the Westchester Land Trust," he said. "Nine thousand acres of open space." He snapped the leash on Charlie. "The best thing is that it's close by."

They didn't see any other hikers as they started down the trail, which meandered into the woods with little fanfare. "I grew up five miles from here and never even knew this existed," Cassie confessed. But why would she have known? This wasn't her world. Her parents had never taken them hiking. They enjoyed the idea of having woods around, but it wouldn't have occurred to them to set off down a trail with a map. They'd been city people who found their way to Connecticut and were content to putter around their little slice of heaven.

Glenn didn't have a map, but he didn't need one. He looked right at home with his hiking boots and green shirt that blended with the dappled light. He nodded toward a tree marked with a yellow blaze. "We'll go this way, it's a nice climb."

The trail didn't ascend immediately. For the first few hundred yards it paced a crumbling stone wall that was going wild, consumed with vines and other growth. In some spots you couldn't see the stones anymore, and Cassie wondered how it might look a hundred years from now. Or two hundred. Whether there would be any sign of people at all. When the wall petered out, the trail dipped into the loamy quiet of the woods, the sun filtering through the canopy, delicate blue wildflowers angling for pockets of sunlight. She couldn't believe all this was just an hour outside Manhattan. She strained to hear the road, but the trees swallowed sound and the only noise was the muffled thud of their footsteps and Charlie's enthusiastic snuffling.

After a few minutes, Glenn unclipped him. "They're supposed to be on leash," he said with a conspiratorial wink, "but if no one's around, I usually let him off."

"My lips are sealed."

Charlie immediately blundered after a squirrel, which shot up a tree in front of him.

"Has he ever caught one?" Cassie asked.

"Never."

"Would he eat it?"

"I doubt it. I hope not. He'd probably just give it a good shake. But I wouldn't want to find out." He whistled and Charlie careened back in their direction, crashing through the understory, snapping twigs as he came.

Cassie laughed. "No wonder he's never caught anything; he sounds like a freight train."

Glenn fed the dog a treat from his pocket. "He's not exactly subtle, but you know where you stand with him."

She was tempted to ask if the same applied to him, but she didn't know him well enough yet to tease. Subtle wasn't the right word anyway since that implied indirectness, and Glenn was most definitely direct. He might have been the most direct person she'd ever met.

She felt a tug of uneasiness about Weber. Glenn would be appalled that she was talking to him. She doubted they would be here right now if she'd told him. She knew enough of him already to picture how his body language would change, how he would close up and become unreachable if she confessed she wanted to hand over her dad's property to a developer. He'd been so passionate that night at the hearing and the thought of his stony disapproval left a tight, unhappy feeling in the pit of her stomach. She needed to be honest; this was too big a thing to leave unsaid.

The trail narrowed and she dropped back, trying to enjoy the hike and not conjure potential problems. It had rained the day before, and the path was spongy in spots. She watched where Glenn planted his feet and tried to do the same. At one point they skirted a marsh, and he pointed out the floppy leaves of skunk cabbage and snapped on the leash so Charlie wouldn't roll in the muck.

When the trail became rocky and started to climb, Cassie tied her windbreaker around her waist. She felt better on firm ground, away from the sticking mud. Walking in the woods gave her a surprising sense of peace. She felt smoothed out somehow, the tightness that always rode with her receding. It was enough to put one foot in front of the other and listen to the birds. And Glenn was happy here. She could see the way his whole body relaxed, how his smile welled up out of nowhere and lingered when he looked at her.

They scrambled up a craggy section of trail, and he stopped to point out a rock that looked like a layer cake, huge slabs of stone resting one on top of the other like a giant had slathered them there. "Glacial erratics," he said, "left over from when the ice retreated. Eighteen thousand years ago this whole area was covered by ice. All the way up to Canada. Two miles deep, if you can believe it." He angled her a look. "That's taller than any of your skyscrapers."

She brushed a hand over the rock, marveling at the force of an ice sheet that could tumble such giant boulders.

They unpacked their lunches on a flat rock overlooking the surrounding hills. "The view's better in winter," he said, "but this time of year you can't see any houses, so that's a plus." He made Charlie lie down and handed Cassie a sandwich. "He's a beggar so don't feel sorry for him."

"I completely forgot there were houses around. It feels like the middle of nowhere."

He smiled broadly as he unwrapped his sandwich. "That's the idea. So much of this area has been developed, but there's pockets like this where you can see how the land used to look. Not even that long ago." He took a bite of his sandwich. "Sorry, I'll shut up. I'm being a bore."

"No, you're not." The rock was just big enough for the two of them, and she sat close to him in the sun, their knees touching. A low hum of happiness started up inside her. She tossed the last scrap of sandwich to Charlie, who bellied forward to reach it. Glenn poked her gently in the side. "You're encouraging him."

She leaned into him. She should tell him about Weber, but she couldn't bear to bring it up. It would spoil everything. Always so hard to deal with unpleasant topics, dig them out of the rootbound place they lived. Her mother, her own genetic fears and now the hard truth about the house.

Glenn looped an arm around her. "I'm glad you like it up here. I didn't know if you would."

"Why not?" But she knew why not. It was obvious she wasn't an outdoorsy kind of person. She lived in the city and ran on concrete. She had a million pairs of shoes but didn't own hiking boots. She'd muddied up her runners today. "Do I look that out of my element?"

"Not at all." He drew her close. "You look amazing."

"I wasn't looking for a compliment." She laughed, but he was so close and his eyes were that gorgeous smokey gray and when he bent to kiss her everything else flew from her head.

He kissed her the way she remembered from the other night, maybe even better, and they might have gotten into an uncomfortable position on that rock, but Charlie nudged her arm with a cold nose.

She yelped, startling Glenn, who knocked over their water bottles. They clattered off the rock, scaring Charlie, who'd begun investigating the cookies in her backpack.

"Well that was a mood killer," Glenn grumbled, but he tousled Charlie's head and fed him part of a cookie when he thought Cassie wasn't looking. They relaxed in the sun, and she told him about her trip to the city and how she and Phil had decided to sell the apartment.

"Are you okay with that?" he said. They were sitting on the ground now, their backs against the sunbaked rock.

"It's the right thing to do, but there's a lot of things I'll miss." She gave him a wry smile. "You wouldn't think much of it, but it's a great apartment by New York standards. The whole place would fit into my dad's kitchen and family room, maybe the mud room too. But Andrew grew up there, and I have a lot of memories."

He trailed a finger down her shoulder. "I get that. I thought about selling the house at one point but couldn't bring myself to do it."

"That's just it. It's harder than I thought it would be."

"How's Andrew taking it?"

She shrugged. "He understands why it has to happen, but that doesn't make it any easier. He's having a rough time in general right now." She glanced over at him. "You never told me about Lilah's visit with her mom. How did that go?" She was dying to know about the ex.

"Surprisingly well." He sat up, restless all of a sudden. "I had my doubts, but Sophie…er…my ex…actually stepped up. She says she wants to be more involved." He shrugged obliquely. "We'll see."

"How does Lilah feel about it?"

He flicked a rock over the rim of the hill, then took hold of Charlie's collar so he wouldn't go after it. "She wants to believe her."

What kind of woman would walk away from a man like this? Her own daughter too. Cassie couldn't imagine. She leaned over and kissed him on the lips, and his eyes opened up for a second. Then he closed them, and she banished the voice in her head that was nudging her to come clean.

There was still time for that.

Chapter Fifteen

Glenn was a decent cook. Not a good cook, he wouldn't go that far. Decent. He got the job done. It had been him and Lilah for so long, and her a picky eater, that his repertoire was limited. Endless peanut butter and honey sandwiches. Chicken or burgers for dinner. Sometimes he snuck in a green vegetable. Nothing fancy.

But tonight he'd stepped it up. Tonight Cassie was coming for dinner.

He wanted it to be low key—no noisy restaurant—just the two of them in his kitchen with a bottle of wine. Maybe two. Lilah was at a friend's and Andrew was home with Cassie's dad, and he had a roast in the oven and...holy Jesus.

Cassie smiled up at him as he opened the door, looking like a million bucks in jeans and a clingy black top.

"Um, you look incredible," he managed. The last time he'd seen her she'd been in sneakers and leggings. Not that she didn't look good then, but this top was...well...it hugged her in all the right places. He stood there stupidly for a second, with Charlie milling around, until Cassie asked if she could come in.

"Yes!" He threw open the door. God, he was acting like an idiot. "Please, come in." Then, before he could overthink it, he dropped a kiss on her mouth. Were they at that stage now? Apparently they were because her face lit, and she said, "It's nice to see you."

"You too," he said with a hum of happiness. He'd been nervous about this evening. Actually having a woman over to dinner. Laying it all out there. This was who he was, where he lived. The house wasn't grand but it was his.

He'd built the deck himself, painted every wall. And he was raising his daughter here.

Of course Lilah hadn't picked up her things the way he'd asked. He frowned as he led Cassie past the family room, where Lilah's stuff was strewn all over. Sneakers, a sweatshirt. Hair clips and other crap littering the couch. And in the middle of the hallway, Charlie's orange ball, which Glenn toed out of the way so they wouldn't kill themselves. "Sorry, this is as good as it gets," he said.

Cassie seemed unfazed. "Are you kidding, this is nothing. I'm still finding stuff from thirty years ago at my dad's house. I have to sneak it out to the trash when he's not looking." She paused to admire a picture Lilah had done. A framed chalk drawing of a man in what looked like a space suit surrounded by bees. The beekeeper in orange, the bees glowing like tiny red stop lights.

"Is that you?" she said. The beekeeper was impossibly tall, dwarfing the hive, even the trees.

"I think it is. I guess I used to loom large to her."

She gave him a smile he couldn't quite decipher. "I'm sure you still do."

He opened the wine and she found a couple of glasses and he remembered again how easy she was to be with. If someone had told him a month ago he'd be seeing a lawyer from New York, he would have said they were crazy. He'd have pictured some hyper-caffeinated woman, charging across town in head-to-toe black. In spite of everything going on in her life, Cassie wasn't frenzied like that. Sure, she worried about Alzheimer's and her dad and Andrew—who wouldn't? But she had a contagious laugh and just being in her presence made him feel lighter, like he might not need to sweat all the little things. And he liked the look of her in his kitchen. Yes, he did. Leaning against the counter like she belonged there.

Over a glass of wine, she told him about the pinching incident. "Right up her skirt," she said.

He winced. "Do you think he knew what he was doing?"

"Oh, he knew."

"So what now?"

She gave a resigned shrug. "Now that he's on the FBI Most Wanted List I doubt we'll be able to find someone else."

"At least Andrew's there."

"For now. Honestly, I don't know how much longer we're going to be able to keep my dad at home. He thinks he's more capable than he is, that's the hard part. The other day I found him trying to split wood. With an *axe*."

"Oh Jesus."

"You're telling me." They'd pulled out a couple of stools and were sitting at the counter with their wine. "He always had to be in control. I couldn't stand it growing up. If I turned up a song on the radio, he'd harangue me that the song was terrible. So the next time, I'd turn it up even louder just to irritate him. I'm sure he thought I was being difficult, and maybe I was. Or maybe I was angry over my mom and had no one else to take it out on." She let go a sigh. "I don't even remember half of what we fought about anymore. It doesn't matter."

The timer went off, which seemed to reset her. "Anyway, enough of that depressing stuff. What can I do to help?"

"Dinner should be almost ready." He opened the oven and stuck a meat thermometer in the roast, but it was nowhere near done. He tested the meat with a fork. "I haven't made this in a while, I thought it would be ready by now." Then a troublesome thought. "You do eat meat, don't you?"

"Um...sometimes." She'd found a slotted spoon and was busying herself turning the skillet potatoes.

He shot her a worried look. "Uh oh, that didn't sound convincing." Why hadn't he asked her? Not everyone ate red meat. He was so used to doing his own thing, he'd forgotten to find out what she liked to eat. He should have just made something simple like pasta. She'd eaten pasta at the restaurant. Why hadn't he just done that?

"No really, it's fine. I don't usually eat meat, but this looks delicious and—"

"You don't eat meat, do you?"

"No." She looked like she'd been caught cheating on a math test. "I'm sorry. I haven't in years but the potatoes look great and I see you have green beans. I'll be fine with that. I should have said something."

"I should have asked," he said glumly. He'd bungled this. Cooking a roast for someone who didn't eat meat. He felt like a complete jerk.

"Let me see what else I have." He rummaged through the pantry, but the pickings were slim. All he could find with any potential was a package of spaghetti and a can of crushed tomatoes. "I could make sauce or we could order takeout." Takeout was starting to sound like the better option.

"No, don't order takeout. Why don't you eat the roast and I'll have veggies? I do it all the time."

"Lilah and I can have the roast tomorrow." The idea of tucking into a hunk of meat while Cassie nibbled on vegetables felt indecent, like unwrapping a Christmas present in front of a kid who didn't get one. No way was he going to do that.

"Then spaghetti sounds great. We can throw in the green beans and if you have lettuce, I'll make a salad."

"I have lettuce," he said, relieved. "Cucumber and tomato too."

"Excellent. If you tell me where everything is, I'll set the table."

He sautéed garlic for the sauce while she found plates and silverware. "Napkins?" she said.

"Just paper towels." He nodded to the counter. "Over there."

The garlic was sending up a fine pungent aroma, and he turned down the flame and threw in a little chopped onion. She was a good sport and he was starting to feel better, like maybe the evening wouldn't be a total disaster after all. Now might be the time to toss in the green beans—or should he wait until he got the sauce simmering. He was thinking hard about that, and should he chop up some of that fresh tomato, when he realized she'd gone quiet.

"They've started clearing that property." She glanced up from the newspaper, which he'd left on the counter. "It must have just happened. I haven't been by there in a few days."

"Yup." He felt a sharp surge of anger thinking of the earthmovers and how much they'd already destroyed. He couldn't even look when he drove that way.

"What about the hives you keep there?"

"I brought them here for now." He'd heard persistent rumors around town that Weber was after her father's property too, which gave him a tight unhappy feeling. He knew she was under pressure but she wouldn't do that. Would she?

The juice from the tomatoes had pooled on the edge of the cutting board and spilled onto the counter, making a runny mess. He mopped it up with a dishtowel. Talking about the development had taken the shine off his mood.

Cassie seemed to sense it. She set the newspaper back on the counter and touched his shoulder. "Hey, I'd love to see your hives."

"You would?"

"I can't imagine what three hundred beehives look like."

"Like your dad's, but a few more." Her touch smoothed him out, and after he got the sauce simmering they took their wine out to the deck. The hives looked like pale barracks in the May dusk.

"Do I need a veil?" Cassie said.

"We should be fine. They won't be too active now that it's getting dark."

They crossed the yard, the grass kept long to encourage the dandelions and white clover the bees loved. Other people might call them weeds, but he considered them forage. No one would ever accuse him of having an overly manicured lawn.

"So how many bees are in all these hives?" Cassie said.

"Anywhere from ten to fifty thousand per hive, depending on the season."

"Good God, that's a lot of bees!" She glanced around apprehensively. "Don't you worry about them getting up near the house?"

"Their flight path doesn't take them that way. They tend to head up and out. The hives are in a good spot, morning sun and afternoon shade. That's pretty much ideal. And down there—" He tipped his chin toward the marsh. "That's wetland. Depending on the time of year there's usually water there. I didn't know I was going to get into bees when I bought the place but I liked that the wetland can never be developed, even after my time. It'll always be protected."

"Your own little oasis. I can see why you never wanted to sell."

He pointed to a cluster of hives set apart from the others. "The ones on the end there, those are my grandfather's. I've had to replace the frames, of course, but the boxes are his. I've painted them a few times over the years." Besides Lilah, he'd never pointed this out to anyone, certainly not Sophie. He wasn't sure why he was telling Cassie, but she seemed genuinely interested.

A few late foragers heading home ducked into the tiny entrances at the bottom of the hives. "Are all these bees descended from your grandfather's?" she said.

"Some of them. Bees only live about a month, a little longer in the winter, so it's a lot of generations, but some are from his stock. I wish he'd known I became a beekeeper. He would've liked that."

"You really love them, don't you?"

"I do. There's nowhere I'd rather be than out here." He gently brushed off a bee that had become too inquisitive and was crawling up his arm. "It's peaceful. I never get tired of watching them. And if you think about what they do in the world...it's humbling. People don't realize we wouldn't eat without pollinators." He stopped, fearing he might be on the verge of a lecture, but she just looked thoughtful.

They made their way back to the deck and watched the sky deepen until the trees turned violet and finally black, and the light slipped away entirely. When the sauce was ready he found some utility candles in the closet and set them on small plates. Not five-star, but the candlelight was a nice touch.

"You grew up here," he said, curious. "How did you end up being such a city person?"

She was quiet for a moment. "It's not that I set out to be a city person, it sort of turned out that way. Don't get me wrong, I do like it here and the hike last weekend was gorgeous. And I have to say when I was in the city last week, it felt loud and chaotic."

"But? It sounds like there's a *but* coming."

"No *buts*. I love the energy of the city. I won't deny that. Growing up here was pretty dull and with my mom sick and all..." Her voice trailed off. "I guess it became easier to stay away."

"And now you're back when you don't want to be." He felt a tug of disappointment. As soon as she got her dad taken care of, she'd be on the first train back to Manhattan.

"I haven't come back enough over the years. I'm not a good daughter." She held up a hand when he started to protest "It's true. I'm not proud of it. My dad needs me. I should have seen that sooner."

"You're here now. That's what counts."

She shook her head. "I don't know."

"Don't sell yourself short; you've put your own life on hold to help him. That's pretty selfless." He poured them more wine, and they talked about other things. She told him she'd given up red meat for heart and brain health, which were interconnected.

He sipped his wine, amused. "I don't have a chance on either count then."

"Tofu's an easy substitute. You can throw on a little soy sauce and bake it in the oven. It has a lot of protein and believe it or not, it tastes pretty good as long as you season it."

He pulled a face. "I can't imagine a universe where Lilah would eat tofu."

"Don't blame it on Lilah. You wouldn't either."

He grinned. "You're right."

"I'm a bit of a nut about all this stuff, I admit that. But you—" She looked at him frankly. "You're in great shape. Is all that from lifting hives?"

"All what?" He felt himself getting warm. Something about the way she was looking at him. "I um...I like to hike. That and working the bees. That's pretty much it, I guess." He got up to get them seconds so she wouldn't see him squirm. She was way more up front than any woman he'd ever known. But in a good way.

"You mean you don't do anything else, like go to a gym? I find that hard to believe."

"I put in a swing set for Lilah, if that counts." He laughed. "But that was years ago."

"Too bad they outgrow that stuff," she said. "They're five and then they're twenty." She regarded him over her wine, her eyes flickering gold in the candlelight. "What happened with your marriage? Do you mind if I ask?

His shoulders tightened reflexively. Talking about his marriage felt like poking at a scab with a fork. Healed over but still unpleasant. "What do you want to know?"

"Were you having problems for a while? Did you have any idea she was going to leave?"

He forced himself to unbunch his shoulders. She'd asked a fair question. "I should have known, but I guess I didn't want to see it. We met in college and I was head over heels. Never really dated anyone else. And the way she was...basically self-absorbed...I didn't know it could be any other way."

She twirled her wine thoughtfully. "You don't have any point of reference when you're that young. Phil and I met in law school; we were kids too."

Surprisingly, now that he'd gotten started, it was easier to talk about this than he'd expected. "She never told me what she was thinking. In all the years we were together, I don't think we ever had a conversation like this. I knew she cared about her art, but I didn't understand what she wanted from life."

"Maybe she didn't completely understand either."

He shrugged. "Maybe. But she never told me she was unhappy. That was dishonest. I only found out later that she'd planned for months to go to Colorado. We had a kid for Christ's sake. We probably couldn't have fixed it but shutting me out—that was indefensible. It took me a long time to forgive her for that. I can handle pretty much anything except dishonesty."

Cassie was still for a moment. "Have you?" she said finally. "Forgiven her?"

He drained the last of his wine. "Like I said, it's been a long time. All I care about now is making sure Lilah's okay."

To his surprise she laced her hand through his.

"I uh...don't usually talk about all that stuff," he said.

"I'm glad you did." She stroked his thumb with her own, which sent a charge straight through him.

"I never expected this," she said.

"This?" he repeated dumbly. The conversation had apparently taken a turn, but all he could think about was the way she was touching him.

"What's happening with us."

If she'd kept his hand another second, he would have abandoned his pledge to take things slow and carted her off to bed. God knew he wanted to. But he was still trying to wrap his head around what she'd said, and anyway, what exactly *was* happening between them? Sophie had trained him to be wary, but now he'd met a woman who made it plain how she felt.

After a moment she smiled self-consciously and disengaged her hand. "I admire that you love what you do. I mean that. Not everyone is lucky enough to wake up every day passionate about their work. I guess I'm a little jealous of that."

"You are? I thought you liked your work."

"I do. It's interesting and useful and I'm good at it." She gazed out the window, where small white moths were beating against the flood light. "But I don't know if I'm passionate about it. I'm not sure I even know what that means."

"Maybe you're not doing what you should be doing," he said cautiously. "What do you care about, I mean besides your family, obviously?"

She rested her chin on her hand, as though her head had become heavy. "That's the thing, I don't know. What is there besides work and family and hopefully you make enough to be comfortable and find some happiness along the way. But sometimes it doesn't feel like enough." She gave him a wry smile. "You make me feel like a slacker."

"What?" He was so stunned for a moment he couldn't even respond. "You're a smart, successful woman. How can you even say that?"

She raised a shoulder. "What have I accomplished?"

"You're just down because life is tough right now. Everyone gets that way."

"No seriously. What have I accomplished?"

"What have you accomplished?" He looked around, like the answer might be right there in the kitchen. "You're a lawyer, which in itself is an accomplishment, you have a great son, and okay he's going through a rough patch, but what kids don't? And you're caring for your dad, which is unbelievably hard and..." He trailed off because of the way she was smiling at him. "What?"

"Keep going," she said, eyes twinkling. "I like this."

He tossed a balled-up napkin at her. "Oh, so this was a ruse to get me to tell you how wonderful you are?"

She laughed. "No, no, definitely not. Just me wringing my hands about what I want to do when I grow up."

They left the dishes on the table and went into the family room, where he tossed Lilah's stuff off the couch and put on some music. Cassie was beautiful and straightforward and incredibly, she wanted him. But what if they somehow found a way to be together? If his passion made her uncomfortable, would he dial it back to please her? Would his love for what he did and where he lived become a source of resentment if she never found her footing?

He didn't know and couldn't think because he was stroking her skin under that clingy top, and Cassie was arching her back in a very sexy way. She felt incredibly soft, and he was about to suggest she lose the top when Charlie jumped up, barking officiously.

Glenn groaned. "Lilah must be home." Was it ten already, why hadn't he let her spend the night at her friend's? She was always clamoring to spend the night.

He brushed a last kiss on Cassie's neck before sliding over a respectable distance.

"In here," he called as the door slammed. "Come on in and say hello."

Chapter Sixteen

Andrew was stalled. In a funk, as Phil put it. He'd grudgingly agreed to be in the wedding and had taken incompletes on his finals, but as far as Cassie could tell he'd made no plans for the summer. And he hadn't said whether he intended to go back to school in the fall.

Dr. Milburn had recommended a therapist, but despite Cassie's nudging, Andrew hadn't made an appointment. This morning she'd dragged him along to the grocery store, hoping they could talk, but he was loitering near the shopping cart in a fog of boredom. "How about pasta primavera?" she suggested, selecting a couple of zucchinis.

He shrugged. "Whatever."

"Or I can make you and Grandpa a steak with pasta on the side. Or veggies if you don't want pasta." She couldn't help thinking of poor Glenn, who'd turned himself inside out about that roast. She'd almost broken down and eaten it so he wouldn't feel bad. She was surprised he was such a meat eater. Besides being unhealthy, it wasn't very green. She hadn't pointed that out though, he'd been upset enough already. She smiled to herself. But they'd gotten past it.

She chose a package of snap peas and a bunch of asparagus, which were a reasonable three ninety-nine a pound. Ciccarelli's, Laurelton's upscale family-owned grocery, had a nice selection of organics and a lovely cheese counter, where they would slice you a taste. So much easier than shopping in the city, where the aisles were narrow and congested and you had to lug your groceries home or pay to have them delivered. She did miss some things about the city, but grocery shopping wasn't one of them.

"Why don't you push," she said to Andrew, who was lagging behind. She'd hoped a change of scenery might do him good, but going out in public seemed to require more effort than he could muster. "You need to make an appointment with that therapist. You've been home almost a month, and you've hardly left the house."

"I'm out of the house right now."

"You know what I mean. You need to talk to someone—a professional. Grandpa and I don't count. I mean we do, but I'm worried about you."

"I'm fine," he muttered. But he didn't look fine. He had the exhausted look of someone who hadn't slept in weeks even though that was all he'd been doing.

She tossed in a box of Grape-Nuts, the only cereal her dad would eat. "Promise me you'll call when we get home."

"Today?"

"Yes today. Maybe you can get an appointment for later this week."

"Can we get Fig Newtons?" he said as they rounded the cookie aisle.

"Sure." At least he was showing an interest in something. As a little boy, Andrew had loved Fig Newtons, declared them his favorite before he realized there were better cookies like Oreos. "I haven't bought Fig Newtons in ages. I used to crave them when I was pregnant with you."

"You did? Is that why I liked them?"

She smiled. "I don't think it works that way. You probably liked them because that's all you knew. Whole wheat or regular?"

"I don't know." He gazed at the acres of cookies in a haze of indecision.

She waited for him to make up his mind. "Sweetie?" An anxious thrumming had started in her stomach. Andrew had never been indecisive about cookies. "Just get something, whatever you want."

"Forget it. I don't want any."

"I wish you'd talk to me," she said miserably.

He turned on her so fiercely she stepped back. "You'll hate me," he said.

"Oh Andrew." Tears welled in her eyes. "I could never hate you. I love you. You know that. Whatever happened wasn't your fault."

"It *was* my fault."

"The review board suspended all of you."

"The review board didn't know everything."

A slow dread rose in her chest. What on earth could he have done? She knew her son better than anyone, had been smitten with him from the moment he was born. She knew his caution about trying new things, his moodiness when he was hungry, the smile that stopped her because it was so much her own. Even now, she could still spot the germ of her sweet gentle boy.

But what did you really know once your child went into the world and left you behind? Only what they wanted you to see. Had she been so wrapped up with her own problems she didn't notice signs of trouble, or had he quietly, subversively gone astray?

"I have most of what we need," she said. "Let's get out of here."

Checkout was excruciatingly slow—the elderly woman ahead of them had an expired coupon, and the checker had to call for assistance. Then the woman counted out her bill in cash. Cassie's stomach knotted, trying to imagine what Andrew had done or thought he'd done. She'd suspected all along that he hadn't told her everything, but such a horrible accident couldn't be his fault.

Still. The weight of his silence bore down on her.

Outside, the day had become warm and sticky, more like August than May, and the asphalt radiated a metallic heat. Another shopper clattered by with a loaded cart.

"Let's go somewhere quiet," Cassie said.

She headed toward home, pulling over alongside the Kingsley property, the part that was still unscathed.

"What are you doing?" Andrew said.

She opened the door. "How about a walk?"

Andrew reluctantly hauled himself out of the car, and they stepped into the woods. It felt immediately cooler, the trees already impenetrable with the lush green of summer.

They walked in silence on the soft ground for a couple of minutes and she waited for him to speak, her heart beating in her throat.

"We wanted to get Jack trashed," Andrew said finally. "He's such a lightweight. We thought it would be funny to see him totally smashed. Like, a couple of beers and he's gone. The guys made this wicked strong punch. You know, like a Long Island iced tea thing."

She nodded, a sick feeling in her gut.

He brushed away the tip of a branch that was in their way. "So when he wasn't looking I poured more Jack Daniels into his cup...you know, Jack Daniels 'cause his name is Jack...anyway, he was getting tanked and stumbling around and Troy said we shouldn't give him anymore, but me and Brandon, we were laughing and..." He glanced at her quickly, then looked away. "Actually, I was the one at that point. Brandon would have chilled. I don't know why I didn't. I poured him more. Oh God, I don't know why. He could barely walk. Everyone else backed off and I didn't."

He took a ragged breath, and she thought he might be done. Prayed he was done because hearing it was unbearable. That her son had done this. Deliberately intoxicated a vulnerable boy. But he went on. "I gave him more and he didn't even notice, that's how lit he was. I was pretty drunk too. We all were." He swiped a hand over his eyes. "Some girls were there and we were being idiots and oh Mom..." He was sobbing now, and no matter what he'd done it tore a hole in her heart to see him cry.

"And then he fell, I don't know how. He was standing there, then everyone was screaming. Guys tried to get him up, and his head didn't look bloody or anything. They were telling him he was okay, but he wasn't moving." He looked at her, his face ravaged. "He wasn't okay. He'll never be okay."

He cried in her arms as a jay clamored overhead. She held him fiercely, as if she could draw him back into her and birth an unblemished child who hadn't yet stumbled and caused pain. Because that's what life was, a series of stumbles. Some minor and some catastrophic. Some you got over and some you never did. She held him with every ounce of strength because he was her son, and the thought of that other mother and son was too terrible to bear.

She kissed his wet cheek. "I love you."

He pulled back. "Am I a terrible person?"

She sighed deeply. "You'd be a terrible person if you didn't have a conscience. But you do have a conscience, Andrew. And I don't think it's going to let you alone."

"I'm sorry," he whispered. "I'm so sorry."

She took his face in her hands. His beautiful face. Pale and swollen from crying. He was hurting, but another boy was hurting more. Another boy was damaged and might never be whole.

"Don't apologize to me," she said. "I'm not the one who needs to hear it."

•   •   •

Cassie's dad had put on his bee suit right after lunch even though Glenn wasn't supposed to be there until two. Now he was peering out the window.

"He's not coming for another hour," Cassie said. "At least take off the veil."

He reluctantly removed the veil but refused to get out of the suit. He'd gotten all bolloxed up while she was on a call and came tramping upstairs to look for her. She'd had to excuse herself to zip him up, then help him downstairs so he wouldn't trip.

"Where's Andrew?" she said with a tug of anxiety. Come to think of it, she hadn't seen Andrew all morning. His confession was eating her up, and she'd almost told Phil, but it wasn't her place to tell him. Andrew had to do that.

Her father glanced around. "I haven't seen him."

She got her dad out to the porch, which was in shade. He could wait for Glenn there. Better than pacing in front of the window. Upstairs, Andrew's door was closed. She knocked, but he didn't answer. She left him alone for now. She would check on him later.

When Glenn's truck rolled up the driveway an hour later, her heart lifted. Even with everything going on, the sight of him eased her. Even his truck had a calming effect. *Marsden Apiaries*. That word *apiary*, such a light soothing sound. She clicked out of her computer and ran a brush through her hair. Should she put on lipstick? That might be trying too hard. They were teetering, that's what they were doing. Teetering on the verge of a relationship. She didn't remember ever feeling an attraction like this. Not for Phil, not like this. It was more than physical, although that was certainly part of it. Glenn was caring and smart and not self-absorbed. And he had a compassion about him. Maybe because of the way his wife had treated him. Not a master of the universe, just a decent, thoughtful guy.

She went ahead and put on a little lip gloss but despite her pleasure at seeing him, she couldn't lose that nagging unease. She hadn't been honest with him about Weber. She hadn't lied, but she hadn't been honest. What was the difference, really? The truth was, she had a vested interest in the Weber development. They wanted her dad's property, and she wanted to sell. Twenty-five acres in all if they could get it. It made her a little sick that she was abetting a project like that. Tearing down woods for a bunch of oversized, expensive homes. A preserve would be lovely, but that wasn't the real world. The real world was what you had to do.

On the porch Glenn was explaining something to her dad, who was listening attentively.

"I was just telling him that if the powdered sugar didn't slow things down, we can try drone comb. I brought some trap frames just in case."

She nodded like she knew what he was talking about. Sometimes he slipped into bee speak without realizing it. But her dad seemed to have an idea because he was already making his way down the steps to the truck. Glenn opened the passenger door and steadied him unobtrusively as he climbed in.

But where was her father's car? It wasn't in its customary spot on the driveway. She'd returned the rental after the first week and was using her dad's old Lexus to get around. Thankfully, he didn't drive much these days. She'd been doing the grocery shopping, and Andrew had taken it once or twice to run errands. She glanced up at the house to see if she could catch a glimpse of him in Shelly's room, but the shade was drawn. Where *was* Andrew? She texted him but got no response.

Glenn had her dad out of the truck by the time she walked down the driveway and across the field, the grass tickling her ankles. Her dad watched intently as Glenn checked the sticky mat for mites.

"You still have a problem." Glenn tipped the mat so she could see. "See those red dots?"

She squinted over his shoulder. Along with bits of dirt and other debris, she saw a smattering of red specks along the white board.

"Those are just the ones that fell off," he said. "If there are that many on the board, there's a lot in the hive."

"Same thing over here." Her dad was inspecting the sticky board on the other original hive. "What was that thing you said we should do?" He looked at Glenn, uncertain about what had been proposed.

"Drone comb traps." Glenn produced two green plastic frames from his truck. "Varroa mites prefer drone brood, so if we take out a couple of frames and substitute these, the queen will lay drone."

The plastic frames looked flimsy, not like the sturdy wooden frames already in the hive. "Then what?" said Cassie dubiously.

"The mites crawl inside once the eggs are laid. Then we wait four weeks until the cells are capped, take out the frames and put them in the freezer for a couple of days. It kills the drone brood but gets rid of the mites."

"You have to kill the brood?" Killing bees to get rid of mites seemed extreme.

"I know. It's a little gruesome but effective. The colony doesn't need all that drone anyway. And it might help keep down the mite population."

"Isn't there anything else you can do?"

"If you want to use chemicals," he said disapprovingly, "which I don't. Once you go down that road, you have to keep treating. This is treatment free—you're not introducing toxins into your hives."

Her dad had managed to lift the top off one of the boxes, and a few bees were drifting around. Glenn lit the smoker, puffing it to get it going. Cassie had a sudden queasy fear that her dad might mention Weber's visit. At the moment, the lights were on and he seemed almost like his old self. That was all she needed, for Glenn to learn about Weber from her dad before she had a chance to explain. If she wanted any kind of relationship with Glenn, she needed to come clean and she needed to do it soon. He might understand if she explained. How the offer was too good to pass up and the Kingsley property would be developed anyway, with or without her dad's five acres.

He might understand or he might not.

She was stewing over this, trying to figure out how she could find a few minutes alone with him when the Lexus lurched up the driveway with a terrible scraping sound.

"Is that my car?" her dad said.

The Lexus, with Andrew in it, limped to a stop. "I don't know what happened," he called. "It just started making this sound."

Cassie jogged over and peered in the driver's side window. The check engine light was lit up ominously.

Her father began moving in their direction too. "Dad," she called, "why don't you stay there and help Glenn with the bees. Andrew and I can deal with the car." Her dad looked ready to object, but she hopped into the passenger seat and they crept up the driveway with that awful scraping noise.

"Where were you?" Cassie said.

"I just went over to CVS to get some Mylanta for Grandpa."

She glanced over at him. "Have you talked to Dad?"

He shook his head. "Not yet."

She wanted to ask if he'd made an appointment with the therapist, but the car was screeching and she could barely hear herself think.

She angled a look at the odometer, which had a hundred and seventy thousand miles. "Who knows the last time Grandpa had this serviced." She opened the glove box. "Let's see if he has any records in here. Don't turn it off," she cautioned. "We might not get it started again."

The glove box contained only the manual, a tire gauge and a small purple flashlight that probably hadn't worked in years. "What about his desk?" Andrew said. "I saw some files there when he asked me to look for a letter opener."

"Where on his desk?" Her father's desk used to be immaculate but now was a hazard, littered with random piles of paper. She needed to take over the bills, but that was going to require some delicacy.

"I'll go see." Andrew jumped out of the car, relieved to have a job to do.

She slid into the driver's seat for a look, bumping the wiper arm by mistake. They swished on briskly, chafing against the dry windshield. That was annoying. She went to turn them off, but they kept on going. She moved the lever in the other direction. Okay. How ridiculous was this. She knew how to turn off windshield wipers. She tried the other arm just in case, but that was the turn signal. She switched that off, but the wipers were still going full speed. She felt a sudden surge of anxiety. How could she not know how to turn off windshield wipers?

A terrible thought overtook her.

This was how it had been with her mom. Simple tasks that she was suddenly unable to do. Putting on lipstick, even making the bed. Her mom used to get confused about how to pull up the comforter and put the pillows in place. Which step came first. In a sweat, Cassie ran through her coworker's names: Leslie Gaines. Malcolm Boskovitch. Fritz Irwin. Judith…what was Judith's last name? But Judith was in another department, and Cassie didn't see her that much. Oh God. She should know Judith's last name. She'd been there for years.

She dropped her head on the steering wheel, startling when the horn sounded. This was it. Her memory was starting to fail. What she'd dreaded since she was sixteen. The precipitous decline—already she couldn't remember her coworker's name! And now, something as simple as windshield wipers. In a sweat, she tried the lever again, then in a panic scanned the dash. Okay, maybe not a lever after all. Maybe a knob. Her heart pounded as she pressed every button she could think of. No. That was the hazards. That was the radio! That wasn't it. It was probably right in front of her. Anyone else would see it in a second.

She scrambled out of the car but couldn't escape the obvious. She was forty-nine, the same age as her mother when it began. She might have one more good year, but everything would become harder. Soon she wouldn't be able to hide it at work. Straightforward matters would become byzantine. Even everyday tasks around the house would become difficult. Making coffee, measuring laundry detergent. Where did you put it? How much were you supposed to use? And *Andrew.* She teared up just thinking about how much she would miss, the years of his life she wouldn't get to see. Graduating from college, getting married. If she was still alive, she would be oblivious.

And Glenn. Just when she'd found a man who rocked her world.

"You okay, what's the matter?" Glenn said, slightly out of breath from hoofing it up the driveway. "I heard the horn and saw you jump out."

"The wipers," she sobbed. "I can't remember how to turn them off."

He ducked into the car and fiddled with the lever. "They're not working. Could be a switch but the whole electrical system has probably gone fluky. I wondered if it might be something electrical when I heard that noise." He gave them another try for good measure. "What year is this thing anyway?"

She sniffed. "You mean you can't turn them off either?"

He moved the arm up and down. "Nope. Not working." He shut off the engine and the wipers froze midstream.

She let out a shaky breath. It felt like someone had been sitting on her chest and now they weren't. "So it's not me?"

He slid out of the car and wrapped her in a hug. "No. It's not you." He held her tight, and she didn't care that Andrew had come out of the house and was gaping at them. She didn't even care that a man had had to rescue her. Right now, she needed Glenn. Period.

"Um...Mom?" Andrew was holding a manila folder. "I found the Lexus file."

She wiped her eyes. "Ok, that's good."

Glenn started to step back, but she kept a hand on his arm. He was warm and solid and just touching him made her feel better. "Andrew, you know Glenn."

Andrew nodded. He looked like he'd bitten into a candy with an unexpected filling and wasn't sure whether to swallow or spit it out. "We met that day with the powdered sugar."

"That's right," she said. "The powdered sugar."

"I'll uh go see how Grandpa's doing." Andrew set the file on the hood of the car and took off down the driveway.

Cassie couldn't help smiling. "He doesn't know what to do with this." She gestured to the two of them. Her heart rate was beginning to return to normal, but the Alzheimer's scare was real and terrifying. And just because it hadn't happened today, didn't mean it wouldn't.

She swallowed. In two weeks she would know for sure.

Glenn gave her shoulder a squeeze. "You okay?"

"Not really. What if I do have Alzheimer's?"

"Don't look for trouble. This had nothing to do with you. Anyway, you have a more pressing problem."

She glanced up in alarm. "I do?"

"Andrew and your dad are alone with the bees."

Chapter Seventeen

Taking the hives on the road was a royal pain. Sealing them up so the bees could breathe but not escape, muscling them onto the truck, securing them so they wouldn't go sailing off when he hit a bump. You had to do it right or you could piss off a lot of bees. So Glenn was glad Lilah was coming along to help. He hadn't even asked, and here she was wheeling the dolly out of the shed.

"You want it in the truck?" She already had her bee jacket on; he hadn't had to remind her about that either.

"Yup. No reason to wheel them across the yard." He took the dolly from her and hefted it into the truck bed. The dolly wasn't regulation bee equipment, just a cart like UPS guys used, but Lilah had painted it bright blue and christened it Dolly. Some beekeepers put clamps on the sides to hold the boxes in place, but he'd found if he kept the angle right they didn't slide off.

"You have your veil too?" He'd already backed up to the shed, then they'd drive over to the hives and lever them up from there.

"Already in the truck!"

"Okay." He gave her a thoughtful look. "You know we won't be back until late, right?"

"That's okay. How many hives are you bringing?"

"Twenty should be enough. He only has ten acres in flower right now."

"Is this the apple guy?"

"Peaches."

"Where?"

"Easton, not far from the apple guy."

Lilah was a good lieutenant when she was in the mood. Last year, the apple farmer had been taken with her, impressed that a girl so young had her own bee suit and knew a thing or two. Glenn had been quietly proud, and they'd stopped on the way home at their favorite ice cream shop, a little shack in Ridgefield, which was out of the way but had the best soft-serve around.

"Remember that time his wife gave us fritters?" Lilah reminisced.

Glenn grinned. "I remember. You scarfed down a whole one and had diarrhea on the way home."

"I did not!"

"Oh, yes you did. I know exactly where we stopped, that Shell station on 57."

"Oh my God..." She collapsed with laughter. "How could I forget something like that?"

He tousled her hair on his way back to the shed. "Because you were six."

"But how come I remember the fritter?"

He gave her an amused look. "Who wants to remember diarrhea?"

"Not me! That's for sure."

Whatever the reason, Lilah was in a fine mood. A good thing too since Cassie was coming and she knew absolutely nothing about moving bees. He'd been half kidding when he invited her along, but she was game. He wanted her to see what his life looked like. All of it, not just hiking or dinner, but what he really did. The gritty work of dragging bees around to pollinate. Nothing glamorous about that. Not that she was under the impression he lived a glamorous life but if anything was to develop between them—and he very much wanted it to—she needed to look under the hood, so to speak.

And yeah okay—he was hoping Lilah and Cassie would hit it off. They'd only met briefly a couple of times. Maybe they'd stop for ice cream on the way back.

"Rope's on the peg behind the extra frames," he said, nodding to the shelves at the rear of the shed.

"Got it." She brought out a length of rope that he'd wound neatly, then looped through itself.

His bee shed was orderly, the way he liked it. You could never be too organized when it came to bees. And you needed to have all your supplies at hand. Once things got away from you, they spun out of control fast. When he was first starting out, he made the mistake of extracting honey in the yard instead of inside the shed. Within minutes, every insect within five miles had shown up for a free meal. Wasps were the worst—just plain nasty—and they could sting repeatedly. He never made that mistake again.

He motioned for Lilah to take the other end of the ramp, and they hiked it over to the truck. Now he just had to staple lightweight hardware cloth over the entrances and get the hives on board. It was nearly dusk, and most of the bees should be back from foraging by now. You didn't want to take off too early and leave stragglers with nowhere to go.

"So what's the story with you and Cassie?" Lilah said.

"What?" He nearly dropped his end of the ramp. Oh geez, now she was going to ask him a bunch of questions. "I um...we uh, well I like her."

She arched an eyebrow. Where did girls *learn* that? "Duh, that's obvious."

"It is?" Was he being obvious? Did Cassie think so?

Lilah grinned. "So what's the story?"

He got a better grip on the ramp and they hoisted it into the truck, which bought him a minute. "We've gone out a few times. That's it." He felt his face getting warm. This was way embarrassing, his daughter interrogating him about his girlfriend. *Wait. Was Cassie his girlfriend?* He hadn't thought of her that way until now, when the word suddenly popped into his head. When did someone become a girlfriend, was there a requisite number of dates? He wasn't even sure she'd be around much longer.

"I like her," Lilah said. "I mean I don't know her that well, but she seems nice." She stopped to rub Charlie behind the ears. "And she liked Charlie."

Glenn chuckled. "Everyone likes Charlie." He opened the back door for the dog to hop in. He would put him in the house before they left but let him believe he was going somewhere for now. "Want to get in?" he said to Lilah.

She climbed into the passenger seat, and he started it up.

"So it's good you're seeing someone," she said.

He had his foot on the brake, about to back up, but he turned to look at her. "What do you mean?"

"I just mean, it's nice, you know." She seemed flustered all of a sudden. "You won't be lonely."

He gestured to all the crap in the back of the truck. "Do I look like I have time to be lonely? What are you now, worrier-in-chief? That's my job."

"I just—" She buckled her seat belt, then threw it off. She looked overheated.

He glanced at her, concerned. "What's the matter, you okay?"

She squirmed for a second, then blurted it out. "Mom asked me to spend the summer in Colorado."

He put the truck in park. "The whole summer?" he said faintly.

She looked at him anxiously. "Right after school gets out."

His chest felt uncomfortably tight. "The whole summer's a long time. Why don't you go for a week or two?" Sophie was notoriously unreliable and had no concept about parenting. How could he hand Lilah off to her for the whole summer? He wouldn't see her from the time school got out until it started in the fall. He felt bereft just thinking about it.

She twisted the zipper on her jacket. "I was worried you might be lonely but now you won't be, right?"

"What does this have to do with me being lonely?" His irritation sparked. All this helpfulness had just been positioning for Colorado. No doubt cooked up by Sophie.

"Because of Cassie. You're seeing Cassie now."

He took a breath. "Look, I'm glad you're concerned about me, but let's slow down. You spent four days with your mom, and now you want to go for the whole summer? I don't think this is such a good idea."

"Why not? You said you were happy I went to Vermont. You told me that. What's the difference if I go to Colorado?"

"The difference is that this is the whole summer, and Colorado is halfway across the country." And fucking Sophie hadn't even bothered to consult him. That galled him more than anything. Putting a twelve-year-old up to it.

"It's only two hours earlier. I can talk to you all the time."

The tightness in his chest had traveled up into his shoulders and neck and created a hard knot. "It's not the time difference. I didn't even know about this until this minute."

Her voice faltered. "Mom said she was going to call you."

"Well, she didn't. Your mom has a lot of big plans, but half the time she doesn't even call *you* back."

Her face fell and he immediately regretted it. *Shit.* He'd broken his rule about not badmouthing Sophie. But she'd gone behind his back—not even the courtesy of a phone call!—and dangled this tantalizing plum of a summer in Colorado without consulting him.

He plowed on perversely. "What are you going to do when you get there, and she's too busy to spend time with you? Have you thought about that?"

Lilah blinked back tears. "You just don't want me to be with her because you hate her. You've always hated her! You *want* me to be disappointed, don't you?"

"Why would I want you to be disappointed?" His gut churned unhappily. Now he was fighting with his daughter, the last thing he wanted to do. How had he made such a mess of this? "Listen—" He reached for her, but she jerked away. "I'm sorry. It came out wrong what I said about your mom. I don't hate her, I know she's trying. It's just that a weekend in Vermont is a lot different than the whole summer."

"You didn't even want me to go to Vermont! You acted all fake happy that I had a good time."

"*What?* That's not true. I was *not* fake happy. I'm glad you had a good time." But even as he said it his face warmed like she'd caught him out. *Was* he glad she had a good time or had he secretly hoped she'd come back with tales of Sophie's neglect. How she'd traipsed off to her art show and left

Lilah with an ailing grandmother she hardly knew. But apparently that hadn't happened. Sophie had acted more or less like a grownup.

"I don't believe you." Lilah was crying now. "You never want me to see her, you don't want me to be happy. You don't want me to do *anything*."

"Oh peanut. *Of course* I want you to be happy. That's all I ever want." He scrubbed a hand over his face. It flat out killed him when she cried. "Look, I have to get the bees loaded. Can we talk about this later?"

"Don't call me peanut!" She jumped out, slamming the door so hard it shook his two-ton truck. "Have fun with your girlfriend! Let *her* help you." She stormed off across the grass, then spun dramatically. "I'm going to Colorado. It's not up to you!"

He heaved himself out of the truck. "That's about enough, young lady." How did she do this to him? Two seconds ago he'd felt terrible, and now he was on the verge of losing his temper. He didn't want to lose his temper. But this was outrageous. One phone call with Sophie and Lilah was spouting attitude. True, he hadn't helped the situation, but where did his twelve-year-old daughter get off talking to him like this?

"First of all," he said, closing the gap between them, "let me remind you that *you* don't tell *me* what you will or won't do. Last time I checked, I'm the adult here and I make the decisions. I'll decide if you go to Colorado, and right now it isn't looking good."

For a moment she looked like she might cry again, then she drew herself up. God she was channeling Sophie. She even had her hands on her hips, which would have been laughable if he hadn't been so pissed. "You don't get to decide everything! Mom's an adult too in case you haven't noticed."

"We'll talk about it later," he said through gritted teeth. And then, because he couldn't bear for the evening to flame out this way, he mumbled, "I'd still like for you to come."

"No way." She marched off, hair swinging, and clumped up the porch stairs in her work boots—a pair just like his own. He had no doubt she would have slammed the door, but sliders didn't slam in a satisfying way. She left it wide open instead, which she knew drove him crazy.

His whole body deflated like he'd suffered a puncture. How had this happened? He hardly ever fought with Lilah. It made him physically sick.

He climbed into the truck and slumped in the driver's seat. Charlie shoved his head forward, and Glenn stroked the soft fur on his neck while the dog assailed him with his meaty breath.

He sighed and patted the passenger seat. "All right, come on up."

Charlie clambered up front, drooling on the console as he went, astounded at his good fortune. Normally Glenn would have wiped it off. With his sleeve, at least. But he didn't bother.

Dog slobber was the least of his problems.

Chapter Eighteen

Cassie was all set for the field trip. She'd arrived at Glenn's house decked out in a new veil since Glenn had sliced open the old one to get at that rogue bee—she still shuddered to think of it crawling up her father's face—and she was wearing her dad's bee suit, which was way too big and looked ridiculous. But she believed in protection. She'd even duct taped the ankles of her pants. No bees were getting in that way!

But now Glenn was in a crummy mood. Hardly speaking at all. All he'd said was that Lilah had gone to a friend's house and wasn't coming. She could see his tension in the set of his shoulders. The uncompromising line of his mouth.

"What's going on?" Cassie asked once they were underway, the hives strapped down in the truck bed like excess luggage.

"I don't want to get into it."

"Did something happen with her mom?"

He only shrugged irritably.

No one could make you miserable like your own child, that was for sure. Something had clearly blown up with Lilah, and what was supposed to have been a chance for the three of them to spend time together had become a strained, silent trip with Glenn, who'd reverted to the uncommunicative stranger she'd met six weeks ago.

"Whatever it is," she said, "you'll feel better getting it off your chest. It doesn't do any good to let things fester."

He sent her a dour look. "I'm not festering."

"If you say so." It was almost dark now, the traffic on I-95 lurching along in fits and starts. The bee suit chafed over her jeans. "Is your ex coming again? Is that it?" Maybe the woman had taken one look at Glenn and decided she'd made a mistake after all. Why else would she be back so soon?

His jaw tightened. "Will you please let it go."

Okay, so maybe not the ex. But she felt a rising annoyance. She'd ducked out of work early for this, made sure Andrew was home to give his grandfather dinner. And now she couldn't pry a word out of the man's mouth. "You know what," she said, "why don't you take me home. You obviously have a lot on your mind. If you don't want to talk, that's okay, but I don't need to sit here if you're in a foul mood."

He looked taken aback. "We're already in Westport. I can't turn around now, the guy's waiting for me. I have to get the bees unloaded. It'll be another hour and a half if we go back."

"So I'm a hostage?"

He closed his eyes for a brief second. "Please. I can't deal with any more drama tonight. Let's just get there and get this done."

"Fine." She looked out the window at a semi churning past. The wheels had those awful spikes that could shred your tires. It wasn't fine, nothing about this evening was fine, but she couldn't make him turn around with a truckload of bees. She was annoyed, not heartless.

To make matters worse, as soon as they left the highway they got lost. The back roads were unlit and the GPS wasn't much help and they bumped down a rutted driveway before Glenn realized his mistake. A dog rushed out barking and lights came on and Glenn waved while the homeowner watched them turn around.

"What now?" Cassie said.

He sent her an exasperated look. "I find the right house. That's what."

The farmhouse, when they finally located it, was a split level with plastic chairs out front and a pile of debris under a tarp. An ancient Volvo that couldn't possibly run had settled in front of the garage. She couldn't tell anything about the man who came out, squinting into the headlights, but she felt a keen disappointment at the house. She'd expected something quaint, maybe a white picket fence, but this was just a tired tract house and except for the darkness, which was denser up here, they could be in any subdivision.

The farmer waved them around back. "Go ahead and pull all the way around. "You'll see the trees."

They rattled over a grass track that took them behind the house, Cassie wincing as she imagined the bees shaken and stirred inside their hives, ready to burst forth in a spray of aggravation. Glenn slowed to a stop when they came to a grove of trees, leaving the lights on.

Cassie's breath caught. The peach trees were exquisite, rows and rows of them, with branches that began low on their trunks and forked delicately into a feathery mass of pink blossoms. Beyond the headlights, the individual trees blurred so the orchard looked dim and mysterious, like something out of a fairytale. Despite the tension with Glenn, a sense of peace suffused her.

She had a thought. "So when the bees wake up, they're somewhere new. How does that work?"

Glenn cut the engine. "They figure it out pretty quick." He got out of the truck without further explanation, but she sat a moment longer, soaking up the stillness.

"Mike Russo," the farmer said when he caught up with them. He shook Glenn's hand and nodded to Cassie. He had wire-rim glasses and a bit of a stoop and looked more like a college professor than a farmer.

"Does this spot here get afternoon shade?" Glenn said.

"Oh yeah, round about two o'clock it's in shade."

Glenn walked the ground, peering off into the trees and coming in and out of the headlights like an apparition. "You have water, right?"

Russo nodded toward the woods at the far edge of the orchard. "Stream's over there, just down that little ridge. Plenty close for the bees. Daytime you could see better."

Glenn nodded, satisfied. "This should work fine."

He opened the truck bed and unstrapped the hives, then untied the ramp. The bees were quiet, but apparently they didn't move around much after dark. Hopefully they hadn't left any strays behind.

Glenn extended the ramp and Russo took an end. He gave Cassie a pleasant smile. "Nice of you to come along and keep him company. I hope he's going to buy you a drink after all this." He tipped his chin at Glenn. "Your wife might like Casey's. Just up the Post Road there. You might've passed it on the way in."

The silence was broken only by the throaty belch of a toad.

Thank goodness it was dark because she could tell her face had gone red. Did they look like a married couple? Maybe because of the taut silence between them.

Glenn, straining down the ramp with the first hive, didn't answer.

"How about it, honey," she said pointedly. "A drink sounds nice."

Glenn shot her a *what the fuck* look and Russo laughed. He had a surprisingly hearty laugh for such a reedy man. "Hope I didn't start something."

"Let's just get these hives unloaded," Glenn muttered.

Cassie asked Russo a few questions about peach farming, which he answered amiably. Glenn had a cramped look on his face but he deserved to be uncomfortable, the way he was acting. So caught up with whatever was bothering him, he couldn't even be polite. She eventually left them to the unloading and wandered through the orchard, the trees enveloping her with the delicate scent of honey and almond. No wonder the bees liked them.

Glenn was a difficult man. A solid, principled man. But difficult. He had a moody side she hadn't fully appreciated. She was used to Phil, who would chase you down the hall to get the last word in. But Glenn was a brooder, probably up there on the truck right now cataloging his grievances. With Lilah. With her. Whoever. She wished she knew what had happened to upend him between the time he invited her and when she arrived. She would gladly listen, but he'd shut her out completely.

When it got quiet, she drifted back to the truck. The hives were all unloaded, arranged in neat pairs in the first row of the orchard. In the dark, they looked like cake boxes lined up for a wedding. Glenn was making his way up the row from the far end, removing the cloth covering the openings of each hive so the bees could get out in the morning.

"Looks like we're all set," Russo said when she reappeared. "In a few weeks, you can come back and do this all over again."

"Oh no," she said, summoning a smile. "You don't need me."

"Moral support, then."

She shook Russo's hand and climbed into the truck. Glenn got in, tired and sweaty, but she ignored him, staring out the window as they bounced out the way they'd come.

"I'm sorry," he said once they'd cleared the driveway. "It's been a rough night."

"Really? I hadn't noticed."

He shifted in his seat. "I didn't mean to embarrass you back there. It caught me off guard when he said that about...you know..."

"It caught me off guard too, but so what? He was just being friendly. You might have said two words. Honestly, Glenn. I don't know how you keep clients."

His mouth thinned, and she thought maybe she'd gone too far, but the whole evening had left her out of sorts. The way he'd shut down and then was downright rude. Being in a bad mood was one thing but there was no reason to be ill-mannered. Not just to her, but that nice Mr. Russo. She kept her eyes on the road but caught Glenn glancing over once or twice.

"Did you ah, want to stop for a beer?" He slowed as they approached Casey's. The parking lot was busy, and the place looked lively. Another time she would have been all in, but now she wasn't in the mood.

"I'd rather just get back."

He flicked his gaze her way, then drove on. "Okay, whatever you want."

After a couple of minutes, he sighed deeply. "Look. I know I've been an ass tonight." They were on 136 now, a narrow two-lane road with the occasional sweep of headlights coming at them.

"That's one word for it."

"Is there another one?"

"Extremely frustrating."

"That's two words."

She felt the stirring of a smile. "Okay, I'll throw in 'rude.' That makes three."

He winced. "That bad?"

"Yes. That bad. You acted like a jerk to me and Mr. Russo." She softened a little. "I assume something's up with Lilah, and if you don't want to talk about it that's fine. But don't take it out on me."

For a long minute he didn't speak, then finally, glumly, he said, "She wants to spend the summer in Colorado with her mom."

"The whole summer?"

"That's what *I* said."

She looked over at him. "And you told her no."

His shoulders sank. "I reacted badly. I might have said some things about her mother I shouldn't have."

"Oh boy."

"Yeah. It pretty much went downhill after that."

"Maybe you can talk to her when she gets home. Is the friend's mom bringing her back, or do you have to pick her up?" They were almost back to Glenn's house now, turning onto his quiet street. Hardly any cars out at ten o'clock on a Friday night in Laurelton. At one time, she would have chafed at the lack of hustle and bustle. At this time on a Friday night—any night—the city was just winding up. But she'd come to enjoy the slower pace, even found herself listening to the crickets when she took out the trash.

"She's sleeping over at her friend's. Right now, I'm enemy number one." He pulled into the driveway and hit the garage opener. "Sorry about tonight. Can we try again? I promise not to be an ass or a jerk or rude...or what was the other one?"

"Extremely frustrating."

He let go a smile for the first time. "That I can't promise."

She laughed. At least he was honest. "Tell you what, I'll take you up on that drink."

"Here?"

"Well I wasn't talking about going all the way back to Easton."

They went inside and she shed her bee suit and he poured them each a glass of wine. "White's all I've got," he said.

"White's good." She followed him onto the deck, with Charlie shambling along after.

The evening had cooled, and she slipped on the jacket she'd brought. A moon had come up, and in the soft light the hives looked like a village of tidy starter homes. You couldn't even tell that twenty were missing.

"So are you going to let her go? To Colorado?"

He rubbed his face. He looked worn out. "I don't know. A month ago this wasn't even on her radar. I mean, she hadn't seen her mother in four years. I feel like she's gone from zero to sixty in about ten seconds. I can't keep up."

"Believe me, I know that feeling," she agreed. "Their emotions are all over the place at that age. Girls especially. What was she like when she was little, before her mom left?"

"Happy, great. Like any little kid. I don't think she realized how disengaged her mother was. I picked up the slack—gave her a bath, read stories, all of it." He lifted a shoulder. "It didn't feel like work to me. I loved doing it. I never understood how Sophie didn't connect."

"Lilah feels safe with you. That's why she's pushing back."

He looked skeptical. "It feels to me like she can't get away fast enough."

"You're home base. You're there for her. I'm sure she doesn't want to upset you, but like you said, it's her mom. Of course she's going to jump at the chance."

He was quiet for a minute, gazing out toward the hives. "I guess I'm scared. I get that it's important for her to have a relationship with her mom, but I don't trust Sophie. My gut's all over the place on this. I want to do the right thing, but I don't know what that is."

"Sometimes it's hard to know the right thing. God knows I've made mistakes with Andrew."

He glanced at her in surprise. "You seem like you have it all together."

"Oh no, I'm still winging it."

He cleared his throat. "I uh...I'm sorry for the way I acted tonight. You didn't deserve that." His hair was rumpled, and he was wearing a UVM t-shirt that had seen better days.

She leaned forward and kissed him on the lips.

"What was that for?" His eyes crinkled in an appealing way.

"You're forgiven." She kissed him again, more slowly this time, and he drew her into his lap. Even after the whole sweaty business wrestling the hives, he smelled salty and good.

He nuzzled her neck. "You know, Lilah's spending the night at her friend's."

"I thought you were upset about that."

"I was," he ran his hands lightly down her waist, "until this very forward woman climbed into my lap."

"I didn't climb into your lap, I just ended up here!" She tried halfheartedly to wriggle off, but he grinned and settled her more firmly. "Oh no you don't."

They were both a little breathless, and her heart was beating in a crazy sort of way. Not like when she went running. When she ran, her heart rate ramped up at a steady, regular pace. She knew what to expect at mile three and mile five. But now her heart was swooping around in a very unpredictable way.

"Shouldn't we get out of this chair?" she murmured.

He pulled back, serious now. "Are we doing what I think we're doing?"

Were they? She hadn't been with another man besides Phil in twenty plus years. Was it too soon to sleep with Glenn? They'd only been going out a few weeks. What if she was boring in bed? How would she even know?

"I didn't mean...we don't have to..." he said when she hesitated. "I just thought..."

Her heart beat in her throat. "I do want to. Very much."

"It's been a while," he said once they'd made it upstairs to his bedroom. A no-nonsense room—the bed neatly made with a navy spread, a few framed photos of Lilah at various ages on the dresser. He looked nervous too, which made her feel better.

"Me too."

"A very long while."

She had to smile. "What, you think you've forgotten how?"

"It's possible. But I'm a quick learner." He kissed her then and things got going in a promising way until Charlie, who'd followed them upstairs, wedged his nose between them.

"Come on, you." Glenn took the dog by the collar and walked him out the door. Charlie sighed hugely, then heaved himself to the ground. "I usually let him sleep in here," Glenn said apologetically. "But under the circumstances..."

"Under the circumstances..." she agreed and hooked a finger through his belt loop. He had a very sexy flat belly.

He wavered. "Maybe I should shower."

"No, you shouldn't. If we stop, we'll never get going again."

They ran into a bit of awkwardness removing clothes. He stumbled out of his jeans, then the zipper on her jacket got stuck. They were both laughing at this point, him standing there in his boxers trying to free her zipper. "I need my reading glasses," he said.

"Never mind your reading glasses." She yanked the jacket over her head. In a minute she would lose her nerve. She was almost fifty years old, about to climb into bed with a younger man who happened to be very fit. Yes, she was in decent shape, but things weren't as firm as they used to be. And she was wearing dull underwear. She certainly hadn't expected the evening to end up like this.

But Glenn didn't seem to care about all that. Once they made it into bed the awkwardness disappeared, and she felt like she was in exactly the right place. As though all the upset and craziness of the last month and a half had somehow led her here. To a man who was solid and caring and would turn himself inside out for the people and things that mattered to him. And whose lips were moving down her belly in a way that banished all thought from her head.

Afterward, she snuggled into his shoulder, contentment seeping into every corner of her being. For the first time in a long while she felt a sense of possibility, like there might be more to life than trudging from one crisis to the next.

"Do you think things are meant to happen, or is it all random?" she said.

He drew her closer. "You mean like tonight?"

"I was just thinking that if I'd called another beekeeper or you'd been too busy to come that day, we never would have met."

She felt the rumble of his laughter. "You might be in bed with the old guy who runs bees up in Weston."

She elbowed him in the side. "Oh stop. You know what I mean."

He was quiet for a moment. "I've never been a big believer in God or fate or that kind of thing. I think life happens and sometimes you get lucky."

She smiled. "Is that what we've been doing tonight? Getting lucky?" She kissed his neck lightly. "By the way, in case you're wondering, you haven't forgotten how."

He looked pleased. "You think so?"

She traced a finger along his shoulder. A very nice muscular shoulder. "Are you fishing for compliments?"

He grinned. "Of course."

"Well I'm not giving you anymore because you'll be impossible."

His smile broadened. "I'm already impossible. You told me that earlier."

"I didn't say impossible, I said very frustrating."

He rolled over to face her, his beard tickling a little. "Am I still very frustrating?"

"Don't push it," she said, laughing.

He trailed a hand along her hip. "Because I wouldn't want you to be frustrated."

They might have started up all over again like a couple of kids, but she glanced at the clock on the nightstand and bolted up.

"Oh my God, it's midnight. How did that happen?"

He kissed the small of her back. "Why don't you stay? Lilah won't be home tomorrow until ten at the earliest. I'll make us pancakes."

She plopped back down, then groaned. "That sounds amazing, but I told Andrew I'd be back around eleven."

"So text him."

She slanted him a look. "And tell him I'm spending the night with a man and I won't be home?"

He looked a little wounded. "You make it sound like you picked up some guy off the street."

She nuzzled the delicious place where his neck met his shoulder. "You're pretty yummy. I might have picked you up off the street." She felt him smile. He had a delicate ego. But didn't all men.

"So stay," he murmured. "Andrew's a big boy; he can take care of your dad."

She untangled herself reluctantly. "I should be there in the morning. Andrew and my dad aren't ready for this."

"Are you?" His gray gaze stopped her.

Was she ready for this? Life was already so complicated. She had a son who needed to come to grips with his behavior, a father who couldn't stay at home any longer, and she had to find a new place to live. And on top of it all, the constant drip of worry that her memory would betray her, that any day now she would start to decline, just like her mother had. How could she inflict that on someone?

"You don't realize what you're getting into," she said.

"Does anyone?"

"I have a lot of liabilities."

He rolled his eyes. "You sound like a lawyer."

"I *am* a lawyer."

He kissed the hollow of her throat. "It seems to me we've stumbled onto something pretty good. At least I think so."

"I do too."

"But you still have to go?"

She sighed and rolled out of bed. "I'd better."

He walked her to her car, and she stood on tiptoe to kiss him. "Let me know how things go with Lilah."

"I will."

He waved from the top of the driveway, and even though she had no idea what would happen next week or next month, her heart felt lighter than it had in ages.

Chapter Nineteen

Cassie felt like a teenager sneaking in after curfew, but her dad was asleep and Andrew's door was closed and neither of them remarked on her fine mood the next morning. Who was she kidding? She could skip naked through the kitchen, and they wouldn't glance up. Mothers of a certain age were invisible, and her dad was just trying to put one foot in front of the other. Literally.

At least his ankle was improving. He was moving competently this morning, making his breakfast. He seemed almost like his old self, all the synapses firing. A stranger might not even realize his memory was faulty. Only his appearance gave him away—hair uncombed, bundled in the frayed cardigan he wore even when the weather was warm.

"How about a walk this morning?" Cassie kissed his cheek as she sat down with her coffee, and he smiled absently, already involved with the newspaper.

It was afternoon by the time they got out, ambling down the driveway, her father leaning lightly on the cane. The day was thick with sunshine, one of those gorgeous May days that felt like summer without the humidity. Her mother's peonies, which had survived despite lack of attention, had sprouted six inches seemingly overnight. Even in Connecticut, life was in a hurry.

Her dad tested a couple of steps then brought forward the cane, wobbling when he caught a stone. Cassie resisted the impulse to steady him. She never knew how much to do, when to help and when to back off. Which was true of all her relationships, she supposed.

Despite his unsteadiness, they made it all the way down the driveway, which felt like progress. From here, the house looked better. You couldn't see the peeling paint and the rot eating away at the windowsills. It looked like any solid Connecticut colonial, and for a moment she saw it as her dad must, the way he probably still viewed himself—battered but still standing.

"Remember the swing?" She pointed to a barely visible indentation where a towering maple had once stood. Grass had swallowed the spot, but you could see it if you knew where to look. Her dad had fashioned the swing from a flat piece of wood, sanded the edges smooth and varnished it so they wouldn't get splinters. Bolted the rope to a branch sturdy enough to hold them.

They detoured onto the grass, and her father scraped at the remnants of the stump with his cane. "Your mother hated that swing," he said.

"She did?" Cassie glanced at him in surprise.

"She was always afraid you girls would fall."

"She never said anything."

"What do you mean, she talked about it all the time."

An anxious thrumming started up in her belly. How was it that her dad recalled this and she didn't? She should remember something as encompassing as her mother's fear. She remembered the swing itself in rich detail—the warm grain against her bottom, legs pumping so hard her feet flew higher than her head. Her dancing impatience when it was Shelly's turn.

But her mother fretting over the danger? That was lost. A bit of her past that had vanished without her even knowing.

Her father smiled an inward sort of smile. "Boy, did I catch hell for that swing. Too high, too close to the road. They're going to kill themselves." Without changing his voice, he'd channeled her mother—her expression, her inflection. Her mom, in flesh and blood, came rushing back, and Cassie nearly staggered with the pain. Her mother, living inside her dad all this time. Her own memory was so incomplete, huge chunks of her mom she'd never known or didn't remember. But her dad, with his dwindling faculties, had stored it all away. Memories he could still retrieve when the clouds parted. At least for now.

Cassie took his hand as they made their way back to the pavement. His skin was papery, the veins gnarled and blue. Her mother hadn't lived long enough to age this way. Her mind had betrayed her, but she'd died with her skin unblemished.

"What else do you remember?" Cassie said.

Her dad shrugged, impatient that he was being pressed to recall. "Let's take a look at the Kingsley property."

"How about we stick to the road?" The woods, with rocks and roots and lumpy ground, presented all kinds of hazards. Anyone could trip, especially an eighty-five-year-old just coming off an ankle injury. But her dad struck out across the road with the obstinate look she knew so well. "We said we were going to walk in the woods."

She'd never agreed to that but it didn't matter, he was headed there now. Her dad hadn't seen the Kingsley property since the bulldozing began. And even though she'd known what was coming, the first time she saw it she'd felt a woozy shock that trees that had stood so long had surrendered so easily. For a moment it had given her pause about selling to Weber, handing over the house and field as fodder for development. She still hadn't told Glenn about her plan. Her stomach dipped unhappily at the thought of that conversation. She needed to talk to him, but it never seemed to be the right time.

No. Her dad definitely did not need to see the Kingsley property. He would never agree to sell, and she still could see no other way forward. But he was already huffing up the embankment, stabbing at the soft spring dirt with his cane.

"You're out of breath," she admonished him. "Slow down." She should have brought a bottle of water.

"I'm fine." But he'd lost his burst of momentum and was having trouble gaining the top of the gentle slope. He was so damn stubborn, why couldn't they have stayed on the road. She should have brought Andrew along. He could get her dad to do anything.

Her father stopped at the top of the rise to catch his breath. "Is this the property they sold?"

She looked at him in surprise. A few minutes ago he'd been so clear-eyed. "Yes, the Kingsley property."

"I know that, but they sold it?" He mopped his face, which was perspiring heavily.

"It sold a few months ago." She wondered if he even remembered about the development. Maybe he just wanted to walk in the woods.

They came to a deer path, which was easier going, but her dad still seemed uncomfortable.

"You okay?" He didn't look good. His face was pasty and he still hadn't caught his breath.

He rubbed fitfully at his shoulder. "Must have slept wrong last night, that's all."

"Your shoulder hurts?"

"When you get to my age everything hurts."

"How long has this been going on?"

"What are you," he grumbled, "my doctor?"

Nothing about this felt right. His shortness of breath and now this pain in his shoulder. She felt a rising unease. "You know what, we're going home."

To her surprise, he agreed. "Maybe I'll lie down for a few minutes."

A terrifying thought dawned on her. Could he be having a heart attack? She tried anxiously to remember the symptoms. Not always a crushing pain, that much she knew. Sweating, shortness of breath. Pain in the neck or shoulder.

She felt his arm. Clammy skin. That was a sign too.

Her own heart lurched in fear. *Oh Christ. He was having a heart attack.*

The downslope of the embankment loomed before them. A nothing little hill, but she had to get him down and out to the road.

No. She needed to call 911. *Now.*

She fumbled for her phone, then realized with a swoop of panic she'd left it at home.

How could she have forgotten her phone? She could see it, charging innocently on the kitchen counter. She hadn't even thought about it; she was going for a walk with her dad, practically within sight of the house. What on earth could happen?

He was trembling now, his face glistening with perspiration. She shouted for help, but her voice came out tinny. No one could hear, the neighbors too far away. Even the earthmovers were quiet today.

She tamped down a rising panic. No time to get him out of the woods. She needed help. *Now.*

"Dad, listen to me." She took a breath, trying to steady her own galloping heart. "I don't want to scare you, but we need to get you to the hospital."

"The hospital? I don't need to go to the hospital. I just need to lie down."

She looked into his face, which was sheened with a fine sweat. "I want you to sit right here and don't move. I'm going to run to the house and call for help." She didn't want to use the word ambulance. That would terrify him.

He allowed her to ease him to the ground. No flat rock to sit on, nothing even for him to lean against. A stout pine a couple of yards away but he would never make it. He sat heavily where she put him, crushing a small bed of ferns.

"I don't feel right," he murmured. "Got a tightness in my chest."

She squatted in front of him, white hot with fear. She could lose him. He could die right here in the woods. "Daddy." In spite of her effort to stay calm, her voice shook. "You're going to be okay, you hear me? I'll be right back. Don't try to move. Just stay here and wait for me." She sprang up, her heart exploding. Then quickly squatted again.

"I love you," she said fiercely. "You hear me? I love you."

Then she was off, taking the embankment in two long strides. She nearly stumbled at the bottom, then quickly regained her footing. She choked back a sob. So many irritants between them. And for what? She'd abandoned him after her mother died, secretly, shamefully wishing it had been him instead. Appalled she felt that way. She'd been a miserable daughter. That was the truth. She lived an hour away and rarely came to see him. And now he was having a heart attack, and she'd left him crumpled and alone in the woods.

She dashed blindly across the road, not even checking for cars, pounding up the driveway, pebbles flying. Her own heart racing like a trapped, terrified animal.

"Andrew!" she yelled as she plunged through the door. One small mercy at least. They never locked it. "Where are you? Grandpa's having a heart attack!" Saying the words out loud seized her with a bottomless fear. It couldn't happen like this. Not now. Not when she was finally beginning to find her way back to him. The father who'd loved her the best he could. Who'd always tried, even if she hadn't seen it.

Her phone was right where she'd left it on the kitchen counter. The face ID was balky so she keyed in her password with shaky fingers. A howl of frustration as it denied her. She wiped her hands on her shirt and tried again. She was in! She tapped in *911* in a fury of impatience.

"I think it's a heart attack," she barked. "No, he has no history. Yes, he's having trouble breathing. He's in the goddamn woods, that's where he is!"

Andrew stumbled downstairs, his face pale with fear. "Grandpa's having a heart attack?"

"They're sending an ambulance." She raced out the door, phone in hand. "We're across the street. Wait at the bottom of the driveway!"

She pelted back across the road and up the hill, shouting for her dad, but got no response. How long had she been gone? Three minutes, maybe four. The dispatcher was still on the line, a disembodied voice clutched in her hand.

Her father was in the same spot, lying in the fetal position now, gray and still. One of his pant legs had ridden up, exposing a pale leg.

She crouched down, rigid with fear. His breath was shallow, eyes glazed with pain.

But he was alive.

"Daddy." She stroked his face, which was wet with perspiration. "They'll be here any minute. Hang on."

He nodded faintly. He'd heard her at least.

She cast about for something to keep him tethered to her.

"Remember when Mrs. Rostov almost had her baby at home, how fast they got there? They sent a fire truck, and we always joked that Warren would grow up to be a fireman, remember? Only he didn't. I think he's a stockbroker in the city somewhere. And the next time with Frannie she was two weeks late." Why on earth did she even remember all this? The Rostovs had moved away years ago.

She strained to hear a siren. For God's sake. Where *were* they?

Her dad's face was drenched with sweat, tiny droplets clung to his brows and threatened to drip into his eyes. His skin the color of chalk. She stifled a sob as she gently wiped his forehead with her t-shirt. Her mother's body had always felt like an extension of her own—familiar, recognizable. When her mom died, even though she'd been a ghost of herself for years, Cassie felt like some essential organ had been scooped out of her. She'd slunk away in agony and left her dad to suffer alone.

She listened again for his breath. Fainter now. *Oh God. She was losing him.* She'd give anything to have that time back, to be the daughter she should have been. She'd given the dispatcher the right address, she knew she had. And Andrew was waiting at the street to direct them.

"Hang on," she whispered. "Please hang on." But his hand was chilled and limp and now she could see no rise and fall of breath. In a panic, she set her ear to his mouth.

Nothing.

She knelt beside him and felt for a pulse, her heart roaring in her ears. She'd taken CPR years ago. Five compressions to one breath? Did they even give breaths anymore? She didn't think so; things had changed. She couldn't remember. She choked out a prayer as she began compressions, the heel of one hand booting into the other.

Please God. Let him live.

She kept at it. Ten, twenty, thirty compressions. Sweat dripped into her own eyes, but she didn't dare stop. Finally, mercifully, the distant wail of a siren. Rising and falling. Rising again. Then all at once close enough to shatter the quiet. From across the street, she heard Andrew's shout and doors slamming. The thunderous arrival of help. With a sob she kept going, trying to keep her count. "Up here," she screamed. "Up here!"

A minute later Andrew dashed up the hill with two medics behind him, a bulky man and a small wiry woman, both of them moving sharply with duffel bags and a stretcher.

"He's not breathing," Cassie cried, jumping up to make way for them. The man, who looked like nothing could faze him, checked for a pulse then immediately began CPR, straight-armed and competent, while his partner fitted an oxygen mask over her dad's face.

"How long has he been unresponsive?" The woman lifted her eyes to Cassie's, but the question overwhelmed her.

"I don't know, a few minutes, maybe." How long *had* it been? Five or six minutes since she'd run back from the house to find him collapsed. Her heart shriveled as they threaded an IV into her father's arm, then slid him into a contraption that delivered chest compressions with some sort of plunger. The device started up with an indifferent mechanical whirring.

Cassie gripped Andrew's hand, which was as sweaty as her own.

The machine kept on but her father didn't respond, and the relief she'd felt when the medics arrived puddled into terror as they exposed his frail chest and shocked his heart to keep it going. She wept like a child as his body jerked with the jolt of the defibrillator. Andrew, clutching her hand, sobbed too.

From somewhere a dog barked, which startled her. How could the rest of the world carry on like nothing was happening?

Her father still wasn't responding, and the medics started up the CPR machine again. Cassie had lost track of time. Had they been here five minutes, ten? An hour? How long could this go on?

"Clear!" the EMT barked and they shocked him again. Cassie's hope dimmed. They'd shocked his heart twice. And nothing. She held Andrew in her arms and wept as the female medic knelt with two fingers to her father's neck.

The woman looked up. "I feel a pulse. Very faint."

Cassie's heart leapt with joy. He was still alive.

Two more responders huffed up the hill with even more gear, the soft ground trampled under so many feet. They carefully transferred her father onto a board and strapped him down, the relentless CPR machine still pumping. The female medic held the oxygen tank as the men hoisted the stretcher. Then with her father's shirt gaping, they hustled him down the hill and out to the street as Cassie and Andrew hurried after.

The ambulance was waiting, its lights pulsing red and blue like a beating heart. The medics quickly loaded her father and Cassie made to climb in, but the woman shook her head. "Not in back, you can ride up front if you want."

She started for the passenger side, then caught a glimpse of Andrew's stricken face. Her son, melting down on the side of the road.

"We'll follow," she said. "Where are you taking him?"

"Stamford's the closest," the woman said as the doors swung shut.

The siren swooned to life, the sound gutting her as the ambulance sped down the quiet street. She agonized at the thought of her dad, terrified and alone. Or maybe he was in some twilight where no one could reach him, the life seeping out of him.

She gathered herself. They had to go forward.

"Come on," she said to Andrew. "Let's get to the hospital."

•   •   •

Stamford Hospital had undergone a renovation, and the fluorescent waiting room with plastic chairs that Cassie remembered from her own childhood mishaps had been replaced by muted lighting and tasteful furniture in tan and seafoam green.

But the décor belied the commotion within. A teenager with a bloody bandage on his arm sat slumped in a chair, a woman clearly his mother, hovering. Across the room, two young children boiled on a couch as the father tried to rein them in. She could only guess at the traumas that brought people here. Car accidents. Heart attacks. Burns. The routine emergencies of life, unremarkable until they were your own.

At the desk they had no information. "Stuart Linden," she repeated, as if saying her father's name would make him appear magically unscathed, strolling under his own steam out the double doors that swung ominously into the bowels of the hospital.

"Have a seat," the receptionist told her. "It could be a while." She looked past Cassie to a middle-aged couple behind her, the man hunched over his stomach in a protective way.

"How will we—" Cassie began, but the receptionist waved her off. "Ma'am, you need to have a seat. Someone will let you know."

An ambulance with lights and sirens barreled past to the emergency entrance where patients were unloaded. She hurried to the wall of windows, her stomach hiking in alarm. But her dad was already here. She knew that. Somewhere inside this byzantine building they were trying to save him.

She sank onto the couch next to Andrew, who glanced up anxiously. She shook her head. "They don't know anything yet."

"You think he'll make it?" His voice was small.

Something big and terrifying rushed up inside her, and she pressed a hand to her mouth to keep it from escaping. "I don't know, sweetie. I really don't know."

"They got him here in the golden hour. I was just reading about it. There's a much better chance of a good outcome within the first sixty minutes after a heart attack." He showed her the article on his phone, trying to steady himself with facts, so much like his grandfather. But she couldn't concentrate. All she could see was her dad lying in the dirt, the hand with the wedding ring he still wore shuddering as the current coursed through him.

"I need to call Aunt Shelly," she said, suddenly remembering her sister didn't know any of this and would be going about her day as if nothing in the world were the matter. She squeezed Andrew's arm and stepped outside into the glare of the parking lot. Only a little after five but it felt like decades since she'd started down the driveway with her dad. If only they'd stayed on the pavement and not attempted the woods. What had she been thinking, allowing him to climb that hill? They could be home right now, her dad settled in front of the TV or fussing over a puzzle. But maybe his heart had been waiting to give out, treacherously biding its time. Maybe it would have turned on him no matter what he did.

"Shel," she said when her sister picked up. For half a beat, she thought wildly of not telling her. Shelly had always been the diligent one—checking on their dad even from a distance, making sure he was okay. Keeping Cassie, so consumed with her own life, updated. She should spare her sister this anguish now. What could Shelly do from California anyway?

But the sound of her sister's voice did her in.

"Hey," Shelly said, "what's going on? You don't sound good."

"It's Daddy," Cassie said and began to cry. She recounted it all—what had started as a promising walk, his increasing discomfort, how she'd run for her phone. She told her everything—the CPR, the monstrous defibrillator. Shelly let her tell it and only when Cassie had finished asked the thing she'd forgotten to say. The most important thing of all.

"What do we know now?"

"Nothing," Cassie said, exhausted. She'd moved a few steps away from the door, all the while keeping an eye out for a doctor. "He was alive when they took him, but I don't know if he is now," she said bleakly.

"If he wasn't, they would have told you." Her sister at her sensible best, even with her own fear.

"You think?" Cassie had no idea if this was true, but she clung to it like a lifeline.

"Believe me, they always tell you the bad news."

"Oh Shel."

"It'll be all right. I'm sure it will. Is Glenn there with you?"

"I called you first."

"Call him. You need someone there. As soon as I get off the phone I'm going to book a flight."

"You're coming?" Cassie's heart, battered and bruised, lifted ever so slightly.

"Of course I'm coming, you idiot. And don't even think about picking me up at the airport. I'll get an Uber."

After she hung up with Shelly, she called Glenn, who was there in ten minutes. He folded her into his arms, and even Andrew looked relieved to see him.

"He's tough," Glenn said, taking a seat next to them. He'd come straight from someone's hives and was in his work boots with bits of mud clinging to them. "When that bee stung him in the eye it hardly slowed him down." She knew this was for Andrew's benefit, but it bucked her up too.

"Yeah, but this was a heart attack," Andrew said. "Cardiac arrest. That's when the heart stops beating and—"

"We don't know anything for sure yet," Cassie said, setting a hand on his arm to prevent him from pulling up another article. It had been forty-five minutes, and no one had come out to tell them a thing. Every time the doors swung open she jumped but it was always someone in scrubs, walking briskly in or out. No one with news about her father.

"They got him here quick," Glenn said. "These days there's all kinds of stuff they can do." From the adjoining chair, he held her hand. He was strong and calm and she wanted to believe him.

"How you holding up?" he said, moving to the couch when Andrew got up to stretch his legs.

She leaned into him. She'd been trying to hold it together, staying upbeat for Andrew's sake. But Glenn's solid warmth undid her. She dropped her face into her hands and cried.

"It's okay." He stroked her back. "It's all right to cry."

"What was I thinking, I never should have let him go up there in the first place."

"You couldn't have known. At least you were with him. Think of that." He drew her close as she sobbed into his chest.

"But I haven't been there for him. I've left him alone. I don't mean today but all this time. He never complained, never asked for help. I should have come more often. I might have noticed something."

"Don't beat yourself up." He kissed her forehead gently. "You're here now and that's what counts." He let her cry, holding her until she was too wrung out to shed another tear, until she had nothing left.

She sat up, quivery and exhausted. Andrew had come back and was watching her worriedly.

"Hey sweetie," she said, wiping her eyes. "We still haven't heard anything."

"Andrew, you hungry?" Glenn said. "It's after six. How about we go down to the cafeteria and see what they have?"

Andrew looked at Cassie, who nodded. "I guess I am a little hungry," he allowed.

"Go on," she urged with a grateful glance at Glenn. "I'll be here."

As soon as they left, the doctor appeared. A very young doctor with dark curls and tortoiseshell glasses who barely looked older than Andrew. Her heart sank at the sight of him. How could someone so young know anything?

But the doctor, who appeared slightly more mature up close with surprising flecks of gray in his hair, reported that her father was stable.

"You mean he's alive?" Cassie stammered.

"Very much so." He smiled briefly. "One of the arteries was completely blocked, but he was lucky. We performed angioplasty to open it up, then put in a stent. It doesn't look like too much damage to the heart muscle, but we'll know more in a day or two."

"Can I see him?" Cassie asked, a bubble of happiness rising in her chest. She would see her father again. They would have time to spend together. They had both been handed a reprieve.

"He's still in the CCU." The doctor checked his watch. "They'll probably keep him there overnight then admit him to the cardiac ward. Might be better to come back in the morning."

He turned to go, but Cassie said, "He has memory issues. He might be confused."

"I'll note that in his chart." The doctor hesitated. "Just so you know, this might make it worse. Hospitals can be disorienting, especially after a major trauma like this."

But she refused to be dampened. She hurried to the cafeteria to find Andrew and Glenn. They would bring her dad home and he would recover. She would handle whatever came next. And Shelly would be here too.

She caught up with them as Glenn was paying for sodas and sandwiches. The two of them were talking, and Andrew was actually smiling. She felt a rush of gratitude for Glenn's easy way with him. When Glenn saw her he gave Andrew a nudge. "Your mom's here."

She hugged Andrew and then Glenn and the cashier beamed and wished them well. "He's resting now," Cassie said. "We can come back in the morning."

They brought the sandwiches home, turkey for them and a veggie wrap for her. The house seemed empty without her dad, who filled it even in his diminished state. They would need to set up a bed for him in the family room; he wouldn't be able to manage the stairs. And there would be rehab. But she couldn't think of all that now. Tonight it was enough that he'd made it.

They took the sandwiches out to the porch. The birdhouse her dad had built years ago swung as a pair of wrens bustled in and out, stuffing it with bits of twig and brush. One of them always in flight, the males and females equal partners in the business of outfitting a home. It seemed impossible the day had gone on so long.

All at once Andrew set down his sandwich. "We need to get his cane. We forgot it in the woods."

"Right, the cane." Cassie jumped up. It seemed intolerable to leave it there.

"It's not going anywhere," Glenn said. "Why don't you wait until the morning?"

One of the wrens was pouring its heart out from a nearby branch. For such small birds they were surprisingly loud. She sat back, utterly exhausted. The thought of returning to the woods in the near dark was too much. "I guess you're right, he doesn't need it this very minute."

"I'll get it first thing," Andrew promised.

"I'll let you." She settled into the wicker chair and the three of them sat companionably on the porch, finishing their sandwiches and watching the wrens until the birds disappeared for the night.

Tomorrow was another day.

Chapter Twenty

Glenn rang the bell but no one answered, so he let himself in. Mr. Linden, who'd been released from the hospital a couple of days before, had been installed in a hospital bed in the family room and Cassie and Shelly were in the process of helping him up. The room was warm, and the place had the stifling feel of a nursing home with pill bottles and Mr. Linden's hospital ID bracelet littering the coffee table.

"Here, let me help." Glenn set down the box of chocolates he'd brought and gently lifted the older man to his feet. Mr. Linden had been old before, but now he seemed ancient. The ordeal had taken it out of him. His cane had been replaced by a walker, and his hands shook as he took hold of it.

"One day at a time," Shelly said. "That's how we're taking it here." She resembled their dad, with his strong features, but you could tell she and Cassie were sisters. Their noses crinkled the same way when they smiled, and they had a physical ease with each other that only siblings possessed. Close siblings, anyway.

"How you doing, Mr. Linden?" Glenn said.

Cassie's father looked at Glenn like he couldn't quite place him.

"I thought I'd check on the bees today. You feel like getting outside?" It would do Mr. Linden good to get out of the house. Cassie too. She seemed exhausted, briefly touching his arm but not lifting her face for a kiss.

Cassie glanced dubiously at Shelly. "I don't know. You think that's a good idea?"

"It's a nice day," Glenn said.

Mr. Linden took a closer look at him. "You're the bee man."

"That's me."

"What do you want to do, Dad?" Shelly said. "You want to get cleaned up and go outside?"

Mr. Linden shrugged irritably. "Don't need to clean up. I'm fine."

They agreed that Mr. Linden could get some fresh air, but first Shelly took him to wash up. Watching him maneuver the walker was painful, and Cassie motioned to Glenn that they should wait outside.

She sat on the step with the breeze lifting her hair, and Glenn sat too. It felt good to be next to her. What with everything going on, they hadn't spoken much the past few days.

"Sorry, it's been a little crazy here," she said.

"Don't be sorry; you have a ton going on." He kissed the top of her head and just for a moment she leaned into him. "Why don't you go for a run or whatever you need to do? I can sit with him for a little while. You and Shelly should take a break."

"He's still so weak. He gets dizzy, and I'm afraid he's going to fall but he doesn't like us helping him."

He slanted her a look. "I wouldn't want you or your sister helping me pee either."

She laughed, which seemed to loosen her up a little.

He twined his hand in hers. "Shelly's here, can you get away for a couple of hours later? I'll make you dinner. No meat, this time, I promise."

She gave him a tired smile. "Believe me, I'd love nothing more than to chuck all this and crawl into a hole with you."

He grinned. "That sounds promising."

"But I don't know when that's going to be." Her smile faded. "And there's something I have to—" But she was interrupted by Shelly and their dad, who were making their way around the side of the house to avoid the front steps. Mr. Linden was hunched over the walker, wrapped in a sweater even though the day was warm.

Glenn stood to lend a hand, wondering what Cassie wanted to say. She seemed preoccupied but anyone would be.

"Where are my bees?" Mr. Linden was out of breath from the short excursion but had that determined look Glenn had come to recognize.

"Want to drive down and take a look?" Glenn said.

Cassie looked doubtful. "Getting across the field might be hard."

But Mr. Linden was already creeping toward the truck.

"I can pull right up to the hives," Glenn said, "if you don't mind tire tracks on the grass."

"If it's okay I'll skip it," Shelly said. "I haven't even showered yet today. Sorry Glenn." She laughed. "I'm sure that's too much information."

"No judgment here." He liked Shelly. There was no artifice to her. He wondered if she was as conflicted as Cassie about their dad. He'd tried to convince Cassie that nothing about the heart attack was her fault, but it was hard to let go of that kind of self-doubt. It ate away at him too. Always second guessing himself about Lilah. He'd stood firm on Colorado even though she was still badgering him to let her go. But he was right; he knew he was.

Still. It killed him that things were rocky at home. Lilah hadn't watched TV with him in a week. They ate together, then she disappeared into her room right after dinner. But if he gave in, she would run all over him. And bottom line, he didn't like the idea of her alone with Sophie all summer.

They helped Mr. Linden into the truck, and Cassie got in front. He thought she might say what was on her mind, but with her dad in the back seat she stayed quiet. Glenn rolled down the windows. It was a gorgeous day. Early June, his favorite time of year. Long days. Plentiful forage for the bees with the belly of summer still ahead. With an active queen, a healthy colony could triple in size over the summer. It amazed him every year how fast the bees ramped up.

Mr. Linden seemed rejuvenated by the fresh air. He gazed intently at the hives, which from this distance looked like filing cabinets that had been deposited in the middle of the field. "Those are where the bees live."

"Yup, those are your hives."

"Hives," Mr. Linden repeated, like he'd never heard the word. Where did a word like that go? The man had been tending bees for years. How could he forget something as basic as *hive*? But maybe he hadn't forgotten. Maybe his mind was just gummed up, and seeing his bees would cut through the clutter.

"Believe it or not, the confusion's better," Cassie said in a low voice. "I mean, relatively better. He didn't even know where he was in the hospital. He thought I was my mom and Shelly was me."

"I'm sorry. I can't even imagine." He gave her leg a brief squeeze. No wonder she was tense, she had a shitload on her mind.

They left the gravel surface of the driveway, and Glenn bumped over the grass, going slow so as not to jostle Mr. Linden. The field had been mowed, but near the hives it had grown tall and weedy, the landscaper clearly wary of getting too close. Glenn hadn't been back since he put in the drone comb a couple of weeks earlier. The cells wouldn't be capped yet, but it couldn't hurt to take a look.

He'd expected Mr. Linden to watch from the truck, but as soon as they stopped, he unbuckled his seatbelt.

"All right," Glenn said, "if you want to get out, let's watch your step." He guided the older man out of the truck and helped him put on a veil. The bees were agitated. A few buzzed around their heads, and a platoon of guard bees eyed them suspiciously from the entrance. Something might have riled them up earlier, maybe a skunk nosing around. He frowned at a stray yellowjacket cruising at mid altitude near the hive. That was a worrisome sign. Even one wasp could mean a nest nearby. Wasps could wipe out a weak colony in no time.

He puffed a little smoke to calm the bees, then cracked open one of the boxes. Every other time he'd been here, Mr. Linden had wanted to help, but now he seemed content to lean on the walker. Glenn lifted out a comb. "She's been laying drone, see? Just like we wanted. Some of it's even capped already." He pointed to a row of cells that had been sealed off with a pale cover of wax. "If we're lucky, the mites are in there with them."

"See that, Dad?" Cassie said, but Mr. Linden didn't appear to recall any of this. In fact, after a few minutes he lost interest. A few weeks ago, he'd been out here himself, wrestling with the hives, trying to light the smoker. Sure, he had some memory issues, but he'd been functioning okay. The heart attack had knocked him down.

Glenn slotted the drone frame back into the box and pried open the next one. This colony wasn't doing as well. "She's laid some drone eggs," he pointed out, hoping to engage Mr. Linden, "but the pattern is spotty. A healthy queen should be laying more vigorously than this." With his hive tool he scraped out the inside of a cell and saw the telltale red varroa mites clinging to a translucent larva. The powdered sugar and even the drone comb hadn't done the job.

He was about to open up the new hive too, but Cassie suggested they head back. Mr. Linden didn't argue. When they got him into the truck, he leaned against the headrest and closed his eyes. Glenn couldn't get a handle on Cassie's mood. Not quite aloof but holding herself back in some way. Had he done something to upset her? He'd been there for her at the hospital, he'd rushed right over. And he'd been checking in every day, at least briefly. A fissure of worry opened up inside him. He wasn't good with women. Things started out well but somewhere along the way, they tired of him. Sophie had. Even Lilah was pulling away. He wasn't easy. He knew that. He was opinionated, and okay, he could be downright moody. But when he was in, he was all in. He didn't know any other way to be.

"I guess I'll take off now," Glenn said once they got her dad back to the house, but Cassie said, "Let me just get him settled. Can you stay a minute?"

He sat on the front step like the hired help, his stomach churning. Was she about to tell him she didn't have time for a relationship? Her life was crazy, but whose life wasn't? Or maybe Shelly had sized him up and told her she needed to find a lawyer, not a beekeeper. He'd fallen hard, that was a mistake. And sleeping with her had only made him want her more.

"Sorry to turn you into the chauffeur," Cassie said when she emerged a few minutes later. She'd brushed her hair and put on lip gloss, which gave him a spark of hope. If she was about to break up with him, she wouldn't have bothered. Would she?

"I didn't mind," he said. "At least he got out for a few minutes."

They stepped off the porch and by unspoken agreement cut across the field. Wherever this was going, better to talk about it away from the house.

"So what's the story with that second hive?" she said. "It didn't sound good."

"There's time to requeen this season if we do it soon, that way the colony can build back up before winter. You might lose it anyway, but it's worth a chance." He was about to explain the mechanics of introducing a new queen but when he glanced over she was gazing off toward the street, and he got the sense she wasn't listening.

They skirted the hives, ending up at the stone wall that bordered the woods. A chipmunk raced along the top, then dove into a crevice and vanished with a flick of its tail.

Glenn waited, his heart stumbling. Something was wrong but he didn't know what. How could he fix it if he didn't know what it was? They sat on the wall in the dappled light, and he waited for her to speak.

When she finally looked at him, she seemed edgy and unhappy. "We're selling the property. My dad agreed. Even if he regains some strength, he can't live here. It's impossible. He can't even get up the stairs. He needs someplace on one floor with memory care too." She glanced across the field toward the hives. "So I don't know what to do about the bees..."

Glenn felt a rush of relief. That was it, she was worried about the bees? It wasn't about him after all. "Don't stress about that. Once we get the mites under control, I'll figure something out. Or the new owner might want them. You never know. Focus on what you need to do for your dad."

She let go a sigh. "There isn't going to be a new owner. I mean, there is...oh, there's no good way to say it. Weber's made an offer and we've accepted."

He blinked, not sure he'd heard correctly. "You're selling to Weber?"

She scraped at a loose stone, causing a fall of fine dirt. "It's a lot of money, much better than anything we could get on our own." She glanced unhappily toward the house. "You've seen what kind of shape the place is in. We'd have to spend a fortune before we could even list it. He's offered to buy it as is. We don't have to do a thing."

"Of course you don't have to do a thing." He couldn't keep the sharpness from his voice. "He's going to rip it down."

"I realize that but there's no helping it."

"Jesus, Cassie. This is a once-in-a-lifetime property. You've got a mature meadow here. There's nothing like this left in Laurelton." Selling the house was one thing, but to *Weber?* How could she go there? "Why not try another caregiver?"

"Caregivers come and go. And eventually he's going to need someplace where we don't have to worry that he's going to fall down the stairs or whether he likes the lady or if she's going to quit. And they're developing now. If we don't jump on this offer, it'll go away."

He felt a rising sense of hurt. "You never said a word about this."

"I didn't know what to say. At first, we didn't know each other well, and honestly, I knew you wouldn't like it. I guess I didn't want to go there. I feel bad. Believe me, it's not what I want to do."

He tossed a rock into the woods, where it landed in the leaves with a hollow thud. "I get it about the money. And it's your decision, you and your family's. I just wish you'd said something."

"I'm sorry. I really am. It just never felt like the right time."

His thoughts were beginning to coalesce in a troubling way. "You were thinking about this the whole time we've been together. You met with Weber and didn't even tell me." For some reason, her silence seemed the greatest sin. "I was in a marriage that wasn't honest," he said tightly. "She never told me a goddamn thing until the day she said she was leaving. It's not about doing what's right for your family. It's keeping stuff back. This might not seem like a big deal to you, but to me it's all about trust." He gestured toward the Kingsley property. "You let things go along with us when you knew you wanted to sell to Weber. What the hell else are you keeping back?"

"I'm not keeping anything back. You see my life. I have an eighty-five-year-old father with dementia who just had a heart attack. And a house that's falling apart. I've been doing my best trying to hold everything together, but I can't do it anymore." She blinked back tears. "They're already developing the other parcel. It's happening with or without our five acres."

"Oh, so why not be part of the problem?"

Her eyes widened. "That's how you see me, part of the problem?"

"I don't know how to see things anymore. Without honesty, we have nothing." He pushed off the wall, something closing off inside him. He'd been a fool to believe things could be different this time. She was just like Sophie. Maybe all women were. "I need to go."

"Glenn."

"I can't do this if I don't trust you."

Tears sprang to her eyes. "It's just a house. It has nothing to do with us."

He shook his head, heat building behind his own eyes. "It has everything to do with us. You just can't see it."

He started back to the hives to collect his things, half expecting she would follow and try to convince him. But she didn't. As he gathered up his equipment he saw out of the corner of his eye that she'd started up the hill toward the house. Head down, walking slowly.

Part of him wanted to rush after her and say it didn't matter. That they'd find a way. But it did matter. It said everything about her.

He sealed up the hives and stowed his equipment in the truck, his whole body ringing with hurt. Twenty minutes ago he'd been mulling over how to save the weakened colony, but it didn't matter. She could do what she wanted with the bees. It wasn't his problem.

In a month all this would be gone anyway.

Chapter Twenty-One

Cassie trudged across the field, her whole body numb. He'd shut down just like she'd feared, looked at her like a stranger. Like he'd never even known her. She should have told him sooner. He was right, she hadn't been honest. She'd waited and waited for the right time, but there was never a right time. She should have just come out with it. If she'd been up front from the start it might have made a difference, but now she'd never know.

She tried to slip inside unnoticed but ran into Shelly, hair damp from the shower, clumping down the stairs with a load of laundry.

"Nothing," Cassie said when Shelly gave her a look.

"Bullshit. Your eyes are red. You told him, didn't you?" Shelly set down the laundry basket, and Cassie gave in and sank to the bottom step. No point trying to evade her sister, she would hunt her down and make her talk.

Cassie sighed miserably. "I don't know what I expected. I knew he'd be disappointed, but I thought maybe we could talk it through. That he might understand. But he actually accused me of being part of the problem."

Shelly squeezed next to her so they were sitting bottom to bottom like they used to. "What problem?"

Cassie gave a dispirited wave of her hand. "I don't know, all of it— deforestation, climate change, child labor, who knows." Her shoulders slumped. "I feel bad about cutting this up. I do." She lowered her voice, but the TV was on and their dad couldn't hear. "But who else is going to give us three-point-two million?"

Shelly rubbed the back of Cassie's neck, which was one massive knot. "The guy's crazy about you, it's obvious. Give him a day or two. It'll blow over."

"You don't know him. It won't blow over."

"Really? He seems so laid back."

"He's not laid back, he's intense in his own way. He just doesn't look it." Cassie pressed on her temple, which was beginning to throb. "Oh Shel. I don't see a way to put this back together. He can't forgive that I didn't tell him we're selling to Weber. That was the deal breaker."

Shelly looked heartened. "That's a good sign."

"It is?"

"The guy's been burned. Badly from what you say. This is something he cares about, and he feels like you weren't honest."

"That's what he said."

"See?" Shelly nudged her. "So call him and apologize."

"I did apologize, but he didn't want to hear it." She leaned her head on Shelly's shoulder. "And nothing's going to change. We're still selling."

"He probably feels bad too. Give it a day and call him. Maybe he'll have a change of heart."

"I doubt it." Cassie heaved herself off the stairs. "Let me make a couple of calls then I'll make Dad lunch. You've been on duty all morning."

"You're in love with him."

"What?" Cassie said faintly.

"You heard me."

"Don't be silly." But the blood rushed to her face. *Was* she in love with Glenn?

"You should see yourself when he's around." Shelly was warming up now. "You're like a sixteen-year-old. You were never this way with Phil. Don't get me wrong, I liked Phil, but you two always seemed more like partners at one of those stuffy New York firms. You know, Sawyer, Linden and blah blah blah."

"For God's sake, don't drag Phil into this." Cassie began hauling herself upstairs, but Shelly abandoned the laundry and followed.

"You're head over heels. I haven't seen you this happy in years."

"But I've only known him two months."

"So? Toby and I got engaged after six weeks."

"Well, you two are nuts. Anyway, how would this ever work? Never mind that he's not talking to me anymore, he's got a business here and I live in New York."

"Why do you have to live in New York?" Shelly tagged after Cassie into her bedroom and dropped onto the bed. It felt like they were back in high school when they hung out for hours in one room or the other. Their dad used to gripe that he could have saved the money and bought a house with one less bedroom.

"Shel, just stop. Okay? I work for the city, I live in New York. And I wasn't up front with him. He's not going to get past that." Cassie sat at the small desk and opened her computer, but her heart was back in the field, the look on Glenn's face. How fast they had unraveled. How miserable and final it felt to walk away. Her insides felt hollow, like everything hopeful had been scraped out of them.

"The point is you're in love with him," Shelly said. "I told Toby, I said, *Cassie's crazy about this beekeeper. He's very hot, better hope I don't stay too long.*"

Cassie groaned. "You told Toby about this? Don't you have anything better to talk about than my love life? Such as it is."

Shelly picked up Cassie's old stuffed dog and gave him a toss. "I didn't tell him the good parts."

"There aren't any more good parts." Cassie rescued the dog from Shelly. "Don't toss Frederick around like that; he's fragile." She set the dog down gently on the dresser. It would take weeks to box up everything they wanted to save and sort the rest for Goodwill. The thought of all that had to be done was exhausting.

Shelly got up off the bed. "I'm telling you, Cass, don't let him get away. He's a good guy, and they don't come along very often. You can figure out the rest."

"You're coming with me Friday, right?" She'd been dreading the appointment with the genetic counselor for weeks, and now it was here. She felt bereft at the thought of not sharing the results with Glenn. How he'd been suddenly excised from her life.

"You know I am." Her sister sat down again and kissed Cassie on the cheek. "Give him a call, you'll feel better."

Cassie shut the door once Shelly had gone downstairs but didn't bother opening the brief she was working on. No way could she concentrate. She pushed up the old frame window as far as it would go and gazed out over the pebbled driveway and the lush field. If her dad didn't have those damn bees, she wouldn't have met Glenn in the first place and life would be so much simpler. But her heart tumbled at the thought.

She hadn't been straight with Glenn. She couldn't blame him for being upset. She sealed up everything difficult—what happened to her mother, the medical history she still hadn't shared with Andrew. So painful to look it all in the eye. She hadn't told Glenn the truth about selling to Weber because she was afraid deep down of how he'd react. She'd been afraid of losing him and she had. She set Frederick back on the bed, and the ancient dog toppled over. Her phone pinged with a text and she lunged for it, heart in her throat.

But it was only Shelly. `Did u call him yet?`
`It's been 10 minutes`
`Call him!`

She didn't respond. She climbed onto the bed and wrapped herself in the old floral comforter that had been there forever. Her mom had bought her and Shelly matching comforters when they were in middle school, and such things seemed important. It had become faded and frayed, but she couldn't throw it out. She still felt her mother's hand in choosing it.

Cassie had lived all her adult life in fear of forgetting, but she couldn't forget a single word of the argument with Glenn. How he was so done he couldn't wait to get away from her. Why couldn't she forget *that*? Memory was so sneaky. It stole what you wanted and tossed the rest back like so much debris.

She rolled away from the yellow light spilling through the window. Spring with its relentless optimism beating down on her. If she had an ounce of energy she would get up and close the blind. Instead, she pulled the comforter over her head.

Was she in love with Glenn? Even now, her belly quickened at the thought. Her mutinous body. She reached for her phone and hit his name before she could talk herself out of it, but after two rings she knew he wouldn't pick up.

"Hey," she said when his voicemail came on. The same terse message about beekeeping she'd heard the very first time she'd called. A stranger on the other end of the line. "It's me. I...I'm sorry about the way I handled this. I should have been up front. Can you call me? Please." She didn't say anything about the appointment with the counselor. It wasn't fair to do that to him.

And who knew if he would listen to the message or just delete it.

•   •   •

Jeanette Torrington's office was located on Tenth Avenue in Mt. Sinai Hospital's westside location. Cassie had run past countless times on her way to Riverside Park but had never given it much thought, just another hospital in a city full of them. But inside was a woman who terrifyingly would tell her future.

Shelly held her hand as they rode up the elevator. "You okay?"

Cassie nodded, but her heart was thundering like she'd just stepped off a curb and narrowly missed getting hit by a bus. She wasn't okay. How could anyone be okay in this situation? For a moment she thought about turning around, but they'd come all this way. And she wanted to know. *Didn't she?* At least she didn't have to worry about their dad. They'd hired a nurse to stay with him, and Andrew would be there too.

She checked in with the receptionist then took a seat next to Shelly in the bland waiting room. Across from them, a young couple held hands, the woman just visibly pregnant.

"I'll take notes," Shelly said, "don't worry about remembering everything. It's too hard when you're in the middle of it. Toby came with me."

Cassie fought back a swell of nausea. "What are the odds I'm going to be lucky too, Shel? What if you used up all our luck?" She knew this was ridiculous, that it didn't work that way. They both had the exact same chance of inheriting the mutation. But she felt like she was either going to vomit or scream or run from the room. Maybe all three.

"Oh pumpkin, there's enough luck for both of us." Shelly drew her in for a hug. "At least you'll know one way or the other, and you can plan."

Plan for what, losing my mind? Cassie was about to say, but a trim woman in khakis and a blazer called her name.

"I'm Jeannette Torrington," she said, shaking Cassie's hand, then Shelly's. "Let's go on back."

Jeannette Torrington was early forties with a warm smile and unruly hair that she didn't bother to pull back. She led them to a neat office and motioned to a comfortable seating arrangement. "I hate talking to people behind my desk," she said, taking an armchair across from them. "Makes me feel like I'm playing God."

"Sort of feels like that anyway," Cassie murmured.

"You mentioned your mother had early onset Alzheimer's," Jeanette said once they were settled and had declined waters. "Do you know which mutation? If you decide to go this route, we'll need to know what to test for."

"It was on PSEN1," Shelly said. "Toward the end our dad had her evaluated so we'd know. They were just starting to do that then."

"That makes it easier," Jeannette said. "Sometimes folks come in and they don't have a lot of information." She looked frankly at Cassie. "As you may know, there are hundreds of early onset dementias, not all of them Alzheimer's."

"Could I have something else?" Was there such a thing as a better dementia? She felt another surge of nausea. She hadn't eaten breakfast, but the coffee she'd had was threatening to come back up.

"Not likely. If your mother had a mutation on PSEN1, you and your sister both have a fifty percent chance of inheriting it."

"I've been tested," Shelly said quietly. "I don't have it."

Jeanette looked at Cassie. "So tell me." She had a straightforward manner, and Cassie knew she would tell it like it was. "Why do you want to get tested?"

Cassie forced herself to unclench her hands, which she'd wedged between her knees. Why *did* she want to get tested? Such a simple question but she didn't have a good answer. She'd made the appointment in a spasm of anxiety after she forgot about Mrs. Macuja's visit, but there'd been other worries since then. Misplaced words here and there. That awful incident with the windshield wipers when she hadn't forgotten at all but thought she had. The unrelenting, suffocating worry smothered her every hour of every day. "I think on some level it would relieve a lot of stress," she said, "to know why things are happening."

"What kinds of things are happening?"

"What you might expect—reaching for words, forgetting people's names. A while back I blanked on a big appointment."

"Anything else?" Jeannette looked up from taking notes on an iPad. "Any personality changes? Sometimes we see that with early onset. Any form of Alzheimer's."

Cassie winced at how casually Jeannette tossed out the word. *Alzheimer's.* The way your doctor might discuss your cholesterol, something to be managed. Only there was no pill to take for this. "Shel, have you noticed anything?"

Her sister considered. "Maybe a little cranky, but let's see. You watched Dad almost die of a heart attack. You're handling the sale of our childhood home. Your son has been suspended from school. And you just broke up with a guy you're crazy about."

Jeannette smiled. "Just a little stress there."

"Could all this be stress?" The nausea had subsided, but now she'd broken out in a clammy sweat.

"Stress can manifest in a lot of ways—physically and mentally. But we won't know anything definitively unless we test. Even if you do come up positive, you could still be suffering from stress, which always makes things worse." Jeannette looked at her squarely. "Just to be clear, if you do have the mutation, there's a one hundred percent chance you'll develop early-onset. We can't say exactly when, but unfortunately there's no getting around it."

Shelly squeezed Cassie's hand, but Cassie couldn't look at her. She couldn't look anywhere except at a picture on the wall of a lush orange poppy unfolding to reveal a delicate black center. For some reason the picture made her think of Glenn and the bees, and she felt a piercing sense of loss. "I'm aware of that," she said quietly.

Jeanette gave her a moment, then went on. "When I counsel patients, I always ask if they're emotionally prepared for the results. Positive or negative. That may sound surprising, but a negative result can be disconcerting too. People sometimes end up with survivor guilt. How old were you when your mother died?"

"Twenty-two. But she started showing symptoms when I was sixteen."

"Were you both still at home?"

"I was in college," Shelly said.

Jeanette gave Cassie a thoughtful look. "So you had to navigate what was happening to your mom all alone."

Unexpectedly, Cassie's eyes filled. She had a sudden vision of her mother on the way to a party in her dangly earrings and the yellow dress she'd loved. Blissfully unaware of what was coming. *Would her mother have wanted to know? Would it have ruined the good years she still had left?*

Jeanette handed her a tissue from a box on the desk. "It's a hard thing to process when you're that young. A time like now it all comes up again." She waited while Cassie blew her nose. "You have children?"

"A son. He's nineteen."

"Have you spoken to him about this?"

"I need to." Her heart felt like a stone in her chest. If she had the mutation, Andrew might have it too. He would have the same risk. Satisfying her own curiosity would curse him with the same wretched choice. And what would it change?

Absolutely nothing.

The poppy on the wall seemed to undulate, the orange folds rearranging themselves around the dark secretive center. She could stare at the picture for hours, contemplating its layers.

"So if you want to go ahead," Jeanette was saying, "the test is simple. We just swab your cheek. It takes a couple of weeks to get the results, and we ask that you bring someone with you that day. It can be a lot to take in. If you want to make an appointment to come back for the procedure, they can help you at the desk on the way out."

Cassie stood. "I'm not coming back." She knew with a sudden, powerful certainty that she did not want this test. If she turned out positive, the moment she heard the news she would begin waiting for symptoms to start. Every day would be a countdown to the inevitable end. Yes, everyone's life ended, but most people didn't know how.

She wanted the joy of living a life of surprise, where the ending wasn't ordained. It might still come to that, but she didn't need to know. She wanted to live like she had a future. Yes, that meant heartache and not always being in control. But that was life in all its messy glory.

Getting ready to die was not the way she wanted to live.

Chapter Twenty-Two

When they got home, she found Andrew working on a puzzle with his grandfather, their heads bent together companionably. A new one, sunflowers in a field. A week since the heart attack and her dad was starting to improve. Small milestones. He could get himself out of bed and was lobbying to use the cane instead of the walker. But the hospital bed was still parked in the family room, and he couldn't yet get upstairs to shower.

"How about I take a turn?" Shelly said, easing onto the couch.

Cassie gave her a grateful look. She needed to talk to Andrew, and she needed to do it now. No more excuses. No more delays. The visit with Jeannette Torrington had left her with an unexpected sense of clarity. She'd looked her options in the eye and come out the other side. Either she had the mutation or she didn't. But this would be a shock to Andrew. She had no idea how he would take it.

"Sweetie," she said, "want to go for a run?"

Andrew stretched his arms over his head. He wasn't usually much of a runner, but occasionally she could cajole him. "I guess so. Let me change."

She started stiffly, her muscles cold after a few days. She hadn't had much get up and go since her breakup with Glenn. It had been all she could do to set one foot in front of the other. She'd left another message but hadn't heard a thing, and his silence left a dull, heavy feeling in her heart.

It felt good to get outside now. Her mother's peonies were in full bloom, a heady pink, already shedding petals on the flagstone walkway. Their lifespan so brief. Her mother had adored peonies, even after she'd forgotten their names. Cassie hated the thought of them ripped out along with the house. But even if she managed to save them, she had no place to plant them in the city.

"Where to?" Andrew looked glad to be outside too, stretching his legs, his skin rosy in the sun.

"Let's cut through the woods then head toward town."

"Aren't they already bulldozing?"

"They haven't gotten to this side yet." She wasn't keen on going anywhere near the construction site, but they could avoid that part. And you couldn't shrink from reality. She was learning that. Finally.

They jogged across the street and up the hill, ducking into the cool of the trees. A woodpecker swept overhead in a flash of black and red. One of the big ones. Soon all this would be gone, packaged into mini estates with gardeners and manicured lawns.

She slowed to a walk. "There's something I need to tell you, that I should have told you a long time ago."

He looked at her. "What?"

"You know Grandma died in her fifties." She felt a familiar prickle of fear, the way she always felt when she pictured what might lie ahead. The heartbreaking decline. The inevitable end. And now, to bring Andrew into this. She'd wanted to spare him, but in doing so had kept him a child when he needed to learn to be a grown up.

"She was sick, right?" he said tentatively.

She took a breath. "Yes, she had a form of dementia—Alzheimer's— that starts very young. People who have it often start showing symptoms in their forties or fifties. It's called early onset. A genetic mutation causes it."

Andrew paled. "Do you have it? Are you going to get Alzheimer's?"

They'd paused next to a huge woodland rhododendron that towered next to the path, its conical white buds about to unfurl.

Her heart felt like a block of cement. "I don't know. I have a fifty percent chance of inheriting the mutation. If I do have it, I'll definitely develop Alzheimer's, the early onset kind." She plowed on. "There's a test but I decided not to do it."

"So you could know if you wanted?"

"That's why Aunt Shelly and I went into the city this morning. I had an appointment with a genetic counselor. But I changed my mind."

"Why?" His eyes widened.

She sat on the remains of a log and motioned for him to sit too. She looked at his sweet, worried face and saw herself at his age, scared to death she would lose her mother, her anchor to the world. "I won't lie, it would be a tremendous relief to know I'm negative. But if I do have the mutation, it would be devastating. It'd be like knowing I'm going to get hit by a truck. Not when I'm going to die, but how. I don't want to live that way. I can't."

He was blinking back tears, which made her tear up too. "I'm sorry, sweetie. I should have told you sooner since it affects you too."

"It does?" He was still processing, hadn't quite grasped the whole thing.

"If I do have the mutation, you have a fifty percent chance of inheriting it too. But if I don't, you don't either. It doesn't skip generations."

"This is fucked up." He exhaled as it sank in. "So I might have this too?"

She closed her eyes for a brief second. This had always been her greatest fear. She'd been reluctant to have a child because of what she might pass on, but Phil had convinced her. *The research is promising. They're working on a cure.* She'd wanted a family. She'd wanted to believe.

"Yes, it's possible you could have the mutation too."

He shoved off the log. "Why didn't you ever tell me any of this?"

She felt a rising misery. Of course he was stunned and confused. She'd just dropped a bomb on him. "A whole bunch of bad reasons—I was scared. In denial. Couldn't deal with it." She toed away a red and black beetle that had begun investigating her shoe. "I'm not a very good role model, I'm afraid. Shelly is much braver. She dealt with it years ago."

"Does she have it?"

"No."

"When were you going to tell me? Were you going to wait until something actually happened and just casually mention it?"

She dipped her head. "I always meant to tell you when you were old enough. It just...time went by and it got hard."

"This is about me too. Didn't you think of that?"

"Of course I did. I think of it every day."

He suddenly ran out of steam. "So you could start losing your memory any time?"

"Yes." There was no way to sugarcoat it.

"And then how long?"

"It depends. With Grandma, it took about five years from the time she started showing symptoms."

"Five years? That's it?" He looked young and afraid and she hated that she'd done this to him. Possibly passed on this curse and left him to deal with it.

"You have every right to be angry with me," she said. "And if you really want to know, I'll go back and get tested."

"But you said you don't want to know."

"I'll do it if it makes you feel better." The thought of going back to Jeannette and taking the test filled her with a panicky dread, but she would do it for him. Only for Andrew would she go down that road.

He slumped back onto the log. "Could I get tested at some point even if you don't?"

"I suppose so. They know what mutation to test for."

"I don't want to make you get tested if you don't want to," he said miserably. "I don't even know if I'd want to. This whole thing is so fucked."

She put an arm around him, and he leaned into her. "Yes, that's a very good way of putting it. But you have time to make that decision. And maybe in ten years they'll have a cure or at least a way of slowing it down."

"There isn't anything now?"

"Nothing that makes any difference."

He looked at her anxiously, like the small boy he'd once been. "But you're okay now, right? You haven't started, like forgetting things?"

She kissed his cheek, which like her own was damp with tears. "I'm okay now."

•   •   •

They started up running again, leaving what was left of the woods and dropping to the street. They ran the back roads of Laurelton amid the glossy green abandon of late spring. Past stone walls and a neighbor seeding his lawn. Skirting a thorny wild rose that had run amok near someone's mailbox. The conversation with Andrew had been hard. So hard. But she felt a kind of peace. At least now he knew.

"There's actually something I wanted to talk to you about too," Andrew said shyly as they caught their breath back at her father's cul de sac.

For a moment, she felt a throb of fear but he looked calm.

"I saw the therapist yesterday. Janice. The one Dr. Milburn recommended."

"I'm so glad." Cassie felt her chest warm. Finally, a bit of good news. "You don't have to tell me what you talked about, but how did it go?"

"I thought she would tell me what to do, but she mostly asked a lot of questions. What's going on, how I feel about stuff."

"Did it help, to talk to someone?"

"More than I thought it would," he admitted. "I made another appointment for next week."

"That's terrific, sweetie."

His face clouded. "I talked to Dad yesterday too. He wants me to live with him this summer and do an internship in the city, somebody he knows in some hedge fund."

"Is that what you want?"

"Not really. I don't want to work at a hedge fund, and Dad's never around anyway."

"What would you like to do? You know you can stay with me, wherever I end up, but you need some kind of job, part-time at least." She thought of what Shelly had said about living in New York. *Did* she even want to be in New York anymore? The longer she was away, the less she missed it. She never thought she'd feel that way, but the crush of people, the traffic, the noise. And her dad was here. She didn't want to just park him somewhere and go back to her old, harried life. Seeing him only occasionally as his memory dimmed, so that eventually he wouldn't even be sure who she was. For a second she imagined Glenn's reaction, the way his face would light when she said she was staying. Then her heart thudded back into place. He wouldn't even know.

"Jack's home from rehab," Andrew said once they'd said hello to a neighbor walking her dog. "I want to go see him."

"I didn't know you'd been in touch." Cassie looked at him in surprise.

"We've been texting. He has trouble with words sometimes, gets them mixed up, but he understands what's going on." He glanced at her. "His mom hates me."

The boy's mother would never forgive Andrew, Cassie understood that. Some things a parent could never get over. "What about Jack," she said cautiously, "does he want you to come?"

"He said he did."

"Did Janice suggest this?" She was pleased he was finally talking to someone, but Andrew needed to make this decision. If the therapist had suggested a visit, Andrew's heart wouldn't be in it.

He shook his head. "I've been thinking about it for a while."

"If Jack wants to see you, you should go." She hesitated, trying to find the right words. "But be prepared. It's not going to be easy, and he might change his mind once you're there. And his family probably won't be happy to see you. You can't go looking for forgiveness," she said gently. "It's not about you."

"I know. I just want to apologize in person."

"I'm proud of you."

"You are?" He looked like the thought was inconceivable. He would carry this shame forever. The raw edges would seal up, but it would live inside him and shape the man he would become. He could bury it or face it. It had taken her a lifetime to learn that. She'd run from her mother's illness and her father's grief. She'd withheld from Andrew and Glenn. Andrew, at least, was trying.

"Yeah." A lump rose in her throat. "I'm proud of you." Andrew had stumbled and was trying to right himself. She couldn't catch him anymore; he had to do that on his own. All she could do was cheer him on.

"So when will you go?" she asked as they walked up the driveway.

"I thought I'd look at flights now, if that's all right."

She smiled at him. "Now is definitely all right."

After Andrew went inside, she wandered across the field, not quite ready to go in. The grass had shot up in the last couple of days, wild with clover and dandelions. A meadow, Glenn had called it. She sat on the stone wall, but all she could think about was being here with Glenn just before she sprang the news about Weber. Her stomach wound so tight. Her fear that it would change everything, which it had.

She missed him. He lit her up like she hadn't thought possible at her age. At any age. He'd listened to her and made her feel seen. He *had* seen her. At least what she was willing to show him. He was smart and thoughtful and sexy. She was stunned by how fast it had happened, how completely she'd fallen. But it had blown up equally fast, over before it really started.

The truth was, she ached for him. It hadn't gotten better; it had only gotten worse. The nights were especially miserable, lying awake, wondering if he was awake too. She missed his voice, his laugh, the way his face brightened when he saw her. She wanted to share her decision not to get tested. She wanted to tell him about her conversation with Andrew and how her dad had started to improve. The small miracles that make up a life. If they didn't speak they would leave it in a tangle of hurt and misunderstanding. And she would always regret it.

She pulled out her phone and tried him again but got voicemail. She left another message, fidgeting on the stone wall, phone in hand, in case he called back. But the only sounds were the drone of a leaf blower and the shouts of children down the street.

Finally she put her phone away and headed back to the house.

Chapter Twenty-Three

The wasps arrived in force the next day. An invading army that materialized out of nowhere and overran the bees' puny defenses.

Andrew, out for the mail, ducked back into the house in a sweat. "They're all over the place. I had to run!"

Cassie abandoned the tuna sandwich she'd been making for her dad. "Bees?"

"Wasps, I think." He winced as he felt his neck. "One got me."

Cassie pushed back his hair for a look. Sure enough the tender skin behind his ear was already going puffy and red.

"How can you tell if it was a wasp or a bee?" Shelly said.

"Must have been a wasp the way they came after me. Grandpa says they're way more aggressive than bees."

"Don't rub it." Cassie wrapped a couple of ice cubes in a dish towel. How on earth did you get rid of wasps? She didn't know the first thing about them, except they were bad news. Andrew getting stung was bad enough, but her dad was just coming off a heart attack. A wasp sting could be downright dangerous for him. She handed Andrew the ice. "Hold it there, sweetie. It'll keep it from swelling."

"It's already swelling," he grumbled but sat in a kitchen chair and applied the ice to his neck.

Her father, who'd settled at the table for lunch, looked agitated. "We never had wasps before. Where did you say they were?"

Cassie sent Andrew a warning look but he didn't notice. "Down by the hives, but this one got me at the mailbox."

"I need to get down there and take a look."

Cassie exchanged a worried glance with Shelly. The last thing they needed was their dad over-exerting himself with a last-ditch effort to save his hives. "Dad, maybe we should just leave them. What can you possibly do?"

But he was up and moving, nosing the chair out of the way with his cane.

"Wait Grandpa!" Andrew said. "You don't have your veil on. You can't go down there like that."

"Dad." Shelly tried to steer him back to the table. "How about we call the bee guy."

Cassie's stomach took an unhappy dip. She'd heard a big fat nothing from Glenn; he hadn't returned any of her messages. She'd had her phone with her constantly, her heart taking off every time she got some stupid alert. She'd tried texting him too but not a word. Whatever scrap of hope she'd had that they could find a way back to each other had been shredded. He'd made his feelings perfectly clear.

"We're not calling Glenn," she said.

Andrew gave her a puzzled look. "Why not?"

"He's not available."

"He'd probably come for this," Shelly said quietly.

"No."

"Andrew." Her father was chafing by the door. He'd cast off the walker and gone back to the cane. "Where's that veil?"

Andrew looked helplessly between his mother and his aunt. "It's um...coming. I'll go get it."

"Cassie," Shelly whispered, "maybe you should just call him. Tell him it's an emergency."

"It's not an emergency, it's just a few wasps." But her skin prickled at the thought of what might be going on out there. Still, no way was she calling Glenn. He would think she was pathetic, inventing an excuse. Even if he agreed to come out of some sort of professional duty, it would be unbearable. Him all stiff and formal. She knew exactly how he'd be. They would deal with it on their own.

"More than a few, Mom," Andrew put in. "Look. There's some right here by the house."

They all peered out the narrow window next to the front door. Outside, a pair of yellowjackets cruised lazily like they owned the place. A few months ago, Cassie wouldn't have been able to tell them from bees, just another stinging insect. But now she recognized the pinched waist and vivid yellow stripes. Yellowjackets were a kind of wasp, a sleeker, more lethal cousin to the homely honeybee. Bees wore themselves out traipsing from flower to flower in search of nectar and pollen. But wasps were opportunists. They hounded you at picnics, they'd eat your hamburger or dive bomb your soda. Instead of turning pollen into honey like the industrious bees, they invaded weak hives, stole their honey and sucked the life out of the brood while they were at it.

Her dad paced by the window. In another minute there would be no stopping him.

"I'll go take a look," Cassie said reluctantly. "Andrew, can you get the smoker?" Smoke might get rid of them. It seemed to calm the bees, maybe it would drive off the wasps. At least enough to give the bees a chance to regroup. Her heart knocked around her chest thinking of all those stingers, but she couldn't just abandon the bees to their fate. They were her dad's last connection to her mom, the one constant in his life.

"You're going out there?" Shelly said. "You're crazy."

"What else can I do? If I don't go, Dad will." But inwardly, she wilted at the thought of wading into a firestorm of wasps with only a tin can full of smoke.

Andrew appeared with the bee suit and Cassie stepped in, zipping up the jacket tight, snapping on gloves. Andrew ventured onto the porch with her, both of them glancing around apprehensively, but the outliers had flown off. "Grandpa's still looking out the window," Andrew said as they lit newspaper in the smoker to get it going.

"Maybe you can get him to work on a puzzle, keep him occupied for a few minutes."

"Are you kidding? He's not going to budge."

Cassie had to smile at her father with his nose pressed against the glass. "At least don't let him out here."

After Andrew went in, she trudged alone down the driveway, checking again to make sure her pants were tucked all the way into her boots. Not even knee-high beekeeping boots, just old mud boots she'd found in the closet. But her veil was tightly zipped. Sleeves tucked into gloves. Pants tucked into boots. She could do this.

She thought of her dad waiting by the window. She had to.

She waded through the field, riotous with wildflowers. The ancient stone wall, bits of it crumbling, but still intact. And the house, presiding over it all like an elegant dowager. How had she failed to appreciate this all these years? The closer she got to inking the deal with Weber the more reservations she had. It wasn't just Glenn, although he'd made her think. Until now, the development had been theoretical, but seeing the Kingsley property ripped up had excavated a hole inside her too. Rubble where trees had been, the woods leveled to make way for fancy homes. She'd run the numbers half a dozen times but still didn't see any other way.

She approached the hives cautiously, puffing the smoker to make sure it was still lit, her heart in overdrive like she'd downed a whole pot of coffee.

And *ooh shit.*

The wasps! The air churned with them. Dozens, no hundreds of wasps swarming the hives. Zeroing right into the boxes!

A pitched battle was underway. Honeybees boiled from the narrow entrances in an effort to repel the attacking wasps. The bees surged out, trying valiantly to smother the yellowjackets and keep them from getting in but the wasps came on. There was no end to them! The air seethed with yellowjackets. They were easy to spot—more streamlined than the bees, with those devilish stripes. And wicked fast. Launching themselves past the defending bees into the belly of the hives.

Cassie yelped when one tested her veil. *Wait!* What was that terrible tingling inside her suit! What if one was crawling up her leg? Didn't Glenn say they could sting repeatedly? She shook one leg, then the other in a crazy dance.

Oh, why had she come out here?

She forced herself to breathe. Deep breath in. Long breath out. She calmed slightly.

Okay. Nothing had found a way inside her suit.

She crept closer, puffing smoke furiously, but the wasps didn't seem bothered. They dove through the entrances at the bottom of the boxes, overwhelming the bees.

Then an awful thought. The smoke was supposed to relax the bees, that was how you opened up the hive. But if she knocked out the bees, it was all over. They couldn't fight if they were comatose.

She stepped back, coughing from the smoke, trying to think. The bees were fighting their little hearts out. Three of them had a wasp on the ropes, the yellowjacket on its back, moving feebly. But a dozen more had taken its place. The bees couldn't keep up. There must be thousands of wasps, unending reinforcements.

Cassie felt a gust of despair. Moving was going to be hard enough on her dad but to have to tell him his beloved bees had been wiped out by wasps would break his heart. It would be more than he could bear.

She turned away, unable to watch the carnage any longer. The bees would fight to the end, she had no doubt. But the wasps were a superior force. They outnumbered the bees and they were vicious.

She put a safe distance between herself and the hives, checking to make sure nobody was following, then shook off the veil and fished out her phone. Glenn could be here in half an hour. Maybe less. He was done with her, but he might come for her dad.

She wavered, heartsick about everything. The bees, the property, the way life had almost offered up something wonderful. Her marriage had failed. Her memory might fail. Her relationship with Glenn had definitely failed. If she went running to him about the bees, it would be one more thing she couldn't get right. Maybe he could save them and maybe he couldn't.

She opened up her internet browser. You could find anything online; she'd found a beekeeper that way. If you could slow down mites with powdered sugar, there had to be a remedy for wasps. It was just a matter of finding it.

She startled when a yellowjacket buzzed her head, then took aim with the only weapon she had: the smoker. She gave the wasp a satisfying swat and it tumbled to the ground.

One down, ten thousand to go.

• • •

Overnight mail was a wonderful thing. The package arrived right on time, and Cassie ripped it open with her dad hovering over her shoulder. She'd watched a dozen YouTube videos about fending off wasps, and they all promised an entrance reducer was an easy fix. Or at least a possible fix. That was the thing she was learning about beekeeping—nothing was for sure. You could try powdered sugar and drone comb and still have mites. Or wasps.

Life was a constant struggle. But wasn't it always? She had to admire the bees. They kept their heads down and did what had to be done, fighting off the wasps as best they could.

"It's supposed to work," she said to her dad as they examined the slim piece of wood. She was secretly dismayed to see how flimsy it was. *This was it?* This ten-inch piece of cedar was going to save the day?

Her dad smoothed a finger along the wood. "I've seen them work. Had a friend—what's his name, that guy up the road—" He frowned, trying to remember the friend's name, then gave up with a frustrated shrug. "Anyway, he had them on his hives. Kept the robbing down."

Her dad had been waiting impatiently for the package to arrive. Who knew why some days were better than others? A good night's sleep, a pleasant dream. Today he remembered about entrance reducers and even that he'd had a beekeeping friend. Some days his memory coughed to life like an old car.

"Should we go see?" Cassie said.

She'd peeked at the hives when she retrieved the mail earlier. The wasps had called off the attack for now and things were quiet. A few bees circled, guarding against intruders. She took that as a sign that at least the colony hadn't been wiped out. She insisted her dad wear the bee suit, her heart quaking a little at the thought of going sans protection. If it looked wild down there, they would turn right around.

Her dad wanted to walk even though the day was cool and drizzly. She watched to make sure his step was steady, but he seemed to be doing all right with the cane. A couple of weeks ago she would have insisted on driving, but this day he was able. Who knew about tomorrow—she could wake up and forget who she was. Or go out for a run and get mowed down by a FedEx truck. The point was anything could happen, you couldn't cower in fear of what might lie ahead. It wasted the life in front of you. It had taken her a long time to see that, always looking over her shoulder at what had befallen her mother. Terrified it might happen to her too. Her father had been knocked down, but he was doing his best.

She glanced at him, her heart beginning to hum. Whatever life had in store, time with him was finite. That much she knew. He wasn't easy and he wouldn't get any easier, but an idea had taken hold over the last few days.

"What would you think if I lived nearby?" she said. Shelly had asked why she had to live in New York. And why did she? A month ago she would have dismissed the idea as impossible, but now it felt right.

He looked at her. "Around here?"

"Yes." A fine mist was coming down, frizzing her hair and dampening her face, but the coolness felt good. "I've decided not to go back to the city. I want to be closer to you." Her marriage was over, and they were selling the apartment. Who knew where Andrew would end up. The thought of starting over somewhere new had begun to appeal. As much as she missed Glenn, she was glad she'd come to this now, her judgment unclouded by the persuasion of a man.

Her father blinked a couple of times. "You're going to live in Laurelton?"

"Laurelton or maybe Stamford. If I can't work for the city of New York living here, I'll find something else. I'm ready for a change. You won't get tired of having me around, will you? I can be a little bossy."

He squeezed his eyes shut for a moment, then shook his head. Her dad had never been an emotional person, but the dementia brought everything closer to the surface. He was awash in feeling these days, a puzzle or a misplaced word could set him off. The frustration at what was happening, the lack of control. She'd seen him get snappish and upset plenty of times. She'd seen him tune out.

But she hadn't seen joy.

He gripped her hand, his eyes shining. "You know I never get tired of you."

She held his hand, heat starting behind her own eyes. She should have been a better daughter, should have visited more often. She should have done a hundred things. They wouldn't get that time back. They had only what was in front of them.

•   •   •

The bees were still distressed from the day before, and it took several puffs of smoke to calm them down enough to slide in the entrance reducers. There wasn't much to it. Each block of wood had two openings, one a little larger than the other. They reminded Cassie of the Lincoln Logs Andrew used to love when he was little. Efficiently constructed with a whiff of possibility.

Her dad set his cane against the hive and inserted the reducer with the smaller opening facing out. It plugged up the half inch between the baseboard and the bottom of the box where the bees flew in and out.

"See? Now they don't have to guard such a big space." He seemed pleased they'd accomplished this.

They did the same for the other hives as the bees stirred uneasily. "So that's it?" Cassie said. It seemed so simple, but maybe it would give the bees a fighting chance.

"That's it."

"What do we do now?"

Her dad shrugged like it was obvious. "Wait and see if it works."

•   •   •

On Thursday, the day they were to ink the deal with Weber, Cassie woke at five.

She hadn't slept much that night, her stomach in a miserable twist. She got out of bed, pulled on a t-shirt and leggings and padded downstairs. Her dad and Andrew were still asleep, Shelly too in the spare bedroom downstairs. The sky was beginning to lighten, and the birds had been at it for half an hour already. She wondered glumly if the red maple outside her bedroom where they congregated would survive the bulldozers. Probably not. The Kingsley property had been scraped clean.

She made a pot of coffee but was too restless to drink it. She emptied the dishwasher and wiped down the kitchen counters, which were already spotless. She tossed yesterday's newspaper in the recycling bin and put fresh towels in the downstairs bathroom. On the way to the laundry room she paused outside her father's office. It needed a thorough cleaning, but she could never get in there during the day when he was awake. A layer of dust had settled over everything, and papers teetered in stacks.

She dropped the dirty towels on the floor and started on the desk. Her dad wouldn't be up for a couple of hours, and at least this would keep her occupied. Better than wringing her hands about the sale.

She went through stacks of paper with jotted notes and yellowed newspaper clippings. A National Geographic from 2004. She paged through it, trying to figure out why he'd saved it but finally gave up. She sifted through mailers from a house painting company, an offer of membership from a local health club. Tossed all of it into the trash. Now she could see the back of his desk, where it looked like at one point he'd had a system for organizing files. There was the Lexus file (how had Andrew ever found it!) and a thick one marked home repair. One for appliances with warranty information for the ancient washer and dryer. And a file labeled insurance with his homeowners and auto and a life insurance policy. Those she knew about.

But here was one thing she hadn't seen. A long-term care policy. She lowered herself onto the chair and began to read. Her dad had taken it out shortly after her mother died and had been paying on it for decades. A policy that would cover his care if he needed assisted living or a nursing home. The kind of expenses that depleted savings in no time. The kind that had led her to believe that selling to Weber was the only answer. Her father had planned ahead but never said a word. Quite possibly he'd forgotten.

She set down the file, her head spinning.

This would change everything.

Chapter Twenty-Four

Cassie shook her sister awake and shoved the policy under her nose.

"What's this?" Shelly said, fumbling for her glasses.

"Dad's long-term care policy. I found it on his desk. It's all paid up through the end of the year."

Shelly paged through it, looking up with dawning comprehension.

"Right?" Cassie said. "We don't need three-point-two million anymore. We could sell the house to somebody who actually wants to live here."

"Does Dad know about this?"

Cassie shrugged. "He did at one point."

"Weber's going to be mighty pissed."

"I never wanted to sell to him." Cassie lowered herself onto the bed next to her sister, who scooted over to make room. "It always felt awful."

•   •   •

Weber Properties occupied a tastefully done space in downtown Laurelton next to a store that sold high-end lighting and home accessories. The kinds of furnishings that would fit perfectly in a Weber house. Not so much in her own family home. They had never been a fit with Weber.

Even so, Cassie felt a twinge of apprehension as she gave her name to the receptionist. She could have done this over the phone, but that felt wrong. She'd set this in motion, and she would see it through.

The receptionist ushered her in, and Weber came out from behind a sleek desk to shake her hand. He glanced toward the door.

"My father's not with me," Cassie said.

"Oh. You do understand we'll need him since the property is in his name."

"May I sit?" She gestured to one of the leather chairs across from the desk.

"Please." He was beginning to look concerned.

She crossed her legs then uncrossed them. "I'll get right to the point. Our family has decided not to go through with the sale."

"I'm sorry?"

"Circumstances have changed and we've decided to withdraw."

Weber clicked a pen several times in rapid succession. Shelly was right. He looked mighty pissed. "We can go to three-five."

"It's not about the money."

"It's always about the money. I can offer four, but that's it."

Cassie felt slightly faint. *Four million dollars.* But what was the difference between three-two or three-five or even four million dollars? It was all a lot of money, and in the end the house would be torn down and the property gutted. She thought of the bees, which miraculously were still holding their own. The long-term care policy would provide for her father's care, and they would still walk away with plenty of money. The house was paid off. How much did they need?

"I'm very sorry, but the sale is off. We've changed our minds."

"What do you mean, you've changed your minds!" Weber, who had the kind of olive skin that didn't redden easily, had turned the color of brick. "You can't back out, we had a deal."

Cassie kept her voice pleasant. "As you recall, we haven't signed anything."

"We had a verbal agreement," he said tightly. "I could sue."

"No judge will take you seriously."

Weber scowled. "What are you, a lawyer?"

"As a matter of fact, I am."

He shoved away from the desk. "You're making a big mistake. That house is a tear down. You'll be lucky to get a million. I'm offering you four times that."

Cassie stood. "I appreciate the offer, but the answer is still no."

She saw herself out with a polite goodbye to the receptionist, who clearly had been listening at the door. Then she stepped into the sunshine, her heart humming.

It was turning out to be a lovely day.

•　　•　　•

Cassie, Shelly and their father visited Keller Williams the next day. Cassie had made an appointment with Beth Tartullo, the real estate agent she'd run into at the coffee shop in Laurelton back in April. The one with the sticky toddler. For some reason, she'd stayed in Cassie's mind. Not as aggressive as the agent in New York or as hungry as Weber. Maybe because she was a young mom with a little boy on her hip. Whatever the reason, Cassie had remembered her.

Beth escorted them to an understated conference room and offered coffee or water. She looked more put together than she had that day at the coffee shop and laughed when Cassie reminded her that they'd met.

"I remember you too. I can't believe you actually called; that day wasn't one of my better moments." She extended a hand. "You must be Mr. Linden."

Cassie's dad had dressed for the occasion in gray slacks and a tweed jacket. He'd combed his hair carefully and even chosen a tie, although it didn't quite match. For a disorienting moment he seemed the father of her childhood, the man who'd tried his best to shepherd them through life and whose opinion still mattered most. He shook Beth's hand, then seemed unsure what to do next, finally sitting when everyone else did.

Cassie prompted gently, "So we're here because the house has gotten to be too much. It's a great house where my sister and I grew up. But we need to put it on the market."

Shelly gave their dad's shoulder a quick squeeze. "It's time for a change, right Dad?"

"I would've stayed, but they convinced me I don't need so much space."

"Aren't you selling to Weber?" Beth tipped her head in surprise. "I thought I heard that."

Cassie felt a delicious lightness steal through her. "We're not selling to Weber. We decided to sell the house and property intact." It felt indescribably good to say that, like her chest had opened up and she could breathe again. Weber had dangled all that money and promised it would be easy, but in the end, nothing good or right was ever easy. She'd convinced Shelly and her dad to go along, but deep down she'd felt like she was cutting off a piece of herself.

"I never wanted to sell to that man," her dad said. "I only agreed because you girls thought it best."

Cassie touched his arm. "You're right, it was a bad idea. But we don't need to do it now." After awakening Shelly the day before, she'd made a quick call to confirm the long-term care policy was still in force. The money was enough for in-home care too, but the house was unsafe with the stairs. And eventually her dad might need more care than a single person could handle. Selling was still the best option. But thankfully they didn't need to sell to Weber.

"Full disclosure," Shelly put in, "the house needs a lot of work. But we're hoping a family might want it."

Beth beamed at them across the table. "I'm so glad to hear this. As a matter of fact, I have a young family that's been looking for a fixer upper, but there isn't much on the market. It's all pretty done around here."

"Our house definitely isn't done," Cassie said. "Not unless you like early 1970s."

Beth laughed comfortably. "You'd be surprised what people will snap up. And you're good with this, Mr. Linden?" Coming from someone else the question might have felt intrusive, but Beth seemed sincere and their dad had been quiet during the meeting. He understood they were selling, Cassie was certain of that. But how must it be for him to relinquish the home where he'd raised a family with the woman he loved? He'd been cheated of time with his Maggie, but had stayed on, growing old in the place they'd chosen together.

"What about my bees?" he said.

Beth's eyebrows, which were very light, went up so you could hardly see them at all. "You have bees?"

"Three hives."

Beth glanced cautiously at Cassie and Shelly. "Um, not everyone wants bees, but you never know. With such a charming piece of property, it could be a selling point."

"Or we could find them another home," Cassie said gently. Glenn was out of the question, of course, but maybe she could locate someone else who would take them.

"Has to be someone who knows bees." Her dad was getting that stubborn look. "I'm not handing them over to just anyone."

"Of course not," Cassie said. God only knew if the bees would survive after the wasp invasion, but whatever shape they were in, she would find them a home. Maybe they would thrive somewhere else. A change of scenery might do everyone good.

"What about that fellow, that friend of yours?" her dad said.

"Oh, that won't work," Shelly said lightly. Under the table, she gave Cassie's hand a squeeze. Cassie had tried calling Glenn a couple more times, but he hadn't responded. Even Shelly, who never let go of anything, had stopped asking.

Cassie dropped back as Beth showed them out. "I'm looking for a place too," she said. "A condo or a small house." In spite of everything, she felt a breeze of excitement. Something appealed about the idea of a house. Nothing grand, but more room to stretch out. A kitchen with actual cabinet space. Honest to goodness closets. She didn't need much, an extra bedroom for Andrew when he came home. A bit of a yard. She might even rescue her mother's peonies.

"I'd be happy to help. Is it just you?"

"Just me." Here she was, almost fifty, venturing out like a twenty-something. She wouldn't lie—after all those years of marriage and motherhood, it did feel a little lonely, starting out with no one else to consult. Did she need central air, and what did you look for in a furnace? But she could start fresh. Paint the walls pink if she wanted too. Navigate life without a doorman. Maybe she would even break down and get a cat.

Beth's handshake was firm and not the least bit sticky. "We'll find you just the thing."

Cassie caught up with her dad and Shelly half a block away looking at a poster for the new Brad Pitt movie. The same family-owned theater that had been there forever, with an old-fashioned marquee, the neon letters stacked jauntily one on top of the other. One of the things she liked about Laurelton was the way the town had resisted chain stores and multiplexes. She couldn't help thinking of her first date with Glenn, how he'd worried she found Laurelton too dull. For a moment her mood flagged, missing him.

"Where have you been?" her dad said. "It's almost time for lunch."

"Lunch?" Shelly consulted her watch. "It's only eleven-fifteen."

"I'm hungry."

"I have an idea," Cassie said.

They made their way down the street, past the women's clothing store where the styles never changed, past the shop that sold delicate enamel dishware. And the bakery, which gave off the tantalizing aroma of fresh bread.

"Want me to get the car?" Cassie said, "or can you walk a couple of blocks?"

"I can walk," her dad said, moving capably with the cane. "Where are we going?"

Cassie smiled as Bobby's, with its bright blue awning, hove into view. "Where do you think?"

Chapter Twenty-Five

Glenn tapped on Lilah's door, which was slightly ajar. The girl, cross-legged on the bed, looked up warily from her phone.

"Can I sit?" he asked.

She pulled out her earbuds, which he took for a yes. "A lot of times my first reaction is no," he said. "That's not a good way to be, and I'm working on it. Even adults can be a work in progress." He smiled ruefully. "If it were up to me, peanut, I'd never let you out of the house, but I don't think that's going to work long term."

She started to protest, but he held up a hand. "Wait. I'm getting there. I love you, and I will always love you no matter if you live close by or across the country. Or across the world, although I hope you don't. But anyway, you're old enough to start making some of your own decisions. So what I'm trying to say in my long-winded, boring way is that you can go."

Her eyes flew open. "To Colorado? For the summer?"

"A month. Your mom and I talked about it. I know she's trying and wants more time with you. And I'm okay with it." At least it wasn't the whole summer; they'd compromised on a month. And Sophie did seem to be making an effort. She'd been better about returning Lilah's calls and sometimes even called herself.

"For real?" Lilah's smile was huge.

He nodded, not trusting his voice. Then, "I'll miss you like crazy. I'm not going to lie. It's going to be real quiet around here for a whole month. But I think you should go. I *want* you to go."

"Thank you!" Lilah threw herself into his arms. Her hair smelled like strawberry shampoo, and part of him wished she were still four and he could keep her this way, but another part loved the young woman she was becoming. Strong and resourceful and too goddamn opinionated.

It had been a tough couple of weeks coming to this decision. Back and forth a dozen times. He'd wanted more than anything to talk to Cassie about it, but every time he went to call her, he had so much else he needed to say. *Like, I've been a jerk.* He thought of her a million times a day. What she was doing, if she missed him. But all the old alarm bells about honesty and trust kept going off, and he couldn't go down that road again.

Not after Sophie.

But Cassie wasn't Sophie. She was just trying to hold it all together, doing the best she could for her dad. It had taken him a long time to see that through his haze of hurt and anger. He'd finally worked up the nerve to call, but she hadn't called back. He could hardly blame her.

He kissed the top of Lilah's head. "You'll have a great time with your mom. Just promise you'll come back, okay? Charlie won't know what to do without you."

"I promise. You and Charlie are my number one, you know that."

"Who, me or Charlie?"

"Oh Dad." She rolled her eyes. "Hey look." She opened her phone. "Mom's been feeding this feral cat. It waits on the deck for food." She showed him a picture of a mangy gray cat peering in the sliding door. "Mom thinks it might have babies somewhere."

"Hmm, it might. If you're lucky, maybe she'll bring them by."

"Ooh, you think?" Lilah looked enchanted. "Would a kitten be tame enough if you got it young? I mean, you'd have to take it to the vet and everything, right?"

"You sure would." He smiled to himself. Better Sophie than him saying no to a feral kitten. He could just picture that scene. "So if you want to go, there's a flight out of JFK Saturday morning, and there's still a few seats left. It's eight a.m. so we'd have to leave early."

She bolted up. "*This* Saturday? That's like two days from now!"

"Yup." He tousled her hair as he stood. "Better start packing. One suitcase please."

•　　•　　•

Glenn's stomach clotted with unhappiness as he swung into the Linden's driveway and spotted the beekeeper. It appeared Cassie had gone and hired someone else. Three weeks and she'd already replaced him. Not that he was here about the bees, but it stung just the same that she'd moved on so quickly. Like he'd never existed. He peered out the window. What the hell was the guy doing, standing on a ladder for Christ's sake, trying to lift out a frame. *Who did that?* It irked him that she'd gone and hired some amateur.

He idled the truck, debating whether to stay or go. He'd come straight from dropping Lilah at the airport, had been upbeat and positive even though it killed him. Maybe he should have given himself some time before coming over, but he'd waited too long already. He owed Cassie an apology but she'd clearly moved on, the beekeeping part anyway. His gut churned miserably. He'd been a fool, tied up in knots over the whole Weber thing when it really didn't matter.

Oh crap. Beekeeper 2.0 had noticed him. Glenn gave a half-hearted wave, but the guy didn't wave back. Just climbed off his ladder and started across the field. With a deep sigh Glenn killed the engine and got out of the truck, the gravel crunching in a familiar way. He didn't want to deal with this new guy; he just wanted to find Cassie and see if he could make things right. He squinted into the sun. The dude was small, something familiar about him. That purposeful walk. *He knew that walk.*

Cassie! Clomping toward him in her dad's bee suit. His heart kicked into gear as he legged across the grass to meet her. She probably thought he was being a dick, waiting for her to come to him. This was so *not* how he wanted things to go.

She shrugged out of her veil when she got close. "Hey."

"Hey," he said cautiously. "How are you?"

She lifted a shoulder. "Carrying on."

"Sorry I haven't been by. It's...uh...it's been..." He'd rehearsed what he was going to say on the ride from the airport, trying to get it right. Maybe if he explained how her keeping quiet about Weber had dredged up all the old stuff about Sophie, maybe she'd understand. But his heart was pounding, and he couldn't grab hold of his thoughts. Everything he'd worked out on the way over had flown out of his head. "I um...wanted to apologize," he finally managed.

She looked at him. "I must have called you twenty times, and you never called back."

He shifted from one foot to the other. "I did call the other day."

"After almost three weeks." Her face was flushed from the heat, and wisps of hair had gotten loose from her ponytail. Her dad's bee suit engulfed her. She was beautiful.

"I meant to call sooner. I'm sorry. For all of it—the way I reacted and then going AWOL. But you weren't exactly open either." His heart was a tight fist in his chest. They'd both messed up, but he'd messed up big by walking away. "I should have called. It just got hard."

"I called you so many times. It was like you fell off a cliff." She'd left a hive open, and bees were drifting around. "I need to close that up," she said. "Want to walk back with me?"

They fell into step, and he waited with a faltering heart for her to speak. For the first time it felt awkward between them. A distance he didn't know how to bridge.

"I'm sorry too," she said finally. "I should have just come out with it about selling to Weber. I guess deep down it felt wrong, and I didn't want to hear about it. I wasn't honest and that was wrong."

"Yes, it was." He'd hoped for her apology, but now it almost seemed beside the point. She'd withheld and he'd withdrawn. He didn't know who was at fault anymore; it just felt miserable.

A frame with brood was propped against the open hive. "I wouldn't have left it open," she said, "but I saw your truck."

"I'll close it up for you." Glenn went to pick up the frame, but she stepped past him.

"No need, I've got my trusty ladder." She gave him a slightly embarrassed smile. "I could tell you didn't know it was me." She climbed onto the stool and slotted the frame back into the box. He had to admit the stool made sense, gave her a better angle. But there weren't nearly as many bees as there should have been. The colony looked depleted. "What's going on with the mites?" he said.

"The mites are the least of the problem. We got invaded by wasps."

"Oh Christ." He came closer for a look. "You put in entrance reducers. That was smart. Did your dad think of it?"

"I figured it out."

"You did? Good for you." He looked at her, impressed. "So have the wasps been back?"

"Yeah, but not as many are getting in. I haven't seen a big invasion like that one day. They killed a lot of bees though."

"May I?" When she nodded he lifted the cover off the hive he knew to be the weakest. Bees were crawling around on top, a few regarding him suspiciously. He waited until they settled before extracting a frame. "Looks like they got to the brood." He held it up for her to see. "It's all gouged out here. But they didn't get it all, at least not on this one." He slipped the frame back in. The wasps had undoubtedly done more damage, but he didn't want to slip into beekeeper mode. He could sense her pulling away. The bees could wait.

He swallowed. "I didn't have any right to lay all that shit on you about selling the house. It's your family, and you have to do what you think is right. I get it. It wasn't my business in the first place. It felt dishonest, that's all. That you didn't tell me."

"I kept trying to find a time. That's a bad excuse, I know. But the longer I waited, the more I didn't know how to say it. I was afraid you'd think less of me." She lifted her eyes to his. "I'll just say this—I didn't want to lose you, and I was afraid I might. I thought maybe we had a chance. I hoped we did. You have no idea how much."

It hit him like a two second delay. "You thought we had a chance?" he said, slightly stunned. "Do you ah...think we still might?" His heart, unruly from the moment he'd set eyes on her, took off at a gallop. *She'd wanted to make it work.*

She looked toward the woods, where a pair of squirrels tag teamed up a white pine. "If we'd had this conversation a couple of weeks ago, I might have said yes, but it's been a long, crummy three weeks, Glenn, and I've done a lot of thinking. You skipped out when things got hard. I tried so many times to talk to you, and you couldn't or wouldn't pick up the phone. You shut me out. What kind of relationship is that?"

He closed his eyes briefly. She was right, of course. "It hit a nerve the way you didn't tell me. Like with Sophie, how I never knew what she was thinking. I just reacted. It's not the same, I get that, but I guess I needed time to process."

"You could have processed with me," she said softly.

"I know. And if you give me another chance, I promise I'll bombard you with feelings."

She let go a real smile for the first time, and he allowed himself a glimmer of hope. Maybe it wasn't too late. But when she finally spoke, her face was settled in a way he understood. "I'm at a place now where I'm okay. I can't be on an emotional roller coaster. I just can't do it. And we both have a lot on our plates. You have Lilah, and I've got my dad and Andrew. Maybe at some point, but I can't do this now."

At some point. That meant never. She was slipping away; this was how it happened. Mistakes, miscommunication. Him being an idiot. His heart felt like it had a slow leak. She'd wanted him, and he'd been too stupid and stubborn to get out of his own way.

"By the way, after all this we're not even selling to Weber."

"What?" He wasn't sure he'd heard right. "You're not?"

"I found a way around it. We listed with an agent in town. She's going to find a buyer for the house and the property, all of it. Someone who won't tear it down." She began gathering up the bee stuff—the smoker and her dad's hive tool. She looked like a beekeeper.

He wanted to touch her—her hair, her face. If only he could touch her they might find a way. But she was out of reach. "I don't even care about all that. They can put up fifty houses here, and yes, it would suck. But not as much as not having you in my life. I want to make it work, Cassie. Even if you're in New York, it's not that far. I'll do whatever it takes. I don't want to give up."

She looked at him for a long moment, and he thought maybe something had shifted, that maybe he still had a chance. But then she said, "Right now, I need to find a place for my dad and start cleaning out the house. I can't think about anything else. I don't have the energy for it."

"So that's it?" he said dismally.

"It's too much up and down. I had a marriage where he pulled away. I can't deal with that again."

He looked at the hives, where bees were coming and going. Doing the best they could. "What about the bees?"

She shrugged tiredly. "I'll do what I can as long as we're here. If they make it, I'll find someplace for them."

He was about to say he'd go back to being a beekeeper again for however long she needed him. That he didn't mind. But he *did* mind. He couldn't do it. He couldn't stomach the thought of coming over here and not seeing her or watching her pack up the house and move on. That would be torture. Worse than never meeting her at all.

"I'm sorry you feel this way," he said quietly.

Her eyes shone with tears. "I'm sorry too."

There was nothing left to say so they hiked back across the field in silence, Cassie carrying the gear.

A rabbit startled in front of them, dashing off a few yards, its nose quivering, then sat fatly on the grass, oblivious to the fact it was still in plain sight.

Chapter Twenty-Six

At the end of August Cassie made an appointment to visit Riverside Gardens with her dad. The house was almost packed up, and he was resigned to moving. Sort of. She'd investigated several assisted living facilities, and Riverside Gardens seemed the best. He could have his own apartment for now and tiered care when he needed more help.

"You look handsome," she said when he came downstairs. He was wearing a pair of navy slacks and a collared shirt. The clothes were clean and his hair combed. In spite of his reluctance, he'd made an effort.

"All right then, let's go." He fished the car keys out of his pocket.

"How about I drive?" she said lightly. He hadn't driven much since the heart attack but in the last couple of weeks, he'd seemed to remember about the car. A couple of times she'd been alarmed to find him about to set out on some errand or another. Luckily, she'd been able to talk him out of it, but here he was summoning up a last bit of defiance.

"I'll drive." His face had taken on that obstinate look. "Just tell me how to get there."

"Well, we have to head down Ridge Road, take a left on Thornhill, which takes us to Oak. We can either jump on the parkway for an exit or cut over on Mill River. Whatever you think."

He waved off the directions. "Tell me when we're in the car."

"What if I wasn't with you?" she said gently. "How would you know how to go?"

"I wouldn't be going on my own," he countered, but his face fell. He still had enough lawyer left in him to realize the faultiness of his logic.

"I know it's hard, but do you think you should still be driving? It was time for me to sell the apartment; it's time to move out of this house. I think it's time for you to stop driving too, Daddy. It's not safe anymore." She held out her hand for the keys. "I'm going to be around; you can't get rid of me. I'll take you wherever you want to go."

He hesitated and she feared it might go badly, but no way was he getting behind the wheel.

"You don't know the car. The brakes are finicky."

"I've been driving it without any problem for the last four months. But I tell you what, why don't you explain it to me when we get in the car." The brakes were fine. She'd had everything checked out when the wiper issue was fixed. She was tempted to pluck the keys out of his hand, but she would never rob him of his dignity that way.

"You can't drive it like this," he said.

"Why not?" She was beginning to get frustrated. Their appointment was in fifteen minutes, and he wasn't budging.

"The windshield is dirty." He'd always insisted on cleaning the windshield when she was a teenager, making her wait while he meticulously sprayed the glass and polished it with a rag. Then planted himself at the top of the driveway and watched her turn around. It used to drive her crazy.

"Let's clean it, then." She didn't point out that he'd been about to set off himself without the benefit of Windex.

"I'll do it."

"Thank you," she said, relieved they'd avoided a confrontation. At least he would feel in control of something. "I'm glad you thought of it."

He nodded and handed over the keys like it had been his intention all along.

•   •   •

The woman who met them at Riverside Gardens was pleasant and cheerful, and Cassie's dad took an instant dislike to her. But in the mood he was in he might have taken offense to anyone.

"I'm Joy," the woman told them, and Cassie couldn't help wondering if that was her real name or one she used to jolly up the residents, a few of whom were lingering in the TV room after lunch. With its shutters and grand porticoed entrance, the residence appeared more like a genteel New England inn than an assisted living facility. Inside was clean and bright with a large black and white dog lounging by the reception desk.

"Who's this?" Cassie asked.

"That's Leo," Joy said. "He's the house dog. The staff takes turns bringing him home at night, but he hangs out here during the day. He's very friendly; you can pet him." She directed this to Cassie's father, who ignored her.

Joy seemed unfazed. She was obviously used to a certain amount of resistance from prospective residents. "How about a tour?"

"That would be wonderful," Cassie said.

Joy showed them the dining room, with tables for eight set with white napkins and tablecloths. A nice touch, even if her dad wouldn't appreciate it. And the community room with couches and comfortable chairs, the wall-mounted TV and built-in bookshelves.

"A lady from the library brings us new books every couple of weeks," Joy said. "And if there's something you want that you don't see, we can ask them. They're very accommodating."

"Look, they have puzzles too," Cassie pointed out, but her father either didn't hear or didn't bother responding.

It was difficult, no question. The house had been sold to a young family, the one Beth had mentioned, but Cassie's dad still dragged his feet whenever possible. She'd sold the patio furniture online, and when the buyer showed up Andrew had to persuade his grandfather to let them take it. Andrew had offered to come today, but Cassie didn't want him to miss his shift at the grocery store.

Cassie touched her father's arm. "Want to see the rooms?"

"I suppose so."

The model suite was bland, with hotel art and drapes that matched the bedspread. At least they could bring some of her dad's furniture so it would feel more like home. Her father lowered himself into an armchair. It had been four months since his ankle injury and he wasn't using the cane anymore, but since the heart attack he tired easily.

"Can we have a few minutes?" Cassie asked Joy, who was all set to whisk them off to see the patio.

"Sure, I'll be at reception when you're ready."

Cassie sat on the bed and reached for her dad's hand. "It's going to be okay. I'll be here all the time, and if you don't like the food I'll sue them."

That got a smile out of him, which she took as a hopeful sign. "Actually, I've heard the food here is pretty good, and you've got a fridge for snacks."

"How will I get to the store?"

"They have a van, or I can bring over a few things. Or we can go together if you want."

"What about my bee stuff?"

"Um, your bee stuff?" They'd discussed the bees; surely he understood the bees would not be coming.

"You know, my veil and such."

"Daddy, there's no place for the bees here." She glanced out the window, which had a nondescript view of the back lawn. A sidewalk ran along a border planted with regulation impatiens and petunias. Beyond that, a stretch of grass gave way to a box hedge and some carefully tended trees. The lawn was probably mowed and clipped weekly. Nothing riotous. No bees in sight.

"What do you mean there's no place for them?" He sounded like this was the first he'd heard of it. "Where will they go?"

"I'm going to find someone who'll take them." She hadn't quite figured that out yet. The thought of looking for a beekeeper left her with a lingering lethargy, like a flu she couldn't quite shake. Two months since she'd seen Glenn and she still ached with regret. Still glanced at every white pickup that drove past.

Her dad crossed his arms.

"We talked about this," she said. "Remember?"

"We never talked about it."

She sighed. Nose to nose confrontation never worked with him. After all these years, she'd finally learned that. "I'll call the Arboretum. I bet they know someone."

"I want that fellow, what's his name…"

Her stomach cinched. "Oh no. Glenn can't possibly take them. He has too many bees already."

"I like him. He knows what he's doing."

She felt a tingle of panic. How could she call Glenn? He definitely would not want to hear from her, not after she'd sent him packing. Calling Glenn was not an option. "I'm sure lots of other beekeepers know what they're doing. I'll find someone good, I promise."

Her dad was beginning to look agitated, his face going blotchy. "He's the one I want. I trust him."

She thought of how the house was being emptied. Furniture sold, the china boxed up. Her father's world shrinking around him. He was being made to leave the house he knew and loved and start over in two rooms with a mini fridge. The facility was a perfectly suitable place that could provide the care he needed. But it wasn't home.

Her father wanted to get up, so she helped him out of the chair. Deep chairs were tough; his wing chair would be better. She would be sure to bring it over. Her stomach churned unhappily at the thought of calling Glenn. He'd humbled himself and asked for another chance and she'd said no, hurt and exhausted by his silence. With everything going on in her life, it had all been too much.

She squeezed her dad's hand as they started down the hall. Leo ambled by, sniffing her leg briefly, and she stroked his soft back. What did her own discomfort matter? Yes, it would be awkward to call Glenn, but this was her dad they were talking about. He might forget the day of the week or whether he'd agreed to a tour of Riverside Gardens, but he hadn't forgotten about his bees. And he knew who he wanted to take care of them.

She had to at least try.

Chapter Twenty-Seven

Cassie's heart ticked up as she pulled into Glenn's driveway. Maybe this was a bad idea after all. She'd promised her father she would try, but Glenn would not be happy to see her. She'd debated whether to call or stop by, but he might not even listen to a message. The thought hollowed her out, that he might just delete it. But what did she expect? She'd made it clear it was over.

The days were noticeably shorter now. Still sticky with August, but at seven-thirty dusk had already settled in, the sky pinking over the ridge. She'd forgotten how lovely his place was—the hives and wetland beyond it, already deepening with evening.

She parked the car, her stomach wound tight. Glenn's truck was here so that meant he was home. For half a second she thought of turning around and high tailing it back the way she came. She could make some excuse to her dad, tell him it wouldn't work. But too late. Charlie had run to the fence wagging and barking.

"Charlie!" Glenn's sharp call from the deck. He hadn't seen her yet since she was hidden by the big rhododendron at the top of the driveway. She waited, her stomach in free fall. Glenn came around the side of the house and stopped. He was wearing a pair of jeans with holes at the knees and a rumpled t-shirt. His hair was tousled like he might have been lying on the couch. Her heart leapt at the sight of him.

"Hi," she said as she stepped from the car.

He grabbed hold of Charlie's collar. "Hey."

She'd thought this visit would be okay—it had been two months after all, as long as she'd known him in the first place—but her heart wouldn't quiet. Maybe he was seeing someone else. It was her own fault if he was.

They regarded each other for a moment over the fence, then he finally unlatched the gate. He didn't invite her in though, he stepped onto the driveway instead, blocking Charlie with his knee. "What's going on?" His voice was cool. "I thought you'd be back in New York by now."

"We sold the house. A family from North Carolina with three kids. They were thrilled with all the space."

"I saw that it sold. That's good news." He was still standing by the gate, hands in his pockets. She'd foolishly imagined they might hug, at least get past the awkwardness, but he was as remote as the moon.

"How's your dad?" he said, his voice giving a little.

"He's good. We found him a place in Riverside Gardens. It's been a little rough, packing up and everything."

"When does he move?"

"First of the month." Her heart was clattering all over the place. She hadn't expected seeing Glenn to be easy, but this was so much harder than she'd imagined. The living breathing reality of him. She'd thought she could do this. A simple request for her dad. But here he was with his ripped jeans and wary expression, trying to figure out why she was here.

She missed him. Their easy conversations. The unexpected way her body soared when he was around. His solid convictions. She missed all of it. But their relationship had ended up so shredded it seemed impossible to repair. How did you get past the miscommunication and mistrust? So she'd let it go and focused on her dad and Andrew and finding a place of her own. And if she was lonely at night, well, she was used to it.

"Believe it or not, the bees are hanging on. Mites and everything. All three hives seem to be doing okay, from what I can tell."

"Seemed like you had a handle on things."

"I don't. I'm only doing what I saw you do, as much as I remember."

"You figured out the entrance reducer on your own; you made that pretty clear."

She felt his sharpness like a slap. "I'm sorry about that day," she said. "I'm sorry about everything, the way we ended up."

"Why are you here Cassie?"

Why *was* she there? Yes, her dad had asked for Glenn, but she could have left a message or sent an email. The truth was, she longed to see him. After two months it hadn't gotten better, it had only gotten worse. No, Glenn wasn't perfect—he had a tendency to clam up when he was upset. He'd finally apologized, but at the time she just couldn't deal with it. But nothing in life was perfect. You could drive yourself crazy trying to get there. And here was a man who came pretty close.

Charlie, tired of being on the other side of the fence, had begun scratching at the wood. Glenn snapped his fingers. "Stop it."

Cassie extended a hand through the slats and Charlie licked it. "Can he come out?"

"I guess so." Glenn reluctantly opened the gate, and Cassie got down and rubbed Charlie behind the ears. Dogs were so simple. No matter how you left things, they were always happy to see you. She'd never been a dog person, but she took a long comforting inhale of his earthy smell.

Glenn shifted on the asphalt. He was barefoot. She'd interrupted his evening, his life. Her heart, which had taken off when she saw him, settled into its customary low orbit. He didn't want to see her; that was plain. He didn't want her here at all. All she was doing was distressing him.

"I came about the bees," she said. "My dad's having a hard time giving them up. I've been looking around for someone to take them, but he only trusts you. He wants you to have them. I think he has the idea he might be able to come over once in a while and see them." This was asking a lot, she knew. Glenn might take the bees, but he surely wouldn't want to deal with supervising her dad and possibly running into her.

She glanced at the hives, luminous in the waning light. A few late foragers were heading home, but most of the bees were already tucked in for the night. Glenn was silent, and she feared he would say no. She didn't know how she would go back to her dad with that. But finally he said, "I don't mind taking them if it'll make it easier for him. And he's welcome any time."

Her eyes filled unexpectedly. "Thank you. He thinks the world of you."

"At least someone does," he muttered.

"I did," she said softly. "I still do if it makes any difference."

He kicked an old tennis ball Charlie had dropped at his feet, and the dog took off after it. "Why are you doing this Cassie? The bees are one thing and I don't mind helping out your dad, but I can't see you. I can't be friends and act like nothing ever happened between us. Because it did. At least for me it meant something. I get that you have a lot going on or whatever. That's fine. You have to live your life. When your dad's ready I'll pick up the hives and get them sited, and whenever you're up from the city you can bring him over. Just let me know so I don't have to be around."

"I'm not going back to the city. I bought a place in Stamford."

A flicker of surprise crossed his face. "Where?"

"A little house off Hope Street. It's a walkable neighborhood, ten minutes from my dad. I missed out on a lot with him, and I know what's going to happen. I want to be here for that." She drew a breath. "And I took a long look at what I want in my life and none of it's in the city." She glanced at the hives and the wetland behind them, where the plaintive sound of a frog had started up. "It's peaceful and pretty up here and I can see birds besides pigeons and I bought a couple of pots and I'm going to put them on the patio, and—" Her heart was thudding in her ears. "And you're not in the city."

He looked at her and she felt heat rush up her neck and face, and thank goodness it was almost dark because now she felt like an idiot. "I miss you," she plowed on. "There's so many things I want to tell you, but you're not there. When you came over that day, all I could think of was how you'd shut down, not how you were making an effort. And then it had been so long, and it felt like we could never find our way back. I made a mess of it. I'm sorry." He hadn't said a word and her face was burning, but what did it matter. "I know it's too late for us, but I just wanted you to know."

He was as silent as a stone. He probably hated her.

"So anyway..." This was excruciating but she'd done it. She'd been honest and told him how she felt. There was nothing left to say. "I'm going to get going. Thank you for agreeing to take the bees. I'll text you and we'll figure out—"

"Cassie." He took a step forward. "I've missed you too."

"You have?" She was finding it hard to form a coherent thought the way he was looking at her. "You're not uh...seeing anyone?"

"You asked me that once before and I'm still not. I only ever wanted to be with you."

"Do you still?" She hardly trusted her voice.

"What do you think?" he said quietly.

Her heart felt like it was filled with helium, like it might float right out of her chest. "Really? Do you uh...want to see my place?"

"I'd like that. Maybe I can help you get settled."

"That would be great. But I mean...I don't want you to think I'm asking you to be a handyman. I only want you to come if—"

He looked amused. "You think I'm offering to be a handyman?"

Her smile welled up. "What are you offering then?"

He smiled too, a slow smile that turned her insides to butter. "I don't know. Why don't we see where it goes."

•　　•　　•

They met at the house on Sunday, the keys newly hers. A sweet Cape with a bit of a front yard and white frame dormer windows upstairs. Three bedrooms—her own, an extra one for Andrew, who would be with her at least through the fall, and a third she could turn into an office or guestroom. After so many years of apartment living, the thought of all that space made her giddy. But the backyard had sold her. French doors that spilled from the kitchen onto a flagstone patio with a tidy perennial garden. Flowering cherry trees that would bloom in the spring.

"The whole thing's fenced," Cassie said. "I could get a dog."

"Charlie's available," Glenn said. "He'd be happy to dig up plants for you."

"Charlie gets a bad rap." Cassie felt a delicious lightness at having Glenn there. They hadn't spoken about anything more than the house and small improvements she might make, but their hands brushed when she opened the French doors and his presence filled the house in a good way.

They strolled through the perennial garden, which was alive with bees. Some crawling on the tops of flowers, others lifting off like miniature cargo planes, their back legs loaded with pollen.

"Wild bees," he said when she gave him a questioning look. "They pretty much do their own thing."

"I don't have any idea what all these plants are." She touched an orange flower with a button center. "But they're pretty."

"That's black-eyed Susan, and that's sedum that the bees are all over. You've got some hydrangea over there, and those pink flowers are phlox. Somebody put some work into this. Are you up for gardening?"

"I think I am." She felt a hum of contentment being here. She'd picked up deli sandwiches on the way over and they took them to the front steps, which were protected from the sun this time of day. "You got me roast beef," he said with a laugh. "I gave up red meat."

She looked at him incredulously. "But you're such a carnivore."

"I kept thinking about it. You were right." He sheepishly accepted half her veggie wrap. "It's not healthy and definitely not sustainable. Lilah was after me too."

Cassie took a bite of her sandwich. "How are things with Lilah? Is she still mad you didn't let her go to Colorado?"

"I did let her go. Not the whole summer, just a month. I never thought I'd say this, but it was good for both of us. And her mom's stepped up, she's better about keeping in touch now. You know what?" He grinned. "The best thing is that my daughter doesn't hate me."

Cassie laughed. "That's always a plus."

He'd polished off his half of the wrap, so she offered him what was left of hers.

"No, you eat it." He touched her shoulder lightly. "You've gotten so thin."

She leaned into him and he wrapped an arm around her and the tightness she'd been carrying around loosened. But not entirely. It never went away entirely. She was always alert for the word she couldn't recall, the fuzziness lurking like a fog offshore, waiting to envelop her when she least expected it. It might be Alzheimer's and it might not, but either way life was short, and she could spend it worrying about what might be coming or she could get on with living.

But it wasn't just about her. If she and Glenn were going to have a chance, he needed to understand what might lie ahead. She needed to be straight with him.

She turned to face him, her heart stuttering. "I'm forty-nine, fifty in November. I could be a ticking time bomb. My mom was this age when her Alzheimer's surfaced."

"Only forty-nine?" His eyes twinkled. "I pegged you for much older." He managed to keep a straight face for a second, then burst out laughing at her look of dismay. "I don't care how old you are or what your family history is. Honestly, I wouldn't even have guessed you were forty-nine."

"It's not a joke. My mom was fifty-four when she died. I could be smearing lipstick on my eyelids in a few years. I'm not going to presume we have a future together, but I can't ask you to sign up for that. It's not fair."

He turned to her, serious now. "Who said life is fair? Is it fair that your dad got dementia too? It didn't run in his family and nobody predicted that, right? Who knows what's coming. I could get stung one too many times and go into anaphylactic shock and die."

She looked at him, horrified. "You could?"

"It's not likely, I'm just saying. You can't worry about what might or might not be around the bend. Bee colonies collapse for no apparent reason. One day they're doing okay, and the next day all the bees are gone. Vanished." He snapped his fingers. "Just like that. Nobody knows why it happens."

She shifted on the concrete steps. "A colony collapse would be terrible, but you can get more bees. There's no bouncing back from Alzheimer's. If I inherited the mutation from my mom, I'll definitely end up with early onset."

"So you didn't get tested after all?"

A couple of kids lazed by on bikes, their voices carrying on the still summer air. Life could be so achingly beautiful. Until it wasn't. "I decided I didn't want to know because there's not a damn thing they can do. Just raise my insurance rates. I don't want to be a hostage to Alzheimer's. I want to live like I don't have it."

He threaded his fingers through hers. "I wouldn't have said this before, but I'm glad you didn't test. I don't know what's going to happen with us. I don't know if you're going to get Alzheimer's. I don't know if my bees are going to get sick and die or just up and disappear. But I do know what I want to happen. I want to be with you. That's it. I want to stay up late talking to you. I want to see you laugh. I even want to eat these fucking veggie wraps." He flicked aside the offending wrapper. "And if I'm lucky enough, I hope to get you in bed and make love to you. That's what I want. The rest is out of our control."

"Even if we only have a few good years together?" A lump rose in her throat. All well and good to stay positive but Andrew could lose her too, grieving his whole life the way she grieved her own mother.

Glenn's gaze didn't waver. "If I walk away, we won't have any years together. That to me would be way worse."

She looked at him—his beautiful eyes with the lines deepening around them. His beard, flecked with gray. He would be handsome at eighty if they were lucky enough to live that long. She kissed him right there on the front porch, a long lingering kiss. Who cared what the neighbors thought.

He wanted her, eyes wide open.

"Don't let me wander outside in my nightgown, okay?" she murmured.

He kissed the top of her head. "Never."

"And stop me if I put salt in my coffee."

"Of course."

"And if I think my phone is the remote, humor me."

"Always." He cocked an eyebrow. "Don't I get a pass on anything?"

She smiled. "Absolutely not. Someone has to keep their wits about them."

They sat on the steps a while longer, watching the neighbor across the street mow his lawn. Waving back when he raised a hand in greeting. "It's funny," she said after a bit. "I haven't been as forgetful lately. I did misplace the shopping list the other day, but who doesn't do that. I haven't blanked on big things though, like appointments or people's names. The scary stuff. Ever since I saw the genetic counselor, I've just felt calmer about the whole thing."

"You were under a lot of stress. That might have had something to do with it."

"That's what she said."

"Go with it then." He drew her close. "That's my professional opinion."

She lifted her face to the sun, which had shifted while they sat. The day was warm but not uncomfortably so. In fact, it felt perfect.

"That's exactly what I intend to do."

Chapter Twenty-Eight

Shelly returned at the end of September so they could walk through the house one last time. The place had been emptied, the furniture sold or donated and her dad's favorite wing chair shipped off to Riverside Gardens, where he was settling in.

"Remember we used to push the furniture aside and roller skate in here?" Shelly said as they paused at the threshold to the living room.

"We did?" The room was cavernous, and without furniture their footsteps echoed. "I don't remember that."

"Dad hated it, but Mom said the room was going to waste."

"Sounds like something Mom would have said." For a moment Cassie felt a familiar tingle of worry at the roller skating she didn't recall, but so many other memories rushed up at her. The way they jumped rope at the end of the driveway, waiting for the school bus in the morning. The sweet, citrusy aroma that permeated the house when their mom baked her lemon cookies. Who knew why Cassie remembered one thing and her sister another. Memory was like that—messy and unpredictable. Sort of like life. She nudged Shelly. "Remember that play kitchen we used to have in the corner? I left a cup of milk in the oven one time, and Mom went crazy trying to find the smell."

Shelly's eyes creased with laughter. "Oh my God, that's right! She was convinced there was a dead mouse in the wall."

They sat on the floor with their knees up, laughing at how the exterminator had torn up the walls looking for mice until her father finally located the sour milk.

Shelly quieted. "This is it. We won't be back."

Cassie leaned against her sister's shoulder. Letting it go was bittersweet, but she felt a kind of lightness too. The house, stripped to its bones, exuded a quiet dignity. The floors would be refinished, the walls repainted. Another family would take up a life here.

And she had a life of her own.

Andrew stuck his head in the door, looking mildly surprised to see them sitting on the floor. "What are you doing?"

Cassie hoisted herself to her feet. "Just taking a minute."

"Glenn's outside with Grandpa. I told him what we're doing, but he seems a little confused."

"That's all right." She gave Andrew's shoulder a squeeze. "Thanks for getting him." Andrew was finding his way, but it would be a long road. As she'd feared, the trip to Dallas had been awkward and the family unwelcoming, but at least Andrew had made the effort. And he was moving forward. Going to therapy and working part-time at Ciccarelli's. He'd started classes at UConn Stamford too. Maybe he would transfer somewhere else after a semester or maybe not. Life had a way of working itself out. You couldn't foresee everything. You couldn't foresee *anything*.

Outside, Glenn and her dad were talking. She gave them both a kiss. "Come inside with me," she said to Glenn. "We have a couple of minutes."

They walked through the front door, past the family room—the TV gone now, the room still. Through the kitchen and out to the sunporch, which had been emptied and swept clean.

"You left the birdhouse," Glenn observed.

"The wrens will be back in the spring; it seemed a shame to take it down."

They climbed the stairs and she showed him Shelly's old room, then hers. Frederick had been packed away and the posters stripped from the walls, but the silhouettes remained. The girl she'd been was gone, but the house and all that happened here had shaped her.

She gazed out the window, where the field was dipped in dusk. "Once my mom got sick I just wanted to get away. I thought if I did everything right I had a shot at my life turning out different. I mean, I didn't actually believe that, but it terrified me that I had no control over my genetics. So I threw myself into trying to manage everything else." She smiled lightly. "I'm in a good place now but just so you know, I'm never going to be a loosey goosey kind of person."

"Loosey goosey?" He looked amused, then turned serious. "You're brave. You know that? You're the bravest person I know."

"No. My mom was brave. Waking up each day and trying to make sense of a world that was going sideways. That's brave." For a moment she faltered. "I hope I can be like her if it comes to that."

He took her in his arms. "You're already there in my book."

"I'm glad you think so." She rested her head on his chest. "Anyway, for now I'm working on loosey goosey."

He kissed her forehead. "I'm very glad you're staying. Have I told you that?"

She smiled up at him. "You might have mentioned it."

•　　•　　•

Outside, her father was waiting with Andrew and Shelly. The light was fading and the bees would be settling in for the night. Time to get going.

"Where's my bee stuff?" her dad said. "Is it in the house?"

Cassie looked at Shelly, who shrugged.

"Nothing's left in the house, Daddy," Cassie said. "The movers took it all. I have your smoker and all that at my place."

"But I'm going to need it."

"Glenn has a smoker." She didn't say they wouldn't need to smoke the bees, that they weren't going to open the hives. Even though she'd explained they were moving the bees tonight, her dad was confused or had forgotten. Or maybe he just wanted to believe nothing had changed. That the house remained the same, waiting for him to walk in the door and resume his old life.

"Let's see how things go," she said gently.

Once they'd assembled at the hives, Andrew helped Glenn unload the ramp so they could muscle the boxes into the truck. It was almost full dark now, bats flitting from the woods, swooping erratically in and out of the trees. Terrifying if you didn't know the good they did in the world. Cassie aimed a flashlight so Glenn could staple the hive entrances closed for the short ride to his house.

"Why are you closing them up?" her father said. "They won't be able to get out."

"We'll open them in the morning," Glenn assured him. "It's just so nobody gets lost on the way."

"On the way to where?"

Glenn stopped what he was doing. "I know a place where they won't be disturbed. Where it's quiet and there's fresh water and they can get healthy again. What do you think, should we take them there?"

Cassie waited, her heart suspended. Her father needed to come to this on his own. A decision he could still make. They could have moved the bees without him; it would have been simpler. But he needed to be here. Just as she'd needed to walk through the house one last time.

Her dad considered. The wheels turned more slowly now. Sometimes they got stuck, especially when he was tired. Mornings were better for him, but the bees had to be moved at night.

"I've never been to this place," he said finally.

"I'm going to take you there now," Glenn said, "so you can see."

Her dad rode in the truck with Glenn and the rest of them followed, a small procession winding along the back roads of Laurelton with a slim moon keeping pace. They were only going a few miles, but picking up and moving thousands of bees had to be done with care. Glenn drove slowly, avoiding the bumps, easing to a stop when the lights turned red. Cassie imagined the bees tucked up inside the warm belly of their hives, drowsy in the darkness. No idea that they would wake up somewhere new. But bees were resilient, and she wanted to believe they would thrive.

At Glenn's house, Cassie and Shelly held their father's hands so he wouldn't trip in the dark as Andrew and Glenn rolled the hives across the yard.

An outside light switched on, and Lilah came down the stairs from the deck. "This is Lilah." Cassie introduced the girl. She was lankier than the last time Cassie had seen her. She'd shot up over the summer, on the cusp of becoming a teenager. About to transform as all kids did to the adult they would become.

"Do you want to wait on the deck, Mr. Linden?" Lilah said. "The grass is sort of lumpy."

"Do you, Dad?" Cassie asked. "We'll sit with you."

She should have known he wouldn't hear of it. He planted himself next to Andrew and Glenn, watching intently as they wrestled the hives off the dolly. "How will the bees know where they are?" he said.

Glenn settled the first hive at the end of a long row. "As long as it's more than two or three miles they reorient pretty easily. Might put some branches in front for few days so they notice something's different."

The new hives looked like all the others, a neighborhood of neat white and pastel boxes, front doors facing east where the sun would find them in the morning.

"I'll bring you over whenever you like," Cassie said. "You can check on how they're doing."

Her father's brow furrowed. "There's too many of them. I won't be able to tell which ones are mine."

"I know which are yours," Glenn said gently. "Don't worry."

"But how will *I* know?" her father said.

Cassie sent Glenn a worried glance. Here, at the end, a wrinkle. The boxes blending in for her father, who still knew enough to know he wouldn't recall. Anguished to lose this last link to himself and her mother in a confusing complex of indistinguishable beehives.

"I have an idea," Lilah said and dashed back to the house, pale hair flying. She was back a minute later with a black marker. "We can write your name on your hives. That way you'll know which ones are yours."

Cassie held her breath. Would this fix be enough, or would her dad leave unhappy and distressed, forgetting in the morning that the hives had been moved, remembering only that something important was gone.

They were all silent, holding their collective breath. Then her dad's face eased.

"Write it big in front," he said.

And so Lilah did. Neatly penning **LINDEN** near the entrance to all three hives. In large letters so anyone could see.

"Is that okay, Daddy?" Cassie slipped her hand through his.

Her father nodded. "That'll do."

•   •   •

In the morning, when the sky lightened and the temperature rose, the bees would begin to stir. Glenn would remove the entrance coverings and the foragers, whose job it was to go out into the world and return laden with nectar and pollen, would shake the sleep from their wings and crawl to the entrance of the hives.

They might see branches where none had been before or notice a new fragrance on the breeze, alerting them that something had changed. The first ones would communicate this to the others and word would circulate through the hive, passed on with the touch of an antenna or the arch of an abdomen until the colony was astir with activity.

Then as the sun warmed their wings and the day brightened, the bees would lift off into the morning to explore their new home.

Acknowledgments

I knew nothing about bees when I started, but all the research and YouTube videos in the world can't prepare you for the thrill of opening up a hive. I'm grateful to beekeeper Cheryl Carter, who graciously let me suit up and introduced me to the "girls." And to beekeepers Erika Deutschlander and Deborah Canet, who read the manuscript and made sure I got the "bee stuff" right. All mistakes are my own.

Certified genetic counselor Tanya Bardakjian patiently answered my questions about early-onset Alzheimer's, and Stamford EMT John DeMaio and paramedic Justin Socha were kind enough to walk me through emergency rescue and demonstrate the equipment.

A big thank you to critique partners Jamie Beck, Falguni Kothari and Ginger McKnight- Chavers, all gifted writers and sharp readers who suffered through early drafts of the manuscript and improved it with their on-point suggestions.

Thank you also to Kathryn Craft, Judy Roth and Denise Marcil for their keen editorial insight and early readers Barbara Josselsohn, Diane Schneider and Anne Silverstein.

The Women's Fiction Writers Association and Connecticut Chapter of Romance Writers of America have been instrumental in my writing journey, and I have made wonderful friends along the way. I wouldn't be where I am now without them. I am grateful to Black Rose Writing for bringing my book into the world and to the welcoming family of BRW authors.

Finally, huge hugs to my family, who I love dearly. My supportive and talented husband Joe Avellar has had my back every step of the way and reads everything I write, along with my amazing children Justin and Jackie Avellar and brother Gary Zohman. My mother, Naomi Zohman, is still my biggest fan and the best-read person I know.

And to my father, Edward Zohman, who I know is with us in spirit. I miss him every day.

Resources

- *Beekeeping for Beginners* by Amber Bradshaw
- *The New Complete Guide to Beekeeping* by Roger A. Morse
- *The Beekeeper's Lament* by Hannah Nordhaus
- *Organic Practices for Honeybee Health* by Les Crowder
- *Honeybee* by C. Marina Marchese
- *Show Me the Honey* by Dave Doroghy
- *The Beekeeper of Aleppo* by Christy Lefteri
- *Beekeeping for Dummies* by Howland Blackiston
- *The Backyard Beekeeper* by Kim Flottum
- *The Honey Bees* by Meredith May
- *Bee People* by Frank Mortimer
- *Memory's Last Breath* by Gerda Saunders
- *Alzheimer's Through the Stages* by Mary Moller
- *The Emotional Journey of the Alzheimer's Family* by Robert B. Santulli and Kesstan Blandin
- *The 36-Hour Day* by Nancy L. Mace and Peter V. Rabins
- *Somebody I Used to Know* by Wendy Mitchell
- A New Era for Alzheimer's/*Scientific American,* May, 2020

About the Author

Photo courtesy of Richard Getler

Linda Avellar is a former Emmy-nominated TV news reporter who's always loved a good story. After stepping away from the news business, she couldn't resist taking a job at the public library in Stamford, Connecticut, where she's surrounded by books.

A Southern California native, she's lived in Connecticut most of her adult life with her husband, two kids, and a succession of amiable dogs and cranky cats. She is a founding member of the Women's Fiction Writers Association, and when she's not writing, you can find her digging in her garden, hiking with her grown kids in the Pacific Northwest, or sailing on Long Island Sound.

Note from Linda Avellar

Word-of-mouth is crucial for any author to succeed. If you enjoyed *Cassie Linden Finds Her Sweet Spot*, please leave a review online—anywhere you are able. Even if it's just a sentence or two. It would make all the difference and would be very much appreciated.

Thanks!
Linda Avellar

We hope you enjoyed reading this title from:

www.blackrosewriting.com

Subscribe to our mailing list – *The Rosevine* – and receive **FREE** books, daily deals, and stay current with news about
upcoming releases and our hottest authors.
Scan the QR code below to sign up.

Already a subscriber? Please accept a sincere thank you for being a fan of Black Rose Writing authors.

View other Black Rose Writing titles at
www.blackrosewriting.com/books and use promo code
PRINT to receive a **20% discount** when purchasing.